SPELLBOUND

"When we win I shall demand a reward," said Rothgar with a wicked smile. "A beautiful Norman witch to take to wife."

He allowed his fingers the freedom to do what they'd been aching to do. He brushed aside the silken strands of Maria's hair to curve his fingers round her slender neck. His lips just naturally followed. And Maria made but the slightest movement before he found her surging body matching his, heartbeat with heartbeat.

"Nay, the chains will not matter," he whispered against her hair. "They are as nothing against the bonds you have twisted round my heart."

Harper Monogram

Conquered By His Kiss

DONNA VALENTINO

HarperPaperbacks
A Division of HarperCollinsPublishers

If you purchased this book without a cover, you should be aware that this book is stolen property. It was reported as "unsold and destroyed" to the publisher and neither the author nor the publisher has received any payment for this "stripped book."

This is a work of fiction. The characters, incidents, and dialogues are products of the author's imagination and are not to be construed as real. Any resemblance to actual events or persons, living or dead, is entirely coincidental.

HarperPaperbacks   *A Division of* HarperCollins*Publishers*
10 East 53rd Street, New York, N.Y. 10022

Copyright © 1993 by Donna Valentino
All rights reserved. No part of this book may be used or reproduced in any manner whatsoever without written permission of the publisher, except in the case of brief quotations embodied in critical articles and reviews. For information address HarperCollins*Publishers,*
10 East 53rd Street, New York, N.Y. 10022.

Cover illustration by Jeff Barson

First printing: November 1993

Printed in the United States of America

HarperPaperbacks, HarperMonogram, and colophon are trademarks of HarperCollins*Publishers*

❖ 10 9 8 7 6 5 4 3 2 1

To my fellow "Big Ten" members
Ann, Colleen, Jan, Kit, Lee,
Liana, Lorraine, Polly, Shelley,
whose friendship and encouragement
keep my spirits high,

And to Carol, Peggy, and Toni, who helped me get
on course,

But most of all to Joe,
husband and best friend,
who never doubted.

Prologue

March 1067

His legs shuddered with the quivering, cramping tremors that told him he'd pushed too far already this day. Nonetheless, he forced first his right foot, then his left, ever onward, scarcely feeling the stones and clods of frozen earth trying to penetrate the scraps of sacking tied around his feet.

His hair clung to his head in sweaty tendrils, his body steaming in the cold, clammy air with the evidence of his exertion. His clothes, worn to tatters and never replaced during his stint of forced labor, offered no protection against the elements. From afar, he heard the cry of a hawk and stopped, his breath clouding the air about him, watching the distant predator circle and swoop.

"For your eyesight, my friend," he murmured, "I would trade much."

The notion of speaking aloud to a hawk was almost as amusing as the thought that he might have anything at all worth trading.

The hawk glided in lazy, effortless circles, its path surely affording it a glimpse of Langwald. *Tell me,* he wanted to shout, *is the manor hall a charred, smoking ruin? Are the cottages destroyed, the people starving?*

The hawk soared on silent wings and then drew itself into a feathered projectile as it suddenly hurtled toward an unwitting prey. An ironic smile played across the man's lips. He had no doubt the hawk would win, capturing and taking what it wanted, just as the Norman invaders' superior arrows had plummeted from the sky to shatter the spirit of England.

Men like himself, who had taken up arms alongside doomed King Harold, were stripped of their titles, their land, their very lives, when their valiant, desperate defense had failed. The lucky ones had died. Those not so fortunate were sent back to the manors they once ruled to serve their new Norman lords. The truly damned were locked in chains, forced to work as slaves, starved, humiliated, worked to death. Those attempting escape were run through with swords, serving as human targets during the Norman knights' interminable practices.

And yet he had managed to escape. He forced his legs to move yet again, recalling with no pride—and no shame—the night he'd crawled among the pile of dead men, cursing winter's overlong hold against spring. The bitter cold weather at first seemed likely to thwart his plan. One shiver, a quiet chattering of teeth, a hint of misting breath, could betray him. Somehow, he'd managed to keep his body and his teeth still, and then the weather turned out to be a blessing.

His body, thoroughly chilled, his arms and legs stiffened from long hours of immobility, raised no suspicion among those tossing the dead onto the dung heap the next morning. At nightfall, while starving wolves slunk near the pile of dead men, he'd laboriously freed himself from the stiff, clutching arms and legs and staggered into the woods, praying the snow and scrabbling wolves would cover his tracks.

If by chance his Norman captors rummaged through the dead and discovered him missing, they would seek him first at Langwald. He knew this. With every ounce of his being, he understood that his home, his livelihood, his mastery of his own destiny existed no more. And yet he could no more stop his slow, trudging progress back to Langwald than a salmon could decide not to fight its way upstream in the spring. Hopeless. Certain to end in death. Even so, utterly impossible to disobey the urgent yearning, the aching need to make the journey.

Just to see. Just one look.

And now he was near journey's end. Another two days' walking—perhaps three, considering his slow, weakened condition—and he could have his glimpse of Langwald's acres. He allowed his gaze to travel toward the low hill rising several miles distant in the west. With luck, he could make the top of that hill before sundown. His brother Edwin, slain at Hastings, had claimed he could see Langwald spread out before him from the top of that hill. He had always meant to investigate Edwin's claim but never found the time amid the constant press of duties.

So, what to do? Spend half a day journeying to the top of the hill and hope for a glimpse of Langwald? Or continue onward, certain to see for himself within two or three days the extent of the Norman occupation of his birthright? Traveling to the hill would add a full day to his final arrival at Langwald. Edwin may have been boasting, taunting him for the fun of seeing him waste time to prove him wrong. The arguments against going to the hill circled in his mind even as he changed direction and headed toward it.

Fine sleet pelted him as he reached the base of the hill. He spotted a deer trail curling through the trees and underbrush. Setting foot on the path, he was suddenly consumed by the urgent need to *see*, a need that overpowered his weariness, a need that set his leaden legs to pumping with the fresh energy of a young colt. Small branches whipped against his face and chest, stinging sharply in the cold. Briars caught in the half-rotted fabric of his tunic, rending huge tears in the already shredded material as he forged his way to the top of the hill. Gasping for breath, he threw his head back and closed his eyes briefly, half-afraid to look, afraid Edwin had lied and he might not see Langwald at all, afraid Edwin had spoken true and he'd find Langwald Manor a charred, burnt-out hulk like so many of the places he'd passed on his journey. Gathering his courage, and reining his emotions in tight check, he took his first look.

Edwin had spoken the truth.

The miles separating him from his manor might not have existed, so well could he see Langwald Hall. A pall of smoke hung over the thatched roof and spread over the close-clustered cottages of his villagers. Sheep grazed in the high meadow. The fields, barren at this time of year, offered interesting patterns not noticeable from the ground. The big squarish patch off to the east—it had to be Britt the potter's neat rows. And there, near the hall itself, stood his mother's herb garden.

Movement caught his eye, and he squinted to focus on the activity centering around Langwald's highest point. The whole population of the village, it seemed, clustered around a huge hole in the ground.

The foundation work for a Norman castle. The ultimate desecration of the land he loved.

A low sob sounded in the back of his throat, and he shook it away, certain it was his body trying to compensate for the breath he'd deprived it of during this last, headlong rush up the hill. He stepped out from beneath the sheltering trees and felt the sleet melt into his hair, sending rivulets of water down his face, mixing with the moisture that was already stinging his lacerated cheeks. Sweat, no doubt, from his exertions.

"Langwald," he whispered, wiping the wetness from his face, unable to tear his gaze away from what was no longer his.

A soft rustling behind him ended with a painful blow to his head, and he saw nothing more.

1

Rothgar's wits returned, slinking from the hidden recesses of his mind like ghost-gray cats seeking the warmth of his reawakened consciousness. All about him, the gabble of Norman voices shrieked outrage, excitement, perhaps a bit of alarm, but Rothgar wasted none of his newfound sense trying to decipher their words, though the long-ago lessons taught by his lady mother, reinforced by months of captivity beneath Norman rule, had strengthened his command of their tongue. Instead, he concentrated all of his mysteriously depleted strength against the urge to breathe deep and fill his lungs with a fortifying breath of air, forcing himself to lie still despite the pain of his arm lying crooked beneath him, to ignore the piercing throb where sharp-tipped rushes gouged the broken skin over his skull.

A clumsy foot trod near his head. With his eyes screwed tightly shut, he couldn't see it so much as feel the wooden floor sag, but nothing prepared him for the heart-stopping stab of pain when the foot carelessly scraped in its wake the rushes lying under him.

To move, to allow the slightest whimper to escape his lips, would remind the Norman swine of his presence. And he'd seen many a good Saxon man slaughtered just so by the Normans, whose misguided sense of fair play caused them to withhold their swords until their enemies gasped and squirmed with unwitting evidence of regained consciousness. So he bit his tongue and concentrated on his inadequate, shallow breaths, and prayed for the pain to recede.

Again, he felt a presence close to him, a soft rustling, a step so light it did not disturb the wooden floor beneath his head. And then hands, soft, gentle, cool against his forehead, so unexpected that all of his fortitude deserted him and his eyelids flew open at the touch.

"Eadyth," he croaked, his voice tight and shaky with disuse, and knew immediately he was wrong.

Much about the woman's eyes were the same as Eadyth's; she looked at him with the same faint disgust, the same cool assessment that told him she held other men in higher esteem. But where his betrothed's eyes were the clear, sun-washed blue of a winter sky, this woman's eyes reminded him of the color of his favorite horse: deep brown flecked with chips of gold. Her face, not so long as Eadyth's in nose or chin, was framed in softly curling hair of the same brown-gold. The hair seemed to warm her skin to the color of honey-baked cream, completely at odds but somehow nicer to look upon than the convent pallor marking Eadyth's years of schooling with the nuns.

At the sound of his voice, the woman withdrew her hands and hastily wiped them against her skirts.

"He lives," she said, her Norman words well said and slow enough that he need not exercise his wits to understand.

At once the din in the hall subsided. Rothgar winced as heavy Norman feet set the floor to quivering beneath him, as he found himself ringed by hard-staring Norman knights who, to a man, gripped the hilts of their swords in white-knuckled fists. The need to lie still had passed, but his legs wouldn't obey his thought to stand, his arms failed to heed his wish that they rise to ward off attack. Seldom had he felt so helpless; he held himself rigid, determined to meet with dignity the death blow he knew one of those knights would soon deal him.

It was the woman who moved first, rather than one of the knights. As if she had sensed his earlier discomfort, she eased a piece of cloth under his aching head; she gently worked his arm free from its awkward position beneath his back and set it to rest over his stomach.

"He called out her name. Fetch the Lady Eadyth," she said, speaking Saxon English to a familiar-looking, gape-jawed wench who had somehow found a space where she could peek at him with frightened rabbit eyes from between two knights.

Sensation returned to his arm; understanding flooded his brain with the same needle-sharp prickles of agony. Through the legs and over the heads of the Norman knights he could see familiar smoke-darkened carvings, pale sections of wall marking the spaces where weapons had once hung. In this place, the name Eadyth was known. The wench who'd gone to perform the woman's bidding—she, too, he recognized.

Langwald Hall. He'd blundered right back to it.

I but wanted to look, to reassure myself all was well.

Too late now to curse himself for a fool. Well beyond time to heed the warnings of those who had urged him to speed with all haste in the opposite direction should he make good his vow to escape his Norman gaolers.

"I would know your name," the woman said to him. "I can speak your tongue."

Her voice soothed his aching, weary spirit with seductive sensation akin to the feel of warm goose grease over sunburned skin. Rothgar gritted his teeth and held his tongue against the almost overpowering urge to answer her simple request. He'd allowed her touch to break his control before; he'd be a dead man sure if he but said to her, "I am Rothgar. Master of . . . myself until Norman usurpers killed my liege lord and enslaved me to pay for my loyalty."

"All Englishmen are stupid," sneered a dark knight. "And these Saxons we are saddled with are the stupidest of the lot. It makes one wonder, Maria, at the regard William held for Hugh, to bestow such a hardheaded, dirt-poor lot upon him."

Beside him, the woman—Maria—stiffened as though the knight who'd spoken had dealt her an insult. Rothgar looked at the knight through lowered lashes, taking the measure of the man, and thought he understood. Outwardly fawning, seeming eager to please, there was nonetheless a slyness about the man's ebony eyes, a minuscule twitch at the corner of his lips, a cast to his dark visage that betrayed an insolence bordering on malicious cruelty.

Maria's husband? Unaccountably, the thought saddened him.

She rose to her feet with a grace belying the long moments she'd spent crouching at Rothgar's side. Ignoring the knight with a decidedly unwifely attitude, she addressed another of the hulking Normans standing guard over his prone, powerless body. Rothgar sharpened his hearing when they began conversing in Norman, certain their words concerned his fate.

"'Tis unlike Walter to give the order to silence a trespasser ere he learns the man's purpose. Dunstan, did this one say anything, did he name himself before you cracked him on the skull?"

Dunstan shifted from one booted foot to another, a tide of red flooding his face. Rothgar, helpless against the weakened condition of his body and taking in the way the Norman's muscles stretched his sleeve, wondered that he hadn't perished at once from a blow delivered by that meaty arm.

"Nay, my lady," Dunstan mumbled. "I would not have struck the man, anyone can see he hasn't fed well of late and lacks strength. Sir Walter'd gone off into the wood and my lord Gilbert bid me—"

"'Twas I who told Dunstan to knock the man senseless."

It was the dark-visaged knight who'd called him a stupid Englishman, and now Rothgar had a name—Gilbert—to put to the man.

Gilbert stepped closer and prodded Rothgar's leg with the tip of his sword. "Think on it, Maria. We found him atop a small hill not ten miles distant, looking on Langwald with the fervor of a priest discovering the true cross. He's a spy, and I only wish we had disposed of him before your tender nature overruled your sense." He pressed his weight against the tip of his sword so slightly no movement was evident, but with strength enough for the razor-honed edge to pierce Rothgar's skin and slip a finger's width into his flesh. Rothgar felt the warm trickle of blood course along the calf of his leg, felt Gilbert's mocking Norman gaze upon him.

An enemy. The pain was sharp, but Rothgar would not give his enemy the satisfaction of jerking back, of crying out. He met the Norman's stare with his own, and let his lips curl into a semblance of a smile, knowing full well his audacity would raise Gilbert's ire and hasten his own death.

No matter. Better to be dead than to submit to this familiar brand of Norman cruelty; better to be gone from a world where Normans ruled good Saxon holdings like Langwald Manor.

"Have a care, Gilbert." Maria's voice carried a rough edge and her hand slapped at the sword, inadvertently widening the wound and sending a shaft of agony up Rothgar's leg before the sword was withdrawn. This time Rothgar could not stifle the groan, but she ignored him, turning her wrath upon Gilbert. *My protectoress*, Rothgar's pain-clouded mind mused before he sorted out the Norman words: "You've set him to bleeding like a stuck pig, and these rushes were put down but three days ago."

And then Eadyth was there, standing tall among the Norman knights, looking on him with a hostility he'd always known she'd felt but seldom allowed him to see.

Rothgar had never meant to face death lying as helpless as a hamstrung doe. He did his best to rise to his elbows at least, knowing that it would take only a few words from Eadyth to pronounce his death sentence. But his arms were as unresponsive as seasoned logs; his head and shoulders so heavy he might as well be weighted down with the carcass of the stuck pig Maria had likened him to.

With a sense of inevitability, he watched Eadyth raise her hand and point one long finger at him. He took in the malicious, self-satisfied smile she indulged in, and watched her thin, almost colorless lips part to speak.

A wave of despair washed over him, so powerful it would have knocked him flat on his back had he been able to rise to his elbows. And Rothgar, who'd faced death almost every day of the past half year and more, who'd thought himself accustomed to the idea, who only moments ago tried to hasten Gilbert's death blow, found he yearned for life with every particle of his being.

Eadyth narrowed her eyes and stared down her long nose at him, granting him a moment's hope that his starved and filthy appearance was so changed she wouldn't recognize him. And then her smile broadened. Addressing Maria, she said the words. "Why, I believe he is Rothgar. My betrothed, before my lord Hugh took me to wife."

Rothgar held his breath at her half explanation, praying Eadyth would likewise control her tongue. But she stepped closer, pretending to study him with her deceitful eyes. "Yea, my lady, I am certain." She straightened and folded her hands before her, demurely, as she'd learned from the nuns. Again, a smile curved her lips. "He is Rothgar, former lord of this, Langwald Hall."

Several of the Normans still encircling him gasped aloud. Gilbert ordered Dunstan, "Run him through."

So her words marked him for death, and Eadyth, who had despised him and scorned Langwald Hall, would live on in the place he loved, safely married to one of the conquering Normans. Rothgar allowed the injustice of it to fill him with rage, to strengthen him so he wouldn't cringe and cower or close his eyes when Dunstan's sword pierced his heart.

"Nay, Dunstan."

Maria's voice rang with authority, stilling Dunstan's hesitant hand. The Norman drew back, furtively glancing at Rothgar's prone body.

"Maria." Gilbert's word conveyed warning and disapproval, but she turned a cool gaze in his direction.

"This is not for you or me to decide, Gilbert," she said. "Hugh is lord here. Hugh must decide."

Rothgar had fought alongside Harold at Stamford Bridge and Hastings. He knew firsthand the frustration of being forced to carry out nonsensical orders, the futility of trying to convince one in power that he'd set himself on the wrong course. At that moment, Gilbert bore the look of a man confronted with such obstacles. He faced Maria with barely leashed fury that threatened to be terrible should he permit it to escape, while she met his rage with a total lack of concern.

It was curious. But Rothgar had no energy to puzzle it out, so drained did he feel after the riptide of emotion he'd just experienced: certain death, and now a reprieve.

"So it is for Hugh to decide." Heavy sarcasm laced Gilbert's words. "Stand aside, then, so I may drag this Saxon to his feet and march him to Hugh forthwith."

His comment provoked a stir from the Norman knights, a muted buzz from the Saxon servants, much like the tension preceding a cockfight.

"This is not the time to bother Hugh—" Maria began.

"Maria, I insist. This has gone on too long as it is."

With a muted shuffling of feet and a few muttered aye's, some of the Norman knights shifted toward Gilbert, aligning themselves behind his stand. A hush settled over the hall. Gilbert, smirking as though he'd gained an advantage over Maria, stroked the hilt of his sword. The words he'd spoken meant little to Rothgar, save that he sensed they hid a deeper meaning, that the exchange between Gilbert and Maria concerned far more than Rothgar's battered presence.

Maria surveyed the hall, her gaze flicking over the knights. None save Rothgar stood close enough to see her wounded pride, her sense of betrayal as she looked at them, Norman looking upon Norman, but holding herself separate, as though a yawning chasm had opened at Maria's feet.

"You are of like mind, Dunstan?" Maria asked softly.

"Aye, lady." The embarrassed knight stared at his feet. "This has gone on overlong."

"Very well." Her clipped words provoked another stir of excitement, along with a dumbfounded look from Gilbert making it apparent the dark knight hadn't expected her to capitulate.

Maria turned her attention on Rothgar. Her nose wrinkling in distaste, she spoke to the knights. "Hugh shall see the Saxon, but not in this condition. He reeks of the cess pit. In light of his identity, one of you must guard him while he's cleaned."

She studied Rothgar intently, as though she were measuring him for the coffin he'd so recently escaped. Although he'd had no choice in the matter, Rothgar felt a flush of embarrassment over his filth-encrusted body, over the tattered rags that did little to cover him.

"He'll need clothes—there must be some of his things on hand from before."

She looked into his eyes.

He'd said one word during this time, his misguided outburst of the name of his traitorous betrothed. As his eyes met Maria's, he wished to say something more, but he knew not what. He couldn't thank her for saving his life, since he might well be dead anyway after meeting with the mysterious Hugh. His sketchy grasp of the Norman tongue couldn't find quick words to tell her he admired the manner in which she opposed Gilbert, or that he thought her face and voice would most pleasantly speed him on his way should death be decreed.

Maria seemed unaware of his respect and admiration. "Cut his hair," she said to the knights. "And shave his beard. He looks so . . . English."

Gilbert waited until his fellow knights had hauled Rothgar from the hall, until the excited, gibbering Saxon workers resumed their duties, until only he and Maria stood before the inefficient Saxon fire pit. He pretended to warm his hands over the fire, hoping that its flickering heat would still their shaking and stifle the urge he felt to throttle Maria's beautiful neck.

She copied his hand warming, her head bent to the task so that the firelight teased golden shimmers from her hair. The sight of her standing so, the pressure of her outstretched arms causing her breasts to swell, her face all gentle and pensive, her teeth teasing her lower lip, her hair tangling over her shoulders to caress her breasts . . . too much like the dreams that tormented his nights.

He spoke harshly to cover the hoarseness of his voice. "You should not have countermanded my order before the other men. When Walter is away on one of his mysterious absences, *my* word must prevail. You gave me no choice but to bring Hugh into the matter."

He expected the stubborn clenching of her jaw at his words. He didn't expect the confusion and reluctant agreement in her eyes when she met his gaze.

"Your words did prevail, Gilbert. He is being readied for Hugh, as you insisted."

Her acquiescence left him feeling magnanimous. "It pleases me that you see my side in this matter. You need not actually bother Hugh."

"Oh, but I insist." Her words were a sarcastic echo of his own earlier statement. Her lips thinned into a mulish line. "You were right to demand a meeting between them. Saxons saw you carry Rothgar into the hall. You flaunted your mastery of their tongue when making your demand. They understood every word you said and would suspect something was amiss if we failed to consult Hugh. Besides, there might be a benefit to such a meeting between the two."

Damn the woman! She'd managed to twist his small triumph into a meeting much to her liking. Someday, he vowed, he would achieve the upper hand over her. Gilbert snorted in derision. "How so? Do you think *Hugh* will pry secrets from him?"

As always, she bristled like a hedgehog at any slur upon her brother's abilities. "We would learn nothing from a dead man, that is certain. You yourself have taken pains to convince me that a holding so rich in crops and beasts should boast some gold as well, yet we have found naught."

"Mayhap I should be present for this most illuminating interview. 'Twould be interesting to watch the new and old lords of Langwald meet face-to-face. Mayhap the old lord shall slap the new across the back with all good fellowship, turn over his hidden stores of gold, and wish us Normans well. Hugh's reaction should be most interesting." He stuffed his hands into the front of his tunic; the fire had done nothing to quell the urge to wrap them about her slender neck. But murderous intent had been replaced with an itch for feeling the pulse hammering in her throat, her very breath controlled by him, until she begged and gasped his name in just the way he wanted to hear it.

"Hugh may prove difficult," she admitted, dragging his attention back to the matter at hand. "But there is no need to remove yourself from your duties. I shall honor my word and present the Saxon to Hugh."

"So eager to see me gone, Maria? I would have you welcome me instead. Ah, well, one day perhaps." Gilbert allowed a mirthless smile to curl his lip. "Some daylight remains. I'm off to see whether Hugh's devoted villagers managed to do any work this day."

He left her standing alone at the fire, alone as she'd been during that glorious moment when Hugh's knights had aligned themselves at his side. He hoped that moment would lodge itself in her mind, that she would think of it again and again, until she came to realize she, too, would do well to join with him.

Had Rothgar been flung before Maria's feet in the early days when Hugh first claimed Langwald Hall, she'd have ordered his execution without a second thought. All across England, Normans had done so, fearful that the landholders they displaced would somehow rouse the people against them, could in some way foment rebellion against their new rulers.

Truth to tell, had the trusted Walter been present, had anyone other than Gilbert uttered the command to kill, she would have held her tongue. And had the Saxon suffered any injury other than a blow to the head, her heart would have hardened. But Gilbert had spoken, and she had intervened, provoking Gilbert's righteous anger and the soul-numbing shift in loyalties of Hugh's knights to Gilbert's side.

She'd expected the shift; she'd just prayed it would occur at some far off point in the future, when Hugh's circumstances were improved. Mayhap acceding to Gilbert's public demand to pester Hugh with the Saxon's presence might placate Hugh's men, buying Hugh more time. None of the men need know Gilbert had withdrawn his demand, and that her own stubborn intent to thwart him left her no choice but to take the Saxon before Hugh.

She felt so alone.

Hard to recall, now, the relief she'd felt when they rode in to claim Langwald and found no lord in residence. Langwald's peasants had grudgingly admitted their lord had disappeared right around the time Harold had called upon his landholders to join him at Hastings. Though none would admit it, it was plain their lord had taken up arms against William, meaning his life and lands were forfeit. Over time, her nightmares about the faceless dispossessed lord had faded, until she no longer worried about the day when he might reappear. And now he lived by her mercy, a wreck of a man, not at all the formidable foe she'd imagined.

And yet, there was something about the man, despite his wretched appearance, that seemed to demand he be accorded dignity.

"Lady Maria!"

The pompous, peremptory call sent a quick shudder coursing through her.

"Philip," she answered, as graciously as she could through gritted teeth.

Of all the times for the overbearing, interfering Philip Martell to poke his meddlesome nose through Langwald's door! But then the man seemed possessed of a knack for turning up at the least opportune moment, such as now, when her thoughts were all in a muddle, her patience worn thin from bearing up beneath Gilbert's snide, self-righteous remarks and wishing his comments hadn't planted doubts in her mind about the wisdom of keeping Rothgar alive.

"It cannot be true." Philip stood before her, nose aquiver like a ferret scenting a rat. Indeed, he had the overall mien of a low-slinking, burrow-seeking ferret: thin body, weasely eyes, a nondescript mop of dark hair shot with gray. Even the status of knight, which he had long coveted but never earned, would not bolster his appearance.

"You must know I would be duty-bound to report to William if you're keeping a sworn enemy alive," he said now. "'Tis bad enough, the things I must convey to his ear, what with the castle walls not rising as expected."

"By Easter, all will be on schedule," Maria promised rashly—anything to still Philip's wagging, annoying tongue. How he'd ingratiated himself to William she had no clue, only that his bastard status might have endeared him to the similarly illegitimate king. No matter; Philip was foresworn to travel hard to Normandy after Easter, where William had withdrawn, to deal with some clerkly duty or other, so she must needs placate him now. "The walls will rise quickly once the moat is dug."

"I certainly hope so." Philip sniffed. He seemed insulted at her inattention. And well he might be, for though she meant to curry Philip's favor, though she knew she should be concerned about Gilbert's rising power over Hugh's men, she could not concentrate on anything but the assortment of kitchen lads and wenches carrying pails of clean water into the bower housing Rothgar of Langwald.

She pretended to listen to Philip while she watched them cart away other pails that at first looked and stank like bog mud, and entertained the fancy that nothing would be left of Rothgar to take before Hugh.

While Philip chattered on, Maria wondered what color Rothgar of Langwald's hair might be.

There was no question as to the color of his eyes: blue. Blue, blue, always blue, these English eyes, though in varying degrees. In Eadyth's eyes, one perceived the chill of a winter morning, the tinge of frozen skin just before frostbite turned it white. The blue of Rothgar's eyes burned hot. When green logs were placed on a crackling fire, the heat sent rivulets of moisture trickling from the cut edges, and little bursts of hissing gas puffing from cracks in the logs. The color of Rothgar's eyes matched the short-lived flames that danced atop those sudden, forceful bursts.

Sir Walter's quiet voice stilled Philip's tongue and broke her idle contemplation.

"The Saxon will not offend now, my lady."

"Walter! I did not know you had returned." Maria seized her trusted knight's wrist and guided him toward Philip. "See to it that Philip enjoys a warming draught before he begins his return journey to Stillingham."

"But I wanted to see the Saxon—"

"You will sit near the fire while I watch over my lady." Walter's tone allowed for no argument. Maria hid her smile as Philip shuffled away, mumbling to himself, like a recalcitrant lad admonished by his father. Not even Philip Martell could override Walter's stolid, relentless determination to complete a set task. Thank God that Walter, who had served her father many years ago, had sought service with Hugh just before the Norman's glorious victory. In these treacherous times, 'twas not an easy thing to find an honest man.

Walter had said the Saxon would not offend. True enough, Maria's nose no longer quivered at Rothgar's scent. But something within her rebelled at the sight of him helpless and humbled. She remembered kneeling next to him, the fleeting, illusive moment when she'd fancied he'd placed himself on her side against Gilbert, lending her a moment's strength to call Gilbert's bluff and bring about this meeting with Hugh, and irrationally wished she could do the same for him now.

His hair, tawny shot with gold, took exception to the rigid Norman haircut. It refused to lie flat against his forehead, curling instead into a nest of wild, thick ringlets damp from his bathing. The skin of his forehead and around his eyes bore the dark color of a man who'd spent much time in the sun, while his chin and hunger-hollowed cheeks flushed fiery red from the scraping away of his beard.

He was on his feet, the first time Maria had seen him upright. Rothgar of Langwald would have dwarfed his more compact Norman captors had he not, as Sir Dunstan had remarked, looked as though he hadn't fed well for some time. And he didn't stand straight, seeming to hunch at the waist as though he'd just taken a blow to the gut. He wore a tunic of tawny edged with blue, the colors and length of it stamping it as belonging to him, but though it clung properly to his wide shoulders, it hung like an ill-made peasant smock over the rest of him.

One hand, broad, blunt-fingered, ropy-veined, and callused, rested atop a heavy oak table. It looked to Maria as though Rothgar clung to the table lest he lose his balance.

"Are you able to walk?" she asked, hoping for an excuse to avoid taking him to Hugh, speaking slowly in the harsh English tongue that grated against her ears.

"Aye." His voice was scarcely more than a whisper, but it rumbled deeply from his throat.

Maria exchanged doubtful looks with Sir Walter. The Norman knight shook his head and moved to grip Rothgar's upper arm, but Rothgar jerked away, nearly toppling to the floor.

"You can barely stand upright, let alone walk," Maria observed.

"An empty belly turns in on itself."

As though his words had been a signal, his stomach set up a ferocious rumbling. Rothgar clutched at it with one hand, keeping his balance with the other. And then he smiled at her. He stood before her, half-starved and in ill-fitting garments, ignominiously shaved and shorn, but in that wry, self-deprecating twist of his lips, she could read traces of the man who had once ruled Langwald Manor.

The sight set something leaping to life within her.

"I'll send for food," she said, wondering at the sudden dryness of her mouth, still hoping to postpone the meeting she herself had agreed to bring about.

But he shook his head, patting at his stomach.

"I fear I gulped at my bath water like a fish tossed

back from the net. 'Tis that which has brought my belly to life."

Maria's stomach roiled at the memory of the filthy, stinking water she'd seen hauled from his bath. She pressed her fingers to her lips to prevent her gorge from rising.

He seemed to understand her revulsion. "Nay, my lady. I had my fill of the water before it did its work on my dirt."

"Surely you didn't stretch your skin so tight it can't hold a bite of bread."

A remoteness seemed to settle over him, as though his mind had traveled back to another time, another place. "I'd as soon not stretch it any tighter, my lady, until I know my fate. It would be most . . . bothersome to get this stomach reaccustomed to good food if meals are to be denied later."

His words hinted at experience with deprivation she could only imagine; his sudden wariness pierced the dreamlike fog that had settled over her at first sight of this man. She would do well to remember the threat he posed, instead of indulging the urge to cluck over him like a broody hen, instead of entertaining fancies that he wished her well over Gilbert. As well he might, considering the fate he would suffer at Gilbert's hand. Indeed, locking him away to starve to death or casting him out from Langwald with no means for survival were the options most likely to be exercised after she went through the motions of presenting him to Hugh.

"We must go, then," she said. Deliberately, she added strength to her words. "Hugh, lord of Langwald, awaits."

She learned then that blue English eyes could dull with despair over more than the threat of starvation.

* * *

Maria preceded Rothgar down the length of Langwald Hall, moving in odd fits and starts and tossing doubtful glances over her shoulder. Though his stride might not be as purposeful as he'd like, his stumbling progress nonetheless kept pace with hers, so that even the ever-vigilant Sir Walter blundered into him from behind. Trying to prevent their combined weight from crashing into her at least provided the distraction he needed to avoid looking about him, avidly drinking in the sight of what was no longer his.

But since all about him had once been his, there was naught to look upon but Maria.

She was a fragile, frail-boned creature, all eyes and hair. The gown she wore looked to be one of his mother's, carefully folded away after her death. His mother had been uncommonly slim and tall, but too slim and not tall enough to allow the other women in the hall to hack off the length to increase the width of the gowns sufficiently. As far as Rothgar could judge, Maria hadn't altered the width, only the length. But rack his brain as he might, he couldn't remember his mother looking quite so fetching in that gown.

His stomach, rebelling at the deluge of water he'd foolishly swallowed, seized him with a cramp. He was glad of the pain. It reminded him of his position: defeated Saxon warrior, escaped slave, weak as a newborn kitten. And his mind seemed to be as feeble as his body; otherwise, it would be furiously working to hatch another escape plot instead of dwelling on the way a Saxon gown clung to slim Norman hips.

She stopped at the door to his own chamber, as he'd known she would; it was the only private room in the hall. With its own fire pit, broad hide-covered window and view of Langwald's sweeping acres, it was truly fit for the lord of Langwald. Sir Walter, following a too-close step behind, gave him a little push over the threshold. Rothgar got his first glimpse of Hugh, and two bits of knowledge that stunned his mind into surprised numbness.

The first was simple enough: Maria had ordered the Norman knights about with impunity, and countermanded the knave Gilbert with an authority seldom granted to a woman. He understood her position of power as Maria moved now to stand beside a seated man, the only one in the room besides himself. Hugh. Allowing for the differences of sex and size, they were as alike as two cheeses sprung from the same mold. Hugh and Maria—not lord and lady at all, but brother and sister.

The second thing was harder and crueler to absorb. Maria bent to whisper something in Hugh's ear, and then with a gentle hand guided his head and held it in place until Hugh looked Rothgar's way with a bleary-eyed, placid stare. His mouth gaped, threatening to spill drool, and he clutched a harvest doll fashioned from wheat straw in one incongruously huge hand.

Langwald Manor—the land, the hall, the people Rothgar loved and near lost his life to preserve and defend—all had been torn from his care and given over to a half-wit.

2

"*Had Dunstan swung* his sword with more vigor, you might have met the same fate."

Maria felt better for having said the words, especially when Rothgar lifted a hand to the close-clipped hair surrounding his own head wound.

"Then he was not always so."

The former lord of Langwald's expression had changed from one of contempt to a look of guarded pity; his words conveyed an odd mixture of curiosity and relief.

"One needs only to look at him to see the bearing of a Norman knight," Maria said, though the boast carried less effect than it would have six months earlier. Hugh's upper arm, big around as her thigh, still bulged with strength. But when she'd encircled it within her own two hands to lead him to table a few nights ago, she'd noticed a subtle softening in the feel of the flesh, as if it pined for the weight of the weapons Hugh had once handled with such deadly efficiency. "'Twas a pike wielded by one of your own kind, cowardly, from behind, that rendered him thus."

There was silence among them as Hugh, heedless of their attention, employed his mighty arms to set his doll atop a bit of string lying on the tabletop. Maria looked away as her brother fumbled with the string, trying again and again to bring the ends together in a loose knot about the doll's waist.

"The people of Langwald must chafe under the rule of one such as he."

If Rothgar's voice had carried scorn, if he had laughed at Hugh or mocked his state, Maria would have summoned Walter and belatedly ordered Rothgar's execution. Instead, the man's words spoke of a familiarity with the pigheaded villagers he'd once ruled.

"They chafe under Norman rule," she admitted.

A ghost of a smile, as if the news of his villagers' mulish lack of cooperation pleased Rothgar mightily, played at the edges of his lips. Maria sought the words to dampen his amusement.

"They know not the extent of Hugh's disability."

Rothgar shrugged. "I myself can neither read nor write, yet it is writ plain upon yon face that no whole man resides within."

"They do not see him so." She fought the urge to cover Hugh's ears with her hands; he wouldn't notice or comprehend the discussion swirling about him, yet it tugged at her heart to discuss his weakness before him. "He is dosed. Demons rage in his head otherwise. I withhold the dose when he must stand before the people. The pain he feels then . . ." It was her turn to allow a smile, tempered with sorrow, to flicker upon her face. "The villagers think him a most fierce and ill-tempered lord. They fear incurring his wrath, and none has voiced a longing for more of his attention."

"Regardless, lady, I doubt you've hidden the truth from them. I have ever found it impossible to keep the slightest secret from Langwald's people." He returned his attention to Hugh. "How did it happen?"

How did it happen . . . the ambiguous English words caused Maria to wonder if she understood Rothgar's question. How had he himself been captured and imprisoned in Langwald Hall? How had Hugh been injured and come to be married to Rothgar's betrothed? How had Rothgar's birthright been confiscated and turned over to Norman rule?

How did it come about that a victorious Norman and vanquished Saxon could discuss such things without rancor?

And how did it happen that she should find herself feeling an inexplicable relief at sharing her burdensome secret with a potential enemy?

His countenance gave no clue as to what interested him most.

He seemed not to mind as she studied him through lowered lashes, suddenly ashamed for forgetting his prolonged hunger, his weakened state. He'd refused to eat before knowing his fate, but did not complain now when it was evident Hugh was incapable of making such a momentous decision. He stood before her patiently, giving her pause to think.

"My life is forfeit, I assume," he said, startling her.

"What makes you think so?"

He nodded toward Hugh. "You've divulged your secret to me, lady. Do you not fear my tongue will wag?"

He spoke true; she should fear the power granted by this knowledge. She should be thinking of ways to pick his brain for methods that would help her deal with Langwald's bullheaded villagers. Instead, she looked at the way he leaned against a wall, his arms crossed before him so that his lack of flesh was less apparent, and wished she hadn't ordered him shorn and shaved. She would like to have seen that tawny-gold hair hanging thick to his shoulders, and thought that if ever a man should be bearded, it would be Rothgar of Langwald.

Hugh succeeded in knotting his string. His little cry of satisfaction intruded upon the whim that had her staring at Rothgar with the helpless fascination of a wolf bewitched by firelight. She blinked three times and fancied Rothgar released a pent-up breath as she turned her attention to Hugh.

She complimented her brother lavishly and applauded his success. "You see, he improves day by day." She directed her comment to Rothgar even as her fingers worked to disengage Hugh's knot. Retying it would occupy his attention a while longer, and she waited until he was once again absorbed in the task. All the while Rothgar's words hung in the air: How did it happen?

She decided to answer the easiest of the questions, and left Hugh's side to fetch his helm.

Rothgar straightened as she brought the headgear to him. She shifted the helm until the damaged part faced up. Her movements drew Hugh's attention, and he blanched at the sight of the helmet, expelling quick, panicked gulps of air. There was a quick motion from the shadows and a small form came hurtling toward Hugh, low to the ground, darting and gliding as though incapable of holding to a straight course. A boy, a near-man of thirteen or so, uncommonly small and brown-skinned and with a short cap of night-black hair crowning his head, revealing ears more pointed than round, slanting brown eyes, narrow brows. He crouched next to Hugh's knee and the knight calmed, patting the boychild's head.

"God's teeth!" Rothgar backed away, his eyes wide. "'Tis one of the woods people."

"You English are so superstitious! 'Tis only Fen." Rothgar was not the first of the Saxons to react so to the sight of the young boy. "On the very day he took the blow that made him thus, Hugh saved Fen from certain death. Fen has devoted himself to Hugh's care ever since." She cast a fond smile in Fen's direction before turning the helmet toward Rothgar, shifting her position to block it from Hugh's sight, and Fen from Rothgar's.

"Look, you see where Hugh was hit," she said, pointing to a dent in the metal helm. She edged her hand into the depression sideways, and then lay it flat. "Four fingers deep. A palm's width." Involuntarily she shuddered, remembering the matching indentation in Hugh's skull.

Rothgar frowned from Hugh's thick-haired head to the helm. "I've never worn such. Where did the blow fall?"

Of its own accord, her free hand rose to answer his question, brushing against his new-shaven skin on its way to the back of his skull, where it buried itself in his short, thick, curling hair.

She tilted her face up to look at him since the top of her head came but to his chin. Perhaps it was the difference in their heights, the shortness of her arm, that brought his head forward at the pressure of her hand. With a quick intake of breath, he stiffened. His eyes locked with hers; his lips hovered scant inches from her own; his hand raised as though to reciprocate her touch.

"Here. The blow fell here," she said, her voice unaccountably hoarse, not certain of the spot where her fingers rested but unable to break the contact. Her fingertips seemed to throb in accord with the life-force rushing through him.

"I see."

His warm breath felt soft as springtime's first breeze against her lips, even as the whispered English words confused her yet again. What did he see as his eyes bored into hers, as her fingers tangled within the silky curling softness of his hair? Did he see a nobleman's kinswoman explaining her brother's near mortal injury . . . or did he see a wanton wench engaged in a most unseemly caress?

Maria snatched her hand away.

Not since her lord husband Ranulf died had her pulse raced so at the proximity of a man. Not since Ranulf's death . . . to be honest, not even while he lived. Cradling Hugh's helm before her, she hastened back to her brother's side.

"Maria." Rothgar's voice sounded at her ear, its rich, husky timbre sending little ripples of excitement shivering through her. He must have followed behind her on feet as silent as a cat's.

She must put paid to this pounding and leaping of her heart.

"Walter." Her crying of the knight's name echoed like a mockery of Rothgar's calling of her own.

Walter burst through the door, his hand at his sword hilt. Only then would she meet Rothgar's gaze. She forced herself not to flinch at the puzzled hurt she read there.

"Take him," Maria ordered.

"Please, there is much I do not understand." Rothgar's words trailed away as Walter gripped his arm.

"What shall I do with him, my lady?"

At her word, Walter's loyal sword would pierce Rothgar's heart or lop off his head, if that were her desire. She could remove his disconcerting presence, please Gilbert, and regain the loyalty of Hugh's men with one simple order. But the words would not come. "He has no appetite for Norman food or drink. Lock him away," she said instead.

"Where, my lady? This hall boasts no cells."

Maria clutched the helm to her stomach, hiding behind it as if it were a shield warding off the beguiling powers of the stranger standing before her. She sorted through the options in her mind: too many villagers worked with the cows in the byre; the stables were nothing more than three-sided shelters; the granaries still held much of Langwald's harvest bounty.

"Put him in the henhouse," she decided. " 'Tis fortified against fox and other vermin. It should hold him well enough."

Walter and Rothgar were long gone before the blood slowed in Maria's veins.

Eadyth pressed close against the wall, edging ever nearer to the great doors, which stood unbarred for the first time in her memory. No doubt the job had been left undone by one of the silly wenches or boggle-eyed lads who ran about, all aflutter at the news of Rothgar's capture and return to Langwald. Even the hounds had abandoned their incessant nosing through the rushes to join the excitement, adding their yapping and growls to the confusion.

Hearty laughter burst forth from the Normans clustered around the knights who had poached Rothgar in place of the fat stag William's new forest laws forbade them. Eadyth took another step toward the door, praying that the louts who usually watched over her were among the knights' audience. Mayhap this one time she could escape their ever-watchful gazes, their smooth phrases: "Do not bestir yourself, my lady. I'll fetch it." "I'll accompany you, my lady, and wait just outside the door until you finish." "No need to talk to them, my lady. I can deliver any messages you might have." Unctuously polite, unfailingly courteous, they nonetheless imprisoned her under the bitch Maria's control as well as if she were manacled and hung by her wrists from Langwald's gyves.

So close now. A puff of air gusted through the separation of the doors, its icy sweet freshness and chill tantalizing her with the promise of freedom. Three steps . . . nay, two . . .

"The wind bites sharp this night, Lady de Courson, and you wear no cloak."

Had the voice behind her belonged to one of her usual guardians, Eadyth would have let loose with a wail of frustration and despair. To reveal such weakness to Gilbert Crispin, though, would be most unwise.

"I noticed the door stood unbarred." The lie came easily; less simple was forming a smile capable of distracting the formidable knight from questioning her presence near the door.

Before she summoned the courage to turn and face him, she felt his hands at her shoulders, followed by the enveloping warmth of a fur-lined cloak settling around her. And then she had no need to turn, for Gilbert stepped in front of her and pushed the doors apart.

"Perhaps you would accompany me while I inspect our defenses this night."

It took all Eadyth's strength of will to step calmly through the open door, as if it hadn't been well nigh a half year since she'd last done so.

She managed to keep abreast of him for ten paces or so before a shuddering gripped her legs and allowed her to walk no more.

Gilbert seemed to have anticipated her distress. He gripped her elbow. "It will pass," he said, his breath misting about his head. "I've seen many a prisoner sprint from captivity, and then fall to the ground as though they'd been pole-axed. I believe the sensation which overwhelms you is not unlike what a man feels upon surviving a battle against seemingly insurmountable odds." He angled his body so it shielded her from the brunt of the wind.

She leaned into his strength, knock-kneed, embarrassed, and thoroughly exhilarated. She reveled in the feel of the wind swirling around her, at the rough clods of frozen earth gouging her feet through the soft soles of her slippers. The moon passed from behind a cloud, and she tilted her face skyward to bathe in its glow.

The giddy sensation of freedom and Gilbert's unexpected complicity loosened her tongue. "Each night, while Hugh tosses and snores, I conjure visions of escaping from Langwald. But in my dreams I run as swift as a hare, not with the faltering step of the village crone."

"And which burrow would you seek, my little English hare?" Gilbert's low laughter failed to soften his words. Eadyth's pleasure in the escapade deserted her like the plumes of their breath evaporating into the night.

"I seek nothing more than the comfort of the nuns who raised me," she muttered, suddenly shivering from the wind's chill.

"And you would scurry to these nuns, without stopping first to gossip about your lord husband with friends and family?"

Eadyth's cheeks burned with anger. "You're as distrustful as Maria. I have no friends and family in Langwald. And even if I did, I have no taste for admitting to all and sundry that I've been bonded in marriage to a hopeless idiot."

"You would admit your plight to the nuns."

The silvery light sharpened the bold planes of Gilbert's face. The only male visage Eadyth had ever enjoyed gazing upon was the image of Christ upon the cross. There were women, she knew, who found Gilbert attractive, who admired his swarthy features, his broad shoulders and bulging thighs. She wondered at their fascination and decided they'd never seen him as she did this night, with the moon casting an ominous tilt to his bristling brows, with his lips set hard and thin and a forbidding gleam darkening his impossibly black eyes. She shivered again, not entirely from the cold, and knew she mustn't lie to him.

"I would tell the nuns of my torment, yes." He began to nod, and she sought to wipe the smugness from his expression. "I would tell the abbess I am still virgin, fit to take vows, and ask that she hold a place for me. Hugh cannot live long. Maria will kill him with her possets, or he'll break his head open against the wall seeking relief from his pain."

She expected laughter from the Norman. She waited his jibes over her maidenly state, his taunting that they'd been right to wed her to Hugh to establish some semblance of normality, and right again to isolate her so none besides the Normans would know the truth. Instead, when he spoke, the words came as hard as if someone had a stranglehold on his throat.

"Hugh was my friend. I miss him sore."

"He is not dead yet." Unbidden, she felt a surge of pity at the memory of her husband clutching his shaggy head between his hands, the puzzled look in his pain-crazed eyes when Maria's dose wore thin and he found Eadyth alone with him. "I think . . . I think he could use your friendship now, Sir Gilbert."

"The shell who calls itself Hugh de Courson is no more my old friend than he is husband to you." Gilbert's words pricked with the sting of sleet.

The wind picked up, sending frozen, brittle-tipped branches clacking against one another in its wake. The eerie quavering of a wolf's cry drifted over all, setting off uncommonly loud squawking and clucking from the henhouse. Eadyth felt pressure at her elbow and realized Gilbert still held her fast. She moved to pull away, but he tightened his hold.

"We must return to the hall, my lady."

"But you have not yet checked your defenses." A fluttering started up in her breast, as though one of the cackling hens had found itself trapped within and was beating its wings in an effort to escape.

"I'll see you safe to your husband before I make my rounds."

"No." She tried digging her heels into the frozen earth but succeeded only in bruising her foot. "No," she said again, louder but less forcefully because of the shamefully pleading tone the word took.

In answer Gilbert gathered her arm beneath his. "There will be other nights, Eadyth."

She stilled, not trusting herself to speak.

He smiled, and perhaps it was a trick of the moonlight that hid all traces of humor. "It strikes me that Maria might be overcautious in keeping you so confined. She couldn't object if I were to offer to escort you on a short walk now and again."

Eadyth found her voice. "You would do this for me? Why?"

Gilbert patted her hand. "It seems both of us are in need of a friend. I can offer my services as escort, and in turn you can . . . talk to me. I wish to know more. Maria is extraordinarily closemouthed."

It seemed an innocent offer; why then did her senses hum, urging her to look beyond Gilbert's words for deeper meaning? But the lure of what he promised quelled her caution. Eadyth nodded her acceptance, wishing she could just as easily shake off the feeling of having struck a bad bargain.

With the tip of Walter's sword prodding at his back at every step across Langwald's yard, Rothgar walked as docile as a well-broke mule. One thing he'd learned over the past months was the value of an outwardly submissive attitude, though it covered festering anger inside.

Pride furnished a flimsy shroud for a dead body.

Walter managed to keep the sword at his back while fumbling around to fling open the door to the henhouse. The acrid, eye-stinging stench of roosting fowl drifted outward. *Even the best-trained mule would balk at entering such a place,* Rothgar thought, locking his knees and refusing to enter. His resistance meant little to Walter, who seemed to carry drovers' blood in his veins. Using his own knee as a battering ram, the Norman knight sent Rothgar tumbling into the henhouse.

At once, the rank, pitch-dark space thrummed to life. Rothgar curled his arms around his head to shield it as birds took to the air in panic. The circle of his arms did little to protect his ears from shrill crowing and squawking as Langwald's scatterbrained fowl shrieked outrage over his intrusion. Their wildly beating wings stirred the air, raising the stench to a suffocating level and sending aloft loose feathers and bits of down to clog his nose and mouth. Unseen vermin sensed new blood, and their tiny itching mouths sucked at his fresh-scrubbed skin and scalp.

If die he must, he'd choose a Norman sword over being pecked and smothered by hens.

Crouching low, Rothgar risked baring one eye to seek a shaft of moonlight piercing the dark. There were several, gleaming through holes small as pinpricks. He dropped to his knees and waded toward them with the intensity of a pilgrim approaching a statue of his patron saint. He pressed his face tight against the splintered wood and snorted to dislodge the feathers from his nose. Langwald's air, even in his dreams, had never smelled so sweet as what he breathed through those tiny holes.

The hens would settle eventually, provided he remained still and allowed them to become accustomed to his presence. So he knelt at the wall, drinking in the air, and considered his position.

He'd overseen the building of the henhouse himself, approving every well-seasoned peg, every rock-hard plank, every tough leather hinge. Stout boards barred the man-sized door in three places; despite the cacophony raised by the fowl, he'd heard Walter slide every bar into place. No sense wasting strength there. Only one board barred the smaller door, fashioned to the dimensions of a chicken. No man, even one so scrawny-fleshed as he'd become, could hope to pass through that opening. Maria, woman though

CONQUERED BY HIS KISS 39

she was, had chosen his cell as craftily as any male gaoler.

And if he did escape . . . what of it? It had taken him two full weeks to make his way back to Langwald, a trip of but four or five days for one who still possessed his endurance. Should he somehow free himself from the henhouse, might he stagger a mile or two before they came in pursuit? Such a distance wouldn't raise a bit of sweat on a Norman destrier's flank, and his exhausted, bobbing noggin would provide but a moment's sport for a knight accustomed to lopping off the heads of more vigorous foes.

And yet it rankled to accept this lot: penned with the hens while he awaited the Normans' pleasure.

All about him the chickens calmed, settling onto their roosts with soft clucks. Not at all like Maria, who, though she might hover and offer comfort, never lost her wary edge.

None of the women of Rothgar's world had prepared him for one such as she. In his experience, women served. They baked bread and cooked. Some washed tunics, while others scrubbed pots and floors. A few warmed his bed, then left it to weave cloth or dip candles the next morn.

His lady mother had set such tasks for a veritable army of women. She herself had worked from sunup to sundown with endless sewing and embroidery, until failing eyesight forced her to stop. The same lack of sight had caused her to fall when she trod too near the edge of the river during the springtime raging, and she died in the grip of the fever that set in after her dousing.

Nay, his lady mother had not possessed Maria's strength of will. He doubted that even Eadyth's precious abbess of Marston possessed the ability to impose her will upon mutinous Norman knights and foist off a mindless doll-player on the people of Langwald Manor.

Nor would a touch from the abbess create a most unseemly craving in his loins to overshadow the hunger in his belly.

But then again, it might. Rothgar had seen no woman for a half year or more. Perhaps that was why the sight of Maria's unbound hair struck him as so glorious, why he'd been captivated by the compassion and intelligence in her brown-gold eyes, why her touch, which had meant only to explain Hugh's injury had instead sent his blood roaring through his veins.

Aye, perhaps a steady diet of Maria's domineering competence would make her face and form less appetizing. But a short dose of it had struck him as strangely appealing. Thinking on this matter proved an interesting escape from his surroundings, and he found himself wondering what it might be like to spend time with a woman capable of serious thought, witty and quick to understand.

When a hen cackled and a rooster let forth with a muffled crow, Rothgar knew from his cramped limbs that no movement of his had agitated them. And then he realized that the light pouring from the pinpricks had altered subtly, so that instead of silvery moonlight it shone with the pale whiteness preceding dawn. From the grainy feel to his eyes, he knew he must have dozed off, dreaming of Maria, improbable as it seemed.

Risking the chickens' ire, he slowly shifted position to afford some relief to his legs. His pen-mates clucked in mild protest, and so he did not at first realize that the scraping and shuffling he heard came from outside. A thud at the door caught his attention.

Kitchen wenches favored this hour before dawn when choosing a bird for the soup kettle or meal table. The dim light lulled the feather heads, so that they scarcely noticed when one of their group had its neck wrung.

But 'twas no half-awake female he sensed at the door. Male voices, low-pitched and argumentative, promised more strength than that needed to twist the head off a chicken. Their commotion set off the chickens, drowning out any hope of deciphering the men's words, but he didn't need to understand what they said to know there was only one other throat of interest in this henhouse.

One set of footsteps hurried to Rothgar's side of the shed and someone, obviously knowledgeable of the habits of barnyard fowl, opened the chicken-sized door. The birds, blinking their red eyes against the light, fluttered from their perches and trooped into the yard, abandoning him to what might come.

Rothgar stiffened his spine and flexed his limbs, urging the blood back into them so he could stand. He would greet his visitors on his feet.

3

The gloom of the henhouse left Rothgar squinty-eyed and blinking at the glare admitted through the flung-open door.

No Norman assassins surged through the opening, only his good friend Britt the potter, and Alfleg, the one who dug his clay.

"Your ugly faces are most welcome," Rothgar said jokingly, to cover the emotion that welled in his throat. Though their brows creased with a furtive anxiety that was new, their bodies looked sturdy and not deprived, their clothing adequate, their boots well cobbled against the unusual cold. If all the denizens of Langwald fared so well, he'd flung away his freedom, perhaps his very life, for no reason. Even so, the sight of them gladdened his heart; surrounded by stench and filth and weakened as he was, he thought, *I am glad I came.*

The potter pushed a water bag and half loaf of bread into Rothgar's hands. The bread's good smell tantalized some hidden reflex that made his hands jerk and bring the bread to his teeth, that made his mouth water and his throat work convulsively in anticipation of the taste.

No. He would not play the grunting, gorging pig before his friends. His arms fought him every inch, like a horse forced to turn the other way when the scent of its stable was in its nose, but he succeeded in lowering the bread.

"We thought you dead, Rothgar."

Rothgar would not have recognized Britt's voice, so gruff did it sound.

"You sent us word after Stamford Bridge. We heard nothing since Hastings. The battle waged October past, and no word."

"Circumstances did not permit it," Rothgar said, the same impulse that stopped him from showing hunger making him reluctant to admit how he'd spent the past months.

Alfleg had posted himself at the edge of the door, his head darting to and fro in short, jerky motions that called to mind the chickens that shared Rothgar's quarters. "Make haste, Britt," he said now. "The household stirs."

"We will come for you tonight," Britt said in his new heavy way, "when we have full dark and many hours to spirit you away. You must be gone from this place. They will kill you. Others have died."

"Who?" Rothgar's heart lurched, but he would know the names of the villagers the Normans had slain.

Britt's litany, each name carefully marked by the raising of one of his clay-roughened fingers, made no mention of Langwald men and women, only those, such as Rothgar himself, who once bore the title of thane. Britt's voice droned on, a human death knell sounding for Rothgar's peers from virtually every village and manor within three days' ride.

"Runners came from each place, risking their lives to warn us of the slaughter. With Langwald so remote, we had hoped the Norman scourge would pass us by, to no avail."

"Yet Langwald Hall still stands, and you and Alfleg at least carry no Norman mark upon your brow."

Britt misread Rothgar's vast relief that Langwald had been spared some of the indignities. The potter's ruddy face flushed a deeper red, and his eyes shifted away in embarrassment.

"They arrived three weeks after the first runner brought his news. We had been warned. With you gone, the men had no heart. We set down our arms."

"I meant no reproach, Britt. It eases my mind to know Langwald's people had the sense to make the best of the inevitable. Had you slain this group of Normans, William whoreson would have dispatched more, and more, and more again." Rothgar drew a deep, shuddering breath. "I have seen it done."

Britt's hard-set jaw seemed to soften a little; some of the high color left his face. "Mayhap we did the right thing," he admitted, but in a tone so grudging that Rothgar knew the man still regretted his perceived cowardice.

"Britt!" Alfleg's voice whispered from the doorway.

Britt moved to leave, but Rothgar gripped the potter's arm to prevent his departure. "A moment, Britt."

How much of his loyal friend's remorse came from the knowledge that he'd surrendered to one such as Hugh? Maria had claimed the villagers knew naught of Hugh's disability; Rothgar's experience had taught him the villagers missed little of import. Yet, how did one say to the likes of Britt, "Do you know you cast down your weapons before a man whose brains might well have leaked from his head?"

If the time came when he found himself free of this henhouse, possession of such a secret could prove valuable. And, too, there was that niggling, prideful inner voice that told him his villagers would think less of him if they knew he'd been supplanted by an idiot.

So he held on to the arm of his friend, his former vassal, and tried to ignore the feeling he was deceiving Britt as he asked, "How goes it with this Norman lord?"

"Britt!" Alfleg's voice carried the edge of panic now, and even Rothgar could hear the clanking of pots and hungry calling of animals that signaled the beginning of morning chores.

Britt spoke quickly. "The land fares well. Rothgar, I will give you all details tonight. Know that the new lord mistreats no man or beast. The serving folk carry wild tales about him, but I know not what is true. To me, he seems monkish, like a priest. He spends his days in your chamber. The Normans say he works at writing and such. And the lady Eadyth's belly hasn't swelled, though they've been wed since Christmas." The blush again suffused his face, as if he'd just remembered Eadyth had once been Rothgar's betrothed. "I am sorry. The whoreson bastard William granted Eadyth's holdings as well as yours to this Norman."

"Then Hugh married her for the same reason I plucked her from the convent." Land hungry, Rothgar had been, and when Eadyth's widower father died without further issue, he'd thought it a crime against good sense to allow Eadyth's rich Kenwyck acres to revert to a convent. The nuns had made surprisingly little protest when he'd kidnapped her from their midst, and only Harold's first call to arms had prevented his marrying her and adding Eadyth's inheritance to Langwald's acres.

Rothgar wondered if Maria had engineered Hugh's marriage, wondered if she'd thought, as he had, that marriage to Eadyth was one sure way to bind her villagers' loyalty to the lord of Langwald.

"Oh, ho, so that was the reason you chose her." Rothgar's admission had broken through Britt's reserve, revealing the humor and good nature that had made friends of the lord and the potter. "So I can leave you here with good heart, knowing you're not pining away for want of Lady Eadyth's pale skin and sharp-set nose."

It seemed a long while since Rothgar had last grinned with real humor, and the shape of a true smile upon his lips felt strange and good at the same time. "The only thing I yearn for is this bread," he said. "Go now, before your monkish lord learns that more than chicks are being hatched in this henhouse."

Britt's countenance sobered. "I but hope that you will still be here tonight."

"As do I," Rothgar said softly, the weight of his predicament settling over him as his friend backed away, then closed and barred the door.

Three times in the past month, Hugh had woken with something akin to sense lighting his eyes. Three times in thirty days Maria's brother had spoken to her, had seemed to understand the things she said. Maria hoped God would not think her frivolous for praying that today might be the fourth.

When she and Hugh had first come to Langwald, she'd gone to her bed thinking the place was theirs. Never again must they pack up and leave at somebody else's whim. Hugh would have time to heal. But then word began filtering through of William replacing this once-favored knight or that once-trusted warrior for less cause than existed here at Langwald: Hugh, weak minded and ill from his injury; the villagers, surly and suspicious of their new lord; work on the castle barely begun and badly done. If they had more gold they could speed things along. But they had none. She'd heard tales of some English halls fair stuffed with hoards of gold and ordered a thorough search of the manor. The hidden chest they'd uncovered and hacked open with such hopes had yielded naught but a few silver pennies. What would William do at Eastertime once Philip Martell told him how things fared?

Through a night made sleepless by the muddle of her thoughts, she'd formed a plan, half-sketched and laden with flaws, but to implement it with clear conscience, she must obtain Hugh's consent. And so she prayed he'd be clear witted this morn.

If it were so, the dose she prepared for him would be wasted. But entering his chamber without it might brand her as overconfident, causing God's ear to turn away from her prayer. She lifted the crock holding the precious liquid, come all the way from Byzantium. Her hand trembled at its lack of weight and she set it down quickly, lest she drop it and the liquid seep onto the floor, shattering all hope along with the crockery.

She'd bought the strange concoction as a curiosity, long before Hugh had been struck down. The old man who'd sold it to her claimed to be a sorcerer, and she'd thought of him every time she packed the crock in yet another of her seemingly endless moves from one kinsman's hall to the next.

"Think of it as a field of red flowers," said the old man. "Each drop you take is like plucking one of the flowers. Eventually the field will be plucked bare, but the person sipping the nectar will be restored."

Maria had never seen a field filled with red flowers; she fancied the thought of standing amidst scented scarlet beauty, and bought the syrup for that reason more than the old man's belief in its healing powers.

When Hugh had been knocked in the head, she remembered the old man's claims for the stuff. As well, she recalled his warning to be cautious: one drop collected with the sucking thing he gave her, no more; mix with a mouthful of wine and swallow quickly, lest its potency escape. She'd followed his instructions and plucked her red flowers one by one until now the field stood near bare, but Hugh seemed far from restored.

There were times over the past months, when she'd been tempted to sample the syrup-induced oblivion herself.

There was an urgent tug at her gown. It was Fen, the strange boy Hugh had saved on the very day he fell. Fen never spoke; nor did he now, though his wide eloquent eyes, his rigid stance, seemed to convey a sense of impending disaster. And then a crash; Eadyth's muffled shriek; an agonized roar—all from Hugh's chamber.

"Walter! Stephan!" Maria called for the two knights even as she ran the short distance to her brother. Fen preceded her, his gliding, evasive movements somehow letting him reach the chamber before she did. She came up short at the sight that greeted her: Hugh's eyes meeting hers, agonized and confused to be sure, but sensible; his arms clenched stiffly at his sides from the paralysis that seemed to accompany the syrup's waning power; the convent-bred Eadyth on her knees at the side of the bed.

It seemed God was on her side after all. Hugh right in the head, the dose not yet mixed.

"Come away, Eadyth," Maria said, pulling Hugh's wife from her knees. "You know how he flails about."

"He—he *looked* at me." Eadyth's wintry eyes were round with astonishment.

"He improves day by day," Maria soothed, and then caught herself in surprise. She'd said those very words to Rothgar of Langwald, thinking it a wistful exaggeration, but maybe . . . maybe. . . . She urged Eadyth out of the way so Walter and Stephan could take their places at either side of Hugh, their strong hands pressing his shoulders to the bed so he wouldn't hurt himself when the thrashing urge overtook him.

On this morn, with the four of them staring at him with wide-eyed apprehension, Hugh kept control of his limbs.

"Who is she?" he croaked, lifting one shaking finger a scant inch from the bed. It wavered so, Maria couldn't tell whether he pointed at Eadyth or herself.

"Why does she weep?" Hugh himself solved the riddle with his question. Because, though tears often threatened to overwhelm her, Maria never allowed herself to shed them before others.

"I *told* you he looked at me!"

Perhaps it was her convent rearing that rendered Eadyth so guileless, Maria thought. Her sister-in-law could go for days—nay, weeks—wrapped in martyr-like silence and then for no reason, spill all manner of confidences best left unsaid.

"I feel pity for him sometimes," Eadyth confessed to Maria, her eyes on Hugh. "Last night I . . . found reason to think he might feel lonely, so when I felt his eyes upon me this morning, I tried to imagine what it must be like, to have no friends. It made me cry, the thought was so sad."

Maria thought how perceptive it was of her to sense Hugh's loneliness. *Eadyth has no friends; nor have I.*

"None has seen fit to answer my question." Hugh's voice stilled Eadyth's naive discourse and reminded Maria that his lucid periods were usually of short duration.

"She is your lady wife," Maria answered, knowing his mind, once set on a matter, wouldn't budge until it was appeased. There was much to be said between them; best to satisfy his curiosity now rather than waste time reminding him that she'd introduced Eadyth again and again.

Hugh's expression brightened, and a smile teased the corner of his mouth. "Then I can touch her hair," he said, his fingers twitching.

This was something new.

"Go to him," Maria whispered, pushing Eadyth toward the bed. Eadyth wore her hair gathered loose about her head, its length caught up in the back and plaited for sleeping. With obvious reluctance, she pulled the waist-length braid over her shoulder and brushed the end of it against Hugh's fingers.

"No." He shook his head and then grimaced with pain. His mouth worked soundlessly, as though seeking words that wouldn't come. "Open it," he said eventually, frustration edging his words so that Maria knew he meant more than he said.

"Undo the braid."

"Yes." Hugh's eyes shone with gratitude . . . and anticipation.

Eadyth's fingers hesitated, but she bent her head and then let her fingers work quickly up the braid. When the last twist was freed, she raked the tresses with her fingers and shook her head, the hair billowing around her.

"Over me, lady wife."

Again Eadyth pulled her hair over her shoulders, this time in softly waving hanks on either side of her head. She allowed the hair on her left to slide through her fingers and drift over Hugh's face; the hair on her right pooled in silken splendor over his hands and midsection. Maria saw Hugh's fingers wrap themselves in the golden curls; she could hear him breathe in the scent.

Had Rothgar envisioned similar tender scenes with Eadyth?

"'Tis enough, Eadyth," Maria called after what seemed an interminable time of watching the curious intimacy. "You may go. All of you may go." The knights, who had been shifting from foot to foot in embarrassed silence, fairly bolted from the room. Fen, who seldom allowed Hugh out of his sight, melted into the shadows. Obediently, Eadyth moved away from the bed, her hair clinging to Hugh and then sliding along in her wake as she stepped back.

Eadyth would hate her even more, Maria thought, watching Eadyth's gentle movements and regretting the imperious tone she'd used when ordering her to undo the braid. But when Eadyth cast a quick look in her direction before scurrying from the room, Maria read no animosity there. A tremulous smile quivered upon Eadyth's lips; the high color staining her cheeks and the bright sparkling of her eyes called to mind the contented expressions seen on the women who sometimes slipped from the various knights' chambers in the morning.

And the correspondingly silly look on Hugh's face had naught to do with the blow to his head.

"When she stood so, her hair stifled the cheeping, the ceaseless twittering."

Hugh's good days had, until now, followed a set pattern. His slow regaining of motion, his ability to form words, then ideas, then full-blown thoughts—all had been in accord until his desire to wallow in Eadyth's hair, and his remark about cheeping and twittering.

Bird sounds. Cheeping, twittering . . . clucking, crowing.

Rothgar of Langwald. Locked in the henhouse all these hours without food or water.

Good God, her thoughts were growing as disjointed as Hugh's.

And Hugh's wrecked mind could fall apart in a heartbeat. There was no more time to waste.

"Do you know me?"

"Aye. You are Maria. My sister."

"Do you know where you are?"

A wary watchfulness entered his eyes.

"I am in my bed."

Maria tried another direction. "Name this hall."

"I—" again, his mouth moved with no sound, "'tis not Evreux." He said the words with some conviction but betrayed his doubt with the rising of his voice.

Maria shook her head.

"Mortain? Poitiers? Avranches?" Hugh spewed out a veritable flood of place names, all in Normandy, and none of which he'd visited within the past two years.

"You lie in your own bed, in your own manor hall. Langwald, Hugh. William gifted it to you, along with a place called Kenwyck." Her heart sank when she realized Hugh's eyes held no recognition. "Try to remember."

As if he sensed her desperation, he looked away from her, frowning in concentration. Maria said nothing for the space of fifty heartbeats. One hundred.

Hugh turned back toward her, wonder and excitement lighting his features. "I am to build a castle," he said, his words tinged with awe.

"Oh, Hugh, yes!"

"And . . . and . . ."

Again, the frantic eye-darting, the soundless working of his lips, but the words missed their opportunity to be spoken. Hugh groaned and clutched his head between his hands, sure sign of the demons' painful returning. Curse Eadyth and her hair!

"Gone, all gone," he whispered in a voice laden with resignation.

"No." Her words countered Hugh's despair with sharp authority. Taking his head between her own two hands, she tilted his face up. He winced at the sunlight streaming through the holes punched in the hide strung across the window, but she held firm. "You must listen, Hugh. You must take heed. Rothgar, the man who ruled this place before you, has returned. By William's decree, he should be put to death or punished for taking up arms."

Hugh jerked away from her and curled himself into a shield against the sun.

There had been moments, during Hugh's brief spells of awareness, when he'd said things that made

Maria believe he heard and understood what was said to him even while he was in the demons' grip. Despite his turning away now, she went forth with what she had to say, praying that her words would enter some safe place in his mind and bide there until he was whole again.

"The villagers grudge every moment of labor we claim. Easter draws near, and William expects a report on your progress. You remember Philip, Hugh. He's fair smacking his lips in anticipation of the tales he means to carry to William." Like the villagers, Hugh, groaning and writhing against the agony in his head, seemed singularly unimpressed with William's expectations; unlike the villagers, Hugh would be stripped of Langwald and Kenwyck should the castle walls fail to rise at a satisfactory pace.

"I propose bargaining with this Rothgar," Maria said, spilling the most daring part of her plan. "He bears a love for this land. We hold him prisoner, and he is vulnerable to our suggestions. I think I can reason with him and make him understand that should William appoint another lord, the people of Langwald would suffer greatly under a harsher rule."

In answer, Hugh buried his face against the wolfskin throw, where the thick fur muffled his shriek of pain.

Maria knelt at the side of the bed, gathering her brother's huge, quivering body within her embrace. "I'm sorry, Hugh," she whispered against his pain. "But you must say it. You must say yes, it is right that we keep him alive, so I can tell the others that Hugh, Lord of Langwald, has approved this plan."

His eyes stared back at her, blank, uncomprehending.

"Say it," she said. And then, wishing she could pull the word from Hugh's throat, she slowly and deliberately repeated it until the word fairly echoed from the walls. "Say *yes*. Yes. Yes. Yes. Yes. Yes."

Like a child aping its mother, Hugh managed the word. "Yes," he said. And then, with a faint whimper, "Help me."

As approvals go, Hugh's left much to be desired. But now she could stand up against Gilbert or any other who might dare question her actions.

"Aye, brother," she said, cradling him against her for a moment. "I will help your head, and I will help you keep this place, no matter the cost."

4

One shovel, wielded more forcefully than the others, rang against frozen earth with an icy scraping noise that caused Sir Gilbert's horse to shy. Cursing, he reined in the animal.

"I like this not," his companion Dunstan said.

"Nor do I." Gilbert tightened the grip on his reins. His horse shook its head and stamped in protest, drawing stares from the working villagers. "Would that they paid such close heed to the task at hand." He nodded toward the dallying workers.

"They hunger for a glimpse of *him*." Dunstan glowered in the direction of the henhouse.

Gilbert didn't bother refuting Dunstan's words; he knew his fellow knight spoke true, though it surprised him that the younger knight confided his unease. Usually only the fatherly Walter heard such confidences.

The contingent of laborers might have had their feet and shovels mired in mud this morning, for all the progress they made. News of Rothgar's capture had spread like plague among Langwald's villagers. Every spadeful of earth, every stomp of a foot or slap of the ramming pole was accompanied by a time-wasting, wistful, longing gaze toward Rothgar's gaol. It was as if the former lord of Langwald Manor were holding court atop his throne of chicken dung.

"I tell you, Gilbert, I begin to regret the pact we made when Hugh took the blow."

Gilbert's horse seemed to sense his surprise, half-rearing and whinnying at the pressure of Gilbert's legs. Gilbert soothed the beast and brought it back under control, and tried to do the same with his own reaction to Dunstan's admission. None of the others who'd seemed to align themselves with him against Maria had seen fit to speak to him of it.

Dunstan's jaw and lips bore the stubborn stamp of a man bound to have his say, despite eyes shot with red and graced with dark pouches.

"Have you been tipping the ale skins too high?" Gilbert asked with deceptive lightness.

"Mayhap. 'Tis the only thing about this godforsaken place worth the effort."

"I did not know you held your home in such little regard."

Dunstan grunted. "My home? So it was promised to be. Now I am not so sure." He spat on the ground. "It's been nigh on half a year since William bid Hugh to build him a castle and keep ten knights well mounted and armed. Look about you, Gilbert. See you a castle? See you ten knights? Nay, that bastard Philip Martell speaks true, there is naught here to fulfill William's requirements save a half-dug ditch and four minders for a man with less sense than a babe. Easter comes soon, and we all know that fawning Philip means to carry his tales across the sea to William shortly after. Will I have a home then?"

Let the villagers lie down and nap for all he cared—Gilbert's full attention was now on his mutinous partner-at-arms. "You swore fealty to Hugh," he reminded Dunstan.

"That I did," Dunstan agreed. "To Hugh—not his sister. While we carry on this witless deception, our skills rust apace with our armor, and our horses grow fat and lazy. Should yon Saxons rally behind the prisoner, they might well slay us with those picks and shovels."

Sounds swooped in to fill the sudden, uncomfortable silence that gripped them both at Dunstan's words: from afar, the piercing cry of a hawk; from close to, the angry shout of a villager pelted by a shower of dirt flung from the ditch.

"Surely Walter does not feel this way?" Gilbert asked at length.

"Walter is ever Hugh's man," Dunstan admitted. "But of late he seems distracted and surly like the rest of us and has taken to disappearing at odd moments. Who can say? Perhaps he's hatching a plot of his own. He spends an uncommon amount of time with bastard Philip, though I know not how he can abide his company. Would that Philip's head had been well dented on the journey here."

"Perhaps it won't go unscathed should he carry out this threat to journey to William," Gilbert said, his voice deceptively light. No sense in betraying his own fears over Philip's close ties to William.

"Stephan, our squires, and myself . . ." Dunstan cast a bleary-eyed stare toward Gilbert, stiffened his jaw and shrugged his wide shoulders. "You must know we took your part against Maria over saving the Saxon's life. As always, she has ignored us. My aim this day was to say we would not think it amiss should you end this ruse and assume control of Langwald."

"Disloyal," Gilbert said, even as something within him soared at hearing his secret desire put into words by another.

Dunstan nattered on, but Gilbert paid scant attention to what seemed a rehearsed speech. Instead, he allowed his gaze to wander over Langwald's fields and meadows and forests and dared for the first time to exult in the possibility. *All mine. This could all be mine. As well as the lady to grace my hall.* The flood of possessiveness that washed through him at the thought was so intense he felt he could drown in it.

"Disloyal," he repeated as if to deny the plan that fell into his mind, so well developed that he knew his thoughts must have been at work on the idea long before he would allow himself to admit it. "The time is not yet right."

"The sooner the better, I say."

Gilbert shook his head. He smiled, remembering his walk in the cold with Eadyth. "Maria has always kept her own counsel regarding Hugh's progress. I now have access to a quick mind and ready tongue to keep abreast of the goings-on in Hugh's chamber."

Dunstan seemed unimpressed, gesturing toward the sullen villagers. "You might have the ears and eyes of a thousand bats hanging from Hugh's ceiling for all the good it will do you with them."

"They'll pay heed well enough to the man who cleaves their old lord in two."

"Rothgar . . ."

"Aye, Rothgar." Gilbert narrowed his gaze upon one of the villagers who had taken a moment to stare at him. The man suddenly developed great interest in his work and began stomping loose earth with a vengeance. Soon, if Gilbert had his way, all of Langwald's men would be working with equal fervor.

"William himself decreed that those who took up arms against him would forfeit both their lands and their lives. I will take a moment this day to remind Maria of William's rule."

"Yet she stayed my hand when you would have had me deal with Rothgar earlier," Dunstan reminded him.

"Only because I allowed the sword to be stopped," Gilbert said, the glib lie coming easily. "I know not her womanish purpose in doing so. But to my mind, putting him to his death before the very eyes of his people would strike more fear into their hearts than hearing of the deed done with quiet mercy."

"Then you will put an end to him and to their resistance. Bastard Philip might have no tales to carry after all." Relief was evident in every line of Dunstan's face.

"Aye." Gilbert allowed grim satisfaction to mark his words. "We'll show these English the folly of withholding support from their rightful lords. I myself will put the sword to their precious Rothgar of Langwald, mayhap atop the Norman motte that rankles them so. Mayhap their muscles will work a little harder, fearing that more English blood will soak the soil."

A kitchen wench skidded to a stop outside the chamber door and stood quivering like a wounded doe facing a circle of slavering hounds. Maria instinctively moved to shield Hugh from the girl's sight.

"What is it?" She stepped forward, backing the wench deeper into the corridor and pulling the door shut behind her.

"I—my lady—" The girl's teeth chattered so, Maria could scarce decipher her words.

Just then Walter lumbered up behind her. "What do you here, wench?" He cast a red-faced, apologetic glance toward Maria and reached for the wench's arm. She cowered away from him and fixed frightened, pleading eyes on Maria.

"Leave her be, Walter. Your lord calls for you." With a meaningful look, Maria directed him into Hugh's room. "See to his needs."

Walter eased the door open, but instead of Walter gaining admittance, Fen slipped through the narrow opening, bracing his slight body before it as if he meant to die rather than allow Walter through the door. Walter cursed and made to clout the youth, but Maria forestalled his hand. From time to time Fen displayed this curious attitude, unwilling to allow a Norman knight near Hugh unless she or Eadyth were present, but Hugh never lacked for anything while under his care.

"Perhaps Hugh sleeps. Stand guard here, Walter, with the door closed."

As Walter took up his post, Maria turned her attention back to the girl. Her relief at keeping Hugh's condition hidden softened her anger at the girl's intrusion. "I trust you have good reason for leaving your kitchen."

"Aye, my lady." Maria's deliberately soothing voice seemed to have restored her confidence. "The old priest bids Lord Hugh speak with him."

"Impossible." Maria's mind raced. Father Bruno, Langwald's priest, had proven himself to be a realistic, valuable ally. Although Maria had not trusted him enough to share Hugh's secret, she had no wish to jeopardize their relationship. "Lord Hugh faces many tasks today. Pour wine. I myself will greet him in the hall."

"No, my lady." Again, the wench's limbs trembled. She twisted the folds of her apron in her hands. "Father Bruno waits astride his mule in the yard. He says—he says nevermore will he enter Langwald Hall until the new lord sets things to rights. Please go to him."

Indeed, it was hard to tell who looked the more stubborn: the fat old mule or the like-bodied priest sitting atop. Despite the cloak she'd flung about herself, Maria shivered in the raw March wind. Her acquaintance with the priest had taught her his love of creature comforts. "Come inside, Father Bruno," she cajoled. "Even now, cook mulls cider to warm us. We will sit near the fire and you can tell me what brings you here."

"I will not."

"You would keep us out here in the cold, shouting across the yard at each other like fishwives?"

"You cast unwonted slurs upon the behavior of fishwives." Father Bruno straightened and fixed her with a glare. "Fishwives handle their humble catch with quick and painless mercy. I would speak with Lord Hugh on his treatment of Rothgar, former lord of this manor."

The priest had spoken with all the power and forcefulness used to chastise sinners from the pulpit. His tones echoed in the close confines of the yard, drawing every eye in Langwald in their direction.

A dairymaid stood, her hands resting on the yoke across her shoulders while the milk pails balanced on either side swayed gently. Another woman, herding geese, lost control of the gaggle when she stopped flicking her willow switch at the birds. Stablemen's hands clutched their charges' bridles; a cowherd held the horn of a sweet-natured milch cow; even harnessed oxen seemed to turn their wide brown gazes in her direction.

The henhouse loomed in a far corner of the yard like an unspoken reproach.

Maria cast about in her mind for a reason to keep the determined priest from seeing Hugh. The priest bore an uncommon fondness for his mule. "Think of your beast, friend priest. He would enjoy a measure of oats on a day such as this. You and I can talk in the stable while he munches his treat. I fear Hugh lies sick in his bed with a fever and I but sought to spare you catching it."

Father Bruno's lips trembled, and she knew she'd hit her mark.

"I've heard of plague striking in Gilwyth. Do you think Lord Hugh suffers from such? Does he require—" The priest swallowed, and then took a deep breath before continuing. "Should I go to his side and administer the sacrament?"

"Nay, Father. I think 'tis but a recurrence of a fever that struck him when he journeyed far south to fight in a tourney. It flares up now and again." Relief flooded the priest's face, and she pressed her advantage. "Come. Let us feed the beast."

The mule trotted briskly once the priest turned its head toward the stables. Maria gathered her skirts and ran across the yard after them. A young stable-boy stood holding the mule's reins while Father Bruno heaved his way off the beast, and Maria ordered all workers from the stable once the mule had its nose buried in a new-filled manger.

When horses and oxen and cows occupied the stable, the air warmed from the heat thrown off their great, sweating hides. At this time of day, the knights exercised their huge destriers on the practice fields, the cows grazed in their pasture, the oxen hauled wood for the castle. Deprived of the animals' warmth, the stable struck as cold as any other outbuilding.

And she'd locked Rothgar in the henhouse without a cloak.

She gathered her own garment around her and shivered while Father Bruno caught his breath.

He went straight to the heart of his complaint without preamble. "Langwald's people have told me things that sicken my soul. Is it not enough that the new king has granted Rothgar's lands to you? Must needs you also torture him, starve him, strip him of all dignity before you put him to death?"

"Mayhap he feels the cold, but I doubt it can be called torture," Maria said with an uneasy glance toward the henhouse. "And Rothgar himself refused my offer of food. We have not dealt harshly with him, Father, considering the threat he poses."

"Threat? I'm told there's naught to him but bones covered with skin, and as for torture, what do you call it, lady, to be tossed into the henhouse with naught to shelter you from the cold? Moreover, I hear your own Sir Gilbert set about him with a sword while Rothgar lay helpless and unarmed at his feet."

"'Twas a mere pinprick." The reminder of Gilbert's cruelty sickened her, but she felt duty-bound to support her fellow Norman.

"Ah, the threat you mentioned—I suppose Gilbert sought to forestall Rothgar's leaping to his feet and disarming a hall filled with Norman knights."

"He need not lift a finger to disarm us all, Sir Priest," she said softly. "His memory has been a goad in the villagers' side all these many months. Now that he's back, I fear they'll turn more fully away from us, risking William's wrath and leading to death and destruction greater than they can imagine."

"Then you will put him to death."

There was a finality in the old priest's tone, a defeated acceptance that indicated he'd expected no other answer despite his brave appearance on Langwald's doorstep. In her experience, priests were of two molds: the pampered, petted younger sons of rich fathers who had no need to curry favor, or the sly, pandering sort willing to sell blessings, benedictions, or even the promise of salvation for the right price. It struck Maria that it must have taken a great deal of courage for Father Bruno to mount his ancient mule and take his hopeless stand before his Norman conquerors.

Most unpriestlike.

She felt a rush of respect for Father Bruno, one that set up the urge within her to confess all to him. Only natural, it seemed, to bare her thoughts and soul to a priest—

Hugh's scream rent the chill air.

"Torture," said Father Bruno. He turned a baleful, self-satisfied eye in her direction, and Maria's impulse to talk shriveled like a rose touched by frost.

"Think what you will," she said, a touch of the frost in her voice. "Rothgar need not die, nor starve, nor suffer torture."

Father Bruno awaited further explanation with the practiced ease of one who has spent hours listening in the confessional.

Maria sought to provoke a crack in his mantle of self-righteousness. "What would you have us do with him, then?"

Before her eyes, the priest transformed himself from the confessor to the supplicant.

"Lady, Rothgar was but seventeen years of age when his father died. His lack of years meant little, for I swear he was born with Langwald River water running through his veins, that his very body sprang from

Langwald's rich soil. My priestly duties carry me to seven manors. None of those places were ever ruled by a lord with more love for his land or his people. At times I despaired of him and accused him of holding his love for Langwald above his devotion to God."

If the priest were trying to plead Rothgar's case, he was doing a poor job of it. Hearing of the man's obsession with Langwald sent fear zinging through Maria, casting doubts upon the wisdom of her plan for keeping Rothgar alive.

Father Bruno seemed to sense her apprehension and lifted a hand as if to forestall a mortal blow sent in Rothgar's direction. "This obsession of his—it can be *used*, my lady."

"How so?" Maria asked, curious now to see whether Father Bruno's suggestion could help solidify her own half-formed ideas.

"You can be sure I have spent the night on my knees begging God's divine inspiration. And it came to me, my lady, while I near swooned from exhaustion. The lord Hugh himself must have been struck by the same thought."

Now it was Maria's turn to stand silent, awaiting further illumination from the priest.

"I rode past the castle site on my way here this morning. These old eyes see well enough to know little progress is being made. And these old ears hear many voices that whisper of discontent and rebellion. Only in Langwald. Not in Kenwyck." Maria kept silent, and the old priest sighed as if exasperated with a student's slow grasp of simple logic. "Kenwyck, my lady. The villagers there rallied behind Lord Hugh once he took the lady Eadyth to wife."

"Hugh can hardly marry Rothgar, Father Bruno," she chided, amused at the thought.

"No. But you could marry him, Lady Maria."

"Ha!"

The one syllable, more of disbelief than humor, echoed from the stable walls and brought the mule's head up so that it swiveled its long, awkward ears in her direction. Maria thanked God that the four-legged creature was the only witness to Father Bruno's witless scheme.

"You are the lord's sister, and, unless I miss the mark, not without influence. With Rothgar at your side, Langwald's people would have a change of heart."

"No," she said, her voice firm. Her husband, Ranulf, had *wanted* her, and her life had been a misery of loneliness and alienation before and after his death. How much worse would it be, foisted off on a man who could, by rights, blame her for losing his birthright and so take out his inner aggressions in small, petty ways? Forget the leaping of her heart when she'd touched Rothgar; that sort of thing was fleeting in nature and could be attributed to the tension of revealing Hugh's condition.

"I have a home now. I'll not marry again," she said.

"But lady—"

"No," she said again. "I will heed your advice, though, and use the man's love of this place. Once he understands the way of things, mayhap he will use his influence to turn the villagers our way. If he does, I shall set him free to make his way elsewhere."

"Marriage would prove an incentive for his cooperation, lady. For one such as he, there would be no greater lure than being able to live out his days on the land he loves."

"There is a greater lure," Maria said, annoyed at the priest's doggedness. "If he does as I ask, he'll get to keep his head."

There was little to say as the disappointed priest prepared his mule and laboriously mounted. "You will take him out of the henhouse," he said. "And see that he doesn't hunger, and that Gilbert's sword stays sheathed. If you cannot do these things, 'twould be a kindness to send him to his death. One such as Rothgar cannot bear imprisonment."

"Aye." Impulsively, she added, "You are a true friend to him, Father Bruno."

"I merely seek what is best for Langwald's people." The priest fashioned the sign of the cross over Maria's head. "William could have sent us worse. I shall pray, Maria."

She wondered if the priest heard her whispered thank-you as the mule reluctantly trotted out into the frigid sunshine.

"Lady Maria!"

"What now?" Maria muttered with a weary sigh. The wench who'd told her of Father Bruno's visit stood trembling in the doorway.

"'Tis Philip Martell, my lady. He's asking after Lord—I mean Rothgar."

It seemed she would have no time to consider her options concerning Rothgar of Langwald. One or another of the men plaguing her would be bound to hound her to death. Best to confront the Saxon now and see if he might cooperate.

"Find Sir Stephan and send him to me. And give Philip a comfortable stool near the fire and a mug of ale," she told the wench. "I have a thing or two to attend first." She headed toward the henhouse, her mind searching for some way to gain a private moment with a man who might well be her deadliest enemy.

5

Rothgar reclined against a wall, one elbow braced under him to support his weight, his knees bent to fit in the confining space, emphasizing the length of his legs. His head swiveled toward her and he cupped his free hand over his eyes to shield them from the sudden brightness. He recognized her at once, she could tell, and his hand flew to an object near his chest, quickly burying it in the noxious straw.

But Maria's eyes weren't as dazzled by the light and they easily pierced the henhouse gloom. She saw what he hid. A goatskin bag, suitable for wine or ale. He'd not carried such when she'd ordered him locked up, and she doubted Sir Walter had cared enough for Rothgar's comfort to have provided him with something to slake his thirst.

Someone had visited Rothgar during the night, and his need to conceal the evidence meant he wanted the visit to remain a secret. With Gilbert's warnings and Father Bruno's remarks about discontent and revolt ringing in her ears, she gripped the door, blurting out an inane remark to cover her discomfiture.

"What say you to another bath, Rothgar of Langwald?"

"The ordering of baths must be your specialty, Lady Maria."

"What?"

"Perhaps I misheard your offer." He scratched at his abdomen and then slapped at his neck. "Thoughts of bathing have obsessed me of late."

His voice, rich and husky with overtones of self-mocking humor, seemed to impale her hand to the door. His casual pose and relaxed mien made a mockery of the precaution she'd taken of having Sir Stephan guard her back. Rothgar's attitude could be a deliberate ruse to distract her from the goatskin bag, or it could hint at his willingness to hear what she had to say. She chose to pretend he'd succeeded in hiding the bag from her.

"Father Bruno feared you might suffer from the cold."

A shadow seemed to flicker over his brow. "Nay, my lady. I have learned dung has many merits, including the casting off of warmth."

"Well, come then, if you can bear to leave your cozy bed," she said, gesturing toward where Sir Stephan waited. She stepped aside to permit him passage, but he took his time getting to his feet. He made a great show of rising and stretching, and she noticed that his feet were careful to scrape and tamp additional straw over the goatskin bag.

He hesitated when he met her at the doorway.

"You should precede me, my lady."

"Nay," Sir Stephan objected, gripping Rothgar's wrist with a lightning-fast hand and hauling him down the short ramp to the yard. The knight bent Rothgar's arm behind his back.

Sweat sprung to Rothgar's brow and he let loose with a sharp gasp, but his eyes revealed barely restrained fury. Had Maria not caught his quickly concealed anger, she might have believed the contrite expression that next crossed his face as he managed to say, "I but sought to . . . stay downwind . . . of the lady."

A thoughtful gesture or a ruse to put him close enough to wrap an arm about her throat?

Maria was aware that many of the people of Langwald, sensing something occurring at the henhouse, had congregated in the yard. To haul their former lord past them while he twisted and writhed from the Norman's grip would multiply their resentment. It must be—it had to be—that thought which sent her heart lurching at the grimace of pain on Rothgar's face.

"Loose him, Stephan," Maria ordered.

She looked to Rothgar, mindful of his duplicity over the waterskin, his quickly concealed rage. "We go to the hall. Will you walk along peacefully with Stephan as your escort, or must we bind your wrists and treat you as a prisoner?"

A muscle in his cheek twitched. "You need not tie me."

They stepped toward the gathered Saxons.

Maria had attended more tourneys than she could count, had welcomed her father and brother and husband home victorious from innumerable battles. None had enjoyed a more fervent welcoming crowd than that which ushered Rothgar of Langwald from the henhouse dung heap to his former manor.

It seemed that every peasant not working in the fields or at the castle site had found his way into the yard. They formed two lines, leaving a path for Maria, Rothgar, and Stephan to pass through. Men, bent with age and joint sickness; women, heavy with child and with more children clutching at their skirts; youths consigned to kitchen and stable and yard work—all risked the Normans' ire by shirking their duties as they cheered their former lord.

"We do not forget, Rothgar!"

"Keep heart, my lord!"

"We're taking care of things for you!"

"We're waiting, my lord!"

Maria kept her chin high, her steps strong and purposeful, but the walk seemed never-ending. With their faces alight with joy, their arms waving and hands clapping and necks craning for a glimpse of him, Langwald's villagers bore little resemblance to the quiet, lethargic people she'd grown accustomed to seeing. So enthralled they were, so enthusiastic at seeing their former lord, that her presence mattered not a whit.

She'd once seen a frog encased in pond ice, its feet outflung as though it had fought against its frozen coffin, but before she could point it out to Hugh, he'd shattered the ice with his mace to reach the life-giving water trapped underneath. Today, the villagers stared through her without seeing, heedless of the brittle mantle of secrecy she'd erected around Langwald as a safety net, eager only to drink in Rothgar's presence and luxuriate in memories of the past.

Never had she felt so lonely.

Rothgar walked close beside her. She could sense the heat of him. Father Bruno's preposterous suggestion taunted her. She imagined making this walk with Rothgar holding her lightly against him, no longer a wary, cautious stranger, but as a husband, with his hand resting on the nape of her neck and her head just touching the strength of his shoulder. No loneliness then. No need to continue her distasteful alliance with Gilbert, her constant placating of Philip. Rothgar would raise his right hand to acknowledge the crowd; she would wave her left. And the movement would bring her hip against his, would set the softness of her belly against his . . .

A sturdy little boy, not more than five years old, broke away from his mother's grasp. He stood in the path so Maria had to stop and he, at least, treated her to his full attention for the space of a heartbeat. Long enough for her to notice his tawny-gold hair and brilliant blue eyes and wonder at his familiar looks. He stuffed dirty fingers into his mouth, glancing from his mother to Maria in confusion, and then looked upward at Rothgar. He smiled around his fingers, and then with a glad little cry, held out his hands.

"Father!" he crowed, wrapping his arms around Rothgar's leg.

Maria's face burned as Rothgar, with a chuckle, bent to lift the boy into his arms. The two male heads tipped toward each other, one plump-cheeked and soft, one lean and shadowed with the incipient stubble of a beard despite being so recently shaved, but bearing the unmistakable stamp of close kinship.

Very close kinship.

One of Rothgar's bastards, no doubt. The villagers laughed and smiled indulgently as the child patted Rothgar's rough chin. Her face burned hotter, remembering that the priest had dared suggest marriage to this man, who apparently scattered his bastards throughout the village. Worse, she'd actually been entertaining idle thoughts of that marriage.

"I am not your father," Rothgar growled in mock ferocity.

"Yes."

"Look closely," Rothgar said, and bared his teeth in a fearsome grimace.

The child giggled, unafraid, and with one grimy finger touched Rothgar's strong front teeth. "Uncle Rothgar."

Rothgar set the boy away from him, tousled his hair, and patted his rump. His attention seemed to stray from the child to his mother, a comely Saxon wench whose work-worn eyes seemed riveted upon Langwald's former lord. The irrational relief Maria had felt upon realizing that the child wasn't Rothgar's fled as she saw his troubled, brooding gaze rest on the woman.

Perhaps the child *was* his, after all, taught to believe Rothgar was no more than a benevolent uncle. 'Twas a ploy noblemen often used to avoid claiming their bastards. His blatant staring at the woman seemed to indicate a more-than-casual interest. A heaviness settled about Maria's heart.

As if the child's action had lifted an invisible barricade, Langwald's people pressed closer to Rothgar, hands outstretched to stroke his arm, to touch any part of him they could reach. The pathway to the hall was fast closing in. The fear of being surrounded by an impenetrable mob of irate villagers overrode Maria's renewed disappointment.

"My lady," Stephan called, warning in his voice.

Rothgar seemed disinclined to move ahead, his attention fixed on the woman and child. Ordering Stephan to use his sword or strength to prod Rothgar into motion might antagonize the crowd. Maria tugged at Rothgar's sleeve until she realized he probably couldn't differentiate her touch from that of a dozen eager Saxons doing the same thing.

She slipped her hand into his.

Her touch drew his startled regard, but Maria took no satisfaction in diverting his attention from the wench and child. Once again, she felt heat course over her face. From her brazenness, no doubt; never before had she grasped thus at a man. It had to be shame that set her heart to pounding so, calling to mind the night before when she'd touched the back of his neck and felt his pulse throb in accord with her own.

Her hand, tucked within his, felt so very small.

Thin he might be, but his hand retained the shape and texture belonging to a man accustomed to heavy labor. Work-roughened calluses grazed against the soft pads on her palm; his long, nimble fingers closed around her own with an ease that hinted at great strength lying in abeyance.

"The crowd grows unruly. 'Tis not safe," she managed to say.

"They would not hurt us."

Her traitorous heart set to slamming against her chest again, thrilling to the rumbling timbre of his voice saying *us,* as though he had chosen to make this walk together with Maria, and from the pressure of his grip on her hand, which left no doubt that he planned to keep hold of it.

She had thought to pull away from him once they resumed their slow progress to the hall, but it seemed quite natural to make her way hand in hand with Rothgar of Langwald.

But she couldn't help noticing, as they passed the mother and child, that tears coursed down the Saxon woman's face.

* * *

It came to him that Maria might be a witch.

His hand still felt the imprint of hers. How had she sensed the devastation to his spirit when young Henry called him father before the people of Langwald? By what unholy wisdom did she know to lend her strength to help him face his people, shamed and conquered as he was, to take his hand in hers as if he were an honored guest instead of a vanquished foe?

And that boy Fen who hovered over her brother—surely even Normans had heard of the ancient faerie people who were said to live in the woods—and yet she accepted Fen's presence as if he were no more than a cat. And now, when her quiet instructions to a serving wench and simple preparations told him she intended to be the one bathing him this day, a tightening in his lower reaches and the racing of his blood hinted that some sort of spell had been woven over him. Why else would his body betray him by reacting thus to a woman who could be nothing more than his bitter enemy?

This small alcove, at the far end of the hall, had always struck chill on even the warmest of summer days. No window broke the coarse wooden walls. During his rule it had served to store cheese and butter and various items too valuable to abandon, like the dusty lute hanging from a peg.

Now, someone had strung a cord across the opening and hung a tapestry from it, as if to shield its interior from prying eyes. A bed of sorts had been shoved into one corner, and women's clothing graced another peg in the wall.

Had Maria claimed this dark uncomfortable niche for herself? Witches were known to relish the cold.

Today, despite the fire roaring in the hall's trench, the alcove struck so frigid that huge clouds of steam billowed from the heated bath water, surrounding Maria in an eerie fog. Like a witch, emerging from the mists after working her incantations.

"The water grows cool," she said with a graceful gesture that reinforced the notion. Surely none but a witch could rouse such urges within a man with a mere beckoning of her arm. At her movement, her woolen gown stretched taut over her breasts, revealing nipples firmed and out thrusting from the cold.

God's teeth! Was he so woman-starved that he could think of naught but leaping into the bath, splashing about until she became as wet as he and her drenched gown clung to her form?

Rothgar forced his thoughts to turn in another direction. Normans, he knew from experience, never acted from impulses of kindness or consideration. They were masters of treachery and deceit. It would surprise him not if, while pretending to cleanse away the reminders of his night in the henhouse, Maria instead tried to force his head under the water and hold it there until he drowned.

"Have you taken this dreary cell for your own sleeping chamber?" he asked.

Maria smiled. "It suits well enough for one who has never known a private bed."

"Surely in your own hall—"

"Hugh and I never had a hall to call home, until now." She glanced around her with a proprietary air that stirred Rothgar's hackles. "I admit this space lacks comfort, but once the castle is built we shall not want for warmth or privacy."

He wondered how long it had taken this Norman witch to perfect her faltering smile, the expression of indecision that came over her when he made no move to disrobe and fall in with her plans.

"The bath does not please you?"

Her words carried a note of challenge. The low rumble of male voices came from outside the alcove, reminding him that this was no pleasant day-ending soak meant to ease work-weary muscles, that full-armed Norman knights waited just beyond the turning in the wall, ready to rush in at her word.

"You mock me," he said, annoyance at his reactions to her lending an uncommon gruff edge to his voice.

She dropped the slab of soap she'd been holding into the tub. Droplets of water splashed like great, huge teardrops onto her gown, darkening the material where they soaked into the wool. "I mock you? How so?"

"This," he said, encompassing the private alcove, the steaming bath, with a sweep of his arm. "Yesterday, 'twas the kitchen bower, with no lack of gawkers, that housed my bath. And two sour-faced men who could scarce bear to let go their sword hilts scoured and scrubbed my stinking hide. Today I find myself alone with one small woman. Do you seek to taunt me with this reminder of my helpless state, or do you Norman females so enjoy washing men that you've worn out the skins of yon knights and seek new sport?"

His words had been carefully chosen to raise her ire, to bring to an end once and for all the indecision surrounding whether he lived or died. Deliberately, he took a menacing step toward her, seeking to provoke her into action. Would the sharp blade of a hidden knife flash in her hand, or would she call out to her men?

She did neither. The misty vapors swirled about her but did nothing to hide the pale tensing of Maria's features as she gripped the edge of the tub. "I meant no mockery, Saxon. And think not that I relish the thought of this bathing any more than you do. Your comfortless English halls offer little in the way of privacy. I must speak with you alone, and this was the only thing I could think to do."

He would have preferred some scathing response to his insulting words. Instead, her quiet dignity shamed him. He felt heat flood his face, and hoped the water vapors clouded her vision. "You are most considerate, lady. There are others who would not have hesitated to mete out a death sentence in the presence of others."

"Death sentence?" She cocked her head so that her hair fell away from her face, revealing the fine line of her chin. An exasperated frown crossed her features. "Are all Saxon men so gloomy-minded? Father Bruno expects the worst just because I locked you in the henhouse for a night. You expect a death sentence just because I offer you a bath."

"My present predicament gives rise to dark thoughts," Rothgar said, affronted by her attitude.

"Oh, cease with your stiff-necked pride." Her expression changed to one of wry amusement. "As you so helpfully suggested, I have washed my share of Norman men, so you need not fear offending my sensibilities. I told you I must speak with you, so take off your clothes and climb into the tub lest your guards wonder at the lack of splashing sounds."

For all his life, Rothgar had been bathed by women, both here in Langwald and in the various manors where he'd been accorded the treatment as an honored guest. There was no reason for his reluctance to do as Maria asked. She had assured his safety; besides, having held her hand within his own, he knew her fine-boned strength was no match for his, even in his reduced state. Still, his hands hung like unresponsive lumps at his side, unwilling to make the simple disrobing movements, while the rest of his skin tingled and prickled with an awareness more suited to the bed than the bath.

"Rothgar." She spoke his name, nothing more. Never had it sounded so from the lips of other women. Her Norman inflection softened the syllables so that it echoed through his head like the call of a siren. To banish the sound, to banish the sight of her standing before him wide-eyed and waiting, he forced his fingers into action and tore the tunic from his body.

And then, all he could think was, *I wish she could have seen me before.*

Once he would have stood proudly before her, knowing women found his tall, well-muscled frame pleasing. Once he had been a lord, confident, self-assured, powerful, and brave.

No woman could enjoy looking on his body now, scarred as it was from the things that had happened over the past months, all shrunken and starved from lack of food. And his status had been reduced to lower than that of the most wretched peasant, stripped of all rights, owning nothing, his very life dangling upon a woman's whim.

The very air of Langwald contributed to his ugliness, the cold raising ugly bumps along his arms and sending his manhood curling against his thigh.

He wished he had his hair back. He wished for his beard, to hide his hot, bare face, but she kept her witch's eyes on him and he felt she would be able to see into his soul no matter what disguise he wore.

He wished he were back in the henhouse—anywhere but standing naked, in every way, before Maria.

It was a trick of the steaming water, Maria decided, that made him so pleasing to look upon.

Oh, there was no doubt he'd hungered for some time. The hollowed belly testified to that. But the rest of Rothgar seemed honed to perfection by his deprivation, tempered with strength like the finest sword.

Wide shoulders tapered to a narrow waist. In between, hard muscular ridges scored his abdomen, and the broad flat planes of his chest accented the corded strength of his neck. His slightest movement set muscles to playing, bunching and hinting at power temporarily held in abeyance. His small nipples seemed determined to copy her own, peaked from the cold and peeking jauntily through the curling tawny-gold hair covering his chest.

She hoped that the swirling steam, which did so much to hide his flaws, would likewise shield her blushing face from his regard.

He climbed into the tub with the reluctance of a ram approaching the shearing pen, and once he'd settled his length into the water, he sat rigid, with knees bent, his hands clutching the sides of the tub until his knuckles whitened beneath the strain.

"The hot water will relax you," she said. "Should I begin with your hair?"

"I will tend to it myself."

"But—"

"*Myself.* A cloth, if you please."

Maria would have leaned back in the tub, dipping her hair into the water and using the cloth to wet the strands near her forehead. Rothgar leaned forward and plunged his entire head beneath the water, where he shook it about like a dog worrying a bone. Straightening, he flung his head backward, sending water cascading in all directions. She couldn't prevent a little yelp escaping when water showered over her, drenching her gown so that the wool clung to her with clammy coldness.

Ignoring the cloth she'd given him, Rothgar used his hand to wipe the water from his face and slicked his hair back so it wouldn't drip into his eyes. He leaned back, sighing with pleasure, looking as content as a new-hatched duckling savoring its first trip to the pond, until his gaze settled upon her, taking in her sodden condition. At once, his carefree enjoyment of the bath took flight, replaced by the wall of remote detachment he seemed able to erect at will.

Maria ran her hands down along her sides, smoothing the wet, rumpled gown. "I know this was your mother's gown," she said. "If you had allowed me to wash your hair, I would have made sure the gown stayed dry."

"It matters not," he said, closing his eyes and readjusting his limbs so he could tilt his head all the way back, submerging it until all of his hair was below water. He appeared most uncomfortable. His chest arched out of the water and his arms gripped the sides of the tub, causing the tight sinewy muscles to bulge with evidence of the strength it took to maintain the awkward position.

She noticed his wrist.

CONQUERED BY HIS KISS

A scarred band of flesh at least three fingers in width encircled the wrist completely.

By taking a few steps to her left, she could see a matching scar branding his other wrist.

Though healed, the ridged, furrowed scars spoke of human strength pitted against unyielding metal, of breaking the skin and enduring the burning agony of rusted metal against an open wound—not just once, but time and time again.

Maria encircled her left wrist with the fingers of her right hand and wondered at the force required to create such marks. Would hanging from the gyves suffice? Could a man deliberately provoke such pain in hopes of breaking free?

She touched the small bone protruding from her wrist, remembering the swift, excruciating pain that shot up her arm when she'd accidentally bumped the bone against a table edge. There must have been times, during the formation of those scars, when the bones in his wrists cracked against iron.

He moved, the water lapping quietly at the edges of the tub as he seated himself upright.

"You wore manacles," she said.

"Aye." He submerged both hands in the water. His head, too, bent toward the bath and she imagined he must be looking for the soap she'd dropped a few minutes earlier. Nothing in his demeanor indicated he gave the matter of manacles more than a passing thought, but she couldn't shake the feeling that the marks he bore on his wrists weren't the only scars carried by Rothgar of Langwald.

"The manacles . . . were they some form of Saxon ritual?"

A shudder passed through him, so quickly controlled that only the rippling water betrayed him.

When he looked at her eventually, his face was devoid of expression, his eyes carefully neutral. But he kept his hands in the water.

"If you fancy a like pair of bracelets for yourself, I fear want will be your master. The Normans who so generously bestowed them upon me seemed inclined to adorn only Saxon wrists."

"Normans? Impossible. Dunstan himself told me he struck you only once on the head, and those scars could scarce form themselves overnight."

He laughed, a short barking sound of incredulity. "You are not the only Normans helping themselves to pieces of England, my lady. Where did you think I spent these past months?"

"Why, I . . ." Maria's voice trailed off. Everything about Rothgar—his hunger, his tattered clothes, his unkempt hair and beard, the circumstances surrounding his capture—all had led her to believe he had hidden himself in the woods after the debacle at Hastings, that he might even have numbered among the men responsible for Hugh's injury. She balanced those things against what she'd observed of him since his capture: his surprisingly good command of her Norman tongue, the avid hunger in his eyes when he looked about him at that which was once his, his fascination with the crying, beautiful Saxon woman and the small boy calling him father.

A man harboring such powerful emotions could not content himself with lurking about in the woods. No, the scars silently screamed the truth. Despite Father Bruno's blathering about Rothgar not being able to tolerate imprisonment, he must have spent the past months chained, shackled, starved, and beaten at the hands of her countrymen.

And this was the man she thought might urge the people of Langwald to accept Norman rule? Maria felt the foundations of her plan crumbling about her.

"You escaped?"

"I escaped." He sighed and settled himself back into the water.

"Did anyone pursue you?"

"I cannot say." He soaped his neck, his eyes closed. "I played dead to set myself free. Perhaps the ruse worked and they still think me moldering away within the dung heap. Winter this year seems unending. Hungry wolves got to the bodies even before I scrambled from the pile. Their sharp teeth might have hid all traces of my escape."

"You may be right." She smiled to soften her words. "If your captors had discovered you missing they would have sent a party of knights after you right away."

"And in my weakened condition, I could have done little to avoid recapture," Rothgar agreed.

"So the wolves hid your escape, only to enable you to fall into the hands of yet another group of captors. Did your freedom mean so little to you, Rothgar?"

A profound stillness settled over him, the mantle of remote detachment she was coming to know so well.

"I know little of Norman foodstuffs, my lady, but we English occasionally feast on the pink flesh of a fish that swims in our far northern reaches. Curious creatures, these salmon. Though wily and cunning through most of the year, each spring some irresistible urge grips them so they needs must return to the place of their birth. At such times a child could pluck his fill of them from shallow streams, so intent they are upon reaching their home."

"You liken yourself to a fish?"

A wry smile twisted his lips. "Why not? Worse names have been hurled at me since October past. The salmon's obsession, I understand it well."

She felt a glimmer of hope. "And having returned to the place of its birth, and seeing all fared well, might a salmon return to the sea content knowing that another, who loves the place equally well, rules in his stead?"

"Fish lack such power of reasoning, my lady."

"But I think a man, presented with such a situation, might well understand all its ramifications."

"So at last we come to the purpose of this bath."

"We do."

"'Tis best I splash about a bit, then, to cover what we say."

Maria nodded. The soap slab fit easily into his large hand, and she watched, her attention riveted on the way he casually dipped it into the water and then slid it along his bare chest, leaving a few streaky, sudsy lines in its wake.

"The words do not come easily to you, my lady."

Her cheeks burned at being caught staring. "I think you will find granting the favor I ask of you no less daunting."

"Ask away." He stretched one long arm over his head, and slowly washed his way down its sinewy length.

"I want you to see your people. Reassure yourself all is well with them. And then tell them that Hugh is their master now, and that they must work for him with good heart."

He gave up all pretense at bathing. "I do not know if I can do that," he said, the simple words revealing his utter honesty.

"Whyever not?" To her fury, she felt tears gathering, threatening to fall. She would not be thwarted, *could* not be thwarted by him in this. What would Hugh say, if he could, confronted by such an obstinate fool? "If you can't speak the words, I'll have you locked in manacles again until you can bring yourself to say them."

The threat, she saw at once, served only to harden his resolve against helping her.

Rothgar leaned forward and braced his arms against the tub, bringing his scars directly into her line of vision. "Know this, lady. I wore Norman irons, yes, but that was only the least of what I endured. And the man who devised my tortures never heard so much as a whimper pass my lips. What you ask me to say would wrench the very heart from my body. So do your worst."

"Then I see I have done wrong to approach you," she said through lips stiff with anger. Her mind raced frantically for something, anything that would secure his compliance, and thought at once of Gilbert and the cruel methods of his that she had called halt to time and time again.

Though every particle of her being cringed at the notion, she presented Gilbert's ideas as her own. "Your death means less than nothing. But I think a family man or two could be sacrificed, the starving, homeless pleas of their widows and children serving as an example to the others. Perhaps some mewling babes, too little to be of use, can be run through. Hugh's men grow surly and discontented—if I lift the rule against rape, mayhap they'll smile again and Norman children will grow in the bellies of Saxon women. In time, I think the people of Langwald will come around."

She felt shamed before the abhorrence and disgust with which he regarded her.

She had thought him cool and remote; the icy loathing that marked his expression now was almost frightening in its wintry intensity.

"I'll leave this tub now, my lady, lest my skin becomes so puckered Langwald's people mistake me for the village crone and pay no heed to the words you force me to say."

She turned away, unable to face him as he prepared himself to do her bidding.

6

The squire's tuggings and familiar weight of his mail partially roused Hugh de Courson. For a moment, memories—clear, sharp, concise—flooded his benumbed mind. A carefree, lighthearted ride across the English countryside. Maria at his side. His most trusted knights guarding his back. And in a pouch near his heart, a parchment, granting a gift so wondrous and rare . . .

A home.

And then a wild, fierce cry from the woods, a motley assortment of ragged, desperate men, an odd, dark-skinned boy cowering beneath a sword. Lowering his own guard to snatch the lad to safety atop his saddle, and a violent, shattering blow to the back of his head . . .

And then . . .
And then . . .
The old pain merged with the new.
Best to sit still and wait for it to pass.
Wait for Maria and the bitter drink.
Wait for Maria.

* * *

Eadyth thought Hugh looked harmless enough sitting there, despite the wartime hauberk covering his upper torso. His hands, huge in gauntlets of mail, rested quietly in his lap; an undented helm covered his head and sat low enough so its nose piece hid the pleading, quizzical look in his eyes.

Why, then, did her heart trip and flutter so? Eadyth decided it could only mean she feared him despite his quiescent appearance.

"Why do you dress him in full armor?" she asked the squire who fastened the mailed hood around Hugh's neck beneath Fen's watchful eye.

"Not full, my lady. He wears only woolen chausses, so we can more easily heave him atop his horse."

"Then he is to ride today?"

She could not fault the squire's cautious regard; never before had she shown an interest in Hugh's handling. *This is Gilbert's doing,* a secret voice warned, reminding her of her promise to tell the knight what she learned in this chamber. She wondered if Hugh's squire could sense her duplicity. She would not have blamed him if he had gone running to Maria, but he continued speaking after a moment's hesitation.

"Aye. The lady Maria bid us ready him to visit the castle site."

Mayhap, Eadyth thought, she had noticed more than she realized. She could recall that on a few occasions, when Hugh was strong-minded enough to ward off the demons temporarily, Maria had paraded him before his Saxon people. Never before, though, had he gone forth clad in his armor.

Although many Normans lacked the height of Saxon men, the knights, like Hugh, had uncommon strength in their upper arms and shoulders and bulging thigh muscles to attest to their skill at mounted combat. Hugh's gleaming mail, polished to near-blinding brightness, enhanced the overall image of strength.

Over the long, lonely months, she had come to ignore Hugh during the day. Fen saw to his needs with no help from her, but the odd little boy-child seemed not to mind. Only when either she or Maria were present would he tolerate the presence of a Norman knight or squire near his beloved master. Eadyth slept at Hugh's side each night, but Maria's dose kept him slumberous and so unaware that Eadyth had no cause to huddle as she did in a far corner of the bed with her back turned, disgusted by the sight of him.

He looked somehow different today, and she couldn't seem to stop staring at him. It was as if the clinking metal he wore sparked and captured her regard like a smartly applied comb sends one's hair to crackling and clinging despite all efforts to smooth it flat. Wonderingly, Eadyth pressed against his sleeve and marveled over which was the harder, the chain mail or the iron-thewed muscle it protected.

The squire frowned at her. "Keep your distance, my lady. You know how unpredictable he can be when his drink is withheld."

His warning came too late. Moving so quickly his hand seemed but a blur, Hugh caught Eadyth's wrist.

She gave off a cry, more from surprise than pain, for his hand was so wide and her wrist so slim that she could twist about freely. But Hugh settled back as though rooted in place, his fingers closed in a rigid circle of mail that would not allow her hand to slip free. She gave a little tug but his arm budged not at all, his elbow braced on his thigh, his hand holding her fast. Fen glided to them and studied Hugh's grip, pressing a light, comforting finger against Eadyth's own before slinking back to his place in the shadows.

"Let me try, lady." The squire's efforts to pry Hugh's fingers apart succeeded only in having Hugh draw Eadyth inexorably closer, until she sat flush against him on the hard wooden bench. And then Hugh again froze still, staring ahead with nary a twitching muscle, so solid and unyielding he might well have been carved of stone.

"I will fetch the lady Maria."

"Wait."

Eadyth held her breath, listening, wondering if she'd imagined Hugh's brief expelling of air, a wordless sigh that somehow conveyed a sense of utter longing. Hugh's fingers tightened, briefly, gently, and then reshaped themselves into a loose bracelet. She turned within his grasp, his mailed glove cold, the myriad links nubbed and scratchy against the warm, sensitive skin of her wrist.

She noticed that though her hips rested even with his, her knees came to just halfway along his thighs, her shoulder but midway between his neck and elbow, but she felt no fear at his dwarfing of her. She exerted a bit of pressure against his grip, and found that the heel of her hand would now slip through the circle of his fingers, and he made the sound again.

She eased her hand back into place.

"Hugh?" She realized that her whispering of his name was the first word she'd ever spoken directly to her husband.

He made no response.

She peered into his face, seeking to penetrate the shadows cast by his helm. Funny how she'd never noticed his eyes, wide and dark and the same gold-flecked brown as his sister's. But Maria's never reflected the unspoken pain, the confusion, the unutterable sadness she found in Hugh's steady, unblinking stare. Eadyth quelled the irrational urge she felt to unbind her hair and cover her husband with it as she'd done earlier, shielding him within a protective barricade against the demons that tortured him.

She had been trained by the nuns, after all, to offer succor to the sick, she thought.

"You need not bother the lady Maria," Eadyth said to the squire, her wrist resting easily in Hugh's hand as she moved infinitesimally closer against him. "My husband and I will await her at her leisure."

"If you are certain, my lady," the squire said, doubt and displeasure and a good measure of surprise fairly dripping from his tongue. He didn't leave the room but took up a spare sleeve of armor and set to polishing its links, casting frequent sidelong, wary looks in their direction.

Eadyth paid him no mind. She sat next to her silent, tormented husband and tried to convince herself that this quiet interlude was not worth reporting to Sir Gilbert.

"He has escaped." Gilbert caught Maria's arm as she hurried past him, evidently on her way to change into a dry gown. His anger over discovering Rothgar's disappearance overrode his annoyance at the way she jerked free of his grip, as though his touch befouled her. "I say, Maria, the Saxon has escaped."

"Rothgar? No, he—"

"He is gone."

Maria looked about to protest yet again, her lips

parting in the light, placating smile that preceded the verbal sword she so often wielded with deadly effect against him. Gilbert allowed himself a smile of his own. For once, she would be the one made to look the fool if she sought to deny what he knew to be true.

He pulled from his belt the goatskin bag he'd found buried in the muck of the henhouse floor and dangled it in front of her. She backed away from the stench of it, and Gilbert pressed his advantage. "He left this behind and made only a feeble attempt to conceal it. Someone in the village conspires with him against us."

"No, Gilbert, he is—"

"All we need do is find the man who owns this waterskin. We will rout the entire village until we find the culprit who set him free. Then we will—"

"Gilbert, 'twas I."

He could only gape at her.

She rushed to explain. "I took him from the henhouse. Even now he waits in the alcove, fresh from his bath."

"You took him from the henhouse?"

"Aye." Her face bore a stubborn, willful expression that dared him to challenge her action. He could feel the heat rising from his neck, kindled by anger at her reckless handling of the prisoner, and embarrassment that she'd again made him look the fool.

Philip Martell came up beside them, pointing toward the bag. "You cannot tell me you eased his stay with this. Gilbert says this is evidence of conspiracy, Maria."

Gilbert flung the goatskin bag at her feet and felt grim satisfaction when she took a step back, hesitating and gripping her hands together, unable to tear her gaze from it before whispering, "Aye. I gave it to him." She seemed to make a deliberate effort to overcome her temporary weakness. "There is no conspiracy. The priest came, you see, and Rothgar has promised to speak to the villagers on Hugh's behalf."

"The Saxon waits fresh from his bath, and your gown is wet." The incipient heat suddenly suffused Gilbert at the thought of Maria, her hair loose and flowing about her shoulders, tending the Saxon in his bath. "I must needs make do with a kitchen slut while you accord him the privilege of an honored guest?"

"I received naught but a draught of ale." Philip pouted.

Annoyed, Gilbert pushed the insulted Philip against the wall.

He had wanted Maria, always, from the first, when he'd befriended Hugh de Courson. His desire then ran pure with the illusions of youth; he had expected no notice from her, certain her beauty and sweet nature would secure her future as wife to some rich and powerful nobleman.

Her marriage to Ranulf FitzHerbert, as landless and bleak of prospects as Gilbert himself, sickened and soured his soul with taunts of what might have been had he only possessed the courage to speak to her of his feelings. How he'd suffered through her four years of marriage! And how he'd secretly rejoiced upon Ranulf's death only to find her as aloof, as unnoticing of him as ever.

When Hugh took the blow, she *might* have turned to him, but that whoreson Walter had come back to service with Hugh just in time to profit from William's largess. Never mind Gilbert's warning that Walter's long absence from knightly service hinted at something amiss. She clung to the old man as if he were her long-dead father, refusing to hear aught bad of Walter.

But Gilbert had wanted Maria always and he wanted her still, though the nature of his wanting had changed. Where once he'd fantasized about cherishing, protecting, and adoring, he now dreamed of taming her high spirits, of bending her will to his own, of using and humiliating her until she tasted the bitter gall she'd fed him these many years.

"He will help Hugh, Gilbert!"

"Oh, will he now? Mayhap, then, he's told you where to find Langwald's missing treasure, hmm?"

When she flinched, admitting without words that nothing of substance had passed Rothgar's lips, Dunstan's promise of support echoed in Gilbert's mind. He had not intended to speak to her of these things so soon. But the Saxon's presence goaded him past all caution, torturing his mind with the memory of the villagers craning their necks for the sight of Rothgar, of Maria flushed and breathless at the mere mention of the swine. "I begin to wonder if anyone can help Hugh. I begin to wonder whether he is worth helping."

"William will be most interested to hear of his own knights bickering amongst one another," Philip interjected.

Gilbert chuckled when Maria's startled, disbelieving gasp revealed the depth of the blow their words struck.

"What are you saying?" None of her usual assurance colored her voice, and something within Gilbert thrilled to know that a mere handful of words from him had wrought such a change. This newfound sense of power dampened the angry mist clouding his brain. Mayhap it would be best, after all, to keep secret the full extent of his budding ambitions.

"I say you should remember, *Maria*," he allowed a gloating caress to make a mockery of her name, "remember who helped you play this ruse so far. And remember that its continued success depends on *my* cooperation, not a few bleating words spoken by a near-castrated Saxon sheep."

"I've been helping, too," Philip said. "I could well have gone to William at Christmas—"

"Oh, cease your blathering. We've had enough of your company this day." Gilbert turned his menacing gaze upon Philip.

"You might well regret this," Philip blustered, nonetheless fastening his cloak about him and hurrying from the hall.

With a show of the pride and strength that both fascinated and infuriated Gilbert, Maria lifted her chin and watched Philip shuffle away. "I will remember well, Sir Gilbert. I will remember everything. Now I must needs chase after Philip and placate his ire. I had thought to be rid of his presence before we took Hugh before the people, but now I shall have to invite him along to view our progress." She turned on her heel and walked away from him.

So the bitch sought to have the final say. Gilbert stifled the outraged roar that longed to burst from his throat, twisting it instead into nasty, mean-spirited laughter that bounced from the walls, building into true mirth when Maria faltered ever so slightly in her step.

Rothgar had wondered at the worn, nondescript tunic the Norman squire handed him after his bath. Maria had raided his wardrobe once before to clothe him—why not now, when he faced a task so important to her purpose? And then he saw the donkey Maria meant for him to ride to the castle site. Once mounted on it, it would take a man with the sharp sight of a hawk to distinguish where the donkey's worn, dull, gray coat ended and Rothgar's worn, dull, gray tunic began.

A lively, spirited mare stood next to the donkey. Maria stood close to the mare's head, stroking its soft muzzle and whispering into its flicking ear. A huge stallion, its head hanging to the ground, its great flanks heaving and streaked with foamy sweat, stood alone, severe exhaustion rendering it shaky-legged and incapable of bolting. Maria turned to the stallion and placed a soothing hand on its neck.

Sir Walter and Sir Stephan, each gripping an arm of their charge, led Hugh de Courson to the spent horse while Fen jogged ahead of them, backward, his eyes never leaving Hugh. With sure, deft motions that hinted at familiarity with their task, the knights bent Hugh's rigid limbs, fitted his foot into the stirrup, pushed and prodded until he sat stiffly upright on his mount. Despite their practiced movements, they panted and perspired like the horse.

Walter wound the stallion's reins around Hugh's hands. Hugh relaxed, as if something buried deep within his injured mind recognized the feel of a horse beneath him.

"You can't—" Rothgar stifled his protest against their abuse of the horse. 'Twas no concern of his, after all, and Maria's casual enumeration of the atrocities she stood ready to order against Langwald's people proved the Normans' cruel disregard for man and beast alike.

But Maria must have heard him.

"Fear not for the steed, Rothgar. His wind is not

broken. I regret running him so hard, but we cannot trust him with Hugh otherwise. Fen sees to it all. He has an uncommon touch with horses." From somewhere within the folds of her tunic she withdrew a leather strand, thin and flexible, which she affixed to the stallion's bridle before mounting her mare with the assistance of a squire.

Walter and Stephan mounted and held their lances with practiced ease in the crooks of their arms—the deadly tips pointed toward Rothgar as if they feared his sorry mount would scamper away.

"We go," Maria announced with a tug at the leather strand. At a pace obviously set to avoid taxing the stallion's remaining stamina, their small party left Langwald's courtyard.

What a motley assortment we must look, Rothgar mused. The new lord of Langwald rode easily yet held his head as stiff as a wood carving, his mighty destrier meekly stumbling behind a woman wielding a strand of leather no thicker or stronger than a boot thong. The wood sprite Fen darted to and fro, as though measuring the distance between Hugh and the other Norman knights. The dust they kicked up settled over Rothgar and his donkey, further dimming the dull gray worn by both. The head of Rothgar's mount came but to the shoulder of the Normans' horses, and its swaybacked gait forced it into a clumsy trot now and again just to keep pace with the shambling pace of Hugh's horse. With each jolting step, the donkey's bony spine dug into Rothgar's private parts and jarred his backbone; the discomfort made him want to clench his teeth but he'd kept them too long to risk cracking them should the beast put its foot into a hole.

And then, above the dull, muffled plod of hoofbeats, he could hear the rape of Langwald.

He'd caught a glimpse of it the day he was captured, and the sounds should have prepared him. But the sight that greeted Rothgar as they topped a small rise smote his heart with such force that he gripped the donkey's mane for support, sending the animal wheezing and braying and bucking in protest.

"The castle site," Maria said, unnecessarily, as he brought the donkey under control.

"You chose well."

The words came hard, even though he himself could not have chosen better. Langwald's mostly flat acres offered little easily defendable turf. The Normans had chanced upon the one small hill that jutted above the rest and set the conquered English to work in a way all too familiar to one who had spent endless time enslaved in similar occupation.

Someone had surrounded the base of the hill with a rope guideline, with a second rope running alongside in a wider circle. Between the ropes, fifteen or twenty men stood abreast, digging; 'twas hard to make an exact count because the bulk of their bodies stood within the excavation. As they tossed dirt over their shoulders, boys gathered it up in pails and ran it to the top of the hill, which had been stripped of its trees and vegetation. There, still more boys traded them for empty pails, and spilled the fresh-dug earth over the steadily rising hill.

The entire village of Langwald, it seemed, stood upon the hill. From the oldest crone to the youngest child capable of standing alone, they stamped at the newly strewn earth with feet, with the backs of shovels, with a tool the likes of which he'd not seen before, fashioned of a flat piece of wood with a round pole in the center so that a man could lift and drop it with great force.

It was as though the very skin of Langwald had

been ripped open, its flesh lying raw and bleeding black beneath the weak winter sun; as though the dirt pouring from the pails and streaming down the sides of the hill were Langwald's rich, inky blood.

A *motte,* the Normans called the mound thus created. An abomination, thought Rothgar. Within him there was a profound sense of loss that told him he'd still harbored a secret, senseless dream of regaining Langwald. *Fool!* He cursed himself, staring at the evidence of the Normans' total domination of what had once belonged to him.

"Hugh selected the location and set out the dimensions," said Maria, resuming their slow progress to the work site.

Rothgar cast a skeptical upward glance at the silent Norman knight riding beside her.

"He did." Maria seemed bent upon convincing him of the plausibility of such an outlandish notion.

"You need not persuade me, my lady. I have agreed to speak on his behalf to the people." Rothgar's lips felt wooden and unwilling to say these simple phrases; how much more difficult would he find it to form the words he'd promised to say?

"I thought . . ." She stroked the mare's neck and then began afresh. "I saw the change come over your face when you saw the workings. I realized then that you have loved this place far longer than we have and that you are entitled to an explanation."

Love? What did these Norman usurpers know of love for English land? Especially from the deceptively sweet lips of one who had so recently threatened death and torture against the very people she now professed to love. "I am only entitled to the freedom you promised me after I fulfill my obligation. Nothing more."

Maria ignored Rothgar's comment. "Walter can vouch for it. He accompanied my brother when Hugh first rode out to Langwald in November, a month after William's glorious victory at Hastings."

Glorious victory for one king meant ignominious defeat for another; in November, while a carefree Hugh de Courson galloped across the English countryside, Rothgar had found himself starving and chained to his fellow unfortunates who hadn't been quick enough to melt into the woods when the extent of the Norman rout became obvious.

"Hugh was himself then, and possessed of great strategy skills," Maria continued. "William sent him to survey Langwald and Kenwyck, telling Hugh he had in mind to make a gift of the manors to one of his most loyal knights, bidding Hugh to select the most defensible position and lay out the bounds so the new lord could commence work at once. Hugh returned, filled with praise for Langwald and fair bursting with envy for the man destined to enjoy William's gift. Even Walter seemed dazzled by Langwald. And then William said to Hugh, 'And did you find the land in good heart, Hugh—Lord of Langwald?'" A smile played about Maria's lips. "Hugh should have suspected. William has been ever playful and generous with him."

"I have found him to be otherwise," Rothgar said.

Until now, the healthy, glowing pink of Maria's cheeks could be attributed to their ride in the crisp sunny air. At his words her color deepened. She shot a quick glance toward his wrists, and a change came over her face, as if she'd only just now realized she'd been exulting over her brother's good fortune before the man whose loss made it all possible.

It should have been so easy to hate her. Instead,

Rothgar fought with the urge to touch her, to reassure her that his lands would have been forfeit regardless of the Norman knight selected to benefit from William's largess.

What manner of man was he to ride alongside her, humiliated by her choice of clothing and mount, forced by her threatened atrocities to speak words that would clog and gag in his throat, and yet feel a swell of admiration for her, an upsurge of interest that had nothing to do with captive and captor and everything to do with man and woman.

"When was your brother injured?" Rothgar asked, seeking to divert his thoughts.

His ploy failed. The grateful look she sent him from her warm, golden-brown eyes kindled rather than dampened his awareness of her.

"Before Christmas, as we rode together to take up residence at Langwald, our party was set upon by outlaws. Men who lived in the woods, starving, their clothes in tatters. I thought you were such a one, when first I saw you."

Rothgar regretted admitting to his enslavement. He would have preferred her to think of him as an outlaw, though he knew not why. "What of your guard? Surely you did not travel alone through such newly conquered territory."

"Oh, no. Walter had made several trips on his own to Langwald to determine the safest route. Walter himself rode with us, and Gilbert and Dunstan and Stephan—all of their squires and pages, as you have seen them here. Even bastard Philip accompanied us, as a favor to William, since the lands granted to Philip lay next to Kenwyck and Philip lacks men of his own. But everything seemed so peaceful, 'twas such a lovely day, and Hugh and I were light in our hearts, so happy and excited to at last have a home of our own. We rode ahead, while the others followed behind."

"And then?"

"And then they sprang at us from the woods and beset us with cudgels and rocks. The knights caught up with us, but one of the ruffians still managed to land a blow to the back of Hugh's head when he bent over to save little Fen. The men responsible for the attack were sent away for punishment. Hugh has been as you see him ever since."

Rothgar gave a noncommittal grunt of understanding, though he found her story puzzling. Having wielded cudgels and rocks himself against the Normans at Hastings, he knew the weapons' limitations; 'twould take a man far stronger than he to dent the solid helm of Hugh de Courson with anything less than stout metal. And the knight had been wounded from behind, with four men-at-arms and their attendants supposedly guarding his back.

I would have stayed close to her side to ward off such dangers, Rothgar thought, feeling a flood of protectiveness sweep through him at the thought of Maria clinging to her horse in terror, surrounded by enraged, desperate Saxons. But she had managed to escape injury where her brother had not. For these many months, she'd successfully practiced a deception that kept the new king of England and the peasants of Langwald unaware of the true state of the lord of this manor, while he, Rothgar, had stumbled from one Norman prison into another. Sheer madness to think she would ever require his protection.

They were near enough now for him to make out the features of the laboring villagers, who dropped their tools and came running once they recognized him. Though he had hungered for the sight, and though he kept his eyes fixed on those well-known, well-loved faces, he was conscious all the while of Maria sitting on her mare so near at hand. She and Hugh, along with their two guards and Philip Martell, stayed back while the villagers surged about him, looking to him for answers, for deliverance, their expressions betraying a curious craftiness behind their smiles.

Strange to think that he found it necessary to tear his gaze from the people of Langwald to look once more upon Maria's face.

She met his regard without flinching. He wondered what she might be thinking, if she feared he would play false with his promise to speak on Hugh's behalf. It seemed she stared at him with quiet confidence, as if she understood the difficulty of the task facing him, and—foolish thought—regretted the part she played in bringing it about.

He turned back to his people, praying for the strength to say what must be said without stumbling over the words or betraying the toll this promise exacted from him. Though he would have sooner died at Norman hands than allow a tear to trickle down his cheek, he realized with wry amazement that his desire to maintain a stoic demeanor had surprisingly little to do with playing the role of the practical loser seeking to save the skins of his people.

It mattered not what his people thought of him. He didn't want to seem less than a man before Maria.

7

Maria had planned it all so carefully. Comparing Hugh in all his strength and splendor to Rothgar in his humbled condition should convince the people of Langwald that a new order prevailed. And yet, although Hugh sat bestride his magnificent horse, his armor gleaming in the sunlight and adding to his imposing stature, the villagers of Langwald spared him nary a glance, so besotted were they with the sight of Rothgar.

Dropping their tools, they ran to him, clustering about him like bees tending their royal chambers. He dismounted to stand among them but she didn't lose sight of him; his shorn head stood above the others, the sun striking strands of gold among the tawny.

"Should we ride closer, my lady?" Walter asked. "He may be spreading all manner of tales to them."

At that moment, Rothgar looked over his shoulder toward her. The distance was too great, so it had to be her imagination that conjured the image of his blue eyes blazing with wounded pride and absolute integrity, eyes that said though the words might tear at his heart, he would say the things he'd promised to say.

Bile rose in her throat at the memory of the threats she'd made to secure that promise.

"He gave his word, Walter," she answered the knight. "I trust him to do so."

"Your mind is as addled as your brother's," Philip spat. "Englishmen cannot be trusted. Most especially Saxons."

"Philip!" Walter's harsh rebuke shocked them all. "Do not speak so to the lady. Besides, as a landowner yourself now, you should understand the lengths a man will go to see it comes to no harm." There was grudging respect in the faithful knight's voice as he watched Rothgar.

They sat their horses, she and her knights still and silent as Hugh, listening to the unintelligible murmuring of the crowd. Occasionally Rothgar's rich, deep tones took command, prompting loud shouts and cheers from the crowd, and a subtle yearning to move closer to him, to let that voice wash over her.

It was, she told herself, only natural to want to assure herself of what he said. He was her enemy, despite her irrational trust in him. And because he was her enemy, she felt certain, 'twas naught but antagonism that speeded the beat of her heart when he worked himself free of the crowd and headed in her direction.

The tunic he wore flapped loosely about his hips, reminding her again of his ordeal and shaming her that she seemed ever heedless of his comfort. She'd not thought to issue him a cloak, or to see that he ate well before this meeting with his people. Still, his strides were strong and purposeful as he approached her, and his shoulders filled his clothes well enough. She touched the packet tied to her saddle, thinking of the few choice provisions she'd packed to send him on his way after he'd fulfilled his promise; she'd thought of that much, at least. A slab of bacon with more lean than fat, fresh bread, good hard cheese, a skin of Langwald's best dandelion wine. It seemed woefully inadequate set against his part of the bargain.

He snatched at a few tufts of dried grasses as he neared, and stopped before Hugh's tired mount, holding the fodder close to the stallion's nostrils. He stood with his head bent, watching the horse lip at the grass. The people of Langwald stared at them, silent tension seeming to crackle in the air.

"You must understand," Rothgar said, his voice rough with emotion. "These people are ignorant of the extent of the change your generous, playful King William has wrought within England. I spoke to them as you asked me, but they are filled with unrealistic confidence in my ability to restore things to the way they were before."

So Gilbert had been correct, after all. Her attempt to sway the villagers' devotion in Hugh's direction had been doomed to fail from the start. Disappointment knifed through her.

"But you need not carry out your threats," he continued tonelessly, as though uttering words memorized during his short walk to her side. "They are ignorant, but I have thought of a way to demonstrate English subjugation to Norman overlords."

The stallion nudged his hand, looking for more grass, just as Rothgar of Langwald lowered himself to one knee before Hugh.

Unbidden, a cry of protest rose from Maria's breast.

A proper penitent would have bowed his head, perhaps even cowered in obeisance, but Rothgar knelt as though a Norman lance served as his backbone. Staring straight ahead, to where she knew smoke curled from the fires at Langwald Manor, he bore the pallor of a fever victim, colored only by a flush staining his cheeks. His eyes, so blue, so expressive, seemed deadened by a bleak desolation; his breath rattled harshly as if holding his position demanded every ounce of his strength and stamina.

Philip snickered, though the other men averted their eyes.

Rothgar knew his people well. Behind him, their shoulders seemed to sag with collective defeat. With much shuffling of feet and low, disappointed murmuring, they gathered up their abandoned tools and headed back to their tasks.

She longed to touch him, to lend her hand to draw him back to his feet, but felt a chill certainty that any acknowledgment of his humiliation would harden his heart even more against her. *You could have spared him this,* an inner voice taunted, recalling Father Bruno's suggestion of marriage.

Walter's voice broke the strained silence surrounding them. "Arise, Lord Rothgar. You have accomplished your purpose."

Rothgar rose, a fluid, easy movement that belied the rocky, frozen ground upon which his knee had borne all his weight. Maria searched his face for some hint that his paying homage to Hugh rested lightly on his mind, but he kept his attention on Walter.

"They will not understand when you tear down their huts," he said, with the knowledgeable tones of one who had seen similar work done.

"'Tis necessary to build new ones closer to the castle walls. They will be easier to defend. The new huts will be well-thatched and sturdy."

"Explain your reasons to them, and tell them you will see to it that their possessions are moved as well."

Walter glanced toward Maria, shrugging a little as if to say he knew Rothgar's demand would have been more properly addressed to her. Maria motioned to him to respond. "They have little in the way of possessions," Walter said. "Some rough stools, tree stumps smoothed to serve as tables, straw pallets."

"Little enough to Norman thinking, perhaps, but items of great significance to them."

"We will see to it that they retain all they had from before," Walter vowed. "Rest easy in your mind on that course."

"Would that you tell them so, Sir Walter," Rothgar said, looking back at the villagers as a starving man might gaze upon a meat pie set to cool on a ledge far above his reach. "I find myself incapable of facing them again just now."

The shrill, piercing cry of a hawk drifted from high in the sky, drowning out, for too brief a moment, the renewed scraping and thudding from the work site. Hugh's stallion again pushed its nose into Rothgar's palm, and he reached to gather more grass, holding it for the horse as though glad of the small task.

"The donkey . . . 'tis yours for your journey," Maria offered. "Stephan will fetch it."

The young knight spurred his mount to comply, but Rothgar put up a hand to forestall him. "Nay. I'll travel shanks' mare," he said, looking back to the stallion's muzzle.

He hadn't met Maria's eye since falling to his knee.

"I brought some food, a little wine, to fortify you," she said, tugging the packet free and holding it out to him. Surely he would have to look at her to take it, if only to acknowledge it as a gift.

He continued stroking the horse's nose.

Light as the parcel weighed, Maria's arm trembled from the strain of holding it by the time Walter plucked it from her grasp and handed it over to Rothgar. He tucked it beneath his arm. And with nary a backward glance he strode toward the sun, his long-legged stride taking him irretrievably, irrevocably away, leaving her a bit out of sorts at his abrupt departure.

He was gone. Just like that.

Maria busied herself with ordering her small party back toward Langwald Manor, telling herself she hadn't expected Rothgar's gratitude or understanding. Why then did this sick, empty, plummeting sensation torment her? Was her pride insulted because a vanquished Saxon hadn't wanted to look at her—just one last time—before he walked out of her life forever?

But wounded vanity didn't explain why the feeling of loss intensified, or the emptiness that settled around her heart, at the thought of never looking upon him again.

Perhaps losing one's birthright minimized its dimensions. Rothgar soon found himself standing at the edge of Langwald's borders, long before he'd settled in his mind the path to strike toward a new life. Heading north made the most sense; the wild Welsh country offered both hiding places and well-entrenched landowners anxious to keep William from crossing their border. Heading west would take him into Kenwyck, the lands he'd once coveted so. Heading east was an exercise for fools; Langwald's acres stretched in that direction, and he carried no illusions as to his fate should Maria's knights find him tarrying within its bounds, keeping stoked the fires of discontent.

He narrowed his eyes against the sun setting on his left, actually took a step to the north, and then, with a sigh, struck out toward the east, where Langwald River sparkled through the trees.

I will just check on Henry and Helwyth, he promised himself, *and then I will be gone.*

Again, in no time it seemed, he found himself standing at a boundary: the edge of the woods marking the beginning of the assart Edwin had so laboriously cleared a few years back. Rothgar himself had helped guide the oxen while Edwin chopped at the roots of stumps. Henry, little as he'd been, scurried about picking rocks, and Helwyth wielded a mattock as well as any man. Rough, root-entwined inch by inch, they'd claimed a dozen acres from the surrounding wilderness, land enough to make Edwin a prosperous farmer. Father Bruno had solemnized the undertaking, preparing a parchment proving Edwin's ownership.

Now, Edwin's acres seemed to shiver beneath the cold rays of the slanting sun. Tall, withered weed stalks rattled gently in the breeze. Here and there young seedlings quivered, their first leaves hanging sere and brown from their spindly branches. The unwanted growth encroached, insidious, like rainwater dripping through branches to soak the dry spot beneath a tree: a trickle along the trunk; a rivulet running from the leaves; fat, wet drops falling from the wind until the once-dry spot merged with the mud surrounding it.

Edwin's lazy old hound, belatedly noticing Rothgar's presence, set up a halfhearted barking. The wooden door slapped with a dull thud against the hut's wattle-and-daub walls, and young Henry ran out, skidding to a stop at the sight of Rothgar.

"Father?" he asked as he'd done in Langwald's courtyard, but this time there was an edge of wistfulness to his voice, a hint of resignation that indicated he knew the truth.

"No, Henry," Rothgar said.

Henry's little shoulders sagged. "Uncle Rothgar," he said dispiritedly. Helwyth stepped through the doorway and lay a comforting hand atop her son's head. The boy turned and buried his face in his mother's skirts.

"I, too, might have mistaken you for Edwin, had you not been standing when I saw you," Helwyth said. "As it was, the sight of you near sent me into a swoon."

"I would have spared you that, but I had no choice in the matter," Rothgar said.

Helwyth's features crumpled. "Ah, Rothgar. He is gone. Our Edwin is truly gone."

"Aye," Rothgar managed to say. He crossed the space to catch her as she swayed on her feet, and silently cursed the Normans as he held his illegitimate brother's family within the circle of his arms.

Looking from Rothgar to Edwin had been like comparing a face to its reflection in Langwald River, until Edwin's face creased into one of his ever-present smiles. Then the difference showed, the difference between being born on the wrong side of the pallet to the sheep girl Anna rather than in the great, ancient manor bed to the old lord's wife Ethelfleda.

Young Rothgar, the legitimate heir, spared the heavy, incessant work of the manor, never knowing a moment's hunger, had grown tall and strong. Edwin, unacknowledged by Old Rothgar, never attained the height of his father or brother. Hard labor at too young an age had added a stoop to his shoulders, and each winter seemed to find yet another of his teeth missing.

It wasn't until Old Rothgar died, and Young Rothgar became known as simply Lord Rothgar, that he'd learned about Edwin. Too proud to accept the gifts Rothgar longed to heap upon him, Edwin asked only to be granted this bit of assart land.

When Rothgar declared his intention to fight for England, Edwin had insisted upon accompanying him. "I have land to lose now, too," he'd said, casting a proud eye over his few acres.

Henry peeked up, the movement breaking Rothgar's reverie. He tried to smile reassuringly, to distract the boy's attention from the sight of Helwyth sobbing against his shoulder. Henry's blue eyes, too solemn for a boy of five, met Rothgar's with a disconcerting awareness before he disengaged himself from Helwyth's grip and bolted across the field and into the woods.

Rothgar knew that Henry would never again mistake him for Edwin.

"How did my Edwin die?" Helwyth asked eventually.

"I know so little," Rothgar said. "He fought by my side at Hastings. A lance struck his shoulder, but the wound did not look to be mortal. Before I could see to him, I was injured and taken away. I never saw him again. Until I saw you standing alone in the courtyard, I had hoped . . ."

Helwyth withdrew from Rothgar's arms and retrieved a bit of cloth from her sleeve to mop at her face. "They've taken it all from us, Rothgar, even our hope. But at least they set you free without causing you harm."

Rothgar kept silent.

She wiped her eyes, but a dark smudge he'd thought was dirt remained to discolor the soft skin above her cheekbone.

"And what is this, Helwyth?" he asked, pointing toward the bruise.

She flinched.

"He calls it my brand," she said at length. "I should be grateful, he says, that he enjoys my skin too well to scar it permanently with white-hot metal, as my resistance warrants. When this bruise fades, he'll give me another."

"Who?" Rothgar scarcely recognized his own voice, so strangled with anger did it sound. "I will kill him, I swear it."

A faint smile toyed at the edges of her lips. "He would flatten you like a careless worm trod upon by a horse."

"Gilbert." Rothgar spoke the name with utter certainty. The very sound of it roiled through his mind, taunting him with the image of himself lying helpless on his back, the tall, sneering Norman ordering, "Run him through," with malevolent anticipation blazing in his eyes.

"I will not say the name," Helwyth said, clutching her hands before her. "I have sworn to kill him myself, and you must be away from this place."

"Never! I will not abandon you and the boy. You and Henry must come with me. Gather your things. We leave at once."

"Rothgar." Helwyth cocked her head and stared at him with the fond, indulgent look an older sister bestows on a headstrong boy. "Look at yourself. And look at me." She smoothed a hand over her skirt, across the soft mound of her stomach. "I know the herbs, and for these endless months I've managed to keep his seed fallow. But I fear one has taken root. Some women can work in the fields with scarcely a pause to deliver their babes. I needs must take to my bed soon if I value my life, for I have not the constitution of a brood mare. Surely you remember the babes I lost ere bearing Henry."

"Aye," Rothgar said. "I remember. And I remember you are my brother's wife. I'll not leave you at the Norman's mercy."

Helwyth merely shook her head in denial. "His ardor has cooled somewhat of late, and this news should dampen it entirely."

"Helwyth—"

"Rothgar." She put a placating hand on his arm. "Do you really think I could leave Edwin's land behind? 'Tis all there is left of him for Henry." A dreamy, faraway look came into her eyes. "Someday I will slay the Norman, mayhap right where you stand. Then his blood will soak into Edwin's earth. 'Twould be fitting, would it not?"

There was a purposefulness to her, a quiet assurance that seemed to form an aura of power around her. Rothgar shook his head. "What has become of you women in the time I spent away?"

"I saw you walking hand in hand with the new lord's sister. Do you speak of other women besides Maria and me?"

"No—the two of you are disturbing enough," he shot back. "Are all women now so bloodthirsty and power-mad?"

Helwyth smiled, but then grew serious.

"You must be away from here, Rothgar. He will kill you if he finds you here, and he would not go easy with me afterward. Make for the woodcutter's hut. If you leave now, you can reach it before nightfall."

"I will not leave you."

"I will fetch Edwin's old cloak for you," she said, ignoring his statement. "It will fall short of your knees, but you will be glad of its warmth."

She disappeared into the hut before he could sputter yet again in protest, and was back before he'd summoned the words for a more convincing argument. She cradled a bulky bundle in her arm, stroking its rough-spun texture as if it were the finest silk, her eyes so fixed upon it that it might have been a most colorful, wondrous tapestry rather than a crude mantle of dirty gray wool.

Helwyth held it out to him, and then quickly drew it back, her hands trembling as she buried her face in its folds. Great shuddering breaths made her shoulders heave, and Rothgar stared helplessly, feeling ham-handed and useless before her silent grief.

"Even the scent of him is gone now," she said eventually, smoothing the cloak and wiping away a few tears that stood like droplets of rain atop the lanolin-rich wool. She thrust the cloak into Rothgar's arms. It tumbled loose and fluttered in the wind, and he moved to swing it about his shoulders.

She stopped him with a hand on his arm. "Not just now," she said, tears shimmering in her eyes. "'Twould be too much like seeing him don it."

"You are coming with me," he said, feeling her hand slide down his arm to rest against Edwin's cloak.

"I cannot," she said, plucking at stray tufts of wool, forming them into a small ball. A keepsake. He understood as she tucked the ball into her sleeve.

"This bickering grows tiresome," Rothgar said. "Call Henry."

She shook her head and crossed her arms, against the wind, against his badgering. "I would go mad," she said. "To look at your face, so like his—every time, my heart would say 'Edwin,' but 'twould be you. One day Henry will again call you Father, and you will tire of correcting him. Bit by bit, our memories will fade, our pain will lessen, until Edwin is lost forever, like this land will be reclaimed by the forest. I could not bear it." Again, she stroked the cloak with a light, lingering caress. "Better to leave me here, where I can nurse my loss and pain, where I can nurture Edwin's son and land, and plan my revenge."

Helwyth shivered in the wind, and a tendril of her hair worked itself loose, pasting itself across her cheek. Rothgar hadn't noticed, until now, the silver strands mingling with the pale yellow, or the work-worn state of her hands, or the tired, resigned cast to her expression as she stared over Edwin's acres. Still, she stood resolute and firm, calling to mind another woman, equally determined to salvage something for a loved one.

"The lady Maria will help you, Helwyth," he said. "You must go to her and tell her the way of things here."

"She is a Norman."

"But she is different. She . . ." She threatened to maim strong men, to kill little babes, to turn her Normans loose to rape and plunder. And her eyes had brimmed with tears, and her voice had trembled as she spoke, and he'd felt her supportive presence surrounding him as he talked to his people, had perceived her regret even as he recognized the good sense in urging the people to accept what could not be changed.

"She is different," he said again.

Helwyth stared at him with the amused half-smile of a woman entrusted with a great secret.

For no reason, Rothgar felt the skin of his face grow warm.

"I could spare some food," was all she said.

The packet Maria had prepared fit snugly beneath his arm, comforting but too small, he knew, to sustain him throughout a long journey. He cast a practiced eye across Edwin's acres; less than half showed signs of recent cultivation. "You have sufficient stores to last until harvest?"

"I need but to ask, and he will provide for me," said Helwyth with a shrug.

Rothgar's belly seemed to fill with molten iron at the thought of his brother's wife groveling before a Norman. The food packet seemed to burn, too, reminding him of his own humiliation. He should have heeded his fellow prisoners' advice and turned away from Langwald when making his escape.

"I have all I need," he said, more harshly than he'd intended. To make up for his sharp speech, he touched Helwyth's cheek. "I will go, though not without regret. Give my love to the boy. My thoughts will be with you always."

"And ours with you," she whispered. "Go with God, Rothgar."

The sun had dipped low while they spoke, and the chill winter breeze sharpened into a biting wind. But Rothgar could feel Helwyth's eyes upon him as he strode away, and though the wind pierced his tunic, he waited until he gained the dark, concealing shelter of the woods before wrapping his brother's cloak around his shoulders.

Gilbert pushed the trencher aside, casting a disdainful look at the heap of well-gnawed hog bones it held. Pork, every day pork, or on rare occasions, a side of tough, aged mutton. *When I rule this hall, we shall eat beef,* he thought, and smiled. Such ideas and half-formed plans seemed to crowd his mind ever since Dunstan's tentative offer of support.

His fellow knights clustered at the far end of the hall, well into their cups and regaling the squires and pages with tales of glorious battles. Only Maria and Eadyth remained at table with him, nibbling at their food or sipping at their wine, each seemingly lost in thoughts of her own.

Eadyth, usually so pale and wan, sported a becoming flush to her cheeks. Her trencher looked untouched; perhaps she'd dined solely on wine that evening. As if she sensed his regard, she darted a quick look at him and flushed even deeper, lowering her eyes to her hands, clenched demurely in her lap. It made Gilbert sit up straight, remembering the way she'd clung to his arm when he tricked her into agreeing to spy on Hugh.

Good God—he hoped the silly cow hadn't fallen in love with him!

Of course, she couldn't help it, married as she was to that useless wreck hidden away in their bedchamber. Who could blame her for falling in love with a handsome, virile one such as he, Gilbert Crispin? Would that the one sitting next to her would succumb.

Maria toyed with her food, pallid where Eadyth blushed rose, listless and drawn while Eadyth seemed to simmer with hidden energies. Like Eadyth, Maria cast a look in his direction, but her wide, brown-gold eyes were wary and cautious. Gilbert smiled again; he knew the reason for Maria's agitation.

"Did you find yourself pleased with the progress at the castle site?" he asked, injecting more sweetness into his voice than the cook had measured into the evening syllabub.

She stopped all pretense of enjoying her meal, stiffening her spine and turning toward him with a proud tilt to her chin. Good God, what he couldn't do with a dozen men possessing her courage!

"No," she said. "Hugh was most disappointed."

"But surely that will change on the morrow," Gilbert taunted, amused at her pitiful efforts to include Hugh. "You did, after all, implement your little plan of having the former lord urge his people to support your brother."

"As you advised, the plan was doomed to failure," Maria said, her words clipped, a bit of color at last staining her cheeks.

"A pity." Gilbert pretended to commiserate, even though her confession surprised him. And disappointed him. He'd hoped to prolong her embarrassment, to draw out her admission of defeat word by word.

Then it came to him, all in a rush, that she had forestalled him yet again. Made light of his sensible advice. Diffused his sarcasm. Turned his jibe into an apparent show of commiseration, so that it appeared he'd endorsed her harebrained scheme, or at least lent his support to it.

A burst of laughter from the knights and squires coincided with the descent of the red mist over his thoughts, a phenomenon that talking with Maria seemed to provoke lately. She glared at him, chin aloft, her eyes daring him to make mock of her pitiable efforts to secure the villagers' support, a tilt to her lips challenging him to discredit her decision to set Rothgar of Langwald free. How galling, her unwomanly ways! How comforting, the red mists that blotted out the anger and resentment, so soothing, so calming, urging him to divulge, now, the full extent of his plans. Laughter again from the knights—his men, one and all; perhaps a bit unsteady on their feet just now, but staunchly on his side.

"You should," he said carefully, savoring the way the red mist pulsated, "pay closer heed to the advice I give."

"I pay such heed as it merits."

"You should," he said again, "grow accustomed to marking my words."

She said nothing. Scarlet, crimson, ruby swirled before him so that he could scarce see her face; he gripped the sides of his chair, lest he rise to his feet to flail through the red fog to the source and unleash his fury upon her.

"I think my commands will count foremost from now on," he said.

She rose to her feet, so quickly that the stool she sat upon tipped over and crashed to the floor.

"Hugh is lord in this hall."

"Then let him countermand my orders," Gilbert said.

"You know he cannot at present—"

"I *know*," Gilbert said, "that you have violated William's direct orders. Those who took arms against him are to be put to death. Yet you set Rothgar of Langwald free."

"I only did so because—"

"Spare me your excuses," Gilbert said, motioning toward a squire. "Geoffrey, I will hear your report now."

The young squire reluctantly separated from the merry group at the end of the hall.

"I followed him as you requested, Sir Gilbert."

"Who?" Gilbert prompted.

"Rothgar of Langwald, of course." The squire's voice reflected his puzzlement.

Gilbert shot a look toward Maria, noting her pallor had returned. "And what did you learn?"

"He first went to visit the hut of Helwyth." Gilbert raised an eyebrow and inclined his head toward Maria. Geoffrey directed his next remark to her. "You will remember, my lady, the young lad who accosted you and the former lord in the courtyard? 'Twas the hut of the child's mother that Rothgar visited."

Interesting, Gilbert thought, the way her face colored and paled, paled yet more and colored again.

"Ah, yes, Helwyth—one of Langwald's more becoming wenches. And then?" Gilbert prompted.

"And then, after some embraces and a most tearful parting, Rothgar traveled to an abandoned woodcutter's hut. He seems settled for the night, having laid in a fire and shuttered the windows."

"Did you send word to bastard Philip as I bid, Geoffrey?"

"Of course, Sir Gilbert," Geoffrey answered, affronted.

Gilbert waved Geoffrey back to his revels.

"Tomorrow I ride to find this woodcutter's hut," he said to Maria in a conversational tone. "A place equipped with a chopping block sounds a likely spot for severing a traitorous head from a scrawny neck."

"What purpose would that serve?"

Ah, there it was—that hint of desperation too often heard in his own voice, seldom heard in hers.

"Well, though you foolishly released the Saxon, Philip now knows we have yet another chance at the man's head. I could take that head to William and forestall Philip's complaints." He pretended to ponder the thought. "The king might be inclined to reward a man who presented him with the head of an enemy, perhaps even award him that dead enemy's estate."

"Langwald belongs to Hugh!"

"Then perhaps Hugh, lord of Langwald, should personally present Rothgar's head to William."

"Gilbert." Maria took a step toward him, tottering as though perched on stilts. "You have sworn fealty to Hugh."

If she had actually made it all the way to his side, if she had touched his arm and smiled up at him with a pretty, flirtatious glance, the mists might have faded. But she stared at him stony-eyed, self-righteous. A stubborn set to her shoulders fired the mists and told him she sought once more to place him into a position of subordination below herself and Hugh.

"All things must pass, Maria," he said quietly. "William will value loyalty expressed today over valor shown in the past. But you need not fear. Hugh need not be displaced, save for his title. And you, my sweet." He reached for her arm and drew her, stumbling, against his chest. "My wife would have the best Langwald has to offer."

"No." She whispered, but the sound sent his blood roaring through his ears. By instinct he employed a hold upon her arm that Walter had taught him long ago, for use against Saracens. Though he broke the hold immediately upon realizing what he'd done, he knew it would leave her arm useless for a time, and an enormous bruise would appear on the underside of her soft flesh. True to form, Maria wilted against him like a fresh-plucked water-starved wildflower. He thought to apologize, but none save her lady's maid would notice.

"Tomorrow," he crooned, running a contrite, yet possessive hand down the length of her rigid back, "I will bring back his head. 'Tis cold enough to preserve it. I will ride along with Philip after Easter and carry it to William as a present."

8

Rothgar must be warned.

He had trusted her. His life in exchange for his pride. He'd upheld his half of the bargain. He would not understand that Maria had kept hers as well, not if Gilbert burst through the door of his hut, flailing about with his sword until Rothgar's head hung spitted from its tip. With his dying thoughts he would condemn her for a liar and a cheat.

Cradling the leaden, aching weight of her injured arm in the cupped palm of her free hand, Maria huddled deeper into the warmth of her cloak and waited in the chill gloom of her sleeping alcove. Curse Gilbert Crispin! Of a sudden, their tenuous agreement to protect Hugh had crumbled about them like the spun-sugar confections that graced William's tables: sweet, insubstantial, disappearing into nothing at a mere touch.

She shuddered, remembering the raw hunger in Gilbert's voice when he'd looked at her and said, "My wife." Never. Never. Perhaps his words had been ale-inspired. The throbbing in her arm suggested otherwise.

CONQUERED BY HIS KISS

Deliberately, resolutely, she pushed thoughts of Gilbert from her mind.

The sounds of roistering grew fainter as one by one the knights succumbed to Langwald's potent ale. When at last naught but drunken snores disturbed the nighttime quiet, she poked her head past the dusty hanging that assured her privacy.

The dying fire cast its dim glow upon the sleeping men. All save Gilbert sprawled upon the floor, their tunics loosened against the alcohol-induced heat of their bodies. It would be many hours before the chill penetrated their drunken stupor. Gilbert lay half-sitting, half-draped over the table, one outflung hand stretched toward an overturned tankard. The ale it had held puddled around his hand. From experience, Maria knew the sun would rise high, the spilled ale evaporate, before he stirred again.

Lying thus, he unwittingly exposed the length of his traitorous back. Had she a knife, she would sink it deep.

But though Maria had appropriated the clothing of the former lady of this house, she'd scorned the Saxon girdles of precious metal holding tiny, jeweled daggers. Pretty, useless toys they'd seemed, fit only for paring fruit or severing fat from lean. Her good hand twitching impotently, she now understood the deceptive strength represented by such a dagger. Placed just so, sliding between the ribs until a pointed tip pierced the heart, it would prove as deadly as the heaviest sword.

Vowing to fasten a girdle about her hips when next she dressed, Maria slipped silently from her alcove.

Along the bare, smoke-darkened corridor she crept, thankful that her slippers made no sound, that no wood creaked in protest. Through the quiet kitchen bower, its fire banked against the night. Past the sleeping bowers, where the knights normally took their rest, hoping their women weren't even now lying awake, waiting for them. On to the stables, where animal warmth and animal smells scented the air, where curious nickering and the shuffling of heavy feet in straw masked her deep, gulping breaths. Away from one man, whose touch meant hurt and humiliation; on toward another, whose firm grip offered support, who had whispered, "They will not hurt *us*."

"My lady?"

The stableboy stood uncertainly before her, rubbing sleep from his eyes. So much for her plan to flee undetected to warn Rothgar; but perhaps all was not lost. "Do you know the hut of the woman Helwyth?" she asked.

"Aye." The boy nodded. "Near the big bend in Langwald River."

Maria knew the place. The information would save her much time. "Saddle my mare."

"Aye, my lady." As the boy moved off to comply, he turned back to her. "And which beast should I saddle for myself?"

"You need not accompany me."

"But my lady, 'tis late night, and dark, and there are outlaws roaming the woods."

It would not do to downplay the boy's concern. Even worse, though, would be to allow him to accompany her. She had no intention of stopping at Helwyth's hut; Geoffrey had told Gilbert that Rothgar had taken refuge in a woodcutter's hut in that area, and she meant to find it, if she had to ride all night to do so.

"Helwyth's boy ails," she said. "I fear it might be plague."

The lad's eyes boggled at the news.

"Say nothing of this," Maria warned severely. "It may be nothing more than a fever, and if tales of plague are spread I shall know whose tongue did the wagging. And you know what Normans do to those who spread tales."

She disliked making the threat, hated contributing to the stories of Norman atrocities, but she had to buy his silence at any cost. The boy shook his head in denial and clutched at his throat, the mere implied threat of losing his tongue rendering him speechless and so fearful that he didn't question how she'd come to hear of Henry's sudden "illness" or why the person asking for her help hadn't offered to lead her to Helwyth's hut.

It didn't take her long to regret leaving the boy behind. Had he known her mission, he might have proved cooperative and could have helped her with her mount. The mare sensed the lack of strength in the arm Gilbert had injured and, resentful of being taken from her warm stable, fought for the bit with every step. "I would make faster progress were I afoot," Maria muttered, and then realized it was true.

She couldn't release the mare. It would head straight back to its stable, and the silly boy would no doubt raise a hue and cry, believing his lady had been thrown. Besides, she would have need of the mount; after warning Rothgar, she would need to make haste to return to Langwald Manor before she was missed, and her feet were so benumbed with cold, she doubted she would be able to run.

She directed the horse to a sheltered copse, eager as the mare for relief from the bitter cold. The small trees about her bent and shivered in the wind, and she sought out the sturdiest before she dismounted. At first contact with the ground, cold pierced her slippers and worked icy fingers up her legs. The mare, she knew, would bolt for home if she dropped the reins. Moving as quickly as her lame arm would permit, she wound the reins around her chosen tree. The mare jerked at her restraints and then fixed Maria with a baleful eye.

Maria rearranged her cloak about her, wishing her feet were clad in stout boots instead of thin slippers and that she'd garbed herself in one of the kitchen wenches' rough woolens rather than her own fur-lined silk. A working woman's cloak had handy slits in the sides, enabling its wearer to stay warm while only the exposed arm bore the brunt of the cold.

Her own lady's cloak boasted no such contrivance. In order to haul the reluctant mare along behind her, she'd have to grip the bridle, keeping her good arm aloft, allowing the cold to swirl beneath the uplifted folds of her cloak. She used her sound fingers to bend the deadened ones to clutch the front of her cloak closed, cursing Gilbert's cruelty anew.

It promised to be a frigid, uncomfortable trek to the hut sheltering Rothgar of Langwald.

And indeed it seemed a lifetime passed, though the moon had scarcely shifted position when she sighted Helwyth's hut. It squatted dark and low against the frosted earth, narrow wisps of smoke curling skyward through gaps in the thatch. No light seeped through the shutters.

It would make sense to rouse Helwyth from her sleep and ask her the location of the woodcutter's hut.

It would mean confronting, face-to-face, the woman who had cried upon seeing Rothgar, the woman whose tear-streaked visage had so gripped Rothgar's attention.

It might mean awakening the small boy, so like Rothgar, who had pointed and called him Father.

Maria tugged the disappointed mare away from the hut.

Something had happened to her feet, making her wonder how long she'd stood staring at Helwyth's hut. No longer did they ache with cold, no longer did her toes shriek in protest when they blundered against the innumerable clods littering the winter-heaved land. She welcomed the respite from pain, though she knew it meant she must find shelter lest her toes turn white and be lost to her.

Sighting Helwyth's hut had given her an idea. She cupped her hand over her brow to shade it from the white moonlight and scanned the surrounding forest. The mare stamped impatiently at her side, straining against the reins as if to test Maria's grip upon them. "Steady, girl," Maria murmured, willing her eyes to find the pall of smoke that would mark the location of the woodcutter's hut.

There. Not five furlongs hence.

Stumbling, willing her still-numb fingers to hold her cloak closed, Maria made for the hazy smoke sitting like a cloud just above the trees. The mare at first resisted and then seemed to scent the smoke. Her ears swiveled and pricked forward, an anxious whicker rumbling deep within her throat. She could, Maria knew, climb atop the mare now and give it its head, but she doubted her ability to lift her foot into the stirrup, much less swing the balance of her cold-deadened body into the saddle.

The mare provided enough forward-moving impetus for both of them. Maria clung to the saddle horn with her good hand, her slight weight slowing the mare's eager gait. Even so, the pace was swift enough, rough enough, that she thought her frozen legs might shatter like icicles from the impact of each half-running step.

The woodcutter's hut, humble and poor though it was, promised sanctuary unmatched by the most elaborate cathedral.

The mare paused at the door long enough for Maria to work her fingers free from the horn, but before she could catch the reins, the horse trotted off to the rear of the hut. Maria hoped some horse-pleasing shelter awaited there, enough to keep the mare content until she finished her business with Rothgar.

The hut stood like a dark well of silence amid the eerie winter stillness. No sounds came from within. Of course—he slept, unsuspecting of the threat hanging over him. She had been right to come with a warning.

It was but the matter of a heartbeat to lean toward the door, to rap upon its unyielding wood with knuckles that split instantly from the cold, to no avail. The door was so thick, no sound could penetrate. Uncaring of the damage to her silk cloak, she rubbed her bleeding knuckles against the soft material, and pressed her weight against the door.

A wave of blessed warmth flooded through the opening, and then light, flickering and golden from the well-laid fire, illuminated the whole of the hut. Scant feet from where she wavered in the doorway, Rothgar of Langwald loomed upright, half naked, his eyes glowing, his lips snarling with feral intensity, clutching an ax in both upraised fists.

His eyes widened with surprise. He recognized her, she could tell, but too late. The deadly ax, swung with every ounce of strength in his muscled arms, had begun its downward descent the moment she'd stepped through the door.

He contorted his body in an odd manner and bellowed as though she had somehow caused him pain. "God damn fucking shit!" he roared.

Curious, Maria had time to think, that her life would end with her ears ringing to the very first Saxon words she'd ever learned.

He'd wrenched his ankle in that reflexive, twisting motion meant to spare her the ax. Otherwise he would have caught her before she crumpled to his feet in a silken heap, would have spared himself that bleak, heart-twisting sensation when he saw blood dripping from her fingers, blood seeping through the tattered rags at her feet. Between his pain and concern, it took a moment for his mind to register the sight of the ax, its blade firmly embedded in the door, its handle vibrating audibly with evidence of the force with which he'd wielded it. Though she bled, 'twas not from wounds he'd inflicted.

Grimacing at the pain in his ankle, he hobbled to her side and crouched next to her. "Maria?" She lay unresponsive, still as death. A finger held below her nose felt the faint stirrings of her breath; felt, too, the inhuman chill of her skin. God's teeth! The woman was near frozen.

He pulled her into his arms, his skin twitching in protest from the slick iciness of her cloak. Her head lolled against his shoulder, and he wrapped her hair around his hand, intent upon supporting her without straining her slender, willowy neck. Her hair seemed to possess all the life she at the moment lacked; it wound about him, cool and smooth and silky, redolent of crisp early spring air and pampered woman.

She weighed next to nothing. In two strides he had her beside the fire. The floor was the best place for her. The hut's ancient bed would flare up like a handful of tinder should a spark land upon it. And her fur-lined cloak would make a better bed than a covering at this point, since it was so thick and well made it would resist heat from without as well as cold. How, he wondered, had she managed to lose her body's warmth when wrapped in such a garment?

One of her hands clutched the cloak tight about her throat in a death's grip. He loosed her fingers one by one, cursing their determined grasp, fearful the slender bones might crack before he pried them open. One of her sleeves fell back as he worked her arms free of the cloak. A livid bruise discolored her soft flesh, and though the arm flopped lifelessly at her side, her fingers curled back into the clawlike grip he'd sought to relieve.

"Maria," he called again softly, watching her eyes for a telltale twitch that would betray consciousness. None appeared. Remembering the blood, he studied both hands, turning them within his own, baring skinned knuckles, the palms laced with rein cuts. Though the fingertips were tinged blue, no trace of the dreaded white spots appeared. Nothing serious.

Her feet, too, were less severely injured than he'd feared. Some womanish lack of sense had sent her out into the night in slippers meant for naught but the bedchamber. He stripped the ragged slippers away, then tore at her hose until her legs were bared. Her toes felt so cold and stiff that they might snap off like ice-encased twigs from a branch.

He lacked knowledge of the healing arts, knowing only that she must needs be warmed from within, that her extremities should be coddled slowly back to warmth lest her blood come to a boil and make her shriek with pain.

He snatched the cooking pot from the fire and hurried from the hut to pack it with snow. If only he had two pots! But this one must do. Set next to the fire, the snow within would melt. He could mix the resulting water with some of his wine and let her take slow, careful sips once she regained consciousness. The wine would work its comforting magic. Then, if her wounds demanded soothing, he would run back into the night for fresh snow to pack against them.

She had moved not at all when he resumed his place at her side. He ran his hands along her arms and fancied they felt a bit warmer. Her feet, though, felt hard and cold as ice hewn from the still pools fed by Langwald River. He would have to lend her his warmth. The thought of gathering her into his arms and holding her tight against him sent his senses leaping; he shook the notion away. 'Twould not do for her to awaken and find herself wrapped in a Saxon's embrace. Her feet needed warming. Surely he could think of a way to do this without tempting himself beyond endurance.

Rothgar arranged himself carefully, the soles of his feet brushing against Maria's. He propped his back against the rough wooden bed, his wineskin within easy reach should she awaken. He splayed his legs until Maria's lay between his own, her toes pointed daintily toward him. Gripping her feet tightly, he pulled until her knees bent. He balanced one of her feet atop each of his thighs, wincing against the coldness of them, sharing his warmth with her, encircling each slender ankle within his grasp.

Her tunic rode up, baring the length of her smooth, slim legs. This he had not foreseen when he sought to spare her his Saxon's embrace.

"God's teeth," he muttered, releasing one foot to tug and pull at her gown until it covered all but her calves. He recaptured her ankle.

His gaze wandered down the tent of her gown, to where her waist curved inward from her hips, to where her breasts swelled above her slender rib cage, to her hair curling against her shoulders, shining in the firelight.

"God's teeth!" He cursed again, louder this time, and reached for the wineskin. Her portion warmed by the fire, and she wouldn't need more than he'd already poured out.

He took a hearty swallow of the wine.

Maria whimpered. She twisted her head, unconsciously seeking the warmth of the fire, her hair falling away and baring the delicate lines of her face, her lashes long against pale skin, her lips parted and moist in the flickering, golden light.

He tipped the wineskin again.

She pressed her feet against him. Her hips moved, lightly brushing the sensitive inner skin of his thighs. His manhood rose against the confines of his breech clout. Heat there—and to spare, but what manner of man would ease himself upon a helpless, unconscious woman?

Resolutely staring into the fire, Rothgar tipped the wineskin again. And again. And again.

9

Maria's fingers woke her.

Cramped and curled, they were the first to jerk from needle-sharp stabs heralding the return of feeling to her injured arm. Only half-aware, she moaned and thrashed in protest at the pain, puzzled to find her feet restrained in some unknown manner, her very posture off balance, but too tired to open her eyes and sort things out.

At that moment, her entire arm set to throbbing with renewed life. Seeking to rise, she sought purchase with her feet. They seemed to be wedged against something firm yet yielding, something *hairy,* something that exuded delicious warmth. Clamped about her ankles were rigid bonds giving off the same wonderful heat. Her eyes came open reluctantly to inspect the strange restraint.

The sight that greeted her prompted an inarticulate shriek, a furious scrabbling as she sought to free herself from a slouching, leering Rothgar of Langwald.

He did indeed slouch, the unclad upper half of his body reclining in a lazy fashion on the straw-littered floor. And well he might leer, for her legs were perched all akimbo upon his very own naked hairy limbs, her hose gone, her gown gaping apart in a most unseemly, unladylike manner.

She shrieked again and managed to pull free from his grasp and clamber to her feet.

Rothgar cocked his head and held a hand to his ear. "It seems we've been invaded by mice."

"Mice!" she squeaked, unable to follow his logic.

"Ah, there 'tis their sound again. Fear not, my lady, I shall save you from them." Holding a wineskin aloft in a mock salute, he tipped it to his lips, higher and higher, and then shook it before his woebegone, disbelieving gaze.

Any fool could see the skin was empty.

"You are wine flown," she accused.

"So I am," he said, looking extraordinarily pleased with his state. "'Tis your fault."

"*My* fault?" This time, she heard the high-pitched, mousy tone in her own voice.

Though she stood fully clothed and he wore naught but a breech clout, he looked to be the more comfortable of the two of them. He sprawled casually, the flickering firelight playing over his chest, over his long legs, over his sinewy arms. His eyes regarded her, slumberous, slanting . . . desirous.

Maria snatched blindly for her cloak and wrapped it about her. He moved not at all, but a twitch of his lips seemed to say her effort to hide herself mattered not at all, that he'd enjoyed an eyeful and more of her, at his leisure.

"Did you happen to save me a sip of wine?"

"Happens that I did, well mixed with water," Rothgar said, inclining his head toward a cook pot sitting near the fire. "Good wine, but surely enough remains in Langwald to have spared you the journey."

"I came to warn you of terrible danger," she said. Considering his carefree attitude and remembering the sight of him standing over her with ax in full swing, it now seemed a wasted effort.

"Warn me? You did naught but faint."

"I did not!" Maria stiffened with injured pride. She had never fainted in her life, had little patience and no sympathy at all for the women who kept servants scurrying about with burnt feathers to revive them from their swoons. "*You* smote me in the head with an ax."

"I did not!" Rothgar echoed her denial and rearranged himself in a more upright position. "Had I done so, your head would be split like a gourd, and you would not be standing before me now, hankering after my wine and casting lewd glances at me."

His words struck her speechless.

"Terrible danger," Rothgar said, almost as though to himself. "Were that true I would be in dire straits indeed. With the head of yon ax buried so deep in the door, 'twould take me till daybreak to wrest it free. I tell you, I am easy game this night for anyone bearing me ill will. Your 'warning' has robbed me of my weapon, and to avoid splitting your skull I may well have crippled myself for life. Have a look."

He raised one leg and waved his foot before her. Perhaps the ankle was slightly swollen; difficult to tell, particularly since her gaze was drawn inexorably down the length of his leg.

Maria heard his quick, low rumbling laughter when he realized where her attention lingered. He pulled himself erect, the folds of his clout falling into place, the good-humored crinkles around his eyes shifting into something raw, something primitive, something poised, and yet waiting. Every inch of her skin, every fine hair on her body, quivered in response.

"I will drink my wine now," she mumbled, turning from him quickly lest he read her wanton reactions in her eyes. Unseeing, she knelt by the fire and groped for the cook pot, snatching her hands back when the hot metal seared her fingers, then reaching for it again and lifting it to her lips, heedless of the heat and soot encrusting it, glad of the discomfort, eager for anything that would dull the inappropriate, inexplicable pull she felt toward him.

"Maria." The playful man had disappeared. He'd moved soundlessly to crouch behind her, his hand gripped her shoulder, his breath stirred her hair. "Maria."

The pot trembled in her hands.

"I did not know you would have an ax," she whispered.

"'Tis a woodcutter's hut, Maria." With infinite gentleness, his hand guided her shoulder until she sat facing him. The wine-flown sparkle had left his eyes, replaced by a solemn assessment, as though he needs must study every move she made, every word she said, to decipher some hidden meaning. His lips curved, and he stroked a spot just above her lip and held up his thumb so she could see the soot marking it.

"Tell me of this terrible danger," he said.

"Gilbert." She could say no more, her wits captivated by the shape of his lips when he spoke, the coarse beard hairs shadowing his face.

"I thought as much." He turned his attention to the fire, reaching into the nearby stack of wood for a log. After placing it atop the burning wood he found a longer, slenderer stick and poked it about in the embers, sending the flames flaring higher and hotter and brighter.

So she was not the only thing that responded with heat to his attention, Maria thought. Of a sudden she felt overwarm; she dropped her cloak to the floor.

Aloud, she said, "Gilbert has sworn to ride out in the morning and sever your head. He intends it as an Easter present for William."

Rothgar stared pensively into the fire.

"I had to warn you," she continued, suddenly desperate that he understand the depth of his plight. "I could not bear for you to go to your death thinking I had broken my word."

"You are so certain Gilbert would best me?"

"Of course he would! He will come after you in full armor, Rothgar, with all manner of pikes and maces and chains. You said yourself your only weapon is lost to you. Begin now to work it free, so you can defend yourself on the morrow."

He chuckled.

She must make him understand. "Really, 'twould be better if you ran for your life, but since you have crippled yourself you must take a stand with what you have at hand."

His chuckling burst into full-fledged laughter.

"I should have known better than to try to reason with a drunken sot." Anger seethed through her: at herself, for melting like a lovesick fool at his alcohol-induced attentions; at him, for guzzling all the wine until he could no longer recognize his desperate situation.

He shook his head at her. "Always so serious."

"But you yourself said it would take until daybreak to free it." She gestured toward the imbedded ax.

"Crippled, you said." She motioned to his ankle. "Gilbert will no doubt snore on until well past sunrise, but you should start off now, being so hampered."

"Maria, has no one ever teased you before?"

"Teased!" She must have misheard the word.

"Teased. Bantered with you. Jested."

"You jested, while your life is threatened, while your wits were wine-soaked?" In Maria's experience, drunken men roared and bellowed, they recounted their heroic exploits, their tempers flared hot and self-control wore thin. Prudent women took care to melt into the shadows at such times. A laughing, teasing drunkard? 'Twas not possible.

And yet one seemed to crouch next to her, his blue eyes twinkling in the firelight, fine lines crinkling about his lips and eyes attesting to good humor.

"Teasing's half the fun in getting drunk," he said.

"And what's the other half—swinging axes at well-meaning women?"

"No, wielding another sort of club altogether, with a willing woman." He raked his gaze over her, utterly disrespectful, leaving her feeling as hot and flushed as though the fire had somehow leapt free of its stone circle to burn along the length of her body.

Maria leaned into the fire, hoping he would mistake the blush staining her cheeks for a reaction to the heat.

She need not have bothered. From the corner of her eye she could see him lift his eyes heavenward, could hear his shuddering breath as he gasped at his own impertinence. "Forgive me," he mumbled. "I should not have spoken so to you."

She could not tell him she forgave his disrespect. Neither could she tell him something within her danced in joyous, intractable abandon at his ribald comments.

"You are drunk," she said.

"I suppose I am." He left her side. "More so than I thought I was, but less than I would like to be."

From behind her she could hear the soft sounds of dressing, the brush of woolen hose tugged along strong legs, the whoosh of chausses yanked over hose, the rustle of a tunic pulled over a head, the scraping of boots along the hard-packed dirt floor.

"I brought a mare," Maria said. "Take her and ride hard. I can make my own way home."

She heard the creak of ropes as he sat upon the bed, the scraping and tugging sounds as he tied his bootlace.

"I've done with running from William whoreson and his executioners," said Rothgar.

She whirled about at his words, swallowing hard against the fullness rising in her throat at the sight of him sitting so easily, so casually on the bed, at the thought that before the sun completed another course Gilbert Crispin would see to it that Rothgar of Langwald no longer walked on this earth. "Then you will die," she said.

"Not easily." He rose and strode across the length of the hut, and with a twisting motion wrenched the ax free and hefted it in his hands. He cast an assessing eye over the hut, its door, its lone hide-covered window, much as Hugh used to do when judging battle terrain.

"Please take the mare," she whispered.

The ax fitted Rothgar's hand as though he'd been born clutching it. He made a circle of his fingers and the shaft slipped through until the head rested against his fist; he twisted his wrist and it slid head-first until the deadly metal blade thudded against the floor. He leaned his weight upon it and focused his full attention upon her.

"Why did you come here, Maria?"

"To warn you! Please, take the m—"

"We are enemies, you and I," he interrupted, sparking within her the urge to refute his statement. "So what prompted your generous impulse? Did you but seek to convince me you had no part in Gilbert's plan?"

"Yes," she said. And then, "No . . . no."

"Then what?"

How to tell him, without sounding the fool, that the thought of his not holding her to blame would offer small comfort in the aching, empty void that would surround her with his death?

"Langwald needs you," she stammered aloud.

I need you, she admitted only to herself.

A humorless, self-mocking smile seemed to flit over his face. "Langwald. Always Langwald between us. I had thought that perhaps—oh, never mind."

He stared down at his ax.

And then she blurted it all out.

"I never thought 'twould be easy—the task I set myself, to save Langwald for Hugh—but it is proving daunting beyond my ability to manage. This entire land seethes with rebellion. Knights disappointed with William's largess would but need to hear a whisper of Hugh's condition before trying to wrest control of Langwald for themselves. I believe Gilbert Crispin now seeks to do that very thing, but I cannot cast him out, for we have so few men to defend ourselves as things stand."

"You are beset by treachery from all sides," Rothgar agreed.

"Including Langwald's people," she said. "Scarcely a night passes without some petty act of vengeance against us. At first it seemed comical. Now, though, with the castle taking so long to build, these depredations prove costly beyond measure. The knights grow surly, the villagers discontent, and I know Hugh is but a short time away from recovery. I know it. If only I could hold things together until then."

She fancied admiration colored his gaze. "Few men could hope to achieve what you seek."

She came to the end of her tale. "William left for Normandy earlier this month, else he might have already learned of Hugh's disability. Alas, Philip must travel to William's side to fulfill some clerkly duty shortly after Easter. He would betray Hugh's condition to William. And Gilbert says he'll present your head to William and tell the king he—Gilbert—would . . . would take me to wife, and swear to care for Hugh for the rest of his days."

Rothgar shifted his weight from the ax and moved to lean against the wall, the dark wool of his clothes blending into the smoke-blackened walls so that only the gleam of his hair, the occasional flash of his eyes and teeth in the firelight betrayed his presence.

"It seems you have nothing to lose," he said at length. "Whether Hugh retains the lands, or Gilbert succeeds with his plot, you are assured of a place."

"Oh, no," she said, longing to draw him close to the fire, where she could see him. "I am beset by lying, scheming men. I can never again trust a single word that passes Gilbert Crispin's lips. No sooner would William agree to Gilbert's plan than Hugh's life would be forfeit, and mine would become intolerable."

Something in that statement brought him out of the shadows.

"What would you have me do?" he asked, his voice low and vicious, the ax quivering in his white-knuckled grip. Maria shrank back from his tight-checked rage. "You said yourself I lacked the wherewithal to forestall Gilbert's attack. I assure you I could despatch his black soul, lady, yet you say you need his sword to protect your brother. You would spill your troubles to me, remind me of my helplessness to prevent his violence towards my people, taunt me with thoughts of you and that lout together."

Rothgar's color flared high, but she was certain her own cheeks reddened even more as she rose to her feet. She stood before him, nearly toe to toe, pretending an assurance she didn't feel, meeting his barely restrained anger with the cool, feigned lack of interest she employed so well in the market stalls.

Words could be like fruit. She selected one; cast it aside in favor of another, weighed this one against yet another whose similar surface hid a richer, fuller flavor—inner haggling, testing the offer before striking the boldest bargain of her life.

"Father Bruno says we should marry," she said at length, hoping she'd chosen the words, and the man, well.

10

A man could enjoy a quiet night's sleep in a Saxon hut. The hard-packed dirt floors, the clay-caked walls, the thick layered thatch, all conspired to deaden sound, to muffle noise. When Rothgar's ax dropped from suddenly nerveless fingers, it gave only a dull thump; when he opened his mouth to speak, only a strangled, garbled squawk emerged, quickly muted.

Why, then, did it seem Maria's preposterous words rang and clamored from the walls as though echoing against vaulted stone?

"Of all the witless notions," he managed to say.

Surprisingly, Maria agreed with him. "I thought so, too, when first he put the scheme to me. I think now that I failed to grasp the full implications of what such a union might bring." Her face softened into an apologetic smile. "Unlike you, Father Bruno cannot speak my tongue. 'Tis difficult for me, sometimes, to understand your tongue."

"You do well enough," he said, thinking he'd spent more time in discussion with this woman than with any other save his lady mother. "But you need not be handy with words to understand me when I say this—no."

"Why ever not?" Her brow knotted in confusion.

"Your knights would never accept me as your husband."

"Gilbert might resent you, but Walter will see to it that your back is covered."

"Your king would demand my head for taking arms against him."

"There is that," she admitted. "But you'll probably lose it whether we marry or not."

God's teeth, but she was a brazen wench! "'Tis an absurd idea," he said, finding himself explaining despite his annoyance with her bold questioning. "I am a Saxon Englishman. You are Norman. Such a union would be an abomination."

"Oh?" She lifted a delicate brow. "William himself urged Normans to wed English when possible, to forge loyalties. All across England, Norman knights have taken your ladies to wife. My own brother did the same, with your own betrothed."

She, who claimed a poor grasp of his tongue, nonetheless managed to fasten barbs to certain of her words, no doubt hoping to goad him to fury. Or did she seek to humiliate him by reminding him of the extent of the Norman occupation? No matter, her ploy failed. Odd, but the notion of Eadyth lying abed with the half-witted Hugh mattered naught, whereas the thought of Maria submitting nightly to Gilbert, Norman woman to Norman man—now *that* would be a true abomination, but was no real concern of his.

"What has gone between Eadyth and your brother is different."

"How so?"

"You said it yourself—through her he gained the liege loyalty of Kenwyck's people."

"Would not your marriage to me secure the same from Langwald's villagers?"

"Aha! So now we come to the true reason for your proposal!" Rothgar wished he still gripped the ax; he felt an uncommon urge to fling something, hard, to relieve the sudden tension building within him.

"I did not propose to you."

"You did."

"I did not. 'Twas Father Bruno's idea—"

"Father Bruno be damned!" he roared. Sacrilege, to curse a priest, but let sacrilege be damned, too. There were times when a man's honor demanded a bit of raving. Such as now, when a woman had the temerity to suggest marriage merely to ensure control of some land, to earn the cooperation of a few dozen laborers . . .

Not so different from what he'd planned to do himself when he'd forced Eadyth from the convent.

The thought brought him up short.

Maria stood before him, the firelight glinting against her tumbled hair, one hand wavering, as though she wanted to touch him but felt uncertain of his reaction. Her eyes, wide and troubled, belied the cool confidence she'd exuded.

He tried to look at himself through her eyes.

No longer hungry but bearing the stamp of starvation. Hair hacked away, proud beard shaven, clad in peasant's rags. So puny and insignificant before a Norman knight's strength that she urged him to run, that she pressed her mare upon him to speed his cowardly flight.

Yet she had stared, with interest, at his crotch. He'd swear on it.

No doubt to see whether a cock still hung from one so unmanned as he.

Yet she offered marriage.

No doubt expecting him to melt into the background, a Saxon eunuch, brought out now and again for show, just as she'd paraded her wretched brother before the castle workers.

Ah, the choices he faced! To run from Gilbert and bear forever the shame of cowardice, to leave her and Helwyth at the Norman's mercy—no, unthinkable. To engage, then, in lopsided battle and die like a dog at the hands of Norman swine. Or to marry and jerk like a puppet at Maria's whim, to watch another rule his lands and people, his neck whole only so long as he remained compliant and useful.

"Think before you say yea or nay," she whispered.

Think? It seemed his thoughts had been swirling for hours, but the fire, unattended, still crackled merrily and no predawn brightness seeped through the gaps of the window hide.

"There is this to consider," she continued in the face of his silence. "I have grown to love this land. A child born of our union—your son, Rothgar—would grow strong on your land, would call Langwald his home. And whether you lived or not, I would see that love of land instilled in him."

He'd thought her a witch earlier; she'd just confirmed his suspicion. None but a witch could have delved into his secret mind and divined his innermost regret. His kin had ruled Langwald ere the Romans set foot on English soil, and it galled to know the succession ended with him. A child, his son, though he might not rule the lands of his fathers, though Norman blood might flow in his veins, would nonetheless roam Langwald's acres, breathe Langwald's air, drink Langwald's water.

And she'd set mists swirling through his brain, clouding his doubts and tantalizing him with thoughts of what it would be like to hold her against him, to bury his face in her luxuriant, shining hair, to sire his children upon her. It roused him; just as her blunt recital of advantages taunted him with the sure knowledge that any joining with her would be but a semblance of true passion, a debt she felt honor bound to repay.

Witch, witch, casting spells, spinning her enticing, inescapable web around his all-too-susceptible self, draining everything and giving nothing in return.

"You would spread your legs and play the whore for Langwald," he snarled, knowing as he hurled the hateful, hurting words that his capitulation was assured.

"Aye, I will spread my legs, and you will spill your seed, all toward the same end. When we come together, Rothgar, with no passion save for Langwald's future, who can say which one of us plays the whore?"

She shamed him. She stood tall as her slight stature permitted, straight and proud, unflinching before his insults.

Rothgar reached for the ax. She never took her eyes from him. He pulled Edwin's cloak from the bed and flung it around his shoulders. She lifted her chin a notch but made no sound. He opened the door. The wind gusted into the hut, provoking a brief, brilliant shower of sparks from the fire. Wood enough in the pile to keep her warm until morning.

He stepped through the door and closed it gently behind him, and then thought, *What now?*

He would leave, that was what.

No matter that Gilbert would think he fled rather than face the Norman sword. Pride be damned.

He would leave, that's what he would do.

She had mentioned a mare. He would not take her mare, but the memory of the way she'd burst into the hut, windblown and so cold her fingers couldn't unbend, warned that she might not have taken care to restrain the animal. A horse with sense would take shelter around back, where the hut blocked the northern wind, and he found her mare sensibly dozing there. "Probably never thought to unsaddle a horse in her life," he muttered to the sleepy mare as he removed saddle and bridle, giving her an extra scratch around the ears before bending to hobble her legs with one rein.

Now he would leave.

A small heap of unsplit logs blocked his immediate path. The pile drying inside near the fire should hold until morning, unless the wind changed course, or a paralyzing blizzard gusted through. If that happened, even Gilbert wouldn't be able to save her. He sorted through the logs, selecting the smaller ones that would burn without additional splitting, and hauled them to the door. He dropped them where she'd be sure to see them.

Now he would leave.

It seemed to take forever to walk a hundred paces.

Once, when he was very young and just learning the ways of the world, he had asked his father why the lowest serfs, who were little better than slaves, made no effort to escape the drudgery of their lives.

"This is where they belong," Old Rothgar had said.

This is where I belong, something within him cried now. It seemed Langwald exerted an invisible pull on his legs, so that each step dragged an unseen weight. Small wonder serfs never ran away.

Serfs often seemed happy.

A loveless marriage with Maria? Was that really so different from the cold, calculated union he'd planned with Eadyth? *Yes,* said that vexing inner voice, but he could not fathom why that should be so—only that it was.

He trudged a few more paces, and then stopped. Trudged some more and stopped again.

Sons, growing tall and strong from Langwald's bounty.

He turned back to the hut. And found himself at the door so quickly he was certain the witch who was to be his wife had provided some magical transportation.

She knelt with her back to the fire, staring at the door, waiting for him. Her eyes glittered: from tears, from the onslaught of wind through the door, he could not tell.

"Are you truly a witch, to make you so certain I would return?" he asked, using his back to push the door closed behind him, turning away from all that beckoned beyond Langwald, something surging to life within him at the sight of her.

"No. But I heard you outside, taking care of me, and I prayed." To prove it she raised her hands, showing her long, slender fingers steepled in the age-old fashion. "Will you hate me forever for forcing this upon you?"

So easy to say, *I could never hate you;* so difficult to uphold, when sanity returned, when she no longer knelt before him in firelight, when he must needs defer to Hugh over his acres, when his servile state diminished him before other men and in his own eyes.

"I will try not to, later," he said.

She made a soft little sound and turned her head aside quickly, then busied herself with brushing her skirts as she rose from her knees. When she at last turned back to him, her head was downcast, her hair shadowing her eyes, only the rounded curves of her cheeks, flushed pink in the firelight, clearly visible.

She fumbled at the ribbons along her neckline, then began working one arm free of her tunic.

"What are you doing?" His voice rattled hoarsely when, with a final tug, she bared her arm, and more, revealing the creamy roundness of one rose-crested breast.

"We struck a bargain, did we not?" At his wary nod, she added, "We have time. I propose we seal it, here and now."

Once, in an attempt to help Maria attract a wealthy husband, her cousin Alyson had attempted to teach her the art of flirtation.

Maria had not proved to be an apt pupil.

Her face froze in stiff lines when coy smiles were in order. Words meant to convey double meanings sounded wooden and contrived when they came from her lips. The suggestive glances, the subtle body movements, the graceful gestures so natural to young Norman noblewomen looked merely silly when she attempted them. Ultimately, Alyson threw up her hands and admitted defeat.

"Try not to grow fat," she'd said, shaking her head over Maria's shortcomings. "At least you have good breasts. Few men could resist a glimpse of them."

Rothgar of Langwald appeared to be one of the few.

A man sensing a conquest invariably betrayed his excitement with a triumphant leer, a self-satisfied narrowing of the eyes, sometimes a furtive loosening of his tunic lest his aroused state show too blatantly. When Rothgar did naught but flinch, Maria knew the words she'd meant to sound lighthearted and flirtatious grated against his ears in some offensive manner, and even the baring of her breast left the front of his tunic flat.

Let us seal our bargain with a merry fuck, was the essence of what she'd said. Better had she admitted she would do anything, give all that she had, to stop him from walking through that door again.

Embarrassment heating her face, she blindly sought her sleeve and began drawing it up her arm.

He forestalled her with a curt order. "Leave it be. And have off with the rest of it. I would see what it is you put on offer."

A shrug of her shoulders sent her gown puddling down about her waist. At his sudden intake of breath she risked a glance at his tunic. Alyson had been right all those years ago. Though her flirtatious words had failed, her breasts had done the trick. Either Rothgar had managed to shove his ax into his breech clout, or the sight of both breasts had inflamed him.

She wanted to cry.

"Ah . . ." His voice trailed off into a snort of disgust. "Cover yourself."

He turned his back to her. As she pulled her gown back into place, she waited for a sense of relief to flood through her, as though she'd wiggled free of an unwanted task. Instead, his rejection stung.

"My husband did not find the sight of me so repulsive," she said, jerking the ribbons into line before retying them.

"Your husband?" He seemed to choke on the words.

"Ranulf FitzHerbert. Long dead, of an agony in the gut." She rested a hand against her lower right abdomen, remembering Ranulf's unpleasant end.

"Do you pine for him?"

"Nay." She allowed herself a small, ironic laugh. "Four years we were wed, with him forever knighting. We had a day here, a week there; in all, we spent perhaps four months together. He was a good-hearted sort, but I'd learned to live without him long ere I learned to live with him."

"Will you carry such fond memories of me, should I lose my head as you expect?"

She studied his stiff, unyielding form. The shadows cast by the fire drew his silhouette against the wall, complete in every detail from the hair spiking about his head to the unruly manhood outthrusting against his clothing, and she knew she could never forget a moment spent with him.

Why had he turned away from her? Why?

As if he'd read her thoughts, Rothgar spoke again, gesturing around the room. "This is not my way." Disgust and loathing fairly dripped from his tongue.

Good God, she'd bargained to wed a lover of men! "I did not understand your inclinations. I have never coupled so." She closed her eyes, unaccountably saddened at the thought of Rothgar lost to her in this way.

And then, equally unaccountably, she heard him laugh, a low, mirthful sound. Her eyes flew open at the unexpected sound.

"Do you always assume the worst? I but meant that love is best made in places where fleas and lice have been routed. Where a soft pallet and warm furs shelter the lovers. I would not take a true whore in a place like this, where I had to drag the stinking straw pallet out into the night lest its hidden vermin burrow into my scanty hair. God's teeth, I wish you'd sent me off with two skins of wine this day."

Miserably, she guessed, "You needs must be drunk to couple with me?"

"No," he said, his merriment dissipating as his demeanor turned as serious as her own. "But a bit of wine might help us feel more at ease with each other, so we could truly say what is in our hearts."

"I need not be wine-flown to speak honestly," she said.

"Oh? Then tell me now, why do you *really* want us to marry?" he challenged.

At once, she longed for wine.

Rothgar was right; with wine singing through her blood, it might be easier to admit some magical shaft had pierced her skin the first time he'd touched her hand, working its secret way to her heart, where it tugged and pulled in protest at the mere thought of being apart from him. When drunk, she might dare confess that of all men, he alone seemed able to banish her cursed loneliness, that having him at her side would fill her with new heart.

"Earlier you tried to give me good reasons, so now I will help you," he prompted, obviously impatient at her hesitation. "Gilbert cannot force you to marry him if you are wed to another."

"That is part of it," she admitted.

"And even if he should kill me, he'd not be interested in a Saxon's leavings."

Of that she was not so sure. "Mayhap not."

"The people would rally around Hugh."

"That is to be hoped."

"You *can* bear children?" He frowned, as if suddenly realizing her childless state.

"I quickened once, but the babe would not take root. The old woman who tended me said it often happens the first time and not to worry."

Her answer seemed to appease him. "Consummating the matter tonight would mean we could dispense with the calling of banns, since a child could be forthcoming."

"Aye."

She waited for him to add to the list, but he stared off into the fire. Presented thus, the sensible reasons for marrying seemed calculated and insignificant, pale shades of the emotions squeezing her heart.

"Are there any others?" he asked casually.

I should tell him there are other reasons, she realized suddenly, her heart hammering against her chest at the thought; realizing, too, that the words could not pass her lips without a sign, no matter how insignificant, to show he felt for her even a tiny portion of the feelings for him burgeoning within her. She clenched her hands into the folds of her gown as she waited.

He seemed to give her silence careful consideration, and then he said, "Then the matter is settled between us, is it not?"

Disappointment washed through her, so overwhelming that one not as accustomed as she to hiding her feelings might have staggered and betrayed the extent of her emotion. Clutching the scraps of her dignity about her, Maria said, "You are satisfied with the bargain, then?"

A long silence ensued, a silence wherein the flames seemed to intensify their heat, wherein the very walls seemed to press in upon them.

He spoke into the silence. "Aye, I am satisfied. Save for one thing."

"And what is that?" Her throat felt dry; her words fell hoarse and tremulous in the stifling, oppressive room.

One side of Rothgar's mouth twitched with the beginnings of a wry smile. He shifted, a minute movement that reminded her of his height, his strength, of the aroused manhood so inadequately concealed by his clothes. Maria felt compelled to draw great, gulping breaths, almost as though his height and strength and arousal denied her a full measure of the hut's close, heated air.

His half smile disappeared, his lips tightening into a firm, determined line, his body taut. And his eyes, hooded and unreadable in the firelight, swept over the length of her, seeming to brand her wherever they touched, leaving no doubt in her mind as to the one thing he sought to seal their bargain.

11

Rothgar stepped closer to her, forcing her head to tilt back, and back again, leaving her spellbound by the tortured longing that swept his countenance, by something feral in the way he held himself, as though a raw power suffused his whole being. His breathing grew ragged; the harsh male sound coursed through her until even the fine hairs along her skin strove toward him.

"Look at my hand," he whispered, as if awed. "Some sorcery draws it to you."

It trembled, as if indeed being dragged unwillingly by some unseen force, as he reached for a lock of her hair. "Look," he said, curling the hair about one wide, blunt-nailed finger, where the flickering firelight caused it to glisten against rough, callused skin like golden-brown silk. He pulled his finger free and her hair uncoiled, drifting to lie against her breast in soft tendrils. He did it again, and again, until half her hair tumbled wantonly to the front of her.

"Loosen your gown, Maria," he urged in a hoarse

whisper. "I would see you with naught but your hair to clothe you."

"I—" Was it just moments ago, or a lifetime ago, that he'd turned his back on her half-naked form? This talk of sorcery, this lustful behavior—was it merely a ploy meant to rouse her, leading to further humiliation? "Nay," she said, the memory of his rejection suffusing her with heated embarrassment.

"Shall I be the first, then?" He seemed unfazed by her reluctance and shed his tunic and chausses in the space of a heartbeat. This time, when he moved close to her, she stepped back, the heat of him an almost palpable thing that pushed her in its wake until she bumped against the wall of the hut.

With the fortress of his furred chest before her, with the sculpted muscles of his arms rising to barricade her against the wall, she wondered how she had ever thought him wasted with hunger. She felt as though he fed upon her very essence, soaking up her fears and her doubts until naught was left but a thrumming, trembling awareness of man, of woman. Of warmth, and privacy, and a heap of fur-lined silk cushioning the floor near the fire. To steady herself, she gripped his arms, just above the bend of his elbows, then had to forcibly will her fingers from tracing the bulging lines of his biceps.

"Will you play the coy miss with me now?" he asked, his breath teasing strands of her hair.

"Will you play the ruthless attacker?" she parried, hoping he wouldn't—and hoping as well her words wouldn't provoke another of his confusing changes of mind.

He laughed, his chest rumbling near her ear, prompting a place low within herself to vibrate in response. "Would that I had, while you slept so helplessly."

She remembered her unchaste position upon regaining consciousness, and lowered her head in embarrassment. He stood so close that her forehead rested against his chest, so warm, the faint, faint aroma of horse, of woodsmoke, the elusive odor of aroused male permeating her senses so that she wanted to breathe in deep, and deeper yet, and drown if she could in the heady scent.

Ranulf, always intent upon bedding her the moment he'd shucked his armor, had never smelled so good.

"You said you did not touch me while I slept," she said, thoughts of Ranulf gone as quickly as they'd come, her words muffled against Rothgar's skin.

"You were like a flower open to me," he whispered, tilting her chin until her eyes locked with his. She felt even more exposed to him, as if he could look into her very soul. "I could have touched."

"A solitary pleasure," she managed to say, wondering if she would have remained unconscious with Rothgar's long, sensual fingers playing against her.

"But a lasting one. Had I done so then, now I would but have to do this, and this!"—he slowly stroked his upper lip with his finger, and lowered it to run his tongue lingeringly along its length—"to be surrounded by your scent and your taste."

"Oh." Such wordplay, such provocative actions, robbed her of her wits. "Then you could have continued on your journey tonight, having no reason to return to me."

"Nay, my lady. Your essence would be more enthralling than the brew you ply upon your brother. One taste and I would be back where I stand now, begging for another draught."

He pressed ever closer, daring to run his hands down the length of her, encircling her waist, pressing closer until his thigh penetrated the juncture of her legs, until her softness straddled his bare, iron-thewed muscle.

"Lacking what I might have had, I must needs settle for this," he said, lowering his head toward hers.

Again, thoughts of Ranulf flitted briefly through her mind: slack, slavering lips, wet with too much wine, woman-starved from long months of campaigning. Kissing a thing to be endured, since it invariably led to the mildly pleasant act of copulation. A woman could always turn her head away from the fetid, slobbering grunts and concentrate on the pleasant friction between her legs, whiling away the time thinking of the child that might be conceived.

And then Rothgar kissed her.

The taste of wine, to be sure, but heady and sweet, so that her tongue itched to trace his lips in search of more. Lips—firm, demanding, capturing her own within his with ardent pressure, with playful tugs. Nigh unto half a year without a woman, if his story was to be believed, yet he held his lust in check, every taut, rigid line of him attesting to his control. And then his tongue—hot, welcome, plundering her own until for the second time that day, her legs buckled beneath her from a man's touch.

But so different, so different.

"Why?" she whispered when he caught her against him for support. *Why do I feel this way? Why did this never happen before?* "Why did you change your mind?"

"Ah, Maria." He buried his face in her hair. She could feel his breath hot against her scalp. "Do you not realize how beautiful you are, how the sight of you would inflame kings, leave alone landless louts like me? I am not made of stone," he said, guiding her hand to his breech clout, pressing it against the one part of his anatomy that seemed to belie his statement. "This night, this night you belong to me."

"You called me a witch," she whispered, wondering why his breech clout didn't burst into flame from the hot brand it concealed.

"Aye, that you are. One glimpse of a tear brimming in your eye and I forget my own woes. One hint of trouble awaiting you and I must needs leap to your defense. Steal my lands, trample my pride, unman me before my people—none but a witch could diminish such matters until all that remains is this." He rocked against her and molded one breast with his free hand, teasing the nipple until she felt it would bore a hole right through her gown.

She wanted his hands, his lips, his tongue, all over her. She wanted the heated, quivering shaft of his manhood buried inside her. Yet, she could not admit it, not when he seduced her with no corresponding passion in his heart.

"Rothgar," she gasped, struggling to explain away her unseemly agitation, "we must take a moment . . . lest the fire dies . . . now."

He groaned. "Aye, but I would have to let you go, and I find I cannot."

A wave of exultation washed through her. He didn't want to let her go! He wanted her, this handsome, teasing, laughing, tormented man; he wanted *her*. "Rothgar," she whispered, inadequately, since she longed to say so much more.

The sound of his name drew a primitive growl from the back of his throat. With fingers that were at the same time infinitely gentle and searingly hot against her skin, he lifted the folds of her gown, baring her legs, baring her most secret places to his sight. And he groaned again, when Maria sought the same of him, when she delved tremulous fingers into the workaday gap of his breech clout and eased his turgid shaft through the restrictive folds.

She knew a moment's doubt, looking down at what she'd exposed, remembering the dry, tight discomfort that always greeted Ranulf's first poke after long months of abstinence. And Ranulf's spear had not the heft or length of Rothgar's.

Nor had Ranulf ever shuddered with the effort of restraining his ardor, or looked upon her with such heated, passion-crazed eyes. The very sight of Rothgar so roused, for her, created a hot melting in her nether reaches and scattered the last of her doubts to the wind.

"Tonight you are mine, Maria," he whispered against her lips. "I will wait no longer to claim you." The hoarse passion in his voice roused tremors within her. Uncertain of his intent, she tensed while he lifted her against the wall, and then she knew what he wanted of her, though she'd never done it so. He supported her weight until she wrapped her legs about his waist, until she lowered herself fearfully against the moist, feverish head of his shaft.

She cried out, as she thought she might, but not from pain.

Poised as she was, there was no chance to ease him slowly into her. But the melting sensation she'd noticed had softened her very core, so that his wetness merged with hers. After the first, brief, searing entrance, she accommodated to his unaccustomed width, she adjusted to the uncommon length of him.

"Be . . . very . . . still." His hoarseness, the anguished inflection of his words, betrayed his tenuous grasp on his control. She clung to him, scarcely daring to breathe, until he expelled a shuddering lungful of air.

"Hold firm with your legs," he ordered, and she gripped him tighter, feeling him settle more deeply within her. He supported her back with one hand; with the other he tugged and jerked her clothes away from her. She felt him wad the wool against her back, and he pushed her against the balled-up bundle so that it nestled between her shoulder blades and protected her skin from the rough wall.

With one arm around her waist and one hand braced against the wall, he thrust into her. His long, sensual stroke brought his chest hard against her bared, sensitive nipples, touching a secret place inside her that had never before revealed itself until it exploded in an undulating, quivering wave of pleasure.

She cried aloud again, helpless against the all-consuming bliss. She feared losing control of her limbs and so clung to him, while he held her tighter, thrusting, thrusting, seeming to possess an innate sense that timed each of his motions to the shuddering contractions rippling through her. At last he shouted with his own release, impaling her even more thoroughly as he pulsated inside her, before turning with her so that his own unprotected back came against the wall, lending support to them both.

Maria snuggled against him, enjoying the thundering of his heart against her breast, the feel of crisp, curling hair and ridged muscle against the soft skin of her stomach, the sensation of being so thoroughly overwhelmed by the size and strength of him. With a reluctant sigh, she made to unlock her legs from about him, but he forestalled her with one huge hand wrapped about her thigh.

"Not just yet."

Curious, yet willing to maintain her position, Maria relaxed against him. She felt his stomach, his shoulders, his back, tense, and then he heaved them away from the wall, grinning down at her as he walked them both, attached in the most intimate manner, to the fire pit.

"As you warned, the fire wanes," he remarked.

"So soon?" She pretended disappointment, and worked her inner muscles around his tumescent manhood. It began swelling again in response, and she flexed her thighs. "Perhaps a touch of the bellows will cause it to kindle anew."

"Maria!" He gasped, then grimaced with pleasure. "We have no kindling, only stout logs. Should the fire die . . ."

"One must lay stout logs with great skill," Maria agreed, smiling, tightening her thighs and lifting herself a notch before dropping back into place. " 'Twould be most unseemly for me to let this blaze perish for want of a bit of stoking."

"Maria!"

It was her turn to lean back, a mischievous glint lighting her eyes. "What, Rothgar, have you no knowledge of teasing? Of bantering? Of jest—"

The balance of her words were lost as he captured her lips with his. They laughed against each other's lips at his clumsy efforts to kneel atop her cloak, they shrugged ruefully when their efforts to untangle their limbs resulted in a moment's separation. It took but the space of a heartbeat for Maria to tug loose the twist holding Rothgar's breech clout in place; it seemed a longer time, since he insisted upon a moment to feed the hut fire before tending to the blaze within her, until he buried himself deep within her again, before their bodies resumed the timeless rhythm and she gained her wish for his hands, his lips, his tongue, to possess her, body and soul.

Rothgar watched the play of firelight over Maria's face, studying the sooty sweep of lashes against her cheeks, the full, pliant lips parted just enough to expel her soft, sleeping breath. A rush of tenderness, a surge of protectiveness swept through him. She belonged to him now. And though his resources were meager, he would die ere letting her come to grief.

"Maria," he whispered, brushing his lips against hers. "You must waken now."

She stirred, bringing her sleep-warmed belly against his hand, her wondrous eyes meeting his first with slumberous confusion and then with remembered satisfaction.

"Rothgar," she whispered, the sound of his name upon her lips sending desire shafting through him. God's teeth, he ached to take her again!

"'Tis still deep dark," he whispered hoarsely. "We needs must make haste."

She lifted herself to her elbow. Her hair, tangled from his touch, drifted over her shoulder, trailing to her waist, the impudent peaks of her breasts peeking through the silken fall.

Her eyes glowed with remembered pleasure. A heartbreakingly sweet smile curved her lips. "Aye, Rothgar. We must find Father Bruno and marry."

He took a deep breath before speaking, forcing his gaze away from the temptations of her body.

"I cannot marry you, Maria."

Her lips parted as if to shout a denial, but she pressed shaking fingers against uttering a sound. And then only a slight fluttering of her lashes betrayed she had heard him. He remembered how skilled she'd become at hiding her true emotions, and knew he'd wounded her.

"We cannot marry," he continued, pressing to explain before she turned away from him. "But not because I fear dying for you. I am not quite the helpless oaf you believe me to be. I grew up swinging a Saxon battle-ax. Though Norman skulls be dense as wood, not even the stoutest oak can withstand a well-placed cut. I could wreak much havoc among your men-at-arms, Maria, ere they claimed much blood from me. But that would serve no purpose."

He traced his thumb over her cheek, wishing he could so easily rub away the wounded sorrow clouding her expression. "Nor, at this time, would a marriage between us accomplish what you seek. It would bring the villagers in line, 'tis true. I fear, though, that such a union would throw your men-at-arms into revolt."

"They would not be pleased," she agreed, though a shaky tremor in her voice hinted the words came hard. "Gilbert, most of all, would react with rage."

"We seek to forge unity, but publicly taking up with me could divide Norman loyalties to your detriment. I saw the way of things in England, Maria. The land is beset by marauders, plunderers, thieves of every class waiting to descend at the first hint of weakness. You cannot afford to antagonize your fighting force just now, nor, however I might enjoy it, can you allow me to lop off their heads."

"I know." She spoke scarcely above a whisper. "I had hoped . . . but I suppose I needs must carry on as before, alone."

"Nay!" Shocked that she thought he meant to abandon her, Rothgar pulled her close against his chest. "I propose a ruse to help you keep Gilbert at bay until your brother regains his senses."

Her sharp intake of breath revealed her interest.

Even speaking of the dark knight sent jealousy and disgust clawing through Rothgar's gut. "Gilbert's reactions are impossible to anticipate. Murderous rage might be but one of his responses to a marriage between us. Suppose he takes it into his head to ride to William whoreson and calls you a traitor to your own brother! Think how it might sound if he brands you a heartless wench who keeps Hugh dosed senseless while you rule the manor and consort with one of William's sworn enemies."

She paled. "I had not thought of that. What—what is this ruse you spoke of?"

"If you regain Gilbert's good graces, do you think he will permit you to carry on as you have done, managing the household and doing as you please?"

She nodded after only the briefest hesitation. "I think so. Many knights are like Gilbert, somewhat dull-witted, but all the more dangerous because their brute strength is not tempered by wisdom. It has ever been easy to bend Gilbert to my whim."

"Then I propose you thwart Gilbert yet again. You say he means to ride out for me this day. I say you take me back to Langwald yourself, as your prisoner."

"But—"

"First we must conjure up some good reason to explain your coming after me on such a night," Rothgar pressed, ignoring her protests.

Unconsciously she rubbed at the bruise marring her upper arm. "Gilbert hurt my arm last night. I could say he frightened me into going after you."

"Excellent," Rothgar approved, though his bile rose at the thought of the pain she'd suffered at

Gilbert's hands. He would make the knight pay for every speck of skin that he'd marred, make him suffer tenfold every moment of pain Maria had endured. "You must tell Gilbert you were wrong to set me free. Confuse and forestall him by pretending agreement with him in all things. Keep his sword swinging on Hugh's behalf. Betimes, set me to work with my people so I can help them understand."

He studied her face for a sign of fear but read only intelligence and contemplation, no trepidation at all at the thought of tricking a mean-spirited Norman knight. Unaccountably, he felt pride swell within him at her courage.

"What if I must needs promise outrageous things to placate Gilbert? How will you know when I am playacting?"

Rothgar nodded, approving the sensible question. "'Tis simple enough. Each night you will come to me." He grinned wickedly. "I shall expect a full accounting of your day's tale-spinning . . . amongst other things."

A sweet shuddering passed through her, sending his loins tightening in response. He moved to cover his lips with her own when she stopped him, voicing yet another concern.

"What if the situation grows out of hand, and I am forced to call an end to the ruse?"

Again, the question proved her solid grasp of the dangers they faced, but he took no pleasure in responding. Heaviness spread through him. "When you stop coming to me, I shall know you have turned to Gilbert."

"Never," she vowed, with a vehemence that both startled and delighted him.

"Ah, sweet Maria. There are times when we are

forced to do the very thing that makes our souls rebel." He pressed her fingers to his lips, praying she need never be forced to such dire actions. "Tell me, if I asked you, would you forget all these worries and run away with me instead?"

"I—" she swallowed hard and looked away from him, toward the fire, and shivered just a little, "I would, Rothgar. I could not let you walk away from me again."

His heart rejoiced at her words; his mind screamed to gather her into his arms and run away with her and leave everything behind.

His honor demanded that they stay.

"Every moment of every day, we both would be haunted by what we left behind. You would sorrow and fear for Hugh. I would grieve to think of my people left at Gilbert Crispin's mercy. 'Twould only be a matter of time before we each blamed the other for our guilt, and then we would truly lose all."

"I cannot bear to think of you locked in chains once more," Maria whispered, tracing his scarred wrist.

"The chains are of no import," Rothgar said, though his skin fair crawled at the thought. "What matters is keeping you alive to nurse Hugh back to health. So long as someone with good heart rules Langwald, I can endure it. You have been spinning tales these many months to hold things together for him. Now you can devote all your spinning to keeping Hugh's men content. I will handle the villagers for you. You do your work within the hall, Maria. I will do mine without."

"If we fail—" she began.

"Then we are no worse off than now."

She thought about that for a moment. "Aye. And if we win?"

"*When* we win," Rothgar said with a wicked smile, "I shall demand a reward. A beautiful Norman witch to take to wife."

He allowed his fingers the freedom to do what they'd been aching to do; he brushed aside the silken strands of her hair to curve his fingers round the fullness of her breast. His lips just naturally followed, capturing the turgid peak hot against his questing tongue. And Maria, the witch in her possessing secret knowledge, made but the slightest movement before he found himself buried deep in her heated sheath, her surging body matching his, thrust for thrust, heartbeat with heartbeat.

"Nay, the chains will not matter," he whispered against her hair. "They are as nothing against the bonds you have twisted round my heart."

12

The clump of boots against Langwald Hall's wooden floors wakened Eadyth. She lay abed in a pleasant, predawn daze, enjoying the warmth of Hugh's back pressed against her own. She'd been silly, the past winter, to cower at the far edge of the bed, shivering, while a veritable ember-stoked oven slumbered, smoldering with heat, next to her.

But Hugh had been different then.

She burrowed deeper into the wolf pelts covering them both. Far too early to rise. Still, sleep eluded her. The pounding footfalls from outside their chamber quickened their pace, now accompanied by muted shouts. She sensed Fen crouching near the bed, heard the low growl that was the only sound he ever made. Hugh stirred beside her, muttering a little. Eadyth tensed, remembering how lightly dosed he'd been the day before.

It seemed far too early for Maria to make her morning appearance with Hugh's draught. The tight-stretched hide covering their window glowed gray; Eadyth had never noticed how a sliver of soft light shone from beneath the door, no doubt cast by the torches lining the outer hall.

She bolted upright, clutching a pelt to her breast. She'd never noticed the light before because Geoffrey, or another of her gaolers, always slept on a pallet stretched before the door. Ostensibly to be on hand to help should Hugh awaken in a wild-eyed frenzy, she understood their role was to prevent her from escaping to spread word of the true extent of Hugh's disability.

The shouting increased in volume; the footsteps raced as fast as heavily mailed bodies could move; no guard slept at her door. What was amiss? Hugh moaned and kicked the wolf pelts from his legs. Eadyth was struggling to pull the pelts back over him against the chill of the room, when their door burst open and Gilbert Crispin stood framed in the torchlight.

"Where is she?"

"Who—who do you seek?" Eadyth stammered.

Gilbert nodded toward Hugh. "His bitch of a sister. She is not abed in her sleeping alcove. I thought she might be here, coddling him."

"I've looked everywhere. Even the knights' bowers are empty. She did not spend the night there," gasped one breathless squire, skidding to a halt next to Gilbert.

Gilbert raised his forearm as if to clout the young man, but instead shook his head in disgust. "The lady Maria would not disport herself in such a manner. Check the stables. She rides the bay mare."

As the young man ran off, Hugh moaned. "Wife?"

At once, Gilbert's attention riveted upon Hugh. "Well, well, what have we here?" he taunted, stepping into the chamber and drawing the door closed behind him. Eadyth, wishing the room were not cast in darkness, felt her heart step up its pace, slamming against her ribs. She could sense Gilbert's menacing bulk approaching their bed. "Did you forget our bargain, my lady?" he asked, his rough-edged voice pinpointing his position much closer than she would like it to be. "You promised to tell me of changes in his condition."

"There—there is naught to tell," she lied, leaning toward Hugh as if she could protect him.

"Think you I am as witless as he?" The jingling clink of mail told her he'd taken another step closer. "You have ever been less to him than a flea to a dog. And now you are *wife?*"

"Wife!" Hugh roared unexpectedly. While the pallet rocked beneath her, she felt Hugh scramble over her legs. She cried out when his big, rough hands forced her none-too-gently to the place he'd just vacated. The glow of dawn filtered more strongly through the stretched hide, illuminating the sight of her naked husband crouched beside her atop the bed, legs poised to spring, his arms held menacingly out at his sides, looking for all the world as though he intended to attack Sir Gilbert Crispin.

And then, as quickly as he'd taken his stance, he crumpled. With a keening moan, he clutched his head and dropped to his knees, shaking the pallet again atop its brace of roping, his heavier weight sending Eadyth sliding against his quivering back. Fen bolted from the bedside, fastening himself to Gilbert's leg and sinking sharp teeth into his hand.

"Look what you've done!" she shouted, forgetting the fears of a moment ago as Gilbert roared out in pain and shook Fen away from him. She cared only for the agony of the big, hulking man trembling next to her, the man who'd leapt to her defense, just as any knight might do for his lady love. She wrapped her arms around Hugh's great, heaving shoulders and lowered his head to her breast. "Find Maria at once," she ordered. "He needs his dose."

Improbably, Gilbert left the room to comply.

He was gone for long moments, giving Eadyth time to wonder at her lack of fear—of both Gilbert and her husband. Many was the morning she'd watched Hugh thrash and flail against the strength of four men, yet now he seemed content to rest in her arms. Tentatively, she stroked his hair, marveling at its thick softness. It seemed that a spot on his head throbbed; she pressed against it and he sighed with relief.

"Here?" she whispered, probing for another pulsating point.

He sighed again.

"Here? And here?" She touched, she soothed, she stroked against the tensely corded muscles at the back of his neck until they relaxed, until he sagged against her, sleeping easily, his weight pushing her back against the high, carved frame of the bed. The sensation was not unpleasant.

Gilbert strode back into the room, clutching Maria's precious bottle.

True dawn flooded the room, illuminating the derisive sneer that crossed his face when he saw Hugh slept.

"It seems you have no need of this after all," he said, waving the bottle carelessly before her, dangling it from two fingers as if he intended to drop it to the floor.

Had Hugh not weighed her down so, she would have tried reaching for the bottle. But he pinned her to the bed so she couldn't move.

And then the young squire returned, his eyes wide with excitement. "You were right, my lord. The lady Maria's mare is gone. Stableboy says she rode off late last night, to tend the sick child of Helwyth."

"Helwyth? Helwyth? What have I heard of Helwyth? Last night, did not Geoffrey announce to all and sundry that Rothgar visited her and thence to a woodcutter's hut?" Gilbert absentmindedly tucked the bottle into the pouch at his waist, a frown creasing his forehead. A terrible, bitter anger overtook his features, and a stream of violent curses flowed before he said, "Maria's gone after the Saxon."

The squire exchanged fearful, puzzled glances with Eadyth. She clutched Hugh more tightly to her as Gilbert stormed from the chamber, heedless that he carried Hugh's potion with him.

With his ax balanced easily against his shoulder, Rothgar led the mare toward the pools dotting this section of woods. Streaks of rose and gold heralded the dawn. Birds ignored the unusual spring cold, twittering cheerfully from the trees, their feathered throats proclaiming their joy in the new day.

Rothgar had no voice for music, else he would join in their song.

He found himself whistling, though, as he chopped an opening in the thin ice to enable the mare to drink. Months had passed since he'd last felt the urge to whistle a tune, and though he found he hadn't lost the ability, he learned whistling was best accomplished without a broad smile splitting the whistler's lips.

"Drink hearty, since you carry two this morning," Rothgar said, patting the mare's broad back while she lowered her head to suck daintily at the frigid water. "And be quick about it. 'Tis later than I thought."

Talking aloud to a horse—what was next? The way the mare's ears swiveled, an enchanted fool such as he found himself to be this morning might begin to believe the beast understood what he said. Then the mare lifted and turned her head, pricking her ears and flaring her nostrils, snorting the water away as she focused her short-sighted eyes toward the hut.

She let out a long, welcoming whinny. Drifting over the chill, early morning haze came an answering neigh. And then another, followed by shouted curses, the faint jangle of horse-borne metal, the dull thudding of hooves against frosty earth so that though they were at least two miles away, Rothgar could almost feel the ground shaking beneath him.

None save Normans rode horses in such a manner.

Maria, alone in the hut.

His heartbeat, his pulse, drummed against his ears, wiping out all sound save for his laboring breath as he raced through the trees, running to the hut where Maria waited oblivious of the approaching danger. They'd come for him, he had no doubt of it, but one look at her tumbled, tangled hair, at the rumpled, ruined cloak ground into the dirt floor near the fire, and they would know. They would know. His captors had taught him women who consorted with Englishmen soon found themselves fair game for any lustful Norman.

If they suspected she'd submitted to him, she would no longer be their exalted lady deserving of loyalty, but a whore deserving only their contempt.

Rothgar burst into the hut. "We dallied too long," he said, panting. "A mounted party approaches."

"Curse Gilbert! He never rises so early after a night spent swilling ale." Maria wasted no time in gathering her cloak. "We can make a run for it."

"I know a way through the woods. Let us hurry, Maria."

They ran to the mare. He tossed Maria up and leapt on behind, with one smooth motion kicking the mare toward the woods. He must get Maria to Langwald. For the ruse to work, Maria must be safe at home, pretending accord with Gilbert; himself working with the villagers, building Hugh's cursed castle.

Before being swallowed by the trees, he risked a backward glance, cheered to see the clearing still stood empty, knowing they would be well out of sight by the time the Normans reached the hut.

Cradling his woman in the circle of his arms, Rothgar pressed the mare up the crest of a low rise before risking another precious heartbeat's pause to glance through the trees behind them. He reined in the mare with a curse.

"God's teeth! What manner of foolishness is this?"

"I cannot see." Maria craned her neck, her shorter stature denying her the view that greeted Rothgar's careful scrutiny.

"Your Normans arrive." Rothgar served as her eyes as best he could, given that the trees sheltering them from sight afforded much the same protection to those he squinted to see. "They approach the clearing from the west, Gilbert Crispin at their head. Another group skulks toward them from the east. They are armed, Maria. It looks to me as if they mean to waylay your knights."

Maria found herself incapable of speech, able only to stare mutely heavenward, wondering why God seemed so bent upon treading all her hopes into dust.

"You cannot afford to lose these men, Maria."

"Nay," she croaked.

"Your arrogant Normans carry only light arms. They expect none but me to resist them at the hut. They must be warned."

"You cannot warn them! They would never believe you! They would set upon you."

One moment he was behind her, his long-limbed body encircling hers. The next he'd slid from the mare, pressing the reins into her hands, staring up at her, his glorious blue eyes darkened with resolve and a wistful regret.

She knew, from his look, that he thought never to see her again.

"Rothgar—" She reached toward him.

"Ride for Langwald. Believe me, your men must not know we spent the night together. Carry on, Maria. Do whatever you must to keep yourself safe until Hugh comes round."

"I cannot." Though she hated the whimper she heard in her voice, she could not erase it. "I cannot do it alone."

"You can." Rothgar reached up, tracing her lip with a gentle finger. "You carry such strength within you. I feel honored and blessed that you shared some of it with me. Now, let me do this for you."

He slapped the mare's rump, sending the skittish beast into a quick trot, and turned away from her before she could protest.

The mare leapt ahead when Rothgar let loose with a warning cry, an eerie echo to the despair shrieking in her heart. Risking a fall, striving desperately to bring the mare under control, Maria twisted in the saddle, his name upon her lips as she helplessly watched him race through the woods, his ax swinging from his hand.

"Normans! Have a care for your backs!"

To think Rothgar of Langwald would ever shout such a warning! And yet he bellowed it with all his might, praying he'd reached them in time. God's teeth! Gilbert Crispin couldn't die now, at the hands of some woods-slinking, scurvy outlaw, not when Maria still had such need of him, not when Rothgar meant to savor that pleasure for himself.

He burst into the clearing surrounding the hut and came up short at the sight that greeted him. Three Norman knights—Gilbert, Dunstan, Stephan—and their squires, all well mounted but lightly armed, faced him with weapons held aloft.

Breathing hard, he read the disbelief upon their faces and remembered Maria's premonition that they would not heed his warning. "Outlaws approaching," he said gasping, pointing toward where he'd seen the attackers sneaking through the woods. "You must make ready to defend yourselves."

Gilbert's laughter rang through the clearing. "The sun has not yet risen on a day when you can outwit me, Saxon. I can see you are the only threat facing me." With a motion of his arm, he directed his men to form a loose semicircle around Rothgar.

"First blood!" shouted Stephan, spurring his mount toward Rothgar.

As if in a dream, Rothgar saw the wild-eyed horse thunder at him, saw the club in Stephan's uplifted arm, sensed the stirring of the air as the club aimed for the juncture of his neck and shoulder. Easy enough to sidestep the blow. And then a piercing shriek claimed everyone's attention.

'Twas Robert, Dunstan's squire, who cried out. For a timeless moment, when even the trilling birds ceased their song, the young man stood rigid, the wide-eyed disbelief marking his face almost comical until he pitched forward, revealing the shaft of a spear quivering from his left buttock.

Like the other squires, Robert wore no mail. Even so, to pierce his stout woolen garb, the spear had been thrown with uncommon force, from an uncomfortable proximity. Realization of their vulnerability settled upon the group of Normans at the same time a veritable shower of spears hailed over them.

"A Saxon trap!" With a howl of outrage, Gilbert pointed his sword at Rothgar. "I'll have your head for this." He spurred his mount into action, flinching just in time so that a well-aimed spear merely gouged his neck rather than burying itself in his throat.

"This is no doing of mine," Rothgar shouted as he braced himself to join the attack, catching sight of several rag-clad forms hurtling at them from the woods. Strangers to him, their poor rags in odd contrast to their well-fed, well-armed strength. Saxons? He didn't think so, and yet they hacked and clawed at the Normans, shouting an odd mixture of English words mingled with age-old Saxon curses.

Rothgar of Langwald raised his ax in the defense of Maria's Normans.

Something about the violence stirred his blood, roused a deep-buried instinct for survival, calling forth the fierce, primal Saxon battle cry that last left his throat at Hastings. And that proved these attackers bore no Saxon blood, for there was no answering cry, only a renewed battle frenzy. Rothgar's brain engaged long enough to feel a brief pang of remorse that he'd been unable to save this one for Maria when one of the outlaws swung his ax against Stephan's leg. The ax severed Stephan's limb at the knee, the forceful blow burying the blade deep in the screaming horse's ribs.

The outlaw sought to wrench his blade free ere the falling horse drag him down. Rothgar leapt forward, relieving the attacker of his head, his ax hacking roughly through the outlaw's neck.

"To me! To Crispin!" Gilbert's muffled cry drew Rothgar's attention. Claiming the headless outlaw's ax as his own, he sought Gilbert's mounted form amidst the churning brawl. The Norman knight fought near the edge of a clearing, bareheaded, possessing but one sword, surrounded by a group of outlaws.

Rothgar's drab garb stood him in good stead, for the outlaws failed to notice him until it was too late to avoid his swinging ax. He sent several unwary souls to eternity as he forged his way toward Gilbert through the hand-to-hand fighters and silently took position behind the group surrounding Gilbert Crispin.

Rothgar caught Gilbert's gaze, the Norman's eyes flaring with hatred and accusation just as his screaming horse went down.

Rothgar gripped two axes, one in each hand, which made easy work of crushing the closest two skulls. Leaving one weapon buried, he used both hands to wrench the other free and swung it again. Two attackers yet lived; they gave Rothgar no chance to ply his ax again. They abandoned Gilbert and fled to the woods, leaving Rothgar standing over the fallen knight.

It ended as quickly as it had begun. The attacking force melted back into the forest with Dunstan in hot pursuit. A final spear clattered to the ground, a Norman spear, no doubt dropped by one of Gilbert's own men. An uneasy quiet settled over the clearing, soon broken by moaning men and the wheezing breath of injured horses.

Gilbert cringed against the earth, seemingly afraid to rise so long as Rothgar towered over him.

The battle lust still raged through Rothgar's blood, leaving him angry and unsteady. His hand gripped the ax handle so tightly it sent sharp streaks of pain shooting to his shoulder. It felt wondrous good. With every ounce of his being he longed to swing the ax just once more, longed to cleave Gilbert's bare head into two neat halves.

But Maria had need of the knight. Especially now, with so many wounded, with one of her knights bereft of a leg, with two of the trained warhorses fit only for merciful death, she had need of Gilbert Crispin.

She had need of Rothgar's wits, too, to help her manage this Norman knave. With a final clench of his fist, he banished all thoughts of splitting Gilbert's skull.

"Are you sore wounded, Norman?" Rothgar asked.

Gilbert touched a trembling hand to his neck. "One cut. And some bruises taken ere you joined the fray." Making a great show of brushing the dirt from his armor, he rose slowly to his full height. Rothgar held his ground before him, taking unaccountable pleasure in noting the top of the Norman's head scarce reached Rothgar's nose.

"You will pay for this, Saxon," Gilbert spat.

"For saving your ungrateful neck?" Rothgar asked, his tone deceptively light as he forcibly quelled the rage Gilbert's words provoked.

"I say you brought this attack about, and only pretended to save my life when it became apparent your men had lost the day."

Gilbert's accusation, his failure to acknowledge the Normans' desperate situation, struck him so absurd that Rothgar laughed, a short bark of disbelief. The sound brought a flush to Gilbert's scowling face. With a lightning-quick motion, he drew back and buried his mailed fist in Rothgar's unprotected stomach.

A coward's blow, one which near robbed Rothgar of all breath. He staggered backward for a few steps, losing his ax, gasping for air.

Fuck Gilbert Crispin. Maria needed none but himself!

Rothgar's breath returned, enough for him to bellow out his rage. He hurled himself full force at the smirking Norman. His weight knocked Gilbert to the ground, and he set about the Norman's face with his fists, knowing he'd only hurt himself by pounding at the mailed sections of his body, thrilling each time his knuckles met skin.

They grappled, Saxon and Norman, rolling across the ground like two lads engaged in a friendly tussle, though murderous intent marked each blow they dealt. Rothgar filched the Norman's dagger from his belt, but couldn't manage to free it from its leather scabbard to lend sharp steel to the damage inflicted by his fists. The Norman's strength was daunting, but Rothgar's long months of hard labor had honed his sinewy strength to a surprising degree. His height lent him greater reach; his long-suppressed rage lent power to his blows.

And he had him. God's teeth, but he had Gilbert's head helpless as a boiled egg between his hands. A handy rock lay ready to crack the Norman's skull, when Rothgar felt small frantic hands gripping his shoulders, felt scalding tears mingling with the sweat on his neck, heard at his ear the voice belonging to the woman he'd prayed was well on her way to safety behind Langwald's walls.

"Stop, stop," Maria begged. "Please stop, before both of you are killed."

Her voice, her presence, awakened his errant senses. Maria had need of Gilbert. And Rothgar had best exercise his wits quickly to extricate her from her folly.

13

Rothgar's scarlet-drenched hands left Gilbert's neck and encircled Maria's with such blinding speed that she gasped aloud, more from surprise than pain.

"Keep your distance, Norman, lest I slit her neck like I split that whoreson lying there," Rothgar threatened, dragging her away from Gilbert's prone form.

Relief weakened her knees. Rothgar's quick, easy movements, his challenging words, assured her 'twas not his own blood darkening his tunic and hands.

She wondered how many of her men would be dead now, had Rothgar not intervened. An unexpected exultation swept through her. He had done this for her. Rothgar had risked his Saxon life against Norman enemies; he had saved Gilbert and held that knight cowering at his feet—all for her.

From somewhere Rothgar had produced a Norman dagger, which he held pressed near but not touching her neck. Strange to think a woman would find such a position encouraging, but her heart soared. Already he had done so much for her; surely Rothgar's ugly, feral, snarling words, his menacing stance holding her captive, were part of the ruse he'd suggested. Maria felt no danger emanating from him, only her own overwhelming relief at being held within his embrace again.

His grasp of her seemed protective rather than threatening. His blood-soaked arm wrapped round her neck to grip her nether shoulder, but loosely so she need not wheeze for breath. Reflexively, she gripped his forearm, looking for all the world as if she sought to wrest herself free, instead drawing strength from the feel of his flesh against her fingers, caring not at all that her hands grew red-stained and sticky. He held her hard against him, his warm, lean, taut body supporting her weight. She could feel his heart thudding against her ear.

He lowered his head with a mean, vicious laugh, more akin to Gilbert's sounds than Rothgar's. She knew a brief pang of doubt, and then he whispered, his voice lighter than the breeze chilling the air: "Fall in with whatever I say. 'Tis a dangerous game I propose we play."

The few able-bodied men in the clearing muttered amongst themselves at seeing Rothgar's hold upon her, moving slowly to their feet, apparently ready to intervene on her behalf.

Rothgar directed his harsh words to Gilbert once again. "Tell your men to tend to their wounds. We have things to discuss in private, the three of us."

Gilbert waved the men away and scrambled to his feet. There was a look about his battered face that frightened Maria, a black, murderous rage hinting at barely suppressed violence. Rothgar pulled her back toward the hut. Gilbert followed each step, reluctantly, grudgingly, as though his leg were hobbled to Rothgar's.

"Leave her be, Saxon," Gilbert said, his voice a snarl when they were out of earshot of the men. "From the looks of her, you've done enough as it is."

Maria's pulse quickened. She should have known the evidence of their night of love would be branded upon her, but what could she have done? The sight of Rothgar and Gilbert pummeling each other had banished all caution from her mind. She carried no grooming tools, no unguents to obliterate the marks of Rothgar's passions, and her fear for Rothgar's safety had driven all sense of self-preservation straight from her head.

"Aye, I had my fill of her." Rothgar laughed, low and triumphant. "Time and again."

Oh, God, what was he doing? He'd warned her against admitting to their lovemaking, and now he taunted Gilbert with it, as though he meant to grind the knowledge into the dark knight's face.

"I'll hack your manhood from you and feed it to the pigs for this," Gilbert rasped.

"She shouted much the same," Rothgar mocked. "Do you Normans know such few curses that the same one needs must be hurled whether 'tis death or rape that is threatened?"

"Rape? You raped her?"

"What, you think a high-born Norman lady willingly coupled with a defeated Saxon?" Rothgar hooted with derision. With one smooth motion he tore away the cloth Maria had used to bind her bruised feet, held aloft her hand. The blood she picked up from touching his gore-encrusted arm emphasized where her palms had been cut by the reins the night before, where she'd split her knuckles hammering on the hut's door. He bared her enhanced wounds for Gilbert's view. "Does it look as though she submitted willingly?"

Fall in with whatever I say, Rothgar had commanded. Such simple words, so difficult to honor. Her throat ached from the effort of holding back a screaming denial to what he said. By making her appear the unwilling victim, Rothgar surely sealed his own doom, judging by the hatred swirling over Gilbert's countenance.

"I am looking upon a dead man," Gilbert said, confirming her fears.

"I think not. Especially since you have only yourself to blame for putting her at my mercy."

"I will hack—" Gilbert began, red blotches mottling his skin.

"I know, I know." Rothgar sighed. "Hack away my manhood and feed it to the pigs. It will not erase the fact that I had her, Norman, and you drove her to me as surely as if William whoreson had spoken the order himself." His voice changed again, coming sarcastic and contemptuous. "What manner of man are you, *Sir Knight,* to inflict pain upon a woman and threaten her so she needs must feel compelled to chase out on a freezing winter's night to set things right?"

She sensed rage surging through Rothgar anew at the memory of the bruise upon her arm.

Gilbert cast a dismissive look toward her arm, where her clothing hid the mark of his cruelty. He clenched his jaw. "'Twas but a moment's inconvenience for her. She had no cause to chase after you. I told her *I* meant to set things right."

"And a fine job you did of it," Rothgar retorted. "Blundering straight into a trap like a honey-dazed bear."

"A trap of your setting," Gilbert thundered. "Devised by you and Langwald's scurvy lot."

"Not so, Norman, even if it pleases you to think so. Have a look at yonder dead man." He gestured with his head toward where one of the attackers lay sprawled, a lance jutting from his chest. "That man never hailed from Langwald, nor from any holding hereabouts. I know every villager within three days' ride. I've not seen that face, nor that cut of tunic, before."

Maria remembered the Norman lance rattling to the ground as she flew to Rothgar's side. The lance *must* have been thrown by one of their own. She refused to consider the implications if it were otherwise.

Just then Dunstan rode into the clearing, shaking his head with defeat. He pulled his horse to a halt at Gilbert's upraised hand and called across the clearing. "They vanished like woods faeries, Gilbert. I saw nothing of men."

"Think on it, Norman," Rothgar continued, nodding as if he'd expected Dunstan's failure. "It seems as though the swine attacking you knew where to find both of us this morn. Of a certainty, they swarmed over everyone in this clearing with no care for my safety. I would say you were betrayed by one of your own."

Gilbert frowned before treating Rothgar to a brooding stare. "So now you hold Maria hostage and blather nonsense of treachery. One would think you believe you have an interest in Langwald, defeated cur."

"I do." Though blandness marked Rothgar's tone, his body tensed against hers. "I saw the way of things at Langwald. You lack a lord. You lack sufficient force. Most of all, you lack gold. The gold to hire the knights you need, the gold to raise the castle walls."

His words hung between them, supported by the crisp, cold air.

"Did I not tell you, Maria?" Gilbert said. "I knew Langwald could not be so poor as it appeared. Spill your secret, Saxon."

"I can tell you where to find gold," Rothgar agreed. "Providing there is something in it for me."

Fall in with whatever I say, Rothgar had told her, but his claim seemed so outrageous that Maria found her tongue at last. "We searched every inch of the manor hall. We found no treasure."

"Nevertheless, it is there." He returned his attention to Gilbert as if she hadn't spoken. "What say you, Norman? Can we strike a bargain?"

He waved the dagger, causing Gilbert's eyes to narrow in reconsideration.

"I think you lie, Saxon, in the interest of saving your neck."

Rothgar nudged the back of Maria's leg with his knee.

"I will bargain with you, Saxon," Maria said in a rush. "Give me your terms."

"A share," Rothgar promptly replied. "I cannot retrieve the gold without returning to Langwald. But . . ." he stretched out the word.

"But . . ." prompted Gilbert.

"I will not discuss the treasure with any but Hugh."

With a roar, Gilbert advanced upon them. Maria cowered back against Rothgar, feeling that gentle pressure to the back of her leg again. "Let him finish, Gilbert!" she ordered.

Rothgar's hand tightened approvingly over her shoulder. "When your lord is full recovered, I shall reveal the treasure and ask a safe conduct of him, that I may journey to Duke William and ransom my safety. As a token of my sincerity, I release your lady now. Unharmed—more or less." He let forth with a lewd, gloating chuckle, managing to whisper against her hair, "Do what you must, Maria, and come to me tonight."

He stepped away from her, making a near imperceptible motion toward Gilbert with his chin. Of course. A woman released from forced captivity should rush to her savior. She lifted her skirts a few inches and scurried across the few feet separating Gilbert and Rothgar, keeping her face lowered to hide the loathing that came over her at the thought of Gilbert taking her within his protective grasp.

"Now you die, foolish Saxon," Gilbert said, gloating, pushing Maria behind his back.

"Nay, Gilbert! I have struck a bargain with him." Maria clutched at his arm. "Besides, he speaks the truth. Hugh lacks gold."

Gilbert cursed, glowering from her to Rothgar. "I like this not, Maria, bargaining with one who should be dead."

"Nor do I," she rushed to assure him, pretending, placating, weighing what she might say next, anticipating Rothgar's next words.

Gilbert muttered an oath but relaxed some small measure, soothed by her words. A shattering realization swept through her: Rothgar had spoken true. The Saxon man who'd touched her heart and claimed her body knew her abilities better than she did herself. The long months of thwarting Gilbert for Hugh's sake had developed strength within her. She *could* do this, she *could* play out the ruse, even though it left her weak-kneed and quaking.

She'd lost her cloak in her headlong rush to separate Rothgar from Gilbert, so she could claim cold if Gilbert questioned why she shivered. What could she say, though, to explain the nervous dampening of her palms, her forehead, that had sprung up while her mind scrambled for lies?

She would think of something. She could do it.

"I would speak to you for a moment alone in the privacy of the hut, Maria." Gilbert tightened his jaw, not noticing her preoccupation. "Though you bargained, I want him trussed up. I trust him not at all."

Rothgar shrugged, willingly submitting his wrists to the squire Gilbert summoned, managing somehow to make the action look a spiteful, silly precaution. A mocking smile curved his lips, drawing a scowl from Gilbert.

Gilbert hurried her toward the hut, placing his body between her and Rothgar like a shield. With all her heart, she longed to catch Rothgar's eye for the briefest heartbeat, to take heart from the warm, confident approval she felt certain she would find there, but Gilbert's stiff, enraged presence denied her what she craved.

Gilbert guided Maria into the mean shelter and pulled the door closed behind them, taking a moment to allow his eyes to adjust from dawn's light to the hut's smoke-darkened gloom. She went to stand before the smoldering remnants of the fire with her back to him, her gown wantonly loose, her hair dust-caked and flecked with bits of straw.

The swirling red mist began trickling into his mind. She had lain with the Saxon. No matter that she had been forced, she had done it.

"I sought you out this morn to apologize. Perhaps . . . perhaps I should not have gripped your arm so yesterday." He forced the words through clenched teeth. "I near had a fit to find you gone."

"You have ever been careful for me, Gilbert." Mockery tinted her words as she rubbed the arm he'd hurt.

Her swollen lips spoke of recent passion. The neck of her gown hung awry, allowing a glimpse of beard-reddened skin to show, and she dared to taunt him! "Slut," he said hoarsely, gripped by a murderous fury at the thought of what had taken place in this very hovel throughout the night, added to the sick certainty that she acted not at all damaged or displeased on this sun-drenched morn. "I care not what bargain you struck. I mean to kill him for this."

"No. You cannot. He must live. He must."

"What, itching for more already? Had I known you were so lusty, I would have met you in this hut myself."

Her face paled. "Does it look to you as though I enjoyed this night?" She lifted her shaking, bloodied hands before him. "I fought with all my strength. But he had been without a woman for so long. I was no match for him." She sobbed and turned her head away.

Her admission made him impatient. He should have skewered the Saxon the moment he'd freed Maria. "Then I will kill him now and find the treasure regardless. Now I know it exists, I'll not rest if I needs must uproot every tree and unearth every stone to find it." He made to storm through the door, but Maria called out to him.

"No!" Her shrill, imperious command rubbed nerves already worn sore.

He paused at the door. "No?" He repeated her word slowly, barely able to pass it through the rage clogging his throat. How dare she forestall him!

"While he lives I am in your debt, Gilbert."

His hand stilled on the door peg. "What do you mean?"

She rushed up to him and he studied her face. He'd seen that white-lipped, pinched, eager look before, on the faces of those who wanted a thing once thought to be beyond their reach, but now within their grasp. What was it Maria wanted so badly?

"Do not kill him now. Not yet."

Gilbert shook his head, pretending an indifference to the words. Never had she begged; always had she demanded. "You have had your chance with him, and your ridiculous scheme came to naught but humiliation. Now he must pay for raping you."

"Aye. And that is why I ask you to spare his life now."

She touched him on the arm, the first time he could remember her ever having done so without prompting.

"If you order an easy death for him, we might not find the gold and my—my honor will go unavenged. I want him to suffer as I have suffered. I want to see him humiliated as he has humiliated me. By *my* hand. It is within your power to grant my wish, Gilbert. And, Gilbert, I shall not be ungrateful."

The touch of her hand, the pleading in her eyes, her tremulous stance, all seemed designed to soften his anger toward her. The swirling mist ebbed, but his soldierly instincts roused in its stead, sensing something amiss.

"Things have changed between us now, wouldn't you agree?" A tentative smile hovered over her lips.

What was it about this woman that fascinated him so? Her face and form were fair enough, but many women possessed greater allure. She had not the glorious golden hair of the Saxon women, nor the entrancing reds and jet blacks of some of his own kind. Brown hair, had Maria, brown eyes; she would go unremarked—had gone unnoticed for years, in fact—among the fashionable, the sophisticated ladies of Norman society. And yet she could stand before him, plain brown eyes glittering with unshed tears, lips trembling, dressed in a torn Saxon gown, and he would think her the most desirable of women.

He shook his weak-minded thoughts away. He studied the situation as a soldier should, and a smile twitched at his lips when he realized the powerful position he held. He'd come to the hut this morn intending to recapture the Saxon, and he'd done so. His intent had been to execute the Saxon in full sight of the villagers, not to waste his worthless blood here, where whispers of his death might grant him the status of martyr.

And Maria begged for the Saxon's life. Oh, God truly smiled upon Gilbert Crispin this day! He could indulge Maria's whim, put her in his debt by pretending to go along with her puling demand for revenge. He alone would know the Saxon's neck would be severed where it would do the most good, in full sight of the villagers who would then know the name of Langwald's true master.

"Would you strike a bargain with *me*, Maria?" he asked, careful to hide his elation from her as he ensnared her within his trap. "A bargain to ensure the Saxon's life?"

"I—I would."

"Whatever I ask?"

She didn't respond for a long moment, looking toward the door as if the answer she sought lay beyond its wooden shape. Naught lay beyond the door, save the Saxon. Gilbert tightened his hand against his mail, drawing a rasp of metal, not accidentally reminding her of his superior strength.

"I will do whatever I must. What—whatever you ask," she whispered.

Victory surged through him. It was near dark in the hut, with the door closed, the windows covered, and the fire that had warmed her night of shame naught but glowing embers. He could see her well enough, though, to go to her side and grip her shoulders, and turn her about so he could look into her wary, deceitful, plain brown eyes and gloat to himself over the wounded betrayal she would soon suffer. How he would savor her suffering, and there was yet a way to prolong his enjoyment, enhance his pleasures with her.

"It is not too late," he said.

"Too late for what?" Her breath caressed his cheek.

"For what I suggested. Marriage between us. A home for Hugh, while we rule his lands together in his stead. 'Tis a perfect plan, Maria. It need not lie about us in ashes now, even though you have been soiled."

"You still want me to marry you?"

He wondered if his own face betrayed the extent of his wanting as hers had done such a short while ago.

Maria looked to the ground, lowering her head in shame. "You could not want me now. Not after what he did to me."

"I will show you what I can and cannot want." He pulled her roughly into his arms and ground his lips against hers.

For a heartbeat, she was his, utterly his, even though she stood still and stiff within his arms. And then she fought against his embrace with the fury of a cornered badger.

"You lie! Nothing has changed between us!" he roared when she flailed away from him, quelling the hurtful rejection until only injured pride remained. Good God—for a moment he had nearly fallen under her spell again. "Had you fought yon Saxon so well I doubt he'd have claimed his pleasure last night. Very well. No bargain with me means no bargain with him."

She had backed away from him swiftly, clutching her arms about her as though to ward off a blow, shivering and pale in the dim light. "I cannot kiss you, not just now," she said, her words clipped and agonized. "His touch . . . what he did, Gilbert, I fear he has ruined me for the touch of another man."

He expelled a breath of air he hadn't realized he was holding, an unfamiliar shame chiding him for his treatment of her. Sweet liar—or truthful victim? He had seen it himself, women claimed as war spoils, who chose poison or a knife to the wrists rather than submit to a man again. Good God—what if she killed herself before he had the chance to enjoy her body as he'd dreamed of for so many years? "You would not kill yourself?" he asked.

"No," she said. "Oh, no."

She stood trembling in the near dark; he stood certain of only one thing: She was not to be trusted, ever.

"If we were to marry, I would claim my marital rights," he warned.

"I know you would."

"And yet, I would prefer not to force you like he did, though I will if I must."

"I ask but a brief respite," she said. "Allow Father Bruno to call the banns. By then, I will surely conquer this ridiculous aversion."

A matter of weeks, perhaps a month or two to call banns. No time at all to a man who had waited years.

"And by then, there could be no question," she added.

"No question of what?"

"Why, a babe, of course. If we exercised our . . . our passions just now, and a babe resulted, you could never be sure of the father."

He had not thought of that, though the idea of siring a child upon Maria's body sent a thrill racing through him. Did she bear the Saxon's whelp first, he'd gut it and throw it into the fine new moat they would build.

"We will wait," he agreed.

"And Rothgar's punishment rests in my hands."

"Within reason," he said, his wary instincts roused once more. She seemed overconcerned about the Saxon. "He waits for Hugh to keep his bargain. You must agree that his wait need not be a pleasant one."

She nodded once, a quick, curt motion. "Agreed. We shall marry. Here is my token to seal the bargain." So quickly he couldn't react, she braced herself against his folded arms, planted a featherlight kiss upon his cheek, and whirled to face the fire, shivering.

Pleased by the kiss, he moved to place a possessive hand upon her shoulder; she shrank away. Very well. He could be generous in victory. He decided to give her a few moments alone while he sorted through the muddle waiting outside.

"Maria," he warned as he stepped through the door, "I shall be watching you carefully."

A shaft of sunlight blazed around her. "I would expect no less of my husband," she said, not turning to face him.

A man should feel elation upon pledging troth with a woman long desired. But a wary caution tempered Gilbert's heart, a niggling doubt that somehow, some way, she'd once again managed to get the better of him.

Had his life depended on it, he could not explain why, but he resolved to keep a very close watch indeed over all she did, over every move she made, in regard to Rothgar of Langwald.

14

Maria stood at the hut's doorway, pretending an interest in the preparations to return to Langwald while surreptitiously casting about for the sight of Rothgar. She noticed that the men-at-arms had taken up her lost cloak and fashioned a rough litter for Stephan. Stretched to its fullest width, the cloak barely supported him; though the men pulled the silk-lined fur taut, Stephan's maimed leg ended near the hem while his good one bent over the edge and dragged upon the ground. Despite the cold, the bearers' brows beaded with sweat at the strain of supporting his weight.

"Mayhap if you removed his armor, he'd make a lighter load," Maria suggested, to a chorus of ayes.

"All our horses save one bear some injury that should be tended ere they are ridden again," said one of the squires. "That is why we heaved Robert facedown atop your mare. Those English devils devised some type of spear that can't be pulled free. We cannot leave him here at the mercy of those skulking vultures."

"You did well," Maria acknowledged. She clasped her hands tightly about her against the biting wind, raking the clearing for a glimpse of Rothgar. There, near the trees—Gilbert had wasted no time. During the few short moments she'd spent gathering her wits back about her in the hut, he'd had Rothgar's mouth gagged and a long tether fastened to his wrist bonds. But lest Gilbert cover his head with a sack, there was naught to quell the life force in Rothgar's eyes.

Oh, how she longed to drown in his gaze, how she ached for his touch, to hear his rumbling laugh and reassuring voice telling her she'd played her part well. Pray that he *would* laugh when she told him she'd agreed to marry Gilbert. He had, after all, told her to do what she must.

She winced at the sounds coming from Stephan. In addition to the initial agony surrounding his first uplifting in the makeshift litter, he needs must suffer even more now at the men's clumsy handling, as his squire's fingers fumbled at his clasps and rough hands bent him this way and that to free him of the heavy mail.

The other sights and sounds greeting her were no more pleasant. Only Dunstan appeared to have escaped injury altogether. Gilbert's and Stephan's horses lay dead, their loss devastating. Robert's wound crippled him as surely as Stephan's severed leg. The other squires fared better, but who knew what toll the sudden attack had taken on their nerve?

How high would the toll have risen had not Rothgar warned her men and plied his battle-ax on their behalf?

The entire episode called to mind the near-fatal skirmish that had claimed Hugh's wits, reminding her of their vulnerability against the superior numbers of the English, should the rabble gather their forces against them. She might have taken some cheer from the injury to Gilbert's neck, but though it trickled with blood, it looked to be only a surface wound.

And, as she had admitted to Rothgar, what would she do without Gilbert? His relative health meant only three knights—Gilbert, Dunstan, and Walter, who must have stayed behind as usual to watch over Hugh—were on hand to protect Langwald against marauders. What would she do if William sent word from Normandy demanding the contingent of knights Hugh was pledged to provide? She shook the worries from her mind. Hugh and Rothgar still lived. She lived. They would prevail.

Oh, to be atop her mare again, with Rothgar's strong arms about her! Her wayward mind set upon the thought, so that she shivered with the effort of staying rooted to her spot when she longed to run to Rothgar's side.

Gilbert noticed her trembling. Dunstan had relinquished his mount to the senior knight, and Gilbert sat the destrier with his customary casual skill, casting an occasional possessive glance at her while he oversaw the tending of Stephan. He leered at her when she trembled and slapped the back of his saddle. "You may ride pillion to me. I shall be happy to share my warmth so you need not feel the loss of your cloak."

Her wits scrambled for a response. "My discomfort this morn is such that I could not ride." *I am sorry, Rothgar,* she screamed silently in her heart as she glanced at him to see if he had taken offense at her words.

Gilbert's expression shifted from lewdness to suspicion as he followed the direction of her gaze. "I think you stare overmuch at one who has harmed you so grievously."

Her legs threatened to buckle beneath her, and her wits summoned yet another glib lie to placate Gilbert. "I plan my revenge, Gilbert. And Stephan's plight led me to notice the Saxon wears a cloak. 'Tis little more than a hank of dirty wool, but it offers some protection from the cold. Once his armor is doffed, Stephan will feel the chill keenly."

One look at Stephan's quaking body confirmed the need for some sort of covering. Though his teeth chattered with cold, rivulets of the death sweat sprung from skin turned waxy pale.

Gilbert shook his head. "I doubt he'll survive the move to Langwald. 'Twill be far colder than this in the grave. He might as well grow accustomed to it. I'll fetch the cloak for you to wear."

"Let me do it myself."

"You will not approach him, Maria."

Gilbert's horse carried him to Rothgar. With the swift, reflexive action of a well-trained Norman knight, Gilbert unsheathed his sword. For a heartbeat he held it poised above his head, his lip quirked with derision, sunlight forming a nimbus around the shining blade, and before Maria could cry out in protest or throw up a restraining hand, the sword descended upon Rothgar's unprotected neck.

The material of the cloak parted. Not one drop of blood marred the skin revealed beneath it. No sound passed through Rothgar's gag. His eyes remained wide open, unblinking.

"You—you have a light touch with the blade, Sir Gilbert," Maria croaked. She wrapped one arm around the destrier's neck, pretending affection for the animal while clinging to it for support from the sudden wave of relief that threatened to wash her balance away.

"When it suits." Gilbert wielded the sword as if it were an extension of his arm, entangling it within the folds of Rothgar's cloak and pulling until the cloak worked free. With a shake of his arm, the cloak hung in limp folds from the tip of the sword. "Heed my skill, Saxon. Should you fail to produce the gold you promise, I'll skewer your heart and present it to the lady just so."

The two men glared at one another. Maria sought a way to dispel the tension gathering round them. She plucked the cloak from Gilbert's sword and shook it out before her. Rothgar's scent rose from it, enveloping her with his silent strength, enabling her to speak to Gilbert again. "Would you ply your blade for gentler reasons now and slice two narrow strips for me . . . my lord?"

Rothgar blinked.

Gilbert didn't seem to notice that she near-gagged on the endearment, but with cocksure, swift strokes severed strips from the cloak. So easily could he separate Rothgar's head from his neck. It seemed prudent to direct the knight's attention away from Rothgar. She hoped he understood when she left him without another glance. She could not risk it. A soft look, a secret smile—anything could provoke Gilbert.

Gilbert, keeping pace with his horse, cast a questioning glance toward the strips she clasped apart from the cloak.

"For my feet," she said. Once well away from Rothgar, she bent to wind the cloth around her feet.

"You cannot walk. You will ride with me."

The squires, finished with their ministrations, began once again to heave Stephan aloft. His agonized cry, noticeably weaker, called forth yet another easy lie. "My pain pales next to his, Gilbert. I must walk alongside Stephan, so I might hold his hand. The walking will keep me warm." She hurried with wrapping her feet, glad that working with the strips masked the shuddering revulsion that gripped her at the thought of pressing close against Gilbert, of his arms encircling her as Rothgar's had done such a short time ago.

She busied herself with tucking the edges of Rothgar's cloak around Stephan. Gilbert rode up to her when she stepped away, pressing the free end of a leather thong into her hand. She followed the course of the thong, seeing it stemmed from Rothgar's bonds. Again, she dared not look at his face, lest she betray her true feelings.

"Since you must walk because of him, I thought it might please you to lead him like the castrated goat he is, my sweet," said Gilbert. "I will lead the party. Follow me."

The pale sun, still begrudging the earth a hint of springtime warmth, seemed to dim in the sky. Suddenly feeling her uncloaked vulnerability to the cold, Maria shivered, wondering how she would manage the long walk back to Langwald, towing one betrothed behind her while following in the wake of yet another would-be husband as he forged his oxlike way back to the manor.

And she had promised to cling to Stephan's hand, to offer him comfort. Wounded men sometimes waxed romantic in the throes of their distress. Fortunately Stephan was unconscious from his pain and loss of blood. Otherwise, given the outcome of the day thus far, she would not be surprised to find herself promising to wed yet another bull-headed man ere the sun set upon Langwald.

Gilbert himself provided the impetus for hurrying back to Langwald with all speed. With an exasperated exclamation, he slapped his hand against his knee. "I almost forgot," he said, digging into the pouch at his belt. "I brought this along by mistake, but mayhap 'tis just as well. Might Stephan and Robert benefit from a dose?"

Hugh's potion bottle dangled from his fingers.

He twirled it as though it weighed nothing, reminding Maria of how little syrup actually remained. On Stephan it would no doubt be wasted; Robert might benefit from its soothing effects, but then would beg for more, draining the bottle even faster. Though guilt smote her heart, she must deny Robert and Stephan.

She would not let Gilbert see how this affected her.

"I think not," she said, shaking her head regretfully. "It drives demons from the head, not spears from the arse. Nor will it help Stephan form a new limb." While Gilbert considered her words, she plucked the bottle from his hand and buried it deep within her waist pouch.

She bowed her head before God, knowing hot waves of shame streaked her face. What manner of woman had she become, spinning tales and denying the syrup's soothing powers to suffering men?

Gritting her teeth, holding one unconscious man's hand and with Rothgar's leather lifeline wrapped around the other, she made for Langwald.

Hugh wrapped one arm about his head, squeezing, hoping to drive out the demon cavorting within. Once, years ago, his squire had gathered rocks to line a fire pit, claiming hedgehogs cooked in such a manner tasted so succulent a man might be tempted to forswear pork.

The squire had reckoned without the moisture trapped inside the river rocks he carelessly chose. Hugh and his fellow knights had watched with great amusement when the heated rocks shattered into needle-sharp shards, slicing off one of the squire's fingers, as he well deserved for delaying their meal, and skewering the already dead hedgehog so that stone bristled from its skin like extra spines. "What a weapon those rocks would make!" the knights had murmured amongst themselves, all the while knowing that harnessing such force and bending it to one's will were surely impossible.

This day, Hugh's head might have been one of those explosive rocks. And then she was there, her cool, gentle hands touching, soothing, heedless that his head might shatter and sever her fingers.

"Here," she whispered. "Here." Where she touched, the worst of the pain took flight, not vanishing entirely but hiding, as though poised behind a secret outcropping in the large rock of his head, waiting to reclaim its territory. He burrowed his head into her softness, shielding his eyes from an accidental shaft of sunlight, dulling his ears to all save her gentle murmuring, nonsensical though it might be.

"Gilbert took the dose away. I have thought for some time you did not need it. Maria does not trust me. I have knowledge of the healing arts, the abbess taught me. 'Tis opium, I believe. The pain you feel now is from being deprived of the dose, not from your injury."

Her voice carried an odd inflection, as though her tongue found difficulty forming the Norman words.

"Here." She pressed a cup to his lips and water spilled over his face, dampening her gown.

When had he last tasted water? Raising a shaking hand to grasp the cup, Hugh gulped furiously. She broke his grip as easily as if a bird had tried to lift the cup in its claws.

"Your thirst will rage. 'Tis a good sign. Your stomach will cramp if you take too much. Fierce pains will grip you soon regardless; you must be prepared. I may need to call in some men. I will not leave you."

He pressed his head into her stomach. She shifted about, cradling him in her arms. The soothing murmurs washed over him.

"I think something is afoot. Gilbert must not know. We must say your pain is from the injury. You must gather all your wits about you soon."

"Yellow . . ." Hugh managed to gasp. "Yellow hair, all over me. Wife."

"Eadyth," she whispered. And then the silken fall of hair shielded him from all save low, comforting sounds as she bent her head over him and with her hands and her voice soothed his pain.

15

It woke him again: the scent of cattle, the scratchy feel of straw against his face, the memory of his words, *When you stop coming to me, I shall know you have turned to Gilbert.* And as always Rothgar left sleep with a shout of denial, tormented by the memory of one night of sweet, perfect, near-mindless ecstasy, only to find himself wide awake and considering Maria's cold-hearted, unwarranted treachery.

Ten nights ago she should have come to him. He'd made excuses for her the first night, again on the second. All told, ten black-dark, humiliating, bone-chilling nights he'd waited before it became achingly apparent that she did not mean to come at all.

In the clear light of day—nay, in the dim light of the woodcutter's hut—she must have reconsidered. Why cast her lot with him, who had no weapon but wits, when Gilbert Crispin offered his strong Norman arm? Would that he had been a spider, able to overhear the conversation Gilbert and Maria had shared in the hut. When first Gilbert had stormed from the hut, alone and angry, Rothgar had felt certain their plan was intact, confident she'd brazened her way through, proud of her, even laughing inside to hear her later address Gilbert as "my lord."

Rothgar laughed no more. She'd called Gilbert her lord, and nevermore glanced upon Rothgar of Langwald, nevermore graced him with her wondrous presence.

The stable walls still rung with the echoes of his wakening cry. He settled back into the heap of straw that formed his bed. None save animals twitched an ear at his noisy outburst; naught but vermin were inconvenienced by his thrashing about in the straw. Like any of Langwald's cattle, he was entitled to his place in the barn, and if he chose to spend his sleeping hours beset by dreams and taunted by his own idiocy, there were none to say him nay.

At least on this night, he'd claimed a full measure of sleep. The sun would not open its eye for some time, but here and there a bird twittered to announce the start of a new day.

So might the fates be twittering their mirth at him. Seduced by a witch so that even in his sleep the mere thought of her made him throb and burn with need. Seduced by the memory of the lies dripping from her honeyed lips, so bewitched still that some part of him held fast to the hope that something had prevented her from coming to him on each of these many, endless nights, that she would indeed explain it all.

No. Ten long nights were far too many. Their whispered plans of thwarting Gilbert were naught but an illusion, as nonexistent as the son she'd promised to bear for him. Ten nights he'd rotted here in the barn, awaiting her explanation, while she did naught but tend her demon-plagued brother. A woman bent on finding a moment alone with him could have done so time and again; one with her authority could have simply ordered him brought to her for a private discussion. Or another bath, in lieu of the horse-trough dunking he'd received to remove the worst of the attackers' blood from his skin. Or, more likely, a punishment. Or perhaps this self-recrimination was punishment enough. Would even the church deal out such humiliation for one who consorted with a witch?

A horse's warning snort, followed by the soft thud of stealthy feet pounding against the earthen floor, diverted his attention. Not caring to flaunt his helpless, manacled state, he worked himself slowly upright, careful to avoid jingling his chains as he backed against the wall.

"Rothgar?"

He didn't recognize the low, guttural voice, so he said nothing.

"My lord?" called someone else, closer to him. It reminded him of another voice, another night across the yard in the henhouse, another enslavement sanctioned by Maria.

"Britt?" Rothgar whispered.

"No names, my lord," came the reply as a shape, a denser black blur moving through the darkened barn, hurried to his side. "Though we be here for dark purposes, we can turn it to some good. Spread your chains upon the ground. I shall cleave them asunder with an ax."

"And likely hack me to death in the bargain," muttered Rothgar. "I'd not trust my own aim in this murky darkness." But he bent and stretched the chains across the floor, twisting his upper body as far away as he could, grimacing when the air stirred and a whooshing sound announced the ax's descent.

"Shit!"

The ax, too dull for its task, succeeded only in burying the chain and its own head deep in the dirt.

"Stand back. I'll try again, my lord."

"Nay, Britt," said Rothgar, a hope he'd scarcely dared acknowledge flickering to life. Maria's absence made it clear she had no need of him; why not seize this opportunity? "Fetch a stone. We can place the chains against it to give the ax something to bite against."

While Britt absented himself in search of a suitable stone, Rothgar listened to the subtle acts of defiance going on through the barn. Someone led the pampered war-horses from their stalls and sent them galloping off with a slap to the rump, heedless that they might turn a leg in the dark. A bucket thumped against the floor. Quick hands robbed the cow of its milk, and then a splash heralded the wasting of it. A rustling thump followed by the sound of tearing cloth hinted at knives rending grain sacks. Fools! Could they not see that hurting the Normans would mean deprivation for themselves and their own beasts as winter dragged on?

Britt, staggering back beneath the weight of the stone, caught the brunt of Rothgar's wrath. "Take it away," Rothgar ordered. "Be gone with all of you, at once."

"But my lord—"

"Out!" Rothgar roared, with as much loudness as he felt it safe to administer. "Do you think I care to cast my lot with a bunch of senseless oafs like yourselves? Do you remember nothing of the things I explained to you at the castle site?"

"But we have no choice! We are forced to do this, my lord—"

"I am . . . no longer . . . your lord." Rothgar ground out the words. He drew a deep, shuddering breath and ran a hand over his face. "Your lord lies abed, with his lady, in yon manor hall."

"But *you* are Rothgar of Langwald," Britt protested.

"Aye, that I am," Rothgar agreed, a sudden peace descending over him. Rothgar of Langwald he was, and by God's teeth, Rothgar of Langwald he would be. Forget his bewitched dreams of keeping Maria at his side. A lord's responsibility, first and foremost, was to his people. He might have failed to win the lady, he might no longer control this land, but he could see to it that his thick-witted, bumble-headed villagers lived to see *their* sons grow tall and strong. No amount of torture, no witch's enticements, could have bound him more tightly to the Norman cause.

"These disruptions must stop, Britt," he said in a kinder voice. "The attack in the wood 'twas a grievous mistake. You might have killed the lady Maria."

"Look elsewhere if you seek the whoresons responsible for that cowardly rout," Britt insisted stubbornly. "Langwald's men had naught to do with it. You have been home but a short while, Rothgar. Such treachery and deceit goes on beneath Norman noses, you cannot imagine."

Rothgar sighed. Britt had confirmed his suspicion that no Saxons took part in the woodland raid. He decided to let the matter drop. "I have cast my lot with the Normans, and you must all do the same."

With a disdainful sniff, Britt jingled Rothgar's chains. "I see how highly they value your support. Better you should deal with them as we do. At least there's a coin to be earned."

Upon that enigmatic statement, the villagers melted into the waning night. Britt's puzzling words seemed to drift like mist through the air. Rothgar reclined against the straw, intending to feign sleep and pretend ignorance when the night's damage became known. Maria might call him in to give an accounting. A thrill of excitement shot up his spine at the thought of seeing her again. He dispelled it by anticipating how she might mock him, taunt him with the plans he thought they'd formed together.

But he would show her that he, at least, meant to keep his part of the bargain. He would see to it Hugh's castle got built.

He would do his best to ignore the triumph in her eyes when he asked her to allow him to assist the villagers to build the castle, thus speeding the desecration of his land. She would not be surprised, of that he was certain; hadn't she been pushing him in this direction from the very beginning?

Prodigious amounts of Langwald's finest ale made its way down Norman gullets each night. Stephan, hovering near death, and Robert, weak-bellied since his injury, no longer joined the nightly imbibing, but the consumption of ale didn't slacken despite two fewer men tipping the skins. If anything, the somber mood darkening Langwald's soot-blackened hall seemed to enhance the sound men's thirst.

Maria might have complained had the ale-fuddled men showed less vigilance. Instead, she found herself the object of the same relentless watchfulness she'd ordered against Eadyth. No matter how much ale was tippled, someone's wary eye—a squire's, a page's, usually Gilbert's own—shackled her within

Langwald as surely as Stephan's missing leg kept him to his pallet before the fire.

This, the eleventh morning after her glorious night with Rothgar, promised no change in the pattern, no opportunity to explain her actions to him, for already the Normans were astir.

Gross consumption of ale, it seemed, made its own demands upon the body as dawn broke the sky, pulling a man from his warm bed to answer a more urgent need. From beyond the flimsy barrier of her tapestry came the sounds of men rising reluctantly from sleep: the muffled groans, the expelled air, fingernails scratching against hairy skin to the accompaniment of loud yawning.

A shrill shout shattered the morning ritual. "The horses are loose! The stable—'tis a shambles!"

Rothgar!

And yet another setback for Philip to whisper in William's ear.

Clutching her wolfskin pelt close about her, Maria peered through the gap between tapestry and wall. Men hopped from foot to foot, jerking on hose and chausses, reaching for weapons. Walter, whose cry had broken the calm, urged them on with all speed. In what seemed no more than two blinks of the eye, the hall echoed with their cries, until none save the injured Stephan and Robert remained behind.

For the first time since returning from the woodcutter's hut, she found herself alone and unwatched.

Cursing the gloom of her little sanctuary, Maria reached for her undertunic and gown and pulled them over her head. No time to fumble with hose. She jabbed her feet into slippers, felt for the peg on the wall that held the cloak she'd found to replace her ruined one. Rothgar lay chained in the very stable

Walter had dubbed a shambles. Perhaps the destruction surrounded an effort to set him free; perhaps he lay dead even now, his skull caved in by the same unseen assailant who'd stolen Hugh's wits, or the band that had tried to kill them all in the woodcutter's clearing.

"Please don't let him die," she prayed. "Not before I can explain why I stayed away so long."

Not before I can tell him I love him.

That realization was almost enough to trip her speeding feet as she raced through the hall. She clung close to the wall, avoiding Robert's fever-bright stare. Guilt still plagued her over denying him a measure of Hugh's dose; she would not be surprised if God punished her by allowing Robert to read her emotions on her face and raise the hue and cry, shout to the world that she sought to escape to stand beside her beloved.

She loved Rothgar of Langwald. A tremulous laugh bubbled from her throat.

His dignity in the face of all that had happened. The compelling love they shared for this place called Langwald. His care for his people, his passion for her, his confidence in her. Her hand tingled from the memory of the time he had faced his people with her. He had called her strong, had shown a faith in her no woman ever expected from a man. And his touch fired her blood with heat she'd never dared imagine. If he had been freed by those responsible for sacking the stable, she would see Hugh cured and then go in search of him. If he perished in the stable, she would do the same.

"Lady Maria."

A thin hand, with the grip of a steel talon, stopped her headlong rush to Rothgar's side. Maria gave a cry of denial.

"Silence, my lady," the voice whispered, and then pulled her into the shadows.

Maria's eyes widened in surprise. "Eadyth! Of all the times to accost me—"

"'Tis the only time. Of late, Sir Gilbert has been dogging your every step."

Maria felt shamed before Eadyth's knowing, nonaccusatory stare. If she herself chafed beneath such restrictions after so few days, how had Eadyth coped with it for months? She owed Hugh's wife a moment of her time, though her very blood whispered with urgency to run, run, run to Rothgar. As if sensing her capitulation, Eadyth loosened her grip.

"Hugh's dose," Eadyth said, wasting no words, glancing about as though she feared being overheard. "'Tis past time to wean him from it."

"But the sorcerer told me to use the full bottle. A small portion yet remains. I must be gone now, Eadyth."

Eadyth shook her head impatiently and restrained Maria with a light touch. "I know what he needs, my lady. I can read the signs. Hugh's mind has returned, but the potion dulls his wits. He must be weaned away as a child is kept screaming for its mother's tit, a painful but necessary process."

"How do you come to know this?" Maria looked upon Eadyth with suspicion. Had she so seriously underestimated the intelligence of this woman?

"I learned in the convent, just as I learned to speak your tongue," Eadyth said, with a shrug of her shoulders. "The abbess chose me to carry on her knowledge of the healing arts. I had nearly finished my schooling when Rothgar stole me away."

A chink there in her Saxon knight's aura of kindness, but Eadyth herself dispelled it. "I minded at first, but not so much anymore."

"Explain what we must do while we walk," Maria said, obeying the impulse that urged her toward Rothgar.

Eadyth, breathing hard from the effort of maintaining Maria's quick pace while doing her explaining, described a gradual reduction in the dose, constant vigilance to guard against self-injury, plenty of watered wine and tempting delicacies to placate an appetite clamoring for the dose.

"I must stop for a breath, my lady," Eadyth gasped, leaning against the wall. Maria waited impatiently; Eadyth bit her lip. "There is a plant. An infusion of its leaves would do much to lessen the fire that will burn in his blood."

"Could you find this plant now? Snow still covers the ground."

"The nuns will have a supply at the convent. I could borrow some and replace it in the spring."

"You will need to go outside, then, and visit the place where you were so happy," Maria said. Eadyth nodded. Maria grudged a moment to think, to weigh the situation. "Can I trust you, Eadyth, to return?"

"This is my home now," said the Saxon woman, bestowing a simple, frank dignity upon the words.

If she could trust Eadyth! Oh, the joy, the relief of sharing Hugh's burden with another! But then a cold splash of reality intruded upon her senses.

"Would you betray Hugh's condition to the nuns?"

"No."

Was Eadyth's denial a trifle too quick? She had no time to ponder the matter. "Gilbert would become suspicious if I dropped your guard."

Eadyth blushed. "Sir Gilbert himself promised to escort me if I sought a breath of air. I doubt he would understand the significance of the medicinals. Still, I would prefer it if another of your men accompanied me. Sir Gilbert frightens me."

Maria knew the feeling only too well but was reluctant to admit as much to Eadyth. Her dread of Gilbert seemed to enhance the fear she felt for Rothgar; pulling Eadyth along with her, she resumed her rush across Langwald's long hall. "Take Walter with you. Gilbert will suspect nothing, and I can trust Walter to see to it that you return to us."

"But you cannot trust me." Eadyth's words were bitter.

Maria reluctantly stopped. "Walter has earned my trust. He fought at my father's side for many years, and then returned from his own journeys to join Hugh just when we began to despair of finding an honorable man to guard his back. Without Walter's watchful eye over you, you might spread tales to the nuns. How would I explain things if a veritable army of nuns appeared at Langwald, clamoring for your return?"

Eadyth stared at the floor.

Maria's tone softened, though she longed to shriek against the additional delay. "Let us make a start toward trusting each other, Eadyth. We will indeed commence weaning Hugh from the dose. So no one knows, you and I alone will share with Fen the burden of caring for Hugh. With our force so depleted, the men are chafing to take up more manly duties. In that way, any improvement in Hugh's condition will be known to us only."

Eadyth nodded again, seeming to brighten. "All to the good. Above all, we must divert attention from Hugh's recovery. I fear what might happen to him while he is so helpless, if certain among you should realize his return to sensibility."

"We can confide in Walter," Maria said.

"There is something about him little Fen mistrusts. As do I. He is Norman, too."

"As am I."

"But you are his sister."

"Aye, I am his sister. I must watch out for what is his until he can resume the task." She had been so consumed with her need to see Rothgar that she'd failed to appreciate how this latest attack upon Langwald's stable spoke of revolt against Hugh. As if to prompt her sense of responsibility, Stephan's groan echoed through the empty hall. Her urge to flee to Rothgar, desperate as it was, had to subjugate itself to the demands of Langwald, to the needs of Hugh's people. Her heart hammered within her as she paused at the door, fulfilling her obligations before following the path of her heart.

"Do you know, Eadyth, how to ease Stephan's agony?"

"There are things I can try. None is certain."

"Or Robert. Yellow muck drips from his wound, and the skin surrounding it burns hot and hard to the touch."

"I know a poultice that might help." Eadyth's brow wrinkled. "I have noticed, too, that Sir Gilbert suffers from a wound at the neck."

Maria shuddered. Gilbert insisted she tend the wound, despite her lack of ability. "Nothing I do seems to speed its healing."

"Perhaps the weapon that inflicted the wound had been dipped in poison. There are poultices that would draw the poison out." Eadyth drew a deep breath, as though to fortify herself for what she had to say. "There are also herbals that seem to soothe, whilst they taint the blood. A wound treated with such would cause a man to grow drowsy and clumsy, so that he might not notice everything going on about him. A full course of the treatment would . . . eliminate the man entirely."

A small silence descended over them while the implications of Eadyth's knowledge coursed through Maria's mind. A convenient way to dispose of Gilbert . . . why now, when naught but his strong arm held Langwald?

Not quite true. She still had Walter. And thanks to Rothgar's warning, most of the squires and Dunstan remained whole.

"These herbals, could they be applied in such a manner that the person being treated did not die but only grew amenable to someone else's control?"

"Treatment can be stopped just short of death," said Eadyth. "To go further would be a most grievous sin, of course."

"Of course," Maria agreed faintly. "But if not pursued to its fullest, the person would recover, in time?"

"Of course," Eadyth echoed.

Maria realized that, despite the outrageous nature of their conversation, speaking of bringing a man to the brink of death, for the first time she felt at ease in Eadyth's presence. A smile hovered at the edges of Eadyth's lips, as though she shared the feeling.

"I have not been kind to you," Maria said, each word coming with difficulty. "Why do you offer this help?"

"Because I want my husband," Eadyth said, the candor in her eyes matching the tone of her voice. "I have had but tiny glimpses of the man waiting within, and I think I will like him when he emerges."

Ever since realizing the extent of Hugh's injury, Maria had deliberately suppressed the memory of her *real* brother, the laughing, gentle, powerful man who deserved so much from life, who deserved a wife like Eadyth. A faint blush tinged Eadyth's cheeks, as if she weren't yet comfortable with the idea of liking her husband. Maria remembered how her cheeks had flamed as well when she first realized she loved Rothgar. The notion that both she and Eadyth had fallen in love at the same time was oddly satisfying. She impulsively squeezed Eadyth's hand. "You will like him very much, indeed. I promise you."

Renewed hope surged through Maria as she took her hurried leave of Eadyth. Never, when she forced the marriage between Eadyth and Hugh, had she suspected a love match might be the result. If it could happen for them, if Rothgar lived, if he hadn't taken her long silence as a betrayal, if he loved her, too, if Eadyth's herbal could somehow help her control Gilbert, just until Hugh recovered—oh, so many obstacles to overcome, but her heart was light as she rushed outside.

Maria ran into the stable, her hair streaming about her shoulders, the folds of his mother's workaday cloak billowing free around her slender form. Rothgar turned his head to the wall and rubbed at his lip. His chin still ached from absorbing Gilbert's blows, and he would prefer that Maria not see the blood he felt trickling along his jaw. Lying, scheming witch she might be, but his traitorous body cared naught; it throbbed to life at the sight of her, his pride demanding he hide his physical and emotional pain.

"He lives!" She sounded breathless from her run.

"More's the pity," Gilbert muttered, prodding at Rothgar with a none-too-gentle foot. "Up with you, Saxon. You have some explaining to do."

Rothgar took his time over it. He kept his face to the wall as he stood, slowly brushing away the bits of straw and stable dust that clung to him. Eventually there was nothing for it but to turn toward her. He kept his expression carefully neutral, kept his head turned a bit to the right so the worst of Gilbert's handiwork might be hidden, but her gold-flecked eyes widened at her first glimpse of him, her full, soft lips parted, her skin paled. This evidence of her concern didn't lessen the pain, but it did make him feel better.

"What happened?"

"Outlaws," Gilbert said. "They set the horses loose. Light damage to the stable, more to yon Saxon."

"*They* did this to him?" Maria sounded skeptical. Gilbert's lie first brought hot words of denial to Rothgar's lips, but he bit them back. Gilbert had spent no time assessing the damage to the stable; he'd stormed right in on Rothgar, mayhap intent upon learning the location of the treasure Rothgar had promised, but more likely to exact a bit of revenge.

Better she should think he'd been set upon by a group of outlaws than battered near-senseless by one man. No matter that his hands were shackled—women would not understand the disadvantage such restrictions put upon a man.

Maria studied his bruised face for a long moment, and then allowed her gaze to move over Gilbert's hands. Rothgar might have smiled, had not his lip started to swell painfully. Though he had been unable to counterattack Gilbert's blows, he'd kept his lips sealed, denying the Norman the pleasure of hearing him cry out, and his hard Saxon skull had taken its toll on the Norman's fist. The knuckles were scraped raw, and a wide bleeding gash marked where Gilbert's skin had lost the battle against Rothgar's teeth. Anyone could see Gilbert lied in not accepting blame for Rothgar's beating.

But she did not challenge the Norman's statement. And Gilbert's look of guarded concern gave way to one of malicious triumph. Rothgar felt keen disappointment knife through him.

Gilbert bent and caught a length of Rothgar's chain. "Look here, Maria," he said, pointing to the shiny spot where Britt's dull ax had scored the dark metal. "'Tis plain someone tried to cut him free, but he claims to have slept through whatever happened here."

"All save that," Rothgar lied glibly. "A horse trod upon the chain."

"And did that same horse trample your face as well?" Maria asked.

"Ah, that was a different beast altogether." Let her make of that what she would.

Maria smiled at him.

It wasn't a full-blown smile; more of a furtive, hidden thing, flashing briefly only after quick sidelong glances assured her Gilbert could not see. And her hand quivered at her side, her fingers reaching toward him as if she longed to touch him, to soothe the hurt inflicted by her man-at-arms. Rothgar chided himself for being a fanciful fool.

Gilbert maintained his position at Maria's side but barked orders to the men, directing some to catch the horses, others to attend to the minor damage inflicted upon the stable.

"We Normans often find ourselves at the mercy of our . . . beasts," Maria said, casting a sidelong glance toward Gilbert. "We depend on them so, that when they frisk out of control we must turn a tolerant eye until we regain mastery."

"What if the beast turns rogue and never submits again to the will of its master?" Rothgar asked. Though Gilbert harkened to their every word, he seemed unconcerned about what they said. It made Rothgar wonder if he might not be reading too much into Maria's allusions.

She dispelled his concern by darting another quick glance in Gilbert's direction before responding to him. "Everyone knows rogues must be destroyed. 'Tis a task which must be approached with great caution lest the rogue cause so much damage there is naught worth saving."

Her hands twisted the material of her cloak. Her body seemed to lean ever so slightly toward him, her eyes wide pools of gold-flecked brown begging for his understanding. It was as if the intervening days had disappeared, as if it were just the two of them again in the woodcutter's hut. He forgave her the chains, the dreary boredom of the stable, the promised explanation that had never come. He gripped the chains in his hands; were they not anchored to the wall, he'd fling them about the rogue Gilbert's neck and pull until it snapped like a twig. While his thoughts were preoccupied with this distinctly unholy desire, Father Bruno lumbered into the stable.

"Father!" Maria was the first to greet him.

The old priest stared about the stable, sour disapproval writ plain upon his face. His glance rested on Rothgar. "You promised to release him from the henhouse," he admonished Maria.

"Look about you, old man," sneered Gilbert. "Does this look like a henhouse to you?"

Father Bruno ignored the jibe, taking in the small acts of destruction and clucking his tongue in dismay. "Stubborn fools," he muttered. He turned his attention toward Maria. "This is exactly the sort of thing I warned you could be avoided. A simple marriage."

Maria put up a warning hand and cast a worried eye toward Gilbert. "Father Bruno—"

"Look what your Norman pride has yielded. I saw one of your horses hobbling about as though it turned a foreleg on the frozen turf. A pile of seasoned oak was fired at the castle site—you didn't know that yet, did you? Was it so far beneath you to wed an Englishman?"

"Father Bruno—" Maria pleaded desperately.

"What is this talk of wedding an Englishman?" Gilbert asked, a terrible scowl on his face belying the softness of his words.

The old priest, the heat of his tirade expended, seemed at last to become aware of the tension in the stable: Maria's stricken expression, Rothgar's battered face, Gilbert's barely contained violence. "No, nothing," he stammered. "I meant nothing. 'Twas just a notion of mine, poorly expressed."

From Maria, a subtle sagging of relief, and no word confirming that she'd bargained with Rothgar just as Father Bruno had suggested. Rothgar felt the return of disappointment licking at his vitals.

"Think on it no more, friend priest," Gilbert said, his voice fairly oozing with false joviality. He gathered Maria to him with one arm. "She cannot marry an Englishman—she's promised to me."

"No!" Father Bruno's full-fledged shout drowned out Rothgar's barely whispered denial.

"Tell him it's true, my sweet," Gilbert said.

"'Tis true," Maria whispered, after a long hesitation, staring at her feet.

"Perhaps she seems overmodest since our betrothal is but several days old," Gilbert said, garrulous beyond what Rothgar had ever heard. "Never will I forget the glorious morn when she consented—nay, *begged*—to become my wife. I myself would have chosen a more suitable betrothal chamber than a common woodcutter's hut, but you know how women set their hearts upon a thing and will not be denied."

Rothgar's heart seemed to plummet to his feet. When would he ever stop playing the fool over this woman? Hadn't he just pondered over the change that had come over her after spending time alone with Gilbert in the woodcutter's hut? Now he knew what had brought it about. She must think him a buffoon without equal—with only a few sidelong glances and well-chosen words, she'd almost lured him into believing in her again.

Gilbert had called the hut their betrothal chamber. That meant that while he thought Maria played her part in the deception they'd planned, Maria and Gilbert—he closed his eyes and gritted his teeth against the image plaguing his mind. The night that even now held him spellbound had been naught but a bit of sport for her, something to while away the time until her true betrothed arranged matters to his own satisfaction.

He remembered how she'd run into the stable just now, unfettered, unguarded, free enough to have come to him sooner if she'd wished. But she'd stayed in the manor hall night after night. With Gilbert. Her betrothed.

"As I think on this, Sir Priest," Gilbert mused, "I believe it best if you marry us at once."

"Gilbert, you promised," Maria began, but a look from the Norman silenced her.

"She fears she bears the Saxon's babe," Gilbert advised the priest in a confidential tone. "He raped her, you know, scurrilous dog that he is."

Maria blushed a fiery red.

"No!" Father Bruno cried again, but in an uncertain, quavering, old man's voice, his eyes darting from Maria to Rothgar to Gilbert and back again. "This cannot be true, my lady."

Gilbert's fist closed around Maria's upper arm; with a small cry she fell against him and clung, her face buried against his shoulder. "The whoreson bragged of it to me himself. Is that not so, Maria?" Gilbert murmured.

"My lady?" Father Bruno repeated.

"He—he took his pleasure of me," she said, her muffled words dropping like dead things in the suddenly still stable.

"He raped you?" The doubt in Father Bruno's voice begged for denial. The priest turned to Rothgar. "My son?"

She still stood close to Gilbert, seeming to wilt against him when his hand closed possessively over her arm. Something tugged at Rothgar's memory, an obscene darkness marring the pale, soft skin of her upper arm, close to where Gilbert now gripped, but his mind had no space for puzzling over the recollection, reeling as it was from her facile wits. How easily she bent his words meant to protect her to suit her purpose in sealing his doom! She held fast to Gilbert; whether from love of the Norman or duty to her brother, it mattered not—her admission before the priest meant she was lost to him.

"Rothgar?" prompted Father Bruno.

"She can call it what she likes," Rothgar answered the priest.

Father Bruno made a sound of disgust and put several paces between them, as though his celibate body feared contamination. A curious numbness seemed to cast a misty veil over Rothgar's body and mind. He welcomed it.

The coppery taste of blood filled Maria's mouth but she could not lessen the pressure of her teeth against her lips. If she did, she was sure to cry out the truth, and everything would be forfeit: Rothgar's life, Langwald, her own miserable hide.

"Well done," Gilbert whispered into her ear, accompanied by a low, triumphant laugh. He relaxed his grip on her arm and the strength slowly seeped back into her legs, though she found she must needs continue clinging to him for a space, until she was steady on her feet, and until she could bear to face the censure in Rothgar's eyes.

Words, always her most potent weapon, wrapped themselves around her now like rope entangling the legs of a snared rabbit. With each word she uttered, the snare drew tighter. Rabbits who kicked hard enough against their bonds succeeded in choking themselves to death, dying in their bid for freedom but ending up nonetheless as a tasty morsel on someone's dinner trencher.

Gilbert eyed her with the avid gleam of a man who would enjoy forking into a plump young rabbit.

She jerked free of Gilbert and went to kneel beside Father Bruno, who stared at a nonresponsive Rothgar with wide-eyed stupefaction.

Words ensnared her; still more words circled even now through her mind, promising another avenue of escape. Should she keep trying, when Rothgar so obviously thought she had abandoned the ruse? Though she seemed caught in her own trap, Hugh still ruled, Rothgar still lived.

There was hope.

Rabbits who cowered fearfully, too paralyzed to make an escape attempt, met the same fate as those who struggled against their bonds. While sometimes—only rarely to be sure, but sometimes—a kicking rabbit freed itself of the snare.

"Will you hear my confession, Father?" she asked. If she could gain a moment alone with him, she could ask him to explain to Rothgar . . .

"And mine," Gilbert added. "We must be shriven clean of our sins ere we marry."

"Nay! Mine alone." Maria fixed her gaze, wide and imploring, upon the priest's befuddled eyes.

"Maria," Gilbert called, an ominous tone to his voice.

"I but meant that my sins are such that I must speak with Sir Priest alone."

"I think not." Though Gilbert stood behind her, she could see in her mind's eye the stubborn, determined look that must be upon his face. "We marry *today*, Maria, and there are no secrets between husband and wife."

Father Bruno blinked. Hoping it meant a return of his wits, Maria mouthed, *No, please,* to him, and felt heartened when with a little jerk of his head, the priest seemed to indicate he understood.

"Oh, no, not today, Sir Gilbert," Father Bruno

said, straightening his posture and sending Maria's hopes soaring. "Why, 'tis Lent! And we must prove you are both free to wed, and that there is no degree of consanguinity."

"What?" Gilbert, puzzlement crossing his face, stepped into Maria's view. She hid her trembling gratitude to the priest by forming a little steeple with her hands and lowering her head over them as though she prayed.

"You might have left a wife behind in Normandy," Father Bruno explained with priestly patience. "And who is to say you are not this woman's close kin? During this season of penance, the church expressly forbids celebration—"

"The church be damned!" Gilbert roared. "And any man among us can vouch for the other things."

"Then there shall be but the shortest delay," Father Bruno said. "Lord Hugh's word shall be sufficient."

A muffled laugh came from Rothgar. Maria exchanged glances with Gilbert; he looked away, not yet ready, it seemed, to admit Hugh's condition to the priest. The priest's eyes sparkled with intelligence; Maria wondered how much she'd truly kept hidden from him, wondered if he guessed at the undercurrents swirling about them.

"Hugh has not yet recovered from the fever I told you about," Maria said. "It may be some time before he can . . . give his approval." And thank God for that, she added silently.

"A pity." Father Bruno frowned in concentration, and then a crafty smile creased his features. "There is another way."

"What is it?" Gilbert asked, while Maria's heart delved to her toes.

"We are hard on Easter Sunday. In the past,

Christ's resurrection was celebrated in great style. Every peasant had the right to approach the manor the night before and enjoy a feast to break the Lenten fast, and ask for a favor. Now, should that custom be continued by Lord Hugh, I might be persuaded to marry you after the holy day, on Easter Monday, perhaps."

"Hugh is not wealthy," Maria said, frantically searching her mind for some way to dissuade the priest from this course of action, which smacked of bribery to her. "All his resources are pledged to the castle. Imagine Philip running to William saying Hugh gifted the people, with the castle yet unbuilt. William would not—"

Father Bruno interrupted her with a dismissive wave of his hand. "The people's wants are simple. One might ask for the right to run an extra hog amongst the beech mast next fall. Another might ask for a bit of wool to weave napkins for a new baby. You shall see, my lady, granting these small boons will go far in binding the people to your side. They will tackle the building with new heart."

"It sounds a good plan to me," Gilbert said, nodding in agreement. He fingered his chin, a cruel smile lighting his dark features. "And should anyone ask for something beyond Hugh's ability to give, I shall persuade them to seek another favor."

Maria's arm still throbbed with the memory of one of Gilbert's forms of persuasion.

"I ask for the first favor," Rothgar called.

Gilbert cursed, his hand flying to the hilt of his sword. Maria whirled about, startled at his joining the conversation.

He leaned against the stable wall, his hands resting lightly against his thighs, the chains encircling his scarred wrists and dangling into the straw. Shadows hid the evidence of his beating, but she had seen, she knew what had happened. Gilbert may have swung the fists, but *she* had done this to him! His tunic lay open at his throat, baring the clean lines of his neck, a few tufts of the crisp, curling hair she'd felt beneath her cheek. Would that she could rest against him there, explain all so he would understand.

"Hearing you bleat makes my sword itch," Gilbert growled. "You should learn silence is a virtue, Saxon."

"As is hard work," Rothgar retorted. "I but seek to foster your cause, Norman. Set me to work on the castle. I will see that no further damage comes to it."

"Ha! You'd do naught but dig up the treasure and sneak off with it. I'd be better served to set a wolf loose in my sheepfold."

"Treasure?" Father Bruno blinked.

Ignoring the priest, Rothgar responded. "Not a wolf, Norman, but a good dog that herds the sheep in the right direction and keeps them from plunging their stupid carcasses over a cliff."

Gilbert snorted contemptuously.

Father Bruno nodded. "The idea has merit, Sir Gilbert. I myself am sore displeased with yon Rothgar, but the people revere him still."

"He'd run off at the first opportunity, no doubt taking the treasure and a goodly share of the able-bodied men with him."

"'Twould serve you better than keeping me in chains," Rothgar taunted.

"Why so eager, Saxon?"

With an elaborate shrug, Rothgar said, "I'd as soon work myself to death as die of boredom in this stable." He raked his gaze over Maria. "And now and again, a curious stench overtakes the place, which sickens me to my very soul."

"You could have him brought back here for the night," suggested Father Bruno. "Or better still, fashion him a small shelter near the building materials. Set a guard to watch over both at once."

Rothgar had said the word, stench, and looked straight at her. His nose had curled, his lip twitched, as though the very sight and smell of her offended him.

"Maria." Gilbert poked her arm. She blinked at him, mired in her misery.

"I asked whether this would fit in with your plan for revenge."

"Oh." Dispiritedly, she searched for more of the words that seemed to be failing her with ever-increasing regularity. Hadn't Rothgar himself proposed as part of his plan that she set him to work at the castle? She couldn't fathom why he brought it up now, when he seemed bent on believing the worst of her. He seemed to have forgotten that he'd told her to do whatever she had to do.

"I suppose 'twould humiliate him to set him to work on the castle." Or perhaps it would cheer him, to surround himself with his people, away from the stench of her betrayal.

Gilbert's eyes raked over her with ill-concealed lust. Rothgar scarcely glanced at her at all, and when he did, his loathing fair set her back on her heels. Father Bruno's expression warred between avaricious delight for what might be in store for Langwald's people, and priestly concern for the good of all. She felt like a juggler, doomed unless she could keep these three unwieldy objectives afloat, never letting one touch each other or drop to the ground. And there was naught to help her, save the healing skill and untried remedies of a timid Saxon maid who had every reason in the world to undermine all her efforts.

Maria fled from the stable.

16

"Listen. There it is again."

Rothgar slowed his spade in response to Alfleg's prompt. All across the motte, men did the same, listening to the eerie, echoing scream, more chilling than the damp, bitter wind, that drifted over the sudden silence.

Hugh, Rothgar thought. A second scream shattered the air, its unspoken pain bringing nervous glances and shivers to the captive audience.

"'Tis an Englishman they're torturing," Alfleg whispered.

Rothgar made a sound of disgust and turned back to his digging. He'd tried, at first, to dissuade the villagers of such a notion: Who among us have they tortured? he asked. I saw no prisoners while I was there, and look, they released me. To no avail. They would believe the Normans whiled their hours away devising punishments, and he could not convince them otherwise without betraying Hugh's secret.

"Shall I spill the dirt here, my lor—Rothgar?" asked one of the peasants, Stigand. Panting from his exertions, Stigand held his filled shovel aloft, waiting for Rothgar's direction as an eager puppy awaits a tossed stick, though the puppy might boast more sense.

A dozen times, a *hundred* times a day since he'd joined their work, they'd peppered him with witless questions. Faced with Stigand's obtuse behavior, Rothgar considered the fleeting notion of adding his howls of frustration to Hugh's. If he were Gilbert, he'd entertain thoughts of hacking them to death, too. As lord, had he been blinded to their stupidity in the past? He did not remember the continual hesitations, the blank looks that seemed to greet every task.

"Over there, Stigand," he pointed, reining in his exasperation, cringing inwardly at what he knew would happen next. And as he expected, a dozen men, bearing similar loads, rushed to the same spot.

"Not there, Toss," he called, curbing his impatience. "You and Wat begin afresh over there." He punctuated his comment with a quick jerk of the arm and then rubbed his hand over his face, holding back the imprecations he longed to shout as Toss and Wat cast uncertain glances at him and tentatively shook their loose dirt over the indicated area.

God's teeth, one would think they didn't know they were building a castle.

Rothgar's eyes widened with sudden understanding.

"Stigand, Toss, Wat, come here." He gestured toward the men. "All of you, come close." As the men complied, he looked toward the Norman Eustace, overseer of the building. Though Eustace scowled at the delay, he kept his distance, as he had done ever since realizing Rothgar was capable of keeping the men working.

"Do you understand the work you do here?" Rothgar asked Stigand but included all the men within his glance.

"Who wouldn't understand?" asked Stigand somewhat belligerently. "We be diggin' a hole."

"Aye," came a few muttered agreements.

"Daft job," added someone from the back of the group. "Spoilin' a nice pasture, we be doin'. Don't sit right with me."

"They make us ram the dirt so hard, won't be fit for crops or beasts."

"Did no one ever explain this job to you?" Rothgar asked.

"The lady Maria gathered us all together," offered Wat. "She spoke a bit of our tongue, and said we was to come here every day and dig."

"Aye," said Stigand. He nodded his head toward Eustace. "Then that one jabbered away at us, makin' shapes in the dirt." Using the end of his shovel to illustrate, he drew a circle in the hard soil.

"Then he pounded away at it, like," added Toss, poking his own shovel end into the center of the circle.

It seemed clear enough to Rothgar; the circle represented the moat to be dug, the center the motte where the bailey walls and keep would soon rise. Take the dirt from the moat, ram it into the motte. Clear to him, who had seen a Norman castle firsthand; perhaps incomprehensible to simple peasants who'd never walked beyond Langwald's boundaries.

"What did you think Eustace meant?" He didn't want to insult them if they did indeed grasp the concept.

Stigand snorted and curled the fingers of one hand into a sheath, into which he crudely stabbed a forefinger. "'Tis plain enough. They'll pleasure themselves with our women lest we dig their daft hole."

Another chorus of "ayes" greeted Stigand's words, accompanied by fierce, bristling glares.

Rothgar clapped his hand over his mouth, to hide the smile rising at the image of Eustace poking at the earth, Langwald's men thinking he meant another thing entirely.

Maria had called these men bullheaded and stubborn. He himself had just recently questioned their intelligence. The men of Langwald were neither uncooperative nor stupid—they had simply never been told, in words they could understand, what was expected of them.

Rothgar explained. He told them that the dirt they flung from the ditch and rammed into the center would gradually create a high-rising hill in Langwald's low-rolling contours. He showed how water would be hauled from Langwald River to fill the ditch, making a moat difficult for attackers to cross.

Sheer walls would be constructed at the edge of the moat, and a matching wall would run in a smaller circle within, creating a bailey in between. Animals could graze within during times of peace, while the bailey would offer a second line of defense should the moat be breached during an attack.

Nestled within the very center of the circle would rise the keep, with vast storerooms at ground level to hold Langwald's bounty against winter and to protect it as well from casual marauders. The Normans would occupy living quarters in the keep's upper reaches.

The men were silent for long moments after Rothgar's explanation ended. Then Wat asked, "So the

Normans be safe and snug, with all our stores, should someone attack. What about us, my lor— Rothgar?"

This part Rothgar did not relish. "Langwald Hall will stand. Most likely the Normans will use it for a church. But your huts will be torn down—"

"Nay! Our homes!"

"—and new ones rebuilt closer to the castle," Rothgar strained his voice to shout over the men's fear.

"New huts?" Stigand asked, the eager puppy look again upon his face. The other men fell silent at once.

"Aye," said Rothgar, relaxing in the sudden calm. "New huts, built with a hearth. The Normans have a way to divert smoke from fire so you'll not have soot throughout the hut. Your wives will like it well."

"My Bessie, she be set in her ways. She'll not want a new hut or new sort of fire," grumbled Wat.

"She'll have no course but to follow along," said Rothgar. "The Normans must have you near the castle, so they can gather you in for protection when attackers come."

"Who, my lor—Rothgar? Whoreson William himself cannot attack what he has already won."

"Someone will come," Rothgar said, remembering the tales he'd learned of invasions past and present. "Someone always comes."

"How will the Normans know they're being attacked, if walls are all about to block their sight?"

"They'll set someone to watch from atop the keep. That man will see everything and call out in good time to gather you all within."

"Then the keep be taller than a hut?" asked Stigand.

"Like ten huts, or twelve, built one atop the other," said Rothgar. Another silence came over them while the men digested this astounding news. One of the younger men, Jem, seemed absorbed in studying the circle and line Rothgar had drawn on the ground to represent Langwald River.

"Do you understand, Jem?" Rothgar asked gently.

"Aye." Jem frowned and looked up at Rothgar, blushing and scowling fiercely. "Seems to me the water in this ditch . . . moat . . . would get fearsome rank, not fit drink for man nor beast. What if we dug a deep trench, all the way to the river, and lined that ditch with clay tiles? Add a bit of an overflow here to draw off the stale water." He drew quick, sure lines in the dirt.

"I shall mention it to Eustance at once," Rothgar said, clapping the youth on the back. He fought back a ridiculous surge of pride in his men; they clustered around the circle, talking all at once in their eagerness to tackle work worth doing, offering more suggestions, laughing at themselves over their misunderstanding.

Rothgar felt the hairs prickling at the back of his neck; Eustace, no doubt, angry over the unduly long delay in the work, but Rothgar had not the heart to interrupt the men's excitement. Still, the feeling of being watched nagged at him, and he glanced over his shoulder.

The mare's bay hide shone in the sunlight. Maria's hair, unbound as usual, streamed free in the breeze. His heart lifted at the sight of her, his pulse quickened; in the excitement of the moment, it was easy to forget her betrayal, understandable, even, that he would feel this urge to share his men's awareness with her.

Come and see, Maria! he longed to call. *They did need me to explain. They will build you a fine castle now. Let Philip whistle in the wind. Perhaps you were right to trick me into staying.*

But another of Hugh's unearthly howls echoed over Langwald, and a second mounted figure added its silhouette to the landscape. Gilbert Crispin's destrier towered over Maria's mare, so that when the Norman knight leaned to give Maria a kiss, he near toppled to the ground—would have toppled to the ground—had not Maria raised welcoming arms to steady him. Rothgar turned away, not eager to witness her clinging to the Norman, and when he next risked a look in their direction, he saw naught but their backs and their steeds' kicking heels as they galloped away, together.

Gilbert stared as Maria withdrew her hand from the clay pot, watching the pure, milky-white lumps of ointment melt from her body heat and trickle in clear, glistening dribbles against her skin. He tilted his head to the side, baring his neck for her ministrations, longing for the numbing effects of the ointment. Of late, it seemed fire coursed through his blood, sapping his strength, blotting his vision and taunting his mind with hazy, incomprehensible images.

Like now—it seemed, for a moment, that Maria's hand, with thumb pressed to fingers, took on the flat, triangular likeness of a serpent's head, her bent fingers the serpent's curving fangs, the ointment dripping like an herbal venom into his wound.

And then her fingers were against his skin, cool against the puffy heat marking the spot where the Saxon spear had nicked him. He could feel his life force beating against her firm touch where she pressed the ointment into his nearly healed wound. He smiled; Eadyth, too, must be in love with him. Why else would she have journeyed with Walter to fetch this healing tincture from the nuns?

He settled back with a sigh, enjoying Maria's ministrations. What would he do for relief when the wound closed, denying access to the ointment? Would she be so willing to touch him without the wound as an excuse? He closed his eyes, imagining the herbal ointment mingling with his blood, a droplet at a time, speeding through his body, and the blessed numbness overtook him, easing the burning that sometimes made him wish he could shed his skin. Like a snake.

Ah, perhaps that explained Maria's hand calling to mind the head of a serpent. He shook the disquieting image away.

"I know not which soothes more—the potion or your touch," he said, a long-unused softness marking his voice as he savored the feel of her fingers. "Dare I hope you grow solicitous of me, Maria?"

"'Tis not every day a Norman knight near collapses atop me," she retorted, so cheerfully that he could not take offense at her reminding him of his humiliating loss of balance earlier in the day, in full sight of the Saxon horde.

"I know not what came over me," he mumbled. "I've never been unhorsed in a tourney, leave alone find myself falling from my saddle for no good reason." His humiliation would have been less had the Saxon Rothgar not been on hand to witness it. Rothgar should have met his destined end by now, but the very weakness that sent Gilbert near tumbling from his steed had likewise stayed his sword arm.

Maria wiped her fingers diligently against the

woolen clout tucked into the Saxon girdle she'd taken a fancy to wearing of late. The girdle suited her, though obviously made for a woman of wider girth. It rode low upon her hips, emphasizing her slender waist. The jeweled dagger sheathed within the girdle was a pretty toy, the red and blue stones sparkling in the flickering firelight, riding on the alluring curve from her waist to her womanhood. As soon as he shed this curious lassitude that gripped his limbs, he'd execute Rothgar of Langwald in full sight of Langwald's denizens. Then, of a certainty, Maria would overcome the revulsion set up from the whoreson Saxon's touch, and he'd be free to follow the path pointed out by that dagger.

He felt the heat of his thoughts flame through him, threatening to overpower the soothing effects of the ointment. "Perhaps I was simply overwhelmed at the sight of you, my betrothed. You looked quite fetching, Maria, with your hair blowing in the wind and Langwald Castle taking shape behind you."

"I should have let you tumble to the ground. A good crack on the head might stop you from following me about at every turn." As though to take the sting from her words, she dipped her fingers once more into the ointment and held it against his skin.

"I might not have lost my balance had you not flinched away when I reached toward you," Gilbert retorted. He felt her fingers tremble against him, and he closed his eyes, memories of times past stirring within him, when he sought only to please this woman. He sought to explain his diligence. "Something seems amiss here, as though treacherous undercurrents flow about us. I fear for your safety, Maria. I never meant for you to cringe from my touch."

It was the best apology he could fashion for

continuing to inflict the bruises that marred her lovely skin. But good God, the woman provoked him beyond reason at times. He held his breath, waiting for some acknowledgment from her, some grudging granting of forgiveness, but Walter's arrival put paid to that hope.

"You have visitors," Walter announced, a fierce glower creasing his face as he stomped toward them.

"What—playing gatekeeper," Gilbert sneered, angry at the interruption.

"Might as well. I've naught else to do," Walter grumbled, ignoring the sarcasm.

"Poor Walter." Gilbert addressed Maria with a mock sigh. The quenching of the fire in his blood left him feeling giddy with relief. Stiff-necked, self-righteous, fatherly Walter offered an excellent source of amusement. "His pride chafes at being denied a place at Hugh's side—first by Fen and now by Eadyth. Not that I can blame Hugh. Eadyth's not so beautiful as you, my love, but her face makes a prettier sight than yon ancient knight's. Even an idiot can mark the difference."

A mistake, that. Maria ordinarily took great offense at any slur upon Hugh's intelligence, but she seemed not to notice this slip of Gilbert's tongue.

"Are you unhappy, Walter?" she asked with a soft concern that roused Gilbert's jealousy. She treated his wound diligently, and talked and even laughed with him, but her tenderness and generosity of spirit seemed to lie forever beyond his reach. And here she was, freely bestowing it upon old, grizzled Walter, who deserved it not at all.

Oh, yes, he could shatter a few of Maria's illusions about her precious Sir Walter, but men-at-arms did not spread tales over each other's exploits. Not if they valued their necks.

"Fear not, Maria. He takes his pleasure when he wills," Gilbert contented himself with saying.

Walter's skin bore the dull, reddish tint of a man who spent much time facing the teeth of the wind. Did it look redder than usual as a result of his jibe? Walter, blushing? Absurd. The very thought made Gilbert laugh aloud.

"Hugh's latest turn demands much of Eadyth," Maria said to Walter, ignoring Gilbert's amusement. "Lately, he tolerates none save her, Fen, and myself."

"'Tis that Fen that rankles most. I've not had a single moment alone with Hugh since he saved that dark-skinned woods creature," Walter said, casting an offended glance in Gilbert's direction. "I have ridden at first by your father's and now my lord Hugh's side through good times and bad, and it sits hard upon my shoulders to hear him screaming in pain. Hugh has ever relied upon *me*."

"I can mark a time or two when your absence might have been a blessing rather than a relief," Gilbert taunted. "And Walter, you haven't always been so diligent. Go ahead, Maria, ask him about the nights he's stolen away to spend with his lady love."

And then Maria took her hand from his neck, and touched Walter's sleeve. All Gilbert's good humor fled; if he had the strength, he would lop the churl's head from his neck. But a tingling in his feet heralded the return of the raging fire, a blotting mist seemed to descend over his eyes and curl into his ears, so that his vision and hearing lacked their normal sharpness. As if from a distance, he heard them speaking.

"Is it true, Walter? Have you found a lover?"

A triumphant grin twisted Walter's oafish lips. Good God, one might think he'd found true love!

Gilbert idly wondered what Walter's Saxon whore would call what passed between them.

"Aye, my lady," said Walter. A strange expression crossed his face. "It seems my longest-held dream is about to take shape."

Gilbert slumped into his seat with a sigh of disgust.

Maria, viewed through the misty fog, looked lovelier than ever. A smile lit her eyes, and her features softened with pleasure. "'Tis wonderful to be in love, Walter. You can marry now, and set up a home. Unless I presume too much?"

"I had not thought of marriage," Walter said slowly, "but perhaps it would not be amiss. I need not worry over losing her then."

"Oh, Walter, I am sure she cannot help loving you well," Maria chided. "You could claim a cottage until the castle is built."

"Thank you, my lady, but she has a place of her own."

Gilbert tried to sit upright, but the effort seemed too great. And his ears hurt from listening to Walter yapping on, and something within him whispered that it wasn't right that Maria should glow with bright happiness over Walter's possible marriage, when any mention of her own, to him, made her droop with despair.

"I thought you'd taken up gatekeeping," he said to Walter. "If a gatekeeper you choose to be, then you must do it properly. Who seeks our company?"

"A pair of scrawny old nuns," Walter said, the odd look still marking his countenance though he smiled at Maria. "They're out there flapping about like a couple of black crows, chirping they intend to ask a favor two days hence. They want leave to bed down in the stable until then. They claim a stable was good enough for Christ's mother and will suit them just as well."

"Nuns." Maria took a long quivering breath. "I should have expected them, but I had hoped . . ." She shook her head and squared her shoulders. "Father Bruno would have my head if I bedded them in the stable. They must be our guests here, in the hall."

The lessening of the ointment's numbing power left Gilbert feeling too spent to study Maria's reluctance at hosting two daughters of Christ, especially during this so-called holy season. His blood burned within him; his life-force withered correspondingly. There was strength enough only to nod toward Maria, and then to make a small, unobtrusive motion of his hand, a prearranged signal that told his squire to assume watch over her, and no inclination at all to mull over the ridiculous, albeit lingering image of Maria's hand poised like the head of a snake, sinking its venomous fangs into his neck.

Though Maria had sometimes speculated on it, now she knew God himself must truly be set against her. There could be no other explanation.

Why else, on the very day when Eadyth's herbal delivered its promised result, would Gilbert collapse into her arms within full sight of Rothgar? And why now, with Gilbert safely under the ointment's spell, did two of God's own nuns turn up to forestall her racing to her beloved's side?

Unless Eadyth had betrayed her.

And if she'd betrayed her over the nuns, what of the ointment? Was Gilbert's sudden sinking into sleep naught but the natural reaction of a man worn out by knightly duties?

Good manners dictated she welcome the nuns into the hall and offer food. Everyone knew how rigorously nuns fasted, either from poverty or true devotion. This pair looked to have spent many hungry days on their knees.

"Eat," Maria urged, seating them at the long table near the fire, waving trenchers of bacon rashers, crisp fried roots, fragrant chunks of bread, beneath their noses. Though she herself had no appetite, the aroma was enough to set her mouth watering. With luck, they would fall upon the food, the sight distracting her keepers so she might make her escape to Rothgar.

The nuns bowed their heads and prayed, though the younger of the two women cast a longing look toward the trenchers.

"Drink," Maria tried next, placing steaming tankards of mulled wine before them. "You must be chilled through, and thirsty from your journey."

"We melted snow in our mouths," said the younger nun in a small, meek voice.

With a sharp glance, the older, authoritative nun quelled her into silence.

"I am the abbess of Marston," she said, turning to Maria, her voice filled with the quiet assurance of one whose slightest suggestion sends feet scurrying to obey. "Your generosity is much appreciated, but you may not wish us to partake of your food and drink once you learn the purpose of our visit."

Maria's shoulders sagged. What would nuns be likely to request—an embroidered altar cloth, a regular delivery of eggs and butter, a joint or two when pigs were butchered? Nothing so outrageous that one would deny them food and drink.

Unless Eadyth had betrayed her.

No sense in prolonging the inevitable. Maria strove

for a pleasant tone. "Sir Walter said you plan to ask a favor of my brother on Easter Eve. I might well take Hugh's place—he understands so little of the English tongue. Perhaps I can listen now, ere the hall is crowded with riotous celebration."

"We want Eadyth," said the abbess, confirming Maria's worst fears. "We mean to take her back with us, so she may take her vows."

17

What could Maria be thinking, Eadyth wondered, to summon her from Hugh's side without coming herself? They had agreed that one of them must always watch over him.

Eadyth learned soon enough.

Maria stood steely eyed and calm, the barest of flushes staining unusually pale cheeks, as Eadyth bustled into the hall. "You have visitors, Eadyth," Maria said, stepping aside to reveal the unexpected guests.

"Rev—Reverend Mother!"

Gape-jawed with dismay, Eadyth recognized the formidable figure of the abbess of Marston, the subservient form of Sister Mary Innocent at her side.

Not quite the veritable army of nuns Maria suggested might come if Eadyth divulged Hugh's secret, but damning enough. It was no trick at all to sink to the floor before the abbess; Eadyth's knees buckled beneath her of their own volition. Or to bow her head for the abbess's touch of benediction—anything to escape the eloquence of Maria's accusing, stricken gaze crying, "You betrayed us!" as clearly as if she'd spoken the words.

"You are looking well, daughter," said the abbess.

"I never expected to see you here, Mother," Eadyth answered with a quick glance toward Maria, hoping she might believe it.

Maria sniffed with disbelief.

Gilbert Crispin slumbered fitfully near the fire, his limbs jerking with the occasional characteristic spasms brought on by the herbal ointment. The jar sat near Gilbert's elbow, its dull dun-colored surface unremarkable, save to one who knew the nuns reserved that particular shape of jar, that exact shade of clay, for one purpose only. Just as one well-versed in the ointment's effects need not see it applied to know it was being used.

With a grunt and jerk of his arm, Gilbert almost toppled the jar from the table. The abbess snatched it up just in time, weighing it in her hand, a half-smile crossing her face.

"It grieves me, Eadyth, that you did not visit with me when you stopped to gather supplies."

"You were at prayer, Mother, and I had no wish to disturb you." Eadyth rose to her feet but kept her head bowed respectfully. The position called to mind the many hours she had spent just so, the many months wasted in longing for a return to the familiar convent, the penitent routine. Aching knees, unremitting cold, hunger pangs so unrelieved and insistent, singing joyful prayers of thanksgiving for the deprivation. How could Maria possibly think she sought a return to the nunnery?

But Maria stared at her with contempt.

"I have worried over you, daughter. Word has come to me that you are not happy here." The abbess's hand, incongruously slim and smooth for one who never spared a bit of goose grease or even butter to rub into skin chafed raw from scrubbing, scouring, and weaving, enfolded the little jar. "When Sister Mary Agnes told me you sought this potion, I feared the worst."

A hush descended over their small group, broken only by Gilbert's wheezing breath and Sister Mary Innocent's excited shuffling. Could Maria not see that by taking two steps, Eadyth could align herself physically with the nuns; they would close around her and there would be the three of them against Maria alone?

But if she did, Hugh, for the first time since his injury lying undosed and alone, would never come to remember her name.

"Believe me when I say the potion is being put to good use, and no permanent harm will result. I am very happy here, Mother. Whoever bore such tales to you spoke lies."

The abbess lifted a brow. "I was told you are still virgin, daughter. If so, we could have this sham marriage declared null and you could return to us."

Eadyth's face burned and her heart gave a wayward lurch. How many times, locked in with the unresponsive lump she'd been forced to wed, had she prayed that somehow, some way, the nuns would hear of her plight? With Hugh's dawning consciousness, those prayers had changed.

The abbess's stern, dignified face conveyed love and concern. It would be so simple to say, "no, Mother, you heard wrong, Hugh and I couple every night," but ingrained obedience would not permit the lie.

"I am sick with love for my husband," Eadyth whispered. Let everyone make of that what they would. Maria stirred with surprise, while the abbess's eyes gleamed with the barest hint of avariciousness, a tense hopefulness, a breathless waiting.

"He cannot have you. You belong to us," Sister Mary Innocent cried.

"You don't care about me at all," Eadyth said, suddenly understanding. "'Tis my dowry you're after." And she was treated to the astonishing sight of the abbess of Marston blushing at being caught out.

She recovered quickly enough. "It was promised to us," she said, challenging Eadyth. "We have rights. First that lout Rothgar of Langwald stole you away. And then these Norman swine took all without giving anything in return. We raised no arms against Duke William. None save our claim will hold sway if you return virgin to us and take your vows."

"Enough!" Eadyth cried. Tears brimmed dangerously, and she trembled from daring to speak so to the mother superior, but a fount of righteous anger seemed to infuse her very blood. She had had enough of being tugged about as though she were naught but a well bucket brimming with what they thirsted over.

"You are right. Rothgar stole me away and naught save the war stopped him from marrying me for my lands. You, Maria, did the same thing. And you, Mother, are no better." With a balled-up fist, she dashed a tear away from the corner of her eye. Both the abbess and Maria stared at her as though she'd suddenly grown three heads, which strengthened her resolve even more.

"Well, you can all go to the devil. What I have—had—belongs to my *husband*. And he cares naught for dowries, or lands, or riches. He—he thinks I'm *pretty*, and he likes my *hair*."

Clapping a hand over her mouth against the sobs she could no longer stifle, Eadyth fled from them. Toward Hugh. Was it true? Did the nuns have rights, property rights they could claim since Hugh had failed to exercise his conjugal duties?

He looked up when she reached the sanctuary of their chamber. Fen studied her flushed face, her heaving bosom, and with a warm smile and knowing look sidled out of the room. Gasping with the effort, Eadyth heaved the bar into place behind him, securing the door against any who might try to enter. Several candles did their best to light the gloom. Though the chill was fearsome, Hugh reclined against the bed, bare to the waist, a wolf pelt heaped carelessly over his hips and legs. The flickering candlelight played over his chest, turning the brown hairs gold and outlining the rigid contours that spoke of many hours spent in physical activity.

"Eee . . . Eadyth?"

The smile that lit his face at the sight of her warmed her more thoroughly than the sun. His voice, rich and deep, freed of the slurring effects of his dose, set up an unfamiliar longing deep within her.

She would not be parted from him.

"Say it again, Hugh."

"Eadyth. Lady wife."

"Yes," she said, tugging her hair free as she crossed the small space to join her husband in their bed.

Perhaps, being virgins and forsworn to remain chaste for Christ, the nuns did not understand the significance of the cries of pleasure, the low-pitched groans, the triumphant masculine shouts that sounded from Hugh and Eadyth's chamber. Or perhaps they did. Intent upon consuming as much of Langwald's food as possible, the nuns sat with heads bent over their trenchers and said nothing more to Maria about virgin brides or nulled marriages or claims to property.

Nor did the abbess make any mention of the ointment pot.

Maria would have welcomed some small talk, some diversion to distract her from the sounds of passion and the passage of time. Bastard Philip—where was he now, when the sounds filling the hall left no doubt Hugh de Courson was still a man through and through? *Carry this tale to William's ear,* she thought.

Set against that cheering thought was the certainty that with each mouthful the nuns took, Gilbert edged closer to awareness. Another application of ointment so soon might rouse his suspicions and could prove too much for his blood to handle in such a short time. Her heart plummeted—yet another day must pass ere she could seek out Rothgar.

One by one the Norman men deserted them. Even Walter, with an enigmatic look in her direction, made his way through the hall, no doubt spurred on by his lord's lusty example to seek out his lady love. He stopped to investigate something near the door. "Who goes there?" someone called softly.

Gilbert's squire stepped out from a shadowed corner, gesturing toward Maria. The knave was keeping watch over her—and rather than challenge him, Walter shrugged and moved on.

This, too, bypassed the nuns' attention. Small wonder. The deep folds of their headdresses curved about their faces like the eyepieces some knights used to blind their horses' side vision. Only the occasional flash of firelight against an eye, or a strong white tooth biting down on a hunk of bread, betrayed the presence of a face within that woolen darkness.

At last, with a most unnunlike belch, the abbess pushed her trencher away. Sister Mary Innocent reluctantly followed suit.

Gilbert sighed and shifted in his chair.

Though she herself would not be able to sleep had she consumed such a prodigious amount of food, Maria gestured toward her tiny sleeping alcove and made the suggestion. "You could share my bed, Sisters. Some small amount of privacy is offered in yon alcove."

"We brought pallets," began Sister Mary Innocent. A glance from the abbess silenced her.

"There is room for all three of us?" asked the abbess.

"I think not," said Maria. "But do not fret over my sleeping arrangements. I have much to think over this night."

"Indeed you do, daughter," said the abbess. A sweeping movement of her head seemed to take in the ointment jar, Gilbert, and Hugh's chamber door, where soft laughter could be heard. Any thoughts these sights and sounds provoked in the abbess's mind were shielded by the concealing headdress as surely as a knight's helmet guards his face from his enemies.

"Take candles, Sisters."

Sister Mary Innocent reached out with both hands. The abbess gently closed her fingers around the younger nun's empty left hand. "Just one, daughter. We are accustomed to disrobing in the dark."

With a swishing sound, the nuns drew closed the tapestry Maria had erected for privacy. The faint glimmer of candlelight shone beneath the edges of cloth. Maria contemplated the bit of light, watching a corner darken and a bit of cloth poke from beneath the tapestry—one of the nuns must have shed her gown there, not taking the time to fold it—and then someone quenched the light altogether.

A Saxon boy came with logs for the fire pit. Maria watched him go about his task, envying his freedom as he stood and brushed his hands against his tunic and walked with a bouncy step toward the kitchens.

The fire leapt higher, but she clutched her cloak about her, the added heat doing nothing to warm her. She felt cold to the pit of her soul. Alone as she'd never been. Hugh, though obviously recovering, was not yet restored to her. Eadyth—relinquishing her virginity and all chance of returning to the nuns—could she, despite all pointing to the contrary, be trusted? If she had not told the nuns, then who? No Saxon save Father Bruno had spoken to Eadyth since her marriage, and loyal Walter had accompanied her to the convent to fetch the ointment, ensuring Eadyth's silence.

Langwald . . . what had happened to them all since taking shelter beneath its roof? Hugh's wits destroyed, pray God not beyond redemption. She herself had denied succor to the wounded, spun lies, and was perilously close to committing murder upon Gilbert, once so staunch and loyal. Stalwart Walter, who should have leapt to her defense once he learned Gilbert's squire kept watch over her, now cared for naught save his new Saxon lover.

It seemed these thoughts swirled through her mind for hours, returning always to the same conclusion: of all who surrounded her, only one had never lied to her, had always kept his word, cared for Langwald and its people to his own detriment. Rothgar. Her throat tightened. He had warned her he would believe she'd taken up with Gilbert if she failed to meet him at night, and she'd blithely agreed, never imagining the tight watch Gilbert could keep over her. How Rothgar must despise her now!

The hall seemed eerily empty. She had sent Robert and Stephan into huts where women could tend their wounds. Walter had gone off. Only Gilbert, lying in troubled sleep nearby, and his swine of a squire watching from the shadows, shared the vast space with her. Even the hounds seemed subdued, as if they understood that the nuns had left no scraps for them, some content to lie with noses resting on paws, others yawning and scratching as they basked next to the fire.

The noise from Hugh and Eadyth's chamber quieted. Gilbert's breathing took on a thready, wheezing sound. A faint rumbling sound came from near the door.

Snoring. Gilbert's squire had fallen asleep.

So soundlessly that even the hounds failed to stir, she crept toward her alcove, bent and fumbled beneath the tapestry for the heap of cloth she'd seen the nun drop. Slowly, inch by inch, she pulled it toward her. Her heart hammered against her ribs as she donned the gown, pulling the headdress up around her and cinching the frayed waist cord, taking courage at the memory of how thoroughly the sweeping folds had hidden the nuns from her own prying eyes. Should Gilbert rouse, should the squire wake, they must surely mistake her for one of the nuns.

The wool, so old and worn that its black edges had turned rusty, enveloped her with the scent of stale incense, as she hurried through the halls to the kitchen, to freedom, to Rothgar.

* * *

Gilbert kicked his man hard in the ribs.

"Where is she?" he demanded when the squire yelped to wakefulness.

"Who—I—my lord?" stammered the squire.

"The lady Maria. You do remember I set you to watch over her."

The squire's eyes boggled in fear; he cowered in anticipation of another quick kick, but Gilbert turned away from him in disgust.

And near pitched forward onto his nose.

God curse this weakness that gripped his limbs! A raw, unpleasant tingling coursed through his blood, robbing him of strength. He shook off the feeling, steeling his mind against it just as he'd been trained to ignore wounds sustained in the midst of battle. For that was what Maria had made of this: a battle of wills. And Gilbert meant to be the winner.

"Perhaps she's abed with the nuns," the squire ventured.

Gilbert stalked to the alcove, grabbing at a candle along the way. He jerked the tapestry back along its rope hanger and held the candle aloft. Two women, their shorn, spiked hair bespeaking their status as nuns, snored softly in the bed. No sign of Maria.

"Damn her to hell," Gilbert swore. He pushed at the squire, sending the younger man sprawling onto the rush-strewn floor. The hall took on a peculiar red cast; the old familiar scarlet mist descended over his mind, pulsating in time with the fevered blood coursing through his body.

"I will find her, my lord," the squire cried, scrambling to his feet.

Gilbert kicked him back down. "Where is Walter?"

"Gone to his woman, Sir Gilbert."

Gilbert grunted. "Then I need not worry. I, too, will seek easy pleasures this night. You'd best get your sleep and be prepared to deal with me in the morning over your lapse of duty."

The squire blanched and wilted against the floor.

Gilbert's legs carried him to the stable, but when he lifted his horse's saddle, they weakened. He fell, the saddle lying atop him. Drawing short, panting breaths, he willed the strength back into his body and slowly pulled himself into a sitting position with the saddle resting across his legs.

Any knight knew the value of short, refreshing naps. A man who could snatch a few moments of sleep could resume battle restored. The only thing better for a man's spirit was a night spent in the arms of a wench. Maria might yet be reluctant, but there were others who would accommodate him—willing or not. Gilbert leaned back against the wall. He'd take his nap and awaken restored. Then he'd play with his wench, and, a new man, deal with Maria in the morning.

Rothgar's shed, built between Eustace's watch post and a small knob on the castle hill, proved to be surprisingly snug against the winter chill. Small as it was, it seemed to trap the heat cast off from his body and hold it within, so that the single woolen rug he'd been issued sufficed to keep him warm through the night. Even so, rising from his pallet on such a night would send shivers coursing through him, and he defiantly clutched the wool to his chin when he heard the clattering sound of stones disturbed by clumsy feet.

Would they never learn?

Small, petty acts of destruction occurred frequently, and nothing Rothgar could say seemed to dissuade the villagers from this course. Only this morning he had confronted Britt on the matter.

"You're only hurting yourselves when you burn the wood meant for the castle. It means we need to cut a new supply," he'd said. "The Normans will keep us at this work until it's finished, even if that means working straight through planting season."

Britt had only shrugged, claiming again that Langwald's men were not responsible, that darker forces were at work, but his failure to meet Rothgar's eye meant he knew more than he said.

The scrabbling sounds from outside intruded upon Rothgar's thoughts. He'd tarried long enough in his pallet's warmth; time now to fling open the door and perhaps surprise the culprit in the act. Casting the rug aside, he crouched low as he made his way to the door and opened it cautiously, in case the intruder reacted with a swing of an ax or sword.

A nun scrambled over the dirt in the moonlight, her gown hanging loose about her as though she'd fasted too long.

Rothgar fell back on his heels.

Surely a nun could not be responsible for the random destruction! But why would one be here, in the midst of the night, tugging at the gown impeding her progress, cursing in a most unholy manner?

A gusting breeze caught the nun's headdress, blowing it away from her face. A tendril of hair escaped the tight bond to whip free in the wind.

All wrong, that. Nuns had no hair to speak of; it was shorn away as part of their bride-price to Christ.

She seemed to sense his regard, though he knew

he was well nigh invisible in the doorway of his little shed. With a glad little cry, she picked up her skirts and came toward him in a stumbling run. And though he could see nothing of her face or form, something within him shifted and leapt to life.

Maria.

He had sworn never to touch her again, but of course he could not allow her to fall when she tripped over a clod of earth, so he caught her against him. It seemed a natural thing to push the ugly headgear away, to set her hair free, to reassure himself that it really was Maria.

Her face, lifted to his, gleamed with pearly luminescence in the moonlight. He cupped it in his hands, stricken dumb at her beauty, forgetting all the carefully phrased insults he'd practiced to ensure their effectiveness in the Norman tongue, the barbed accusations he'd thought to direct at her if he'd ever found himself in a position to do so.

"I have so much to tell you," she whispered. She reached up, stroking his cheeks where his facial hair had grown to the still-bristling, not-quite-silky stage of a beginning beard. Her touch jolted his knees; he had nothing to grip but her body, and strength seemed to suffuse him as she lent her support.

"You must have hated me when I did not come to you," she said, tangling her hands in his hair.

"Aye," he whispered. "I hate you. I do." He clamped his lips against hers and staggered backward with her into the cramped privacy of his shed, falling by necessity onto the pallet he'd so reluctantly left such a short while ago. His tongue, his lips, all useless when it came to hurling taunts and accusations at her, proved adept at more pleasurable tasks.

Long moments later, Maria reclined against him, her head against his shoulder, her hair streaming over them both. "I must shed this smelly gown," she said.

Rothgar's pulse quickened; his loins, already aching with longing, tightened even more. His blood pounded through his veins, filling him with a rushing urgency to tear the offensive garment from her, to feel her naked and soft and warm against him. Amid this erotic swirl of thoughts a tiny spot cleared, just enough for a warning voice to whisper, "Do that, so she can run back to Gilbert with your seed in her belly."

At once, his passions deflated. His fingers curled around her shoulders, claiming one last small possession of her, and then he pushed her away from him.

"Rothgar?"

No light at all penetrated the snug shed, no shaft of moonlight illuminated the dark space. He drew away from her as far as the limited confines would allow, glad of the dark. The small shed seemed to echo with her bewildered confusion. He could imagine her kneeling before him, her hands opened beseechingly, her eyes wide and brimming with tears. Even this mind-conjured image was enough to make him want to pull her again into his arms and soothe away her hurt; it seemed he would ever be susceptible to her wiles.

"Could you light the fire? I—I cannot see you," said the witch.

"This is my prison. No provision was made for a fire pit."

"Rothgar, please. You must hear me out."

"I would have listened endlessly had you seen fit to come to me as we agreed. I listened well while Gilbert spoke of marriage and you did naught to deny it, while you let Father Bruno believe I dishonored you."

With a sinking heart, Rothgar realized he waited,

breath bated, for her to refute his charges. She said nothing. There was the scraping of shoes against earth, and a dull thumping sound—she pounded against the walls of the shed in search of the door. It creaked open a bit in response to her pressure, and moonlight knifed through the darkness. She moved into the light.

"Look at me," she commanded, as if his eyes hadn't flown to her of their own accord. "Tell me what you see."

"A witch," he answered at once. "A liar." He swallowed, the words coming hard as tears trickled in silvery streaks down her cheeks. "A woman shivering in the night, though the wind can scarce be colder than her scheming heart."

Her chin jerked as though he'd struck a blow against her.

"What do you expect me to see?" he roared, curling his hands into fists to quell the urge to reach for her, to draw her next to him, to tell her that what he really saw was the woman he loved beyond and against all reason illuminated by moonlight. He groaned and slumped against the wall.

"Do you see my shame?"

"Shame over what?" he asked, tired and dispirited, all his anger seeping out at the words. She had done what she must to survive, a woman playing dangerous games in a world ruled by men. What did it matter if she'd decided he played no part in her life? He lived.

"Eadyth loves Hugh," she said. She crossed the few steps to his side and sank down on her knees to meet him eye to eye.

So Eadyth had found love. A wry smile tugged at the corners of his lips as he remembered how she'd begged to return to the convent—when she thought Rothgar of Langwald was to be her husband. It seemed he held no charm for women.

"That seems a cause for rejoicing rather than shame."

She caught his hands within hers. And though hers were so small, so slight, his felt surrounded and soothed.

"She loves him. And when a threat raised its head, she did not resort to lies and scheming to get her way. Oh, how I have wronged Eadyth! I thought her dull and stupid, but she sleeps this night in the arms of the husband she loves."

"If you find being in bed with a husband such an admirable thing, why are you here, Maria? If I remember aright, you've forgotten your bargain with me and gone and betrothed yourself to Gilbert Crispin."

Her hands trembled, clasping his tighter. "But 'tis you I love, Rothgar."

There had been times in his life when he'd taken a blow to the gut, or fallen from a frisky horse, or cracked his head against a beam, or otherwise been stunned into timeless, breathless silence. Never had a bolt of joy been the cause, shafting through him with giddy delight, so that all he could do was grin stupidly in the dark and say, "You love me?"

In answer, she moved into his arms and found his lips with her own.

"'Tis fearsome hard to love a man who hates you," she whispered against his lips.

"Fearsome hard, indeed," he agreed, gasping when she pressed her hand against the part of him that best fit the description. Her lips parted in welcome and he darted his tongue into the soft, wet heat of her mouth, reveling in the feel of her, the taste of her. Her tongue against his reminded him of her glib way with words, her ability to twist the situation to suit her needs. "Would that I could believe you, sweet liar."

"You must believe me." She caught his face between her hands.

"And what am I to believe, that you conspired with Gilbert and maligned my character to the priest with naught but good intent?"

"Aye. That is it, exactly." She seemed delighted over his sarcasm.

"Only a woman would think in such convoluted fashion."

She tightened her hand around his throbbing shaft. "A woman, you say? God's teeth, but I thought 'twas *your* ruse I played out."

Rothgar chuckled, the feel of her against him lightening his mood. His hands, tired and cramped from a day's hard digging, burrowed into the folds of her cloak, seeking her warmth. Damn—she wore yet another gown and tunic beneath the nun's garb.

"You were right, Rothgar, to suggest this ruse," she said, ignoring his probing fingers and leaning urgently into him as if she could transfer the force of her convictions through his skin. "Though I have had to improvise beyond expectations, Hugh improves day by day, and Eadyth and I control Gilbert through a potion—"

Rothgar's chuckling developed into full-blown laughter. "I'd best guard what I eat and drink in your presence, my sweet. It sounds as though you're dosing every man within Langwald."

"You misunderstand. We have *stopped* dosing Hugh, and *commenced* with an ointment to stifle Gilbert's barbarous nature."

"The very thing I fear," Rothgar whispered against her hair, his hands at last finding her skin, smooth and supple beneath the coarse wool. "One touch, one glance from you and I turn barbarian."

"Stop that!" she cried, wriggling free of his stroking fingers. "Rothgar, you must heed what I say."

"Speak, then." He sighed, leaning back against his pallet, drawing her with him but contenting himself with holding her lightly about the waist.

She spun a most astonishing tale for him. He listened in speechless amazement as she described her confrontation with Gilbert in the hut and her reluctant promise to wed in order to placate him. Of her own virtual imprisonment within Langwald, preventing her from coming to him as she'd promised. Of Hugh's apparent slow return to sensibility, and of her and Eadyth joining forces against Gilbert.

"We are so close, Rothgar," she concluded. "A week, perhaps less, and Hugh might be able to assume his rightful place. But Langwald is so vulnerable just now. These mysterious nighttime raids against the castle supplies could be a sign portending worse to come. Stephan will never fight again. There are only three knights left to rely upon."

"Yet you say you are poisoning Gilbert," Rothgar reminded her.

"I must," she said. "He seems changed of late. I fear what he might do. Eadyth says the ointment could kill him, and I would do so without hesitation if our fighting force was not so depleted. I must ever be careful to use only enough to leave him sleepy and clumsy, but lively enough to shake off the effects and spring to our defense if the worst should occur before Hugh takes over."

"Would you really kill him?" Rothgar asked, unable—or unwilling—to imagine Maria cold-bloodedly daubing the poisoned ointment on Gilbert's unsuspecting neck.

"I . . ." Her voice trailed off, and he could feel her shoulders hunch with uncertainty. "I do not know."

"I have watched Gilbert Crispin and seen him do naught but bellow and bluster. He looks to be a good man in a fight, but I do not sense in him the ability to be a leader of men."

"He is not," Maria agreed. "Instead, he bullies those who are helpless against him. Once, while Fen was helping me bathe Hugh, we discovered bruises. Since then Fen never permits any knight to be alone with Hugh, not even Walter, but I have good reason to believe 'twas banishing Gilbert from Hugh's side that brought an end to the abuse."

Rothgar thought of the helpless, drooling wreck of a man toying with his doll; of Helwyth's bruised face; of the mottled discoloration staining Maria's tender skin; and of Gilbert's broad, battle-honed body bending over his victims. He felt an overwhelming, impotent rage. "He will never touch you again," he swore. "You belong to me."

She grew very still against him, almost as though she were holding her breath for fear he would call back those words. "You do believe me, then?"

"Ah, Maria, I spent so many nights cursing your failure to come to me. I convinced myself your words were impossible to believe. 'Twas jealousy eating at me, thinking of you and Gilbert together. But when you come into my arms, and tell me you love me . . ." He let out a short, humorless laugh. Never had he been so ruled by a woman that his good sense fell victim to his heart. Yet here he lay, with such a woman in his arms, ready to cast aside all doubts, all honor, in order to help her preserve his own lands for another man.

But she would be his. And that dizzying, delightful prospect made it seem a fair trade. Maria moved against him; she nuzzled his chin, finding his lips in the dark, and any lingering doubts fled his capricious mind.

"Will you love me now?" she asked.

"Bold wench," he said with mock ferocity. "You are ever the one to ask for pleasure."

He fancied she blushed; she drew away, suddenly shy, but he trapped her against him.

"You are so beautiful," he murmured. "I dislike loving you always in mean shelters upon dirt floors. We should be abed, with a good fire crackling nearby, and heaps of furs offering comfort. I have thought of you just so, lying back against furs, with your hair streaming about your shoulders."

"Do you like my hair?" He could feel the brush of her hand, feather light, as she reached self-consciously toward her head. "Do you think I'm pretty?"

"Beautiful," he stated, capturing her hand and drawing it to his lips.

"I find you pleasing to look upon, too," she said.

"You do?" He paused in the midst of pressing heated lips against the palm of her hand. He'd often wondered what others saw when they stared him in the face; it seemed a fickle whim of God's that allowed a man to look upon anything he chose save his own countenance. He'd caught glimpses of himself now and again: usually in a bucket of water; once, in a hammered metal plate shinier than most. But the image reflected back to him, of pale, wavering skin, a smudge of blue marking his eyes, a wild array of tawny-gold hair surrounding his head and covering most of his face, told him only that he shared features common to other men.

"And I am developing an uncommon fondness for dirt floors," she added.

He laughed then, a low, triumphant rumbling deep within his chest as he pressed her into the pallet. Though every male urge goaded him to strip himself naked and tear away her gown and tunic as well, to reveal her lissome, supple form to his covetous eye, concern for their comfort in the bone-chilling cold stayed the impulse.

In many ways it was an unsatisfactory coupling: Maria, with her skirts hitched up about her waist, her gown barring his questing lips and mouth from her breasts; himself, with his manhood freed through the opening in his chausses, missing the feel of her hot, wet passions against its root. Her legs wrapped around him, but he felt only the pressure and not the sensation he craved against his sides, his back.

In other ways, he'd never felt so fulfilled.

"I love you," she whispered against his lips as he drove into her, her breath mingling with his. With her words his heart set up a clamoring separate from the wild pounding brought about by passion. "I love you," she said again, and a tender warmth, having nothing to do with their physical exertions, enveloped them. "I love you," she gasped yet again, when the force of his groaning thrust shifted her perilously near the edge of the pallet. Her sweet softness closed around him with shuddering pulsations and he cursed the clothing between them, wishing his belly were bare against hers so he could share the rippling contractions that left her breathless and moaning with delight.

"I love you, too," he whispered against the heat of her neck when they lay quiet at last, waiting for the blood to cool and the heart to subside. She tightened her arms around him.

"Tomorrow is Easter Eve," she said. "Eadyth and I are hopeful that Hugh might be well enough to sit in attendance when the villagers make their requests. That alone might still Philip's wagging tongue."

"I hope for Hugh's presence as well," said Rothgar, "for I intend for him to give over to me the most precious thing in his care."

"And what is that?" she asked, her fingers idly toying at a few stray hairs that peeked over the neck of his tunic while her heart hammered against him. "The gold you promised Gilbert?"

"There is gold, but precious little in coin. The old stud bull ruling the pasture—years ago he gouged himself against a storm-felled tree. When the wound healed it left a small pocket of skin dangling from his neck. The gold is hidden there, Maria, twelve solid coins, awaiting any man foolhardy enough to brave that old bull. A small fortune, but not enough to hire all you need for Hugh."

"Enough to buy your ransom from William, Rothgar!" Maria's eyes shone. "I've heard it's being done. Mayhap—"

He silenced her with a finger against her lips. "Time enough to worry of those things later. I do not need Hugh's permission to claim that gold. Nay, the only gold that interests me shines from your hair in the sun, sparks from your eyes."

She shivered, with a little rippling laugh that told him he'd pleased her. "You mean to ask Hugh to return Langwald, then."

"You hold Langwald more precious than anything in Hugh's sphere?"

"All other men seem to," she said. "Langwald, always Langwald. Hugh, yourself, and Gilbert . . . why else does even bastard Philip nose about for tales to carry to William, lest he seeks to gain Langwald for himself? Of late I have even suspected Walter of casting a covetous eye over the land."

But Rothgar had naught to say of coveting Langwald to Hugh.

"I shall say to your brother, 'Lord Norman, your castle moat has been dug and the walls set to begin to rising two days hence. Save for a few regrettable exceptions, Langwald's people accept you as their overlord. Now that you are well enough to rule on your own, I ask you to set me free as was promised, and I ask your permission for your sister, Maria, to go away with me.'"

The shaft of moonlight gleaming through the shed door fell square upon Maria's head nestled against his shoulder.

"And then I shall ask the same question of you," he continued. "Tell me now, Maria—what would your answer be? Could you give up the home you've wanted for so long and set out upon an uncertain course? We will have no home, no manner of living until I find some type of work." He remembered how she had grown still scant moments ago; it was his turn now to wait with pounding heart, with tingling nerves, for her answer.

The moon highlighted the curve of her lip as she smiled. "First I must tell my brother how, together, you and I saved Langwald for him. How your wise leadership caused the castle walls to rise, and how your strong arm held off the attackers in the clearing. And then I will say to you, Rothgar, 'It seems all that shifting about in my younger days had a purpose after all, as practice for what lay ahead. Aye, homeless, purseless, traveling Saxon, I will go with you.'"

"A trifle long-winded, but an excellent answer," said Rothgar, enfolding her more tightly within his arms, reveling in the heady feeling that anything would be possible with this woman at his side.

18

Rothgar walked with her to the edge of the courtyard, pressing one last kiss upon her lips, unwilling as she herself was to break the warm circle of his arms.

"I must go," Maria whispered. "You must return to your shed ere Eustace wakes, and I must not test Gilbert's ire by my absence. Oh, Rothgar, if God wills it, Hugh will preside over the Easter festivities, and this will be the last time we must part."

"If Hugh has improved so much, mayhap I should come with you now," Rothgar urged, his voice hoarse and strained. "I shall be mind-boggled all day, fearful for your safety. And I do not favor the thought of Gilbert touching you, or you touching him, no matter the reason. If Hugh truly is ready, find a sword for me, Maria, and I'll put an end to Gilbert Crispin and your troubles."

"And raise a multitude of others."

"Aye." The word dragged, a dispirited, reluctant flutter of sound. "I can scarce expect my people to switch their loyalties to Hugh if I carve up his knight."

Maria leaned into his strength, savoring for one lingering moment the feel of her softness molded against his hard-muscled form. She knew an ephemeral thrill when his hand cupped the back of her head, holding it against his shoulder; felt the warm stir of his breath as his lips sought her forehead; felt the renewed thundering of his heart against her breast.

"This way is best," she said. "We must placate Gilbert, just for one more day, and arrange things so Philip has naught to say to William against Hugh."

"Go, then," he said, his words coming thick and hoarse. "Go now, or I'll not let you go back at all."

There was no need to don the nun's wool for warmth as Maria hurried across Langwald's silent courtyard. Her senses felt benumbed when apart from him—all save her feverishly questing mind, plagued by worries now that his spellbinding presence was removed. For instance, did nuns lie abed until dawn, or did their religious obligations pull them from sleep during this quiet, timeless interlude between full dark and the pale glimmering promise of sunlight at the edge of the sky?

She quickened her step. The robe, scorned last eve for its odor, now carried lingering traces of Rothgar's scent. Loath as she was to give up this one thing that called him to mind, the nun's gown must be returned and a furtive prayer whispered that its wearer had not already discovered it missing.

She slipped into the hall. The great fire, little more than a heaping bed of embers after a long night's neglect, cast an orange-gold glow over the smoke-blackened walls. A hound pricked alert ears in her direction, sniffing the air to catch her scent, and then lowered its head back to its paws with an apologetic wave of its tail.

The rush-strewn floor seemed to stretch endlessly, with only one rug-wrapped form to break up its expanse. The collection of seats and benches surrounding the main table lay scattered and empty.

Maria swallowed and gripped the robe more tightly. She had hoped to find Gilbert still asleep as she'd left him, his squire still snoring at the door. Their absence foretold disaster. She needs must devise an excuse explaining her absence. She thought of Langwald's chapel, a poor, little-used room of worship. She would tell Gilbert she'd spent the night there praying, and hope God would not forsake her again for the lie.

And then she sensed, rather than saw, another person slinking through the shadows. Maria whirled, coming face-to-face with one of the kitchen wenches. So great was her relief, and their mutual surprise at stumbling over one another, that each let out a muffled little shriek and dropped her bundle. Maria's unfurled into a heap of rusty black wool; the wench's tattered cloth split apart, revealing a tangled mass of branches and leaves.

"Greenery, my lady, for the Easter feasting," explained the wench, crouching to gather it up. Before hauling it into her arms, she peeked up at Maria, gnawing at her lip. "'Tis said to speed winter on its way. Lest, of course, my lady forbids us to spread it about in the old way."

Norman priests, when backing William's claim to England, pointed to the near-pagan Saxon custom of adorning altars and tables with greenstuff. "'Tis their way of worshiping their old gods along with the true Christ!" they'd proclaimed, speaking of mad dancing around Beltane fires, of tree gods and sun worship.

A sharp-spined holly leaf reflected the embers in

its shiny surface. Crisp red berries glimmered in the light against the waxy petals of an English flower she'd noticed poking brave blossoms through the snow. What was wrong with a bit of color to relieve Langwald's drabness on this day, when her brother might meet his people, when the memory of her wondrous night with Rothgar filled her senses?

"We shall need more than this. Much more than this," Maria said, kneeling to help.

She was on her knees, clutching branches of holly and ivy, when the abbess found her. Sister Mary Innocent trailed, as usual, in her wake, this time not from humility but from her inability to watch where she walked. Her attention seemed riveted upon the pale blue gown she wore—one of Maria's favorites. With each step she took, the young nun plucked the fine, clinging wool away from her waist and watched it settle back into place, outlining her form in a way the stiff old black wool could never duplicate. Another of Maria's gowns was draped awkwardly over her head, the sleeves tied beneath her chin like the ends of a peasant woman's head scarf.

"Someone has stolen Sister Mary Innocent's habit and veil," said the abbess, staring disdainfully down her nose at the greenery Maria held.

A spray of holly lay across Sister Mary Innocent's borrowed gown.

Only a short while ago Maria had praised Eadyth's ability to solve problems without resorting to lies; now she found herself casting about in her mind for some plausible excuse for possessing the gown.

"Cease worrying over it, Mother," she said, swiftly flipping the bundle to bury the holly beneath it. She stroked the wool, seeking an explanation. "I have it right here. When Sister cast it off last night it fell so that one of its folds spilled into the passageway. I . . . caught it with my foot as I walked past. I thought one of the serving wenches might wash it clean of my clumsy treading."

"Christ's daughters tend their own clothing," said the abbess, snatching it away from Maria. "Go, daughter, and garb yourself properly," she said, switching her attention to Sister Mary Innocent, who accepted the garment and headed back to Maria's alcove with slow, reluctant steps.

Several other Saxon women had crept into the gradually lightening hall, their arms filled with vibrant, fragrant greenery. They stared with wide-eyed trepidation from their kneeling lady to the formidable nun towering over her.

"Do you intend to allow them to spread that greenstuff about?" asked the abbess.

"What is the harm, Mother?" Maria asked, rising to her feet with the holly and ivy cascading from her hands, knowing that by holding on to the greenery she'd be allying herself with the women against the nun. "They mean no blasphemy. 'Tis just their way."

"Then let us step aside so they can get on with it," said the abbess, an approving sparkle in her eye belying the stern lines upon her face.

"I see no harm in the custom myself," she confided in low tones when she and Maria stood alone, watching the happy, chattering women spread the greenery about. "I was led to believe you Normans read all manner of demonic significance into it."

"You might have asked me," said Maria, her pride smarting from the fearful tripping her heart had set up when it seemed she'd offended the nun.

"As you might have asked me over the borrowing of Sister Mary Innocent's gown."

Maria's cheeks flamed so, she felt certain they could challenge a holly berry for redness. "I apologize, Mother," she whispered. "It was the rash act of a moment. Had I time to think it over . . ."

"You would have done the same thing," finished the abbess, with no hint of malice or anger in her words. When next she spoke, she did so in a halting but adequate Norman, as though she did not want their conversation overheard by the women in the hall.

"I am not blind, my lady. I see the way things go here. I came, thinking to find Eadyth held virtual prisoner, wed against her will to a barbarous monster. Instead, I find you holding that unhappy position, and Eadyth content with her lot."

"Oh, Mother, 'twas not always so." Her eyes suddenly beset by tears, Maria groped blindly for the nun's warm, dry hand, wondering if her unrequited wish to confess all to Father Bruno would find fulfillment in being told to the abbess. "I wronged Eadyth, forcing her to wed my brother. That I find myself facing a similar position seems a fitting punishment."

"Bah," said the abbess, enfolding Maria's hand in both of her own. "Eadyth was no more suited to taking the veil than you are, my daughter. Had she a true vocation, I would have raised the hue and cry when Rothgar of Langwald spirited her away. We would have fetched her back to take her vows."

"Yet you came after her now. I thought she might have asked you to do so."

"Word of Eadyth's plight came from other lips, my lady, someone who seemed to have his own interests at heart. Still, I felt duty bound to investigate, for Eadyth's sake. If I found she pined for Christ, or if I found her unloved and mistreated, I would offer her the shelter of our house and the protection of vows," said the abbess, an enigmatic smile upon her face. "Just as I now offer them to you, daughter."

"I fear I would make a poor nun," said Maria, knowing that while Rothgar of Langwald walked this earth, no vow of chastity would keep her from him. "Will you name the traitor for me?"

"Would that I could, daughter. He kept himself in shadows and spoke in a harsh whisper to disguise his true voice, but I am certain I would recognize it if I heard it again. I shall pay him no mind if he approaches me with more lies."

"I am grateful, Mother, and in your debt."

"Alas, we are poor nuns," said the abbess, turning her frank, intelligent gaze upon Maria. "Eadyth's dowry, if not Eadyth's presence, meant much to us. That is why I came, daughter, to see for myself the woman who was said to rule Langwald for her brother, who might understand our meager needs."

"When I heard you were at the gate, I had hoped you might ask for meat or altar cloths and suchlike."

"Meat, yes, but bed clothes rather than altar cloths, and the occasional sack of flour," said the abbess. "And when milk and eggs can be spared, we could make custards for Sister Mary Pius, who lost her last tooth a sennight ago."

"'Tis not so much to ask," said Maria, thinking that Langwald's bounty could well extend to the small convent.

"Not among sensible women," agreed the abbess. "A man might think otherwise. I must go now, and see to Sister Mary Innocent. Would that some unmarried, land-hungry lord had descended upon us before she took the veil." She took her leave with a final comforting squeeze of Maria's hand. "Thank you, daughter.

And remember that when strength of spirit is called for, there is One who has it aplenty, One who hears every prayer." With a mischievous, worldly twinkle lighting her eye, she added, "One who determined which herbs would grow upon this earth, and One who fashioned women's bodies with knees, and men's bodies with dangling parts susceptible to pain should the prayers take overlong in being answered."

The Saxon women, whispering and subdued while Maria spoke with the abbess, grew festive when the clattering of the nun's rosary beads faded. Laughing, pulling Maria into their midst, they adorned Langwald Hall in the time-honored manner. Eager hands made short work of the malodorous job of changing the floor rushes. Dogs frisked about their feet, snarling playfully at the brooms, snatching at long-forgotten bones, rolling in the fresh rushes liberally laced with herbs and pine needles in honor of the holy day.

Young girls ran from woman to woman, offering chunks of bread, bits of cheese, dippers of clear, cool water, so they need not stop their work to break their fast. A pale waiflike boy who Maria had often noticed lurking about in a furtive, lost-looking manner, sat happily in a corner, strumming with great skill the lute that usually hung, dusty and disused, upon the wall in her alcove. One clear treble voice took up the chorus of the lay he played, and then another joined in, and then another, until all sang along. Even Maria, perched precariously atop a cask while she strung garlands of ivy between gyves designed for a less pleasant purpose, hummed the melody as she strained her ears to learn the words.

Gilbert Crispin staggered into the midst of the merry group.

The joyful tune came to a discordant halt, the boy's fingers jangling the lute strings. One by one the musical voices trailed away, until a lone voice trilled on. The singer, squinting her eyes to peer about at the sudden silence that greeted her pause for breath, ended her song with an unmelodic shriek when her nearsighted gaze settled upon Gilbert.

And Gilbert's eyes, renowned to be as sharp-sighted as a gyrfalcon's, rested upon Maria with the steady, remorseless regard of that feared, feathered predator.

"Where were you last night?" he demanded, taking a stumbling step toward her.

"Play on!" Maria called to the lute player, praying the boy had the courage to pluck at the strings while she summoned the courage to lie about spending the night in the chapel. The first tenuous strains sounded as she clambered down from the cask, and a woman, her gaze darting knowingly between Gilbert and Maria, bravely took up the tune, motioning for those around her to join in the song. To the tune of their uncertain, quavering song Maria fought against the despair that threatened to overwhelm her.

"I did not think you would need the ointment again," she said. "And so I went to worship my lord." A lie and not a lie, considering the passionate fervor that drew her eyes to Rothgar's body every time the moonlight struck him, though she thought it unlikely she would ever repeat this conversation to her Saxon lover.

Gilbert, his doubt and his desire to believe her warring over his face, looked as though he'd spent the night in similar pursuits. Bits of straw clung to his tunic and the matted back of his head, and a foul stench drifted from him, as though he'd exercised his lusts on a floor littered with rotted manure.

"Did you not think to look for me in the chapel?" she asked, folding her hands and bowing her head, keeping watch over him through her lowered lashes.

"I did not," Gilbert admitted, the grim set to his mouth, his very stance softening as he took in her submissive pose. "I should have thought . . . a mindless beast dwells within me, and snarls to life when it thinks I might lose you yet again. I swear that shame dizzies me now, when I recall what I thought and did last night."

He took another heavy, uncertain step toward her. His squire dashed from the shadows, a bruised eye and swollen lip proving he'd paid dear for sleeping through her escape the night before. He gripped his lord's arm and guided him to a low settle near the fire.

"Maria," Gilbert called, so weakly that she scarce heard him above the women's singing. "I would have you tend my wound now."

"Aye." She sighed. But when she reached for the clay jar, naught but a wilting snowdrop sat in its place. And on the floor, shards of pottery poked through the rushes surrounding the stiff, glassy-eyed body of a hound, a globule of greasy ointment half-melted at the end of its lolling, swollen tongue.

Rothgar shouldered an empty cask, joining the line of similarly laden, excited men heading toward Langwald's open portal. Some cast furtive, embarrassed glances in his direction, as though ashamed to be so anticipating a Norman feast in what had been his hall, but Rothgar ignored their unsolicited sympathy.

Truth to tell, it grated upon his nerves.

More than they, Rothgar sweated with eagerness to burst through that doorway. That it once belonged to him mattered less—mattered not at all—compared to the woman waiting within.

Throughout this interminable day, he'd squinted toward the hall, grudging the distance between it and the castle site, a desperate certainty gripping his vitals that something would go wrong. How would he hear, how could he see, if something should go amiss? How cocksure he'd been, assuring her the two of them could thwart Gilbert with naught but a few well-chosen lies. The plan, seemingly so well reasoned under cover of night, vanished like predawn mists in the light of day.

The shrieking squeal of a pig being slaughtered for the night's feast had drifted through the air. A flurry of activity near the stable had caught his eye, and he recognized the blue-black mat of Gilbert Crispin's hair standing out among the crowd of men. Maria's vulnerability struck him with the force of a battering ram to the gut. His feet, instead of sprinting to Maria's rescue, had seemed to take root in the ground; his fingers lost all sensation, curling into useless, impotent fists at his side.

But the day had passed. The sun had wended its way, inch by excruciating inch, across the sky. Eustace's cry, "Day is done!" had freed Rothgar from his self-imposed bondage, and he'd dropped his shovel, taking off for the hall at a dead run, coming to his senses only when the men called after him, reminding him to hoist a cask.

It wouldn't do to burst full-tilt through the door on his own, sweaty and work-stained and demanding to see Maria.

He forced himself to wait next to the stack of empty casks; fortunately, in their own eagerness to commence the festivities, the men of Langwald soon joined him. Their lighthearted banter covered his agitated silence; they crowded around the doorway, and he silently and remorselessly shouldered his way through until he was one of the first to cross the threshold.

It was Langwald Hall as he loved it best, with fir logs heaped high upon the fire, sweetening the air with the clean, sharp scent of pine. Hundreds of candles added their extravagant glow to the fire pit's leaping flames, casting an unaccustomed brightness that made even the smoke-darkened walls gleam beneath their greenery. Father Bruno stood near the fire, a mug of ale in his hands, beaming with paternal pride.

Rothgar settled his cask onto the floor. Another man did the same, and two more topped the casks with a plank, forming a makeshift table. All the while, his eyes roved over the hall, seeking Maria.

"Not there, you dunces, over here," shouted a woman. She clapped her hand over her mouth when she recognized Rothgar. "I am sorry, my lord. I did not realize—"

Rothgar's offer to move the casks was lost in the glad, welcoming cries of women who surrounded him in an eager, pressing cluster. He pretended to smile, made senseless, noncommittal grunts to acknowledge their good wishes, while his gaze raked every distant form, his ears strained to hear over the incessant strumming of a lute, the excited Saxon babble.

There was a motion at the far end of the hall, near the small alcove Maria had claimed for her own. Two nuns, real nuns he supposed, moved into the light.

And in between them walked his Maria, clad in a fine gown of dark gold wool. A matching headrail, an adornment most women chose to conceal sparse hair and pox-ravaged cheeks, served only to hide the glory of Maria's thick, shining tresses, but he knew, he knew how it looked flowing free about her shoulders, he knew the smooth, creamy texture of her skin, he knew how easily his hands could span her slender waist, so winsomely defined within her golden girdle and sparkling jeweled dagger.

Another group of men strode through Langwald's door. Normans. Philip Martell. Gilbert, Walter, Dunstan, their squires and pages. Harsh metallic jingling accompanied their steps as their mail gleamed in the bright light. They spoke not at all, staring about them with fierce, mistrustful expressions that shouted louder than any words that they disapproved of the festive gathering. Their condemning silence overtook the crowd, like ice sealing the surface of a pond, until an uncomfortable hush permeated the merrymaking.

Gilbert Crispin stood at the head of the group, his mailed fist twitching at his sword as though he longed to flail it about in the close-packed group of Saxons. Rothgar knew a moment of despair. Had Maria played him false yet again with her tale of neck wounds and slow poison and weakness and jerking limbs?

Her words trilling joyously over the quiet crowd, Maria called, "Glorious Easter, my lord!"

Rothgar tore his attention from Gilbert, forcing himself to turn toward her, to see with his own eyes whether her expression as she greeted Gilbert matched the delight in her voice.

She wasn't looking at Gilbert. For the space of a

heartbeat, her wide, brown-gold eyes met Rothgar's, and then with a bright smile, she turned and dropped into a deep, welcoming curtsy before her brother, Hugh.

"I do not believe my eyes!" Philip said shrilly. "I was assured this was not possible—"

"Hold your tongue!" barked Walter.

A collective gasp rose from the Saxons. None had seen their lord Hugh de Courson except from a distance. Rothgar's mood momentarily lightened, remembering the tales Maria had spread of Hugh's foul temper, when most in the crowd took an involuntary step back. Eadyth stood proudly at Hugh's side, blushing and clinging to his arm, no doubt causing confusion in the minds of those who credited Hugh with monkish inclinations.

Hugh extended his free hand to Maria, murmuring, "Don't be silly," in Norman.

"Speak their tongue," she answered as he pulled her to her feet.

"Glorious Easter," called Hugh, restoring the festive mood.

The crowd parted, allowing Hugh and Eadyth to make their slow way to the great table, and then closed in again behind them. Somehow, in the flux of people, Rothgar found himself next to Maria.

"I wish I could kiss you," she whispered. "Hugh will want me beside him; he is not as conversant as I with the Saxon tongue and Eadyth's grasp of the Norman tends toward the religious. Nay—do not look at me while we speak."

He did as she asked but found her hand with his. She looped one finger around his thumb and he pressed it against his thigh.

"Let us leave now. Hugh looks capable enough.

None will notice if we slip away amidst all this confusion." His own attempt at a whisper sounded discordantly loud, as though every ear could hear. His heart responded with a riotous clamoring he felt it unwise to reveal. He continued staring at Hugh, but a prickling sensation at the back of his neck reminded him that Gilbert stood not far away. The voice of doom taunted within. "Now," he repeated. "I am in a fever of anxiety to get you away ere something terrible befalls us. Surely your brother is now fit to take command?"

She did not answer for a moment; if not for the light pressure of her finger round his thumb, he would have thought she'd melted into the crowd. "I do not know," she said at last, heartbreak evident in her voice.

"Maria?" Hugh's call pierced the music and babble surrounding them.

"I cannot leave him now. He knows none of these people; he might become frightened and allow the demons to reclaim his wits." She tugged her finger free, but he recaptured it.

"To him for now, but to me ere long. Say yes, Maria."

"Maria!" Hugh called again.

"Say you will leave with me tonight." Rothgar gripped her tighter.

"We will leave tonight, you stubborn Saxon," she said, stifling a giggle behind her hand.

"I wish I could kiss you," he repeated her comment, wondering why the thought roused no excitement, only a dark sense of foreboding, of something lost forever.

Their lips did not touch, but when he risked a look toward her she was peeking up at him through slanted, laughing eyes, with a seductive, heated curve to her lips that made his own throb in response, sending heat flaring through his loins. Her flirtatiousness made mock of his fears.

"As I think on it, I am disinclined to be parted from you just now," she said. "I think Hugh might need two at his side to help decipher the demands of these people." She took his hand, openly this time, and they forged through the crowd. Rothgar's heart slowed its knocking; he would allow nothing to happen to her while he stood at her side.

"Who is he?" Hugh asked when they stood before him, a decided chill to his voice. Rothgar thought the attitude warranted. Eadyth stiffened perceptibly at the sight of him; Maria clutched his hand, laughing and blushing, her headrail askew.

Rothgar decided to answer for himself; it was, in a way, their first meeting. "I am called Rothgar."

Hugh stared at him; Rothgar took the opportunity to do the same. Hugh's pale countenance, along with minute creases about his eyes, hinted at his physical ordeal, but the brown-gold eyes, so like Maria's, gleamed with shrewd intelligence. The witless, drooling doll-player seemed banished forever.

"The man who once ruled this hall was called Rothgar."

"I am he."

"Is this true?" Hugh directed his question toward Maria.

"Aye," she answered.

"Then why is he not dead?"

"Without him, there would be no castle, Hugh, and your knights might well be dead. And these people, instead of feasting tonight in your hall, might be planning ways to burn it to the ground."

"Is this true?" This time, Hugh looked to Rothgar for an answer.

"There may be some who still seek to burn it to the ground. But for the most part, they accept you as their new lord."

"Why did you intercede on my behalf?"

"Because I love them." Stated so simply, it sounded a ridiculous reason for blithely handing over one's birthright, to willingly forego freedom, to stand by now while everything within him urged him to take Maria's hand and flee into the night. And yet it was the truth. "They did not understand what was expected of them. They did not understand the inevitability of someone like you coming along. I but sought to protect them."

"Like a father with a wayward child?"

"Just so," Rothgar said, amazed at Hugh's quick grasp of the situation.

"Then I owe you a great debt. I shall think on it and grant you an appropriate reward."

Gilbert shouldered himself between Rothgar and Maria, breaking their handclasp, before Rothgar could tell Hugh the payment he desired. With great effort, Rothgar stopped his fist from crashing into Gilbert's damp, pallid face. Sweat trickled down the Norman's forehead; his hair matted against his scalp; he seemed breathless all out of proportion to the effort necessary to gain his position. Perhaps there was something, after all, to Maria's tale of slow poisoning. Even so, it seemed prudent to hold his tongue and make his request of Hugh later, away from Gilbert's ears. Gilbert wore a sword at his waist; Rothgar had naught but his two hands, tired from a day's digging.

"I did not expect to see you presiding over this gathering," Gilbert said to Hugh.

"Glorious Easter, Gilbert." Hugh clapped the Norman's shoulder, his happiness at greeting his man-at-arms evident. "Good God, it seems a lifetime ago since I've seen your face."

And so it has, Rothgar thought, realizing Hugh had no idea that Gilbert had conspired against him.

"Sit, sit." Hugh reached over, drew a stool next to him, and patted it invitingly. Gilbert took the seat. Directing a malicious, triumphant smirk toward Rothgar, he grasped Maria's hand and pulled her against him. She struggled ineffectually to free herself.

Hugh studied them, a frown creasing his forehead. For a moment, confusion clouded his eyes; he shook his head as though to clear it. "Let us begin," he said.

The people of Langwald lined up to ask an Easter favor of their new lord. And what had been a whim of Maria's in keeping Rothgar at her side soon proved a fortunate choice. The villagers' rough country accents distorted the Saxon tongue beyond her ability to decipher on more than one occasion. Rothgar translated, gradually regaining his composure as Gilbert slumped in his seat, his hand eventually dropping from Maria's to lie, twitching, upon his lap.

"Owd roof, hers pingly dripplin'."

"Could he cut new thatch for his roof?" Rothgar deciphered.

"Horse thass gone. Mare needin' tupped. Norman, bah." The villager spat into the rushes. "None else."

Maria turned wide, questioning eyes to Rothgar.

"Could he breed his mare to one of the war-horses? His stallion died."

With magnanimous waves of his hands, Hugh granted all requests; as Father Bruno had promised Maria, none were extortionate. As the line of petitioners dwindled, the tantalizing odors of well-cooked food filled the hall. The last petitioner, a woman swathed in a heavy veil and cloak stepped forward. She dropped her veil from her head. Both Maria and Eadyth cried out; Rothgar felt his stomach lurch sickeningly, all his hatred and frustrations, his premonition of doom rising to the fore.

It was Helwyth, her face swollen and bruised almost beyond recognition. Dried blood caked her lower lip; when she spoke, her words whistled around the broken edge of a tooth.

"Who did this to you?" In his horror, Hugh addressed her in the Norman tongue. Helwyth flinched at the sound and awkwardly loosened her cloak. Her left arm dangled uselessly at her side, the skin of her forearm bulging unnaturally where the broken ends of bone poked from beneath the skin.

Gilbert, roused from his stupor, sat bolt upright. Helwyth raised her chin in their direction but said nothing.

"Who did this to you?" Rothgar repeated in words she could understand, scarcely able to force the words from his throat. He knew who had done it; better that Hugh should hear it from Helwyth's own lips.

"Mama!" Young Henry freed himself from a woman who had been holding him. He wrapped his arms around his mother's leg but stepped back in confusion when Helwyth cried out in pain. Bursting into tears, he looked about in panic until his gaze settled upon Rothgar. Whimpering, he hurled himself into Rothgar's embrace.

"My lord." Helwyth held out her good arm toward Hugh in supplication. "Please be merciful. I carry a

Norman child in my womb. And a Norman has done this to me."

"Silence her!" Walter thundered, obviously unable to believe one of his own kind had exercised such brutality upon a defenseless woman.

An outraged babble of voices greeted her announcement and overrode Walter's command.

"Who?" demanded Hugh, shouting to be heard above the din.

"'Tis none of his concern, wench," Philip said.

Gilbert sat low in his stool, shaking his head, gazing with fear-filled eyes toward Walter as though he feared the older knight's punishment for this foul deed.

During his months of captivity, Rothgar had learned many Norman curses. He heaped these upon Gilbert's head, along with the most vivid insults he knew in his own tongue, heedless of any who heard him. "Foul bastard," he roared when he finally exhausted his supply. His stomach twisted sickeningly within him at the thought of what the Norman swine would do to Maria should he get his clutches upon her. His sense of responsibility weighed upon him like a millstone, berating him for his self-absorption in his own affairs, for his failure to protect his dead brother's wife.

Father Bruno elbowed his way to the forefront. "You cannot allow this to pass, Lord Hugh."

"Be gone from here," Gilbert ordered Helwyth, moving threateningly toward her. Father Bruno cowered away, though Helwyth held her ground.

Rothgar gripped Gilbert's shoulder to stay him, aching for the feel of a sword in his hands. Weaponless, he had to content himself with digging his fingers through the chain mail until he found solid, bunched muscle. He shuddered anew at the thought of all that battle-honed strength unleashed against Helwyth's slight body. He twisted his grip viciously, thrilling at the gasp of pain he wrenched from Gilbert.

"Did you do this, Gilbert?" Hugh's voice conveyed low, barely controlled fury.

"N-n-n-no," said Gilbert, falling back into his seat, breaking Rothgar's grip. His eyes darted about as though he sought help among the hostile crowd, cringing from Walter's murderous countenance, coming to rest with hatred upon Helwyth, with the promise of revenge upon Rothgar.

"Then who?"

"Aye, whom shall you point the finger to if not yourself?" Walter echoed, ominous warning fair dripping from his words.

"Go on, then, Gilbert, implicate one of your fellow men," Philip taunted.

Gilbert's complexion darkened. "I implicate no man. Pay no attention to her, Hugh. She seeks to uncover a viper's nest of troubles." A false, cajoling smile crossed his features. "You'd not ignore the advice of your own trusted soldier over the mad ravings of an enemy whore, would you, Hugh?"

"Please, Lord Hugh, my rightful request," Helwyth insisted, ignoring Gilbert's threats.

"Speak, woman," Hugh ordered, glancing with utter loathing upon Gilbert's fawning form.

Every eye in the hall rested upon Helwyth's weaving, battered figure. No sound, save for a few sympathetic sobs, prevented her voice, though weak and tremulous from pain, from carrying to every ear.

"I must have protection, my lord. For myself, and for the babe I carry."

"You shall have it," vowed Hugh. "I swear it."

"I want him." She lifted a trembling finger. The wavering of her hand made it difficult to see where she pointed.

"Gilbert?" asked Hugh. "Do you want me to punish him for these loathsome acts?"

Helwyth shook her head. "I shall wreak my own revenge, my lord. I ask you for a husband to protect me and mine. I ask your permission to wed Rothgar of Langwald, this very night."

19

This, I can do.

The perfect clarity, the utter simplicity of this one thought temporarily banished the chirping and twittering threatening to reclaim Hugh's senses.

The seemingly endless line of petitioners preceding the battered Saxon woman had swum together in a senseless blur, their rough words eluding his tenuous grasp of their tongue. He'd caught a word here, a phrase there, but what did he know of thatches, of swill pots, of wheat sharps? So he'd agreed to all, caring naught for what he granted, only that his wife squeezed his arm and smiled with shy pride, his sister bloomed with approval.

Would that he had taken Eadyth's advice and retired to his chamber after making an appearance, leaving Maria to deal with these people. But then had come this woman. A spot near the back of his head shrieked in agony at the sight of her bruised face, his head felt swollen and throbbing at the thought of what she must have endured. Poor, poor lady. He could not tear his gaze from her, though the firelight seemed suddenly brighter, stabbing through his skull into the backs of his eyeballs with an unwelcome, familiar pain.

"You wish to marry Rothgar?" He repeated the Saxon woman's request, just to make certain.

"She does not, not really," the Saxon Rothgar said chokingly. "I have been remiss in keeping watch over her, but I swear she'll not suffer again."

"It is my right to ask," the woman said, glaring at Rothgar, a stubborn set to her jaw.

This, I can do. But should I?

Oh, for a moment's quiet counsel with his wife! But no, there was some knowledge, vague and unpleasant, surrounding Eadyth and Rothgar, swimming just now beyond the reach of his mind. Maria stood rigid, staring white-faced from him to the Saxon woman. Did she fear he would not offer his protection? His wife, his sister, this Saxon wench . . . so vulnerable against any of his men, not just Gilbert . . . Walter, even those strapping young squires . . . women, spoils of war, but so foolish, so needless for men to abuse what cannot refuse. He must speak to them all, from lowly squire Robert to faithful knight Stephan. Where were those two ingrates?

"I am within my rights," the Saxon woman repeated. She seemed to sway upon her feet, as though ready to swoon. Sympathetic hands reached out to support her. A small child disengaged himself from Rothgar of Langwald. Gilbert's squire was quick to capture Rothgar's arms, for as soon as he was free of the child, the Saxon made as if to pummel Gilbert to a pulp. Rothgar struggled within the squire's grasp while the child went running to the woman, staring up into her face, his own features disconcertingly familiar, like . . . like . . .

"What is your name, woman?" Hugh asked.

"I am called Helwyth."

"And why are you set upon this man?"

"Because there are no others. All Langwald's men are wed, or dead, having answered Harold's call to arms. Besides, the boy is fond of him."

The boy, ah, that was what nagged him so, the boy, so like Rothgar, the woman claiming she was within her rights to ask for Rothgar as husband, the child clinging like a limpet to Rothgar, trusting him above any other when fright overtook him. Was it possible they were father and son, lord and lover? He owed a great debt to this Rothgar, he'd admitted it himself. If there had been a spark between these two once, marriage might reignite the flame.

"Helwyth, no. I'll take care of you and the boy, but I cannot marry you." Rothgar strained against the squire.

Helwyth ignored the Saxon. "I need a man to protect me, Lord Hugh, to tend acres that belong to me."

This, I can do!

"Does this Helwyth truly possess lands?" Hugh asked Walter.

"Aye, several acres of assart land in good heart, and a snug hut. But I beg you to ignore her request." His man-at-arms spoke as though river gravel clogged his throat. Not surprising.

After years of honing one's skills to obliterate Saxons, it chafed a man's honor to bestow such wealth upon a former enemy, but landless bachelor Walter could not possibly comprehend the debt he owed this Rothgar. Aha! even as Hugh mulled these thoughts, Walter gave Gilbert a swift poke at the back of his head.

"Do not do this, Hugh," Gilbert begged.

"You have no right!" Philip shrieked. "Langwald was not meant to be carved up like a haunch of venison. She has no claim to any acres! William shall hear of this when I petition—"

"Leave this hall, Philip," Walter roared, "ere you say something so stupid it cannot be forgotten."

Hugh ignored them all. From Rothgar he had gained lands, even a wife; one day soon, God willing, a son. With one magnanimous gesture, he could set things to rights. By William's decree, Helwyth's pitiful assart acres no doubt reverted to Hugh, but he could grant them to Rothgar, and a hut, not so grand surely as Langwald Hall, but shelter enough, along with the pretty little woman as wife, and a sturdy son. Hugh's bedchamber beckoned, promising sweet relief from the noise, the light . . .

"You! Sir Priest, come forth."

Father Bruno sidled up to Helwyth.

"You! Rothgar of Langwald, go stand alongside your bride."

To Hugh's astonishment, Maria gave a small, despairing cry and slumped toward the floor. Women and weddings, always unpredictable. Something to be said, perhaps, for staggering drugged and unaware through one's own. Gilbert's squire, quick with his hands, released Rothgar and caught her with one fluid motion. The reflexes of a born knight, there . . . must see to his training. And there went Walter, stomping away as though he mistrusted his ability to see this thing through.

Gilbert squawked something nonsensical about treasures and banns, about consanguinity, yammering that the priest said none could marry until after Easter day. "Think this over, my lord," Gilbert urged, using a form of address long abandoned between the two of them. "This man is your enemy. The woman, a troublemaker. They will conspire against you, and all manner of ill will is sure to result."

"I think this solves more problems than it creates. You and I will speak at length later," Hugh said, knowing Gilbert would, as always, back away when confronted. True to form, Gilbert snorted with disgust and stalked from the hall, moving in a staggering, weaving gait quite unlike his usual forceful strides. Longing for the quiet of the room he shared with Eadyth, Hugh turned his aching head toward the priest. "Do you require a special book, Sir Priest?"

"Not for this," Father Bruno answered.

Hugh noted that the young squire, sharp-eyed once again in spotting a need, had his hand at Rothgar's elbow and guided him, stiff-gaited and ashen-faced, toward Helwyth. Rothgar no doubt found himself struck speechless, overwhelmed by Hugh's generosity, but Hugh needed no emotional outburst thanking him for repaying the debt. The crowd of Saxons smiled and nodded their approval of the outcome.

Rothgar jerked free of the squire's grip and planted himself before Hugh with the wide-legged stance of a fighting man, provoking a flood of caution and a corresponding increase in the aching of his head. The smiling, nodding Saxons caught sight of the confrontation and grew still.

"You say you owe me a debt, Lord Norman," Rothgar's voice rang strong and clear. "I ask you to give me your sister Maria in marriage."

The collective gasp that rose from the Saxons couldn't mask Hugh's roar of agonized outrage. Blustering, sputtering for words to quell the Saxon upstart, he found himself struck speechless while the Saxon spoke on.

"I will protect Helwyth and her son, but 'tis your sister I love."

"Silence!" Hugh roared, finding his voice at last. A fearsome pounding commenced within his head, as though tiny men swung pickaxes at the backs of his eyeballs. Was every man in the hall determined to thwart his will on this, his first day in the lord's chair? And his sister, had she been dallying with one of the enemy to encourage him thus? He fought for breath, ignoring Eadyth's fluttering concern. "You overreach yourself, Saxon. I'll see her to a nunnery ere I wed her to one such as you."

"Hugh, please—" Maria began, but he silenced her with a wave of his hand.

"What—do you plan to speak of love for this defeated cur, Maria? Once before I saw you wed to a landless, piss-poor man. I'll not do it again. Things are different now, my sister. I have lands and money and can do better for you."

"Hugh—"

"Enough! One more word, and I'll lop off his head."

"I love her, Lord Norman. Do not make—"

Hugh clapped his hands over his ears. "If you love her, then hold your tongue, or I'll wring her neck as well. Dead or in a nunnery, 'tis much the same to me." He freed his ears when Rothgar paled and stepped back a pace. "Much better, Saxon." Narrowing his eyes to give the tiny pickax men less light to work by, he glared out at his people. "Now. I have given my orders. Sir Priest, you have a wedding to perform. I'll bode no further delay."

Hugh caught Eadyth's hand within his. He must needs see this through ere escaping to the bedchamber. His throbbing head and a pervasive lassitude gripping his limbs from the unaccustomed activity made it unlikely he would savor the joys of marriage this night; looking upon the swaying Helwyth, it seemed Rothgar of Langwald would pass his time in an equally chaste manner. So Maria fancied the man; lucky thing he'd regained his senses so he could find a more suitable fellow for her. All in all, a good day's work, this. No man could have done better.

Langwald's people, somber since the Norman occupation, seized upon the hastily arranged wedding as an excuse to double their merriment. With none of the solemn reverence usually present during the performance of a holy sacrament, they sang and danced, shouting their approval, so that Father Bruno's words binding Rothgar to Helwyth for all eternity could scarcely be heard above the din.

Not that Maria wanted to hear the words spoken. Father Bruno himself seemed flustered by the noise, mumbling phrases unlike any she'd ever heard used in a marriage ceremony, stumbling over Rothgar's name, even casting broad winks from his far eye toward Rothgar, but perhaps that was the way of things when Saxons pledged their troth.

No matter. While her mind reeled, refusing to believe what her eyes were seeing, while her lips continued to mouth soundless, empty denials, Father Bruno made the sign of the cross over the wedded couple, sealing the eternal vows.

It was finished. Hugh and Eadyth took their leave, heading for the sanctuary of their bedchamber. Time to stifle the contradictions that choked Maria, the cries of, "It should be me!" and, "We were to leave together, this very night!" Too late to heed the premonition of doom Rothgar had hinted at, too late to wish they'd stolen away in the night.

She would go to her grave remembering the sight of him standing, head bowed toward Helwyth before the priest. Upon her mind would forever be burned the image of Rothgar twisting Gilbert's shoulder while he clutched Helwyth's child in his arm, of Rothgar leaping at Gilbert's throat, stopped only by the intercession of Gilbert's squire.

Maria knew Rothgar loved her; his brave confrontation with Hugh proved he loved her, but the bonds holding him to the lady who was now his wife stretched far beyond anything Maria could ever know with him. She remembered the day in the courtyard, the young boy calling him Father, Rothgar's yearning, riveted expression upon Helwyth's tear-streaked face.

He was lost to her.

She heard his voice now, calling, "Sarah, Gwynneth," into the now-quiet hall. Two women hurried forth. They reached for Helwyth, and he released her with a look of tender regret, his gaze following as the women hurried his new wife from the hall. As though his release of Helwyth were a signal, the villagers found seats among the makeshift tables. Kitchen lads and wenches ran into the hall, bearing steaming trenchers of food, and soon none noticed that only Maria and Rothgar still stood, staring at each across the expanse of Langwald Hall.

He took one step toward her; she one step toward him. And another. And then another. How tall he seemed! How wide his shoulders, how well-shaped his form, how impossible to reconcile this glorious, virile man with the half-starved wretch lying at her feet such a short time ago. And yet even then she'd been drawn to him, as she was now.

"Sarah's a bone setter, and Gwynneth will soothe her hurts with herbs," he said when they were close enough to speak without shouting.

"I did not know they possessed such skills," she said, wincing at the inanity of their conversation, but helpless to make it otherwise, lest she let loose with the tears stinging her eyes. "We had need of their service for Stephan and Robert."

"You shall have it in future."

A short, uncomfortable silence gripped them.

"Are you afraid, Maria?"

Yes! she longed to scream. *Of Gilbert, of life without you.* But she only said, "Hugh now stands ready to protect me, it seems."

"Would that he had listened to me." Rothgar frowned, seeming unimpressed with her effort to dismiss her fears. His words came out garbled and hoarse, as though he'd had to force them around an obstacle.

"Rothgar, do you love her?"

"Love Helwyth?" He looked away, concentrating on the fire. "Respect, mayhap, and admiration for her fortitude."

His words fell like stones upon her heart. Respect, admiration—those emotions had a way of blurring into a kind of love over time. Not passion, perhaps, but a certain sense of comfort, a feeling of belonging.

Her marriage with Ranulf had been much the same. So she knew well enough how things would go with Rothgar and Helwyth. There might be a slight constraint between them at first, particularly if they had ended their earlier union under less-than-friendly circumstances. And Rothgar might spend a few nights staring across Langwald's acres toward the hall, and then the castle, remembering Maria.

Until Helwyth healed.

One night Helwyth would welcome him back into her bed. Other children would arrive to join the boy, and one day Maria would spy Rothgar amongst a crowd of laborers, work-roughened, careworn, wondering at the passion that seemed bound to kill her just now; he would look upon her, grown sour and bitter, and think his Helwyth the better woman.

Or Maria might share illicit passion with him, seeking ways to admit him to her bed at night, claiming him as her personal body servant. Sinful, unholy thoughts, but rousing her blood and raising a wild, pattering beat in her heart.

"I must go to her and see how she fares."

Maria's throat ached with the effort of holding back her hurt, with deliberately shattering that sinful, wayward dream. He would always have to go to Helwyth; he must always be concerned with how she fared.

"Go, then," she said, her voice hoarse and aching.

He expelled a quivering breath, such as a man might do when struck midsection by an opponent's clenched, mailed fists. For the first time since he became another's husband, he met her gaze. The hopeless desolation clouding his blue eyes so exactly reflected the agony gripping her heart, she felt she could swoon from the force of the shared emotion. And, shame upon shame, a sudden, fierce pang of desire shot through her, leaving her trembling and yearning for his forbidden touch.

"It seems we are doomed to be ruled by devotion to our brothers. Ah, Maria—" his voice caught and he looked away from her, "you know 'tis you I love."

She longed to throw herself against him, to feel his long, strong arms enfold her one last time, but she grew conscious of furtive glances, knowing smirks directed at them. God curse this constant awareness of her position! "Loyalty to my brother's cause kept me from you one day too long, Rothgar," she said, "but I did not know you had a brother, or what purpose you have in raising his presence."

He gave a short, disbelieving bark of laughter. "You did not know that Helwyth was my brother's wife?"

"How could I know?" she whispered, pressing trembling fingers against her lips. "Then the child, the boy, he is not your son?"

"My brother's wife, my brother's son," Rothgar answered. "I cannot believe—even now, when the deed is done—that Father Bruno blessed this unholy union. Maria, God curse me forever for saying this, but I can never be husband to Helwyth. My heart, my soul, everything within me longs for you. There must be a way for us to be together."

Between their feet lay a hand-span of floor, a clump of rushes, nothing more. Yet never had two people, Maria felt sure, been more thoroughly separated. She felt Rothgar's heat, smelled good honest work upon him, even sensed his frustration and love pouring over her in invisible waves. Less than one step and she could crush her breasts against the wide expanse of his chest—but never again could she touch him. Loyalties, circumstances, even God, had conspired to keep them apart.

Until the night? With Langwald's people abed, God's own sky darkened, what was to stop her from joining Rothgar in the night?

So loud was the hammering of her heart that she

didn't notice Walter standing beside her until he spoke.

"Is this Saxon dog preventing you from going to table, my lady?"

Walter had returned to the celebration and now gripped the handle of his sword, ready to unsheathe it should she give the word. His ruddy countenance darkened. Like most of the Normans, he'd adopted the Saxon custom of wearing a beard, and his reddened face contrasted unattractively with his grizzled whiskers. He seemed agitated out of proportion to the day's events. Maria's hand, denied the touch of Rothgar that it craved, seemed numb and unfeeling when she pressed it atop Walter's to calm him and stay his sword.

"I am not hungry, Walter. Let him be."

"He should be in chains. Gilbert is right about him. He's apt to run off and join the rabble outlaws, causing all manner of mischief. How could Hugh have done this?" The hatred in Walter's voice reminded Maria of the knight's unremitting loyalty to Hugh.

"Taking Helwyth to wife holds me tighter than any chains, Norman," Rothgar said. "I must needs guard my neck in order to protect hers. I give my word, you'll have no trouble from me."

"Coward," Walter spat.

"Walter! Rothgar!" The two bristled at each other, their rage an almost palpable thing in the air. Maria flung herself between them. She leaned into Rothgar, closing her eyes and savoring the feel of him against her despite the tension rippling about them. For an all-too-brief moment, he gripped her shoulders and bent his head, whispering so softly in her ear that she wasn't sure she'd heard it aright:

"Midnight. I will meet you in the shed."

"Hiding behind a woman's skirts," Walter sneered.

"A thing I learned from Normans," Rothgar shot back even as he pulled Maria protectively behind him.

Father Bruno's voice put a halt to their dangerous bickering. "Rothgar! If you have finished with your discussion, Helwyth has need of you. Ease her mind if she frets for the child. Britt's wife will keep him while Helwyth mends."

Walter dropped his hand from his sword. Rothgar tightened his grip on Maria's arm, and then released it slowly, dragging his fingers down her sleeve. With naught but an anguished, heated glance at her, he went with the priest.

And left her shivering, longing, aching for him.

Waves of shame coursed through her. Surely everyone in the hall had heard Rothgar's declaration of love, had borne witness to the wanton way in which she'd clung to him, could sense the need that gripped her still. Her teeth chattered and she gripped her arms about her, as though to ward off a chill, when what she sought was to shield herself against temptation.

Midnight. In the shed. Oh, how gladly she would race across the fields, knowing he awaited her!

She, Maria de Courson FitzHerbert, would willingly become a married Saxon's whore. Stealing the clothes of a nun, scorning God's law, anything, just to be with him. How long could it last, though, before each grew to despise the lack of honor in the other? Rothgar had already suspected her motives on nights when she couldn't slip away. Would it be her turn when he found himself unable to meet her, would she imagine him lying entwined with Helwyth while she spent cold, empty nights alone in her bed?

"Nay."

She must have spoken aloud. Walter, the color receding from his face, stared at her with puzzlement. "My lady?"

"I—" *I cannot do it,* she cried silently. *I cannot be his whore.*

But she would. Again and again, whenever he beckoned, powerless to stay away from him. Unless she could find a sanctuary, a place to hide, an unbreachable enclosure to contain her unholy lusts. A sanctuary such as the one offered her this very day by the abbess of Marston, the very nunnery Hugh wielded like a threat.

"I must speak with the lady Eadyth, and then . . . then I must go away. My brother spoke of sending me to a nunnery. Very well, this night I will ride to my new home with the abbess of Marston and Sister Mary Innocent."

"I will accompany you, my lady."

Walter, ever thoughtful, seemed to sense her desperation, for he made no plea asking her to reconsider. Indeed, he seemed quite pleased at the thought of escorting her to the convent; he no doubt feared for their safety. Very well, his strong arm would be welcome if they chanced upon the Saxon outlaws. But more important, his presence would dampen any desire Maria might feel to break her journey and rush back to Rothgar's arms. She knew she could not humiliate her brother before one of his men.

"Thank you, Walter. We will leave as soon as the sisters have eaten their fill. Do you think we shall need a larger escort?"

"Fear not, my lady," Walter assured her. "I can take care of you."

* * *

Helwyth rested comfortably in the back of the wagon, the two healing women fluttering solicitously over her, heaping hay beneath her splinted arm, cushioning her head with a hay-stuffed woolen clout. Rothgar slumped at the end of the wagon bed, hands dangling against his knees, unwilling to share Father Bruno's abrasively cheerful company on the more comfortable driver's bench. So leaden was Rothgar's spirit, so heavy his thoughts, that his body weighed as though cast in stone. Even the wagon's rough ride over frozen turf could not jostle him from his uncertain perch.

The last traces of daylight left the sky until only the bright beacon of the full moon lit the road. Morosely, he watched the rutted, frosted ground pass beneath him. The clods of earth crumbled beneath the wagon wheels; his dreams met a similar fate, each creaking, spine-jarring turn of the wheel crushing his hope, grinding his hopeless love into common dirt. Married less than an hour and riding to his wife's bed with adultery already planned and oh, so eagerly anticipated. What other commandments might he break ere the sun rose on the most holy of days?

Murder. He could ignore God's command "Thou shalt not kill." Find a sword, and, sometime between sneaking away from his wife and joining his love, lop the head from Gilbert Crispin. Dead, the Norman was no threat to Helwyth, to Maria, to Hugh. One stroke of the wrist, maybe two if the Norman's neck proved exceptionally stubborn, and none need fear him again.

But ten, twenty Gilbert Crispins could lie moldering in the grave, and Rothgar would still be married to Helwyth. And for that, there was no easy remedy, no magic sword to sever the bond God had wrought.

He caught the scent of woodsmoke just as Father Bruno slapped the reins against the horse and urged it on with a chirping whistle. Rothgar gripped the sideboard with his arm to keep his balance, wondering, as the horse trotted to the cottage, at Helwyth's extravagance. Smoke puffed through the thatch. Firelight gleamed through gaps in the shutters. How had she managed, bruised and broken as she was, to build such a roaring blaze? Had the pain addled her senses, causing her to forget to douse the flame and bank the embers while she made the long walk to Langwald?

The door to the hut flew open. Illuminated in the light stood his brother Edwin.

"Rothgar!" cried Edwin.

The sight of the brother he'd thought dead and the glad welcome in his familiar voice stunned Rothgar into silence.

"Ah, ye did it, my poor girl," Edwin crooned, shouldering his way past a dumbstruck Rothgar to gather Helwyth into his arms.

"She did it, indeed," boasted Father Bruno. "I shall give you a full accounting."

"First get her into her bed, and mind the arm," said Sarah.

Working with quick, silent efficiency, they eased Helwyth onto her pallet, leaving Rothgar standing in speechless confusion. Edwin crouched to one knee at her side, holding her good hand within his as she smiled wanly at him. The two healing women looked on with the fond, head-tilted smiles of indulgent mothers while Father Bruno rubbed his hands together before the fire, with the air of a man well satisfied with what he saw.

"God's teeth, will someone tell me what goes on here?" Rothgar roared, finding his tongue at last.

"Ah, Rothgar." Edwin tore his attention from Helwyth and gestured about the hut. "Sit. Fortify yourself ere you leave."

"Leave?" Rothgar repeated. Surely Edwin could not know of his planned assignation with Maria.

Father Bruno pushed a neat bundle toward Rothgar's foot. "Here you go, Rothgar. Food enough for a week, I dare say. You'll make good progress in your journey before you needs must forage for more."

"Are you all mad? There is no journey in my future. I am wed to Helwyth now."

"How could you think so, Rothgar? You know she is Edwin's wife." Father Bruno frowned at him with disapproval.

"Aye, that she is, my poor girl," agreed Edwin.

Rothgar pointed at Father Bruno. "Knowing Edwin lived, you stood before me and spoke the vows."

"I did not." Father Bruno straightened to his full height. "I quoted my favorite passage from Saint Augustine's *Confessions*. Do you not know the difference between that famous work and sacred marriage vows, Rothgar?"

Father Bruno might have stood on his head and recited Druid chants for all the attention Rothgar had paid to the marriage ceremony.

Now the priest shuffled his feet, glancing down with a sheepish smile. "I'll admit I had some concern about religious *intent*. Father Bolsovor and I have wrested with this matter without conclusion, though not specifically over your situation, so to be sure I called you Edwin throughout."

"He called you Edwin. I heard him," said Sarah.

"As did I," Gwynneth confirmed.

"And I winked, Rothgar. Did you not see—"

"Enough!" Rothgar shouted. And then quieter, "Enough." He rubbed a rough hand over his eyes, feeling the excited tremor travel through him at the implications of what he'd just learned.

"I am not married?"

"You are not," said Father Bruno.

"And my brother is alive."

"I should hope so," said Edwin.

They all gaped at the vibrant, exultant yelp that accompanied his joyous leap, the slap of his palm against the thatch for good luck. Maria! This news would wipe the stark pain from her eyes. Tonight, when he held her in his arms, he could explain everything.

"Why?" he asked, knowing a silly grin stretched his lips.

"To rescue you, of course," said Father Bruno. "You were doing such a poor job of it on your own."

Edwin explained. "Now you are here, away from their clutches, and you can claim your freedom. We schemed this plot together, the three of us, just this morn. My poor girl clenched her teeth I'm sure to pull it off ere fainting from her hurts."

Never, thought Rothgar, had a man been less appreciative of a rescue attempt. He tried to summon a grateful smile, feeling guilty at Edwin's eager expectancy, at Father Bruno's proud-puffed chest, at Helwyth's pain-wracked smile, but God's teeth, he wished they had left well enough alone.

"We thought, too, that Edwin might pretend to be you once you're gone," said Father Bruno. "The two of you are much alike. With luck, they'll not notice the difference."

Rothgar doubted that plan's success, but then again, the one with the most intimate knowledge of his face and form would be safely away from here, at his side. Hugh had had but one good look at him, and Walter wasn't likely to trouble himself with the farming activities of a peasant. That left only Gilbert.

"I daresay Helwyth has more strength and courage than most men," Rothgar said, shaking off his doubts and regrets. He touched Edwin's arm with a rough, brotherly gesture. "You must tell me how it is you've sprung from the dead."

Listening to Edwin speak was like reliving the hopeless campaign at Harold's side: the din of battle, the choking, coppery scent of blood, fear and pain clawing at men's souls while the deadly shower of Norman arrows felled their partners-at-arms.

"The Normans left me for dead," said Edwin. "I could see all was lost. So I headed for home."

Along the way he'd taken up with a group of outlaws, stealing what they needed to stay alive, causing what damage they could among the Normans they chanced across.

"That last group we tangled with ran me down and tossed me into a stinking hole they called an *oubliette* out past Kenwyck way. 'Twere naught but a dry well with walls so steep and smooth a cat couldn't climb to the top. I tell you, Rothgar, there were times I'd have traded my soul for a breath of clean air, a drink of water."

"I understand, brother," Rothgar said, his voice gruff. "It seems we both made our escape from Norman holes."

"Oh, I walked out a free man." Edwin said. "'Tis Eastertide. Can you fathom? One of their priests said we must be turned loose a sennight back, named some outlaw set free during the time of Christ and said Normans could be no less merciful. I tell you, their ugly faces liked to split asunder at the sight of us walking free."

"How long have you been here, Edwin?"

"Since yesterday, with demons chewing at my guts when I saw the lay of things here." Edwin lowered his head toward Helwyth and planted a light kiss upon her forehead.

"I had no thought for anyone save my poor girl here," Edwin said, tears choking his voice as he gazed with guilty sorrow upon Helwyth's moaning form. "I flew straight here like a duck back from winter, and saw the Norman with her. Oh, that were a hard thing to take, Rothgar."

Edwin's voice cracked, but he cleared his throat and went on. "I meant to kill him, soon as he was well away from her and the boy. I feared what he might do to them should I burst in when they were within his reach. It like to wrenched my heart out, knowing what was going on with my wife. I heard her screaming and thought he was pleasing her right good. I swear I never realized a man could do such villainous things to a woman. I should have known, God forgive me, I should have known."

"How could you have known?" Rothgar asked, seeking to comfort his gentle brother.

"I should have known from the first, when I recognized his cowardly, back-stabbing face. All those months ago I saw that same Norman whoreson clout his own lord upon the head. A man who does such and then casts the blame upon an innocent man knows no depths to his dishonor." A tear seeped from his eye; Edwin made no move to wipe it away. "Poor Lord Hugh. I doubt he knew such a black-hearted viper nested in his own den."

"Lord Hugh? You saw his own man attack him?" Rothgar remembered the vague suspicion he'd felt when Maria described the attack that felled Hugh.

"Aye, his own man. 'Course, I didn't know he was our lord Hugh then. I but saw a brown-haired Norman knight drop like he'd been pole-axed, and the Norman whoreson what bashed his head grabs me by the scruff of the neck and says I'm the one what did it. That's when they tossed me into the hole. I confess to being afraid, Rothgar. If I went after him while he was with my poor girl, it would be back to the *oubliette* for me, and God alone knows what manner of punishment he'd have taken upon her. Just look at what he did to her, for no good reason. I heard her screams last night, and found my son huddled outside in the cold this morning. I should've burst in on him whilst he had his chausses down."

Rothgar's thoughts swirled through his mind, with fear for Maria at the forefront. Let Edwin castigate himself for being a fool; Rothgar felt even more so, knowing the depths of Gilbert's depravity and leaving Maria behind to fend for herself, with naught but a jar of herbal ointment and a muddle-headed brother for protection. A thought, outrageous and only half-formed, flitted through his mind. He confronted Father Bruno.

"Will you tell me now what you know of the outlawing and destruction going on at the castle?"

"Bah, I can tell you that," Helwyth summoned strength enough to spit onto the dirt floor. "Whoreson Norman doing it his own self, with the help of some rough 'uns from past Stillingham way. Pays our men to mess about and have a bit of fun, he does."

"The same Norman?"

"Aye."

The knowledge cast new light upon the villagers' reluctance to name the guilty party.

"You must be willing to stand up and admit these things, Edwin. You, too, Helwyth."

"Just give us the chance, and we'll shout it from the top of that castle you're helping them build."

"You'll not have that long to wait." Rothgar looked quickly about the hut. "What manner of weapon did you plan to use against the Norman?"

"Yon pike always served me well." Edwin inclined his head toward a barb-tipped pole leaning near the door.

"What are you planning, my son?" Father Bruno asked.

"A matter I should have concluded long ago, Father," Rothgar said, gripping the pike, knowing Father Bruno could say nothing to sway him from sending Gilbert Crispin to a kinder death than he deserved.

"Helwyth, you wanted revenge," he said as he hefted the pike in his hand, seeking a comfortable balance. "I swear to bring you his heart. 'Twill be black, no doubt, as black as the hair upon his loathsome head."

Helwyth whimpered in denial.

"Black? No, beneath his helm, his hair is all grizzled and gray," Edwin said.

"Gilbert Crispin's hair is as black as a carrion crow. Sir Walter is the one with grizzled hair."

"Aye, that's the gray-headed devil what clouted his lord and burns the castle's wood, and tupped my wife," said Edwin, nodding. "The whoreson knave called Walter. In league with that bastard Philip Martell."

20

Though Easter marked the stretching of day into night, it was full dark before Maria and the nuns gathered their traveling bundles and made for the stable. Walter greeted them in the courtyard, the lantern he held casting light over a veritable herd of equines: Maria's mare, Walter's own destrier, the two placid donkeys belonging to the nuns, and bringing up the rear, Philip Martell astride his bay gelding.

"Abandoning the festivities so soon, Philip?" Maria asked, not relishing his company on the journey.

"I could not let you travel to the abbey with naught but Walter to protect you, my lady. The night is fraught with danger these days."

"Are you certain you wish *these* men to guide us tonight?" the abbess whispered. "Surely there must be others."

"None I can trust more," said Maria, climbing onto her saddle. Such was her misery that Philip's abrasive presence could be tolerated—nay, welcomed—since it meant he could not be poking about

Hugh's business while she had him well in her sights. She reined in her eager mare so Walter and Philip rode out ahead of her. She studied them as she followed. She'd never noticed before how alike the two of them were, their shoulders much of a size, their height about even, allowing for the difference in horses, their hair glowing the same silvery gray beneath the moonlight. But then, perhaps any mailed, mounted man might cast a similar shadow at night.

In no time, the swifter horses had outdistanced the donkeys. Maria opened her mouth to call out to the knights to slow their pace, but just then the castle foundation loomed in the night. The dark, yawning moat, the heaps of piled wood, the shed where Rothgar promised to meet her at midnight. She averted her eyes and dug her heels into the mare's side, sending her leaping forward, trusting the mare to find safe footing in the dark.

"Lady Maria!" The abbess's call drifted over the night air. Safely past the shed of temptation, Maria tugged at the reins. The mare tossed her head and snorted with displeasure at being held back as the men's horses kept to a trot.

Caught there, between the nuns far to the rear, and the bobbing lantern light marking Walter and Philip's position ahead of her, she felt suddenly vulnerable. The moon seemed to cast a direct beacon down upon her, illuminating her position. The wind teased the trees, sending branches clacking against each other, parting tangles of brush to allow the moonlight to strike against watching, waiting eyes.

"Woods creatures," Maria said aloud.

Wolves, suggested an inner voice.

A cloud scudded across the sky, engulfing the

moon and casting impenetrable darkness over everything. The plodding donkey hoofbeats sounded closer; up ahead, the lantern stood still, as though Walter had noticed her absence and waited for her. The moon freed itself of the concealing cloud and Maria shot a worried glance to the place where wolves might be waiting.

Fen stood at the edge of the woods. The sight of him drove all fear of wolves from her heart. Fen never left Hugh. Had something gone amiss in the brief space of time since she'd left?

The mare, sensing Maria's distraction, snatched the bit into her teeth and bolted toward the Norman war-horses. The sudden motion caught Maria unaware. She sawed uselessly at the reins and then clung desperately to the mare's mane. She managed a quick look behind her, hoping Fen might sense her plight and run to her rescue. But the mysterious, elusive boy-child had vanished into the night, with no glimpse of him running through the trees, no sound of pounding feet to mark his presence.

Perhaps he had never been there.

"The lady Maria—have you seen her?"

"I'll soon make you forget the lady Maria. Dance with me, Rothgar."

Rothgar disengaged his hands from the grasping wench, recoiling from the ale stench surrounding her. All about him, people cavorted, twirling to music, laughing, cramming their faces with food and drink.

"The lady Maria—where is she?"

Britt, his face reddened with pleasure, clapped Rothgar on the shoulder. "Tired of the marriage bed already, Rothgar? Give our Gytha here a try. You liked her well enough in the past."

"The lady Maria—I must speak with her." Resolutely, Rothgar forged his way through the roistering crowd, confronting any who seemed less than fully wine-flown, receiving naught but shrugs and unconcerned smiles in return, until he found himself staggering along the edges of the hall, repeating her name again and again to the rhythm of his thundering heart.

Her alcove stood bare.

He took no time to request permission to enter Hugh's bed chamber. Eadyth shielded her eyes against the sudden light. Hugh slumbered beside her.

"Maria. Where is she? She is in terrible danger." Rothgar's throat, parched with anxiety, near choked at the words.

"She came by here just before Hugh fell asleep." Eadyth's soft words brought a smile to Hugh's slumbering face. "She's gone to the convent, with the nuns. Hugh says he'll fetch her back when she comes to her senses."

Eadyth hid a yawn behind her fist. "She's in no danger, Rothgar. Walter offered to see them safely to the abbey."

Walter rode to help her when the mare's drumming hoofbeats signaled Maria's danger. He caught the reins in his hand and hauled the mare to a stop.

"Oh, Walter." Maria slumped in her saddle, her heart beating erratically after the headlong flight through the chill night. "We must slow our pace. 'Tis not safe to ride so fast in the dark. Besides, the nuns cannot keep up."

"They know the way to the abbey, my lady," Walter said, though he kept his mount to a walk as they rode to join Philip. With a coquettish toss of its head, the mare touched noses with the other horses just as Philip spurred his destrier into a swift trot. Walter grabbed the reins from Maria's hands and urged their horses to follow.

"Nay!" cried Maria, struggling with one hand to regain the reins while grasping for balance with the other. "We must wait for the abbess. She sounds fearful."

"They know the way, Maria," Philip repeated Walter's words. "Besides, nobody would dare accost a holy sister."

"Give me my reins."

In answer, Walter spurred his horse forward.

Philip now carried the lantern, its uncertain beacon diluted by the moonlight. Philip cast it into a ditch, where it glimmered feebly in the dark.

"Lady Maria!" The abbess's voice drifted plaintively through the night. "Those men . . ."

"Walter, please, give me my reins." Maria's heart tapped against her breast, lurching uncertainly to match her tenuous grip on the mare. Never before had Walter acted so. "I am afraid."

"Cling tight, my lady," Walter said, his breath puffing about him. "We fear being followed, and Philip's horse knows its way in this dark."

Maria felt a little better then. What had seemed out of character for Walter now looked to be a sensible precaution. Though Gilbert had not borne witness to their leave-taking, it was possible he'd lurked in the darkness and set out after them. Thank God for Walter, ever thoughtful of her safety.

Obediently, she held tight to the mare's mane.

"Lady Maria! He's the one . . . traitor . . . do not

CONQUERED BY HIS KISS

trust . . ." So faint, so nearly inaudible was the worried cry, that she could not understand all the words.

"I thought Stillingham lay this way, and the abbey lay to the right," Maria said when their small group took the left path at a fork in the road.

"Worry not, Maria. Our destination lies in this direction," said Philip. Walter grunted in agreement.

There was a flicker of movement amidst the trees, a light rustling of leaves along the forest floor. Not a predator, for the horses seemed oblivious to the sounds. It reminded Maria of the eerie, uncertain glimpse of Fen standing near the woods, but as before, she caught no sight of him when she looked over her shoulder.

His life would be forfeit for stealing a horse. No matter. Rothgar raced to the stable. Edwin's nag was no match for the well-bred Norman mounts, so he must help himself to one of their spares if he hoped to catch up with Maria.

Soft lantern light revealed Gilbert Crispin already in the stable wearing mail on his upper body, struggling clumsily to saddle his horse. He turned at Rothgar's noisy entrance, and for a heartbeat their glances met, Gilbert's black and pain-filled, Rothgar's wary and anxious.

Gilbert turned back to his horse. Clenching his teeth, fighting to quell the memory of Maria's bruised arm, Rothgar passed him, seeking a suitable mount. There would be time later to deal with Gilbert.

"I missed her at table. I thought she was with you." Gilbert's voice, quivering with suppressed fury, brought Rothgar to a halt.

"Walter has her."

Rothgar's gaze met that of his enemy's, each reflecting their mutual dismay.

"Good God." Gilbert gripped his horse's neck, looking as if he'd slide to the straw lest he held tight.

"You knew about him all along, did you not?"

"He was not always so, only since William made Hugh lord of this manor. You're no different. Recall what you did to her in the woodcutter's hut."

"Ah, yes." Perhaps it was time to reveal their deception. "It seems we have something in common, Norman—we're both equally guilty of rape."

"But I didn't—"

"Nor did I. It was many things, but it was not rape."

Gilbert expelled a shuddering sigh, a sound conveying an unwilling acceptance of an unpalatable truth. When he spoke, though, no evidence of emotion colored his words.

"Look, Saxon, and see if there's a bay gelding in that stall to your right."

"'Tis empty," Rothgar said with a cursory look at the stall, impressed by the Norman's ability to shake off his personal feelings.

"That means Philip rides with them. I have long suspected some unholy alliance between Walter and Philip. We have no time to waste. You'll have to guard my back while I save Maria in case this cursed weakness slows my sword arm."

"Guard *your* back!" Rothgar roared in outrage. "*I* shall save Maria, you Norman whoreson. Guard your own back, for I intend to bury my pike in it for the hurt you've done her."

"Oh, my, now I must cringe from every shadow

and whirl about in circles to evade your deadly thrust." The Norman chuckled, pleased at his own wit, not noticing the grim determination that suffused Rothgar, paying no heed when Rothgar glided silently across the space separating them.

Gilbert grunted as he tugged the saddle in place. And grunted again with surprise when Rothgar's arm encircled his neck. 'Twould be so simple, Rothgar knew, the mere tightening of his arm and the Norman's windpipe would collapse, his heavy fingers would claw for release, his face would mottle into purple while his body died for the air Rothgar's arm could so easily deny. The Norman grew still, no doubt well aware of the damage Rothgar could inflict.

"Aye, you'd do well to cringe, Norman," Rothgar spat. "'Twould be easy to end your worthless life, but I find no honor in defeating one who pits his strength against women. Besides, if you are right and Philip Martell has joined forces with Walter, it may take the two of us to set Maria free."

A dull flush darkened Gilbert's countenance, the only outward sign showing Rothgar had bested him. "I never meant to hurt Maria. Walter taught me that arm grip."

"It matters naught who taught you, only that you used it against her. Touch her again with harmful intent, Norman, and I shall kill you. I swear it." With a short, forceful motion, Rothgar thrust Gilbert toward his horse.

"She could provoke any man beyond reason," Gilbert muttered, regaining his balance.

Rothgar treated him to a cold, contemptuous glare. "Touch her again and you die. I swear it. Now, muster your strength and courage—we face *men* this night. Which horse among these is swiftest, Norman? Answer true, or I'll slit your throat after I finish with Walter and Philip."

Gilbert gestured toward the far end of the stable. "Hugh's stallion, in the corner. He's not been exercised for days. He'll not accept a Saxon on his back, I'll wager, so mount up. I'll relish the sight of you sailing through the air almost as much as watching you break your neck when you come to ground."

"God put horses on this earth for me to ride," Rothgar said.

"And Saxons for me to spit like a joint of beef."

They might have been two rutting stags, clashing heads while a poacher tracked their doe through the woods. Rothgar shook off his rage, promising to indulge it later.

"Each barb we exchange gives them time to put more distance between us. Let us put aside our differences, Norman, until she is safe."

Gilbert considered for a moment, and then gave a brief nod. "Do you know where they're bound?"

"The abbey."

"I'm near ready," said Gilbert, tugging at a cinch.

Hugh's stallion rolled its eyes and flattened its ears, but such was Rothgar's determination that he had the beast ready to ride before Gilbert gained his saddle.

Gilbert cast a disdainful look upon the pike Rothgar gripped at his side. "Try this, Saxon," he said, tossing a broadsword to him. "Think you can use it?"

"The blood bubbling from your neck will tell me what you think of my skill when I run the blade across your throat," Rothgar answered, pleased with the heft of the weapon in his hand. He mounted the skittish, spirited stallion, mastering the animal with his firm hands and legs. He thought he and Gilbert made most unlikely partners-at-arms as, cursing each other and jostling for position, they tried to force two horses through a doorway built for one.

Philip's horse, apparently forgetting it knew its way in the dark, drove a foreleg deep into a rut. The bone snapped, a sharp, cracking retort that echoed like the snap accompanying a dreaded, earth-sizzling lightning bolt, louder even than the shrill, agonized shrieks from the horse as it pitched forward to its knees.

Maria's mare drew back on its haunches, quivering with fright. Walter dropped her reins, working desperately at his own to keep his horse under control. "Philip!" he called urgently.

"I am not hurt, Father."

Somehow, Philip had managed to fling himself from his horse's back before the great, heavy gelding crashed to the ground. He lay a safe distance from the beast's thrashing legs, his face pressed into the ground so that his words had come out muffled and unclear.

Maria caught her reins, wrapping them tightly about her fist. She'd not relinquish them willingly again, no matter what Walter said. Or what Philip said.

Philip had called Walter Father.

But no, surely she hadn't heard aright. Her eyes and ears had been deceiving her all night: thinking Father Bruno miscalled Rothgar's name during the wedding, thinking she'd heard and seen Fen, even imagining the abbess mistrusted Walter. Perhaps if she lay as Philip did, face plowed into the earth and shuddering from his narrow escape from injury, her cry of Walter might come out sounding like Father, too.

Philip rose now, shaky-legged, brushing the dirt from him.

"Any bones grate as you walk?" asked Walter, his voice husky.

"Just scratches." Philip held out his hands, palms up, revealing dark patches that might be blood, might be tiny rocks embedded in the skin. "Nothing to fret over, Walter."

Nothing to fret over, Maria, she chided herself, happy she'd not embarrassed herself by questioning Walter over what she'd thought Philip had said.

Philip stepped warily behind the wheezing, whimpering horse, crouching down near its head. With a swift motion, the flash of metal glinting in the moonlight, he drew his knife across the horse's throat.

"Sorry to lose that one, I am," he muttered as he came back to them. "Move forward, Maria. I'll ride behind you."

A wave of revulsion passed through her. "This mare is too fine-boned to carry two over any distance."

"I'll not walk."

"You take her, then, and I'll walk." Maria slipped from the saddle in a smooth motion. Better to walk than spend any time with Philip's arms wrapped about her.

"You cannot walk . . . such a distance."

"You said yourself we are close to the abbey."

"Mount up pillion to me, my lady." Walter slapped his horse's broad rump. The deep-seated battle saddle curved upward at Walter's back, offering only a tenuous handhold, but if she pulled her overtunic over the saddle back, it would pull tight against her back and hold her in place.

Maria gripped Walter's hand, taking reassurance in his strength as he easily hoisted her onto her slippery, uncomfortable perch.

"God damn fucking shit!" Rothgar roared. He stood in the stirrups, yanking back with all his strength to bring the plunging, snorting stallion to a halt before it trampled the waiflike creature standing silently before him.

Apparently not content to survive one brush with death, Fen darted before Gilbert's horse, prompting an outraged shriek from the Norman as his mount almost unseated him.

Fen stood in the middle of the road, midway between them. He reached out, touching both horses, stroking their noses, letting them catch his scent until they stood docile and quiet.

"Stand aside, Fen." Rothgar quelled his urge to run the boy down. "We are in a fearful hurry. The lady Maria is in danger."

Fen beckoned toward the woods. The horses turned their heads to follow his hand motion, their ears pricked with interest.

"Out of the way, you abomination of nature!" Gilbert bellowed. He reached for his sword.

"Wait."

No expression crossed Fen's face to mark whether or not he appreciated Rothgar's intercession. He took several gliding, low-to-the-ground paces toward the woods and looked back at them over his shoulder. His hands flashed in the moonlight, meaningless gestures that somehow filled Rothgar with an utter certainty that Fen understood everything of nuns, of knights, of danger. Of Maria.

Maria trusted Fen with Hugh's life.

Fen beckoned, his motions frantic.

Never before had Fen seemed so like the fey woods sprite some claimed him to be. Who better than a trusted woods sprite to guide him to his beloved?

"We go through the forest," Rothgar announced.

"Like hell we do, you Saxon idiot. The abbey lies off this road. Besides, full sun barely penetrates that thicket of trees. We'd never make it through with only the moon to light our way."

"We have Fen to guide us." Tilting his head back and indulging in the full glory of the Saxon battle cry, Rothgar touched his heels to his horse and rode toward Fen.

"God damn you, Saxon, cease that braying and get back to this road!"

"Go along, Norman, dawdle the long way round." Rothgar called over his shoulder. "I'll have matters in hand well before you meander into the fray."

Rothgar smiled at the bellowing curses flung at his back, at the unmistakable sound of hoofbeats closing in behind him. Following Fen, they rode into the woods. Fen's hand trailed behind him; Rothgar's mount followed, muzzle outstretched. Gilbert's destrier huffed nose-to-tail with Rothgar's.

The forest closed about them like an eggshell encases its yolk. Thick, murky air stilled all noise, save the heavy tread of hooves against leaf-coated dirt, the jingling of harness, the snorting breaths of their mounts.

No light pierced the pervasive gloom. Dark, vague shapes that might be trees and nappy black areas of nothingness seemed to swirl before Rothgar's befuddled eyes. When it seemed the darkness was absolute, Fen led them unerringly into a deeper, blacker void. Branches and vines and things making one grateful for blindness trailed over Rothgar's face, his arms, his legs.

Gilbert's breathing became audible, harsh, gasping gulps that told Rothgar the Norman shared his sensation of having suddenly gone blind. Added to this uneasy feeling came a niggling doubt, goaded by his intuitive sense of direction, that Fen's path carried them away from the abbey, that their sightless travel led them ever farther from Maria. God's teeth, he should have heeded the Norman.

He felt an irrational urge to lash out at the pervasive blackness, to push against its unyielding, impenetrable gloom. His blood roared through his veins, his very heartbeat pounded in his ears. So might a man's sensations be reduced, having been buried alive, struggling against a coffin lid weighted down by heavy, immovable earth.

Abruptly, the smothering darkness lightened, the sense of suffocation lifted. Moonlight glimmered tentatively through the thinner trees. Fen moved with sure-footed speed, the horses breaking into a canter to keep pace. An open field beckoned, and the narrow ribbon of a road.

A small group stood illuminated in the moonlight, one hopping man trying to gain a foothold in the stirrup of a horse turning prancing, evasive circles around him, and another already mounted, with a pillion rider up behind. Fen gestured toward them and then took a step back, seeming to melt into the surrounding trees. A brisk breeze kicked up, sending a few dry leaves skittering over the frozen field, lifting a strand of the pillion rider's hair.

"Maria!"

Rothgar dug his heels into the stallion's sides, but

it was as if Fen's disappearance reminded the beast of its supposed resistance to Saxon riders. While Gilbert charged ahead, Rothgar fought against his horse's stiff-legged, hump-backed attempts to dislodge him, its ferocious thrashing as it kicked its heels.

He regained control, but not before Gilbert crossed more than half the space separating them from Maria. Rothgar slapped the reins against the horse's neck, praying for a burst of speed. Together, he and the Norman stood a chance; it mattered naught who reached Maria first, only that she be set safely aside while they dealt with the traitorous Walter and Philip. His horse, now scenting battle, plunged eagerly ahead, needing no further urging. Gilbert rode straight for Walter and Maria, looking as though he intended to ram his destrier right through Walter's horse.

Maria's eyes widened when she recognized Gilbert. She fumbled at her waist, drawing her hand back and then holding it aloft. Moonlight shimmered against a dagger's blade, the decorative jewels in its hilt glittering and sparkling as she made to bury it deep in Gilbert's fast-approaching neck.

"Maria, no!"

Curse these ears of hers! What cruel trick of fate ordered them to continue their deceiving ways, especially now, when all her senses must be focused against the feral, onrushing Gilbert Crispin? Mad laughter bubbled from his lips; he hunched low over his horse's neck, his sword held aloft, heading straight for her. But instead of terror sending her heartbeat skittering, it was the cursed deception of her ears, cruelly tricking her into thinking it was Rothgar she heard crying out in the night, making her blood sing, her senses reel.

Rothgar, crying, "Maria, no! Gilbert means you no harm."

Aha! Certain proof demons had taken control of her ears. And her mind. Overriding all instinct for self-preservation, urging her to tear her gaze from Gilbert, wasting precious, possibly life-saving time in probing the moonlit road for the sight of a man who couldn't possibly be there.

"Maria!"

Her ears hadn't deceived her. He was there, charging at them astride Hugh's stallion, his mount's superior speed closing the distance between them, near standing in the stirrups as he brandished a broadsword over his head, a blood-chilling cry spilling from his lips. Walter cursed, his horse plunging frantically beneath them as they eluded Gilbert's sword. Maria clung to the saddle, almost losing her dagger, missing her chance at Gilbert's neck. She cringed low when Rothgar burst past them. His sword bit hard where Gilbert's had missed, whistling through the air to hack deep into Walter's arm, bringing forth a bellow of mingled rage and pain unlike any she'd ever heard from him.

Rothgar thundered past, rapidly crossing the short distance between Walter and Philip. With the flat edge of the sword he walloped Philip across the back, knocking him to a senseless heap upon the ground.

"Get down, Maria," Rothgar called, near breathless, fighting against his mount's eagerness to kick at Philip. "Get away so we can engage battle. Run."

"Why did you strike Walter?"

Rather, had Rothgar bloodied Gilbert's arm! But Gilbert sat his horse, catching his breath, alert but making no move toward her, seeming to prove Rothgar's wild statement that he meant her no harm.

Walter laughed, a low, ugly sound.

Rothgar succeeded in wheeling the horse about. "Trust me, Maria. Walter is your enemy!"

"Walter? Nay—"

"Tell her how you smote her brother in the head, Walter, and how 'twas your paid assassins who attacked us near the woodcutter's hut. Tell her how Philip's minions plunder Langwald and cast suspicion upon Langwald's people," Rothgar taunted.

"And tell her how you raped and beat the Saxon woman and blamed it on me," shouted Gilbert.

Quivering and uncertain, she sought a denial from the man she trusted. "Walter? This cannot be true."

"Silly bitch," Walter said. "We'll see whether your idiot brother likes having one of his women stolen from him, as he stole Helwyth from me this night." He made a clumsy, groping motion toward her with his uninjured arm, but seated behind him as she was, she made an awkward target. Sudden fear clenched her vitals; a lifetime of affection and faith argued against the evidence of her eyes and ears. She sought to free her overtunic from the saddle back so she could slide from the horse's broad rump and run as Rothgar said, but Walter succeeded in grasping hold of her garment.

Gilbert spurred his horse, approaching from the right. Rothgar lunged from the left. They looked as if they meant to smash Walter between them, but Walter urged his horse forward, somehow managing to hold on to her and guide the beast, cackling maniacally and gibbering of ransom.

"Oh, Walter," she whispered, wrapping her arms around him and resting her cheek against his back, listening to his traitorous heart beat once, twice, three times before she plunged her dagger into the side of his neck, shrinking away and crying, her tears mingling with Walter's hot, salty blood.

Gilbert kicked his horse when the Saxon reached Maria first and snatched her up into the saddle before him, wrapping his arms about her and burying his face against hers as though she were a river, he a land-flopping fish. Walter's horse, confused by the loss of its rider's touch on the reins, circled anxiously, coming up hard against the Saxon's mount, sending Walter sprawling to the ground. The Saxon swine's lips were so hard-pressed against Maria's that no sound of triumph over unseating a knight escaped.

Gilbert looked away, knowing he must master the rage that welled within him at the sight.

Give the Saxon credit for being a good man in a fight. Philip still lay where he'd fallen, his shoulder somewhat askew as though Rothgar's blow had separated it from its rightful position. He'd handled Hugh's stallion well, too, far better than Gilbert himself could have done, given the trembling weakness that seized his limbs from time to time. The Saxon's skill worried him. He meant to kill Rothgar and had hoped the Saxon would not know how to defend himself against a mounted attack.

Funny, how tonight's exertions left him stronger and more clear-headed than he'd felt in days, despite missing his daily application of ointment, Maria's soothing hands against his skin.

Her hands—where were they now?

He whirled, and saw Maria and the Saxon silhouetted against the moon-streaked sky. They had dismounted, the horse wandering and sniffing hopefully against the frozen ground. The Saxon's head bent toward hers, his huge, clumsy thumbs wiping tears away from her face as he murmured soft words.

"Not married?" Maria's sharp, delighted cry rang out.

"No, 'twas a trick. We can still . . ."

Gilbert closed his ears to their conversation, wishing he could shield his eyes as well. She clung to Rothgar, her nether reaches pressed wantonly against his hips, her hair hanging down her back as she smiled up into his brutish face.

The comfortable, familiar red mists settled in, seething through his mind and mercifully blocking the details of their embrace from his sight. *His* betrothed—she had sworn her troth to him in the woodcutter's hut. He had curbed his impatience, falling prey to her lies. It was clear to him now. She'd lain with the Saxon of her own will! His hand curled around his sword hilt. One thrust, now, while the only weapon on the Saxon's mind was the puny thing between his legs.

Gilbert shook his head. Tempting as the thought might be, it would only lead to disappointment. She'd fling herself atop the Saxon's bleeding, dying body, declaring eternal love. He'd seen it happen time and again. No, far better to separate them. Once she was away from him, she'd come round. He'd seen that time and again, too—women railing against forced marriages, against slavery. They grew to accept their lot; some even reveled in it after a while.

It should be easy enough to outwit the Saxon. After all, Normans had conquered all the English with scornful ease. He dismounted and gripped Philip by his displaced shoulder, provoking low moans and much thrashing of the head. He left him lie, and then went to prod Walter with his foot, prompting only a low grunt. He kicked him hard, this time earning a loud groan.

"They live," Gilbert called. "Let us question them."

Lured by the notion of learning what motivated Walter's perfidy, the couple approached, Rothgar's arm draped possessively over Maria, she clinging to him like a tick on a deer.

"You were Hugh's man. Why did you try to kill him?" Gilbert shouted into Walter's ear.

"Go to hell, Crispin."

Gilbert shrugged. He returned to Philip and gripped his wrenched shoulder, twisting it until he screamed and sweat beaded upon his brow. Maria gave a small cry and clung tighter to the Saxon, causing Gilbert to twist harder, even though Walter was blubbering, "Stop, I'll tell you what you want to know."

A simple, heart-wrenching tale, Gilbert thought dispassionately. Maria and Rothgar certainly seemed caught up in it, allowing him to surreptitiously gather together all of the horses' reins while Walter blurted his story. Who would have thought the old Norman knight had spent such a passionate youth, siring a bastard son—Philip—upon a lady of noble birth? Or that her family had refused to allow them to marry—but then, considering his treatment of the Helwyth wench, that looked a good decision—and had him exiled for ruining their daughter?

Somehow, Walter had kept track all those years of the boy, taking it to heart when none sponsored him as squire. Taking it hardest of all when Maria and Hugh's father declined to take the youth under his wing. Duke William, a bastard himself, should have understood and forced the issue, but instead consigned Philip to bookish, clerkly duties.

Walter had returned from exile just in time to offer his services to Hugh de Courson, with only half-formed notions of making Hugh pay for his father's long-ago slight in failing to sponsor Philip. And then had come the battle. Walter had held high hopes of reward for both himself and his son, had allowed himself to dream Langwald might be the reward—and then William had granted Langwald to Hugh. Nothing to Walter. Lands so poor the gifting might have been an insult, to Philip.

"Stillingham. Bah. Naught but a pittance," Walter gasped, breathing hard as his life's blood flowed from him. "Miserable acres, while Hugh de Courson picked the plum."

"But William chose to do it that way, Walter." Maria's voice trembled. "Hugh had naught to do with the selection, nor with declining to sponsor Philip in his youth. Why did you try to kill Hugh?"

"Because I meant to wrest away Langwald and Kenwyck for Philip, to repay him for all those slurs of 'bastard' he's endured these many years. Curse that brown-skinned faerie that diverted my blow that day, and curse him again for barring me from Hugh's side so I could not finish the job. Philip should have had Langwald, and my strong arm would have kept it safe for him."

"Well, 'tis over now, old man," Gilbert said.

"It is not," Walter declared, crazed determination lighting his eyes. "'Tis started again. My woman Helwyth, the babe of mine she carries, handed over to yon Saxon. This time I shall fight for what should be mine as long as there's breath in my body."

Gilbert watched Rothgar's mouth settle into a

grim line. Good! Perhaps he might be able to make use of the Saxon's thirst for justice, pitting Rothgar against Walter long enough to distract the Saxon's attention, enabling Gilbert to sever Rothgar's head as he'd planned for so long.

"You finish him, Saxon," Gilbert cajoled. "You've earned the right." Slanting a glance to see whether Rothgar took the bait, he tied the collected reins to the sword sheathe forged to his saddle, securing all four horses.

"No!" Maria laid a beseeching hand against Rothgar's arm, but he gently disengaged it. "There must be another way."

"Don't act the fool, Maria," Gilbert scolded, knowing he must stop her blathering before she swayed the Saxon's mind. "Walter lies there cursing and swearing revenge. You put everyone's life in danger if you let the knave live another day. Remember, you struck the first blow against him yourself."

Rothgar nodded with reluctant agreement. "Though this is not the Saxon way of meting justice, it must be done, my love. He will ever be a threat to you and your brother. Helwyth will never be safe from his lusts. Besides, he's near dead already."

"I—I suppose you're right," Maria cried weakly.

"Come, Maria, you needn't watch," Gilbert soothed falsely. Such was her misery over Walter that she seemed to welcome Gilbert's comforting arm around her shoulder as he pulled her away from Rothgar. She turned into Gilbert's embrace, enabling him to heave her onto his horse and spring up behind her, the sudden thud of his weight against her back turning her cry of alarm into naught but a gasping breath for air.

The Saxon hefted his sword in the air, but now

that Gilbert had Maria where he wanted her, Rothgar seemed to be taking overlong in despatching Walter's soul to the devil. "Let me lend a hand, Saxon," Gilbert cried, urging his horse the few steps to Rothgar's side.

Saxons had fallen at Hastings beneath the superior strength of mounted men. This Saxon would fall now for the same reason. Gilbert lifted his sword, aiming not for Walter, but for the vulnerable juncture between Rothgar's neck and shoulder.

"Gilbert, nay!" Maria roused from her misery, somehow divining his intent, and cried out. She bore down against his arm with all her slight weight, a weight that ordinarily would have deterred his aim not at all, but his limbs were still subject to their cursed weakness. He missed his mark, striking Rothgar's arm instead, helping drive the Saxon's sword deep into Walter's heaving chest, ending the stroke with a satisfying slash into the Saxon's thigh. At once Rothgar's blood flowed, black and shining in the moonlight.

With an exultant cry, Gilbert raised his sword again. And again Maria thwarted his true thrust, so that the strike meant to split Rothgar's head instead struck the Saxon broadside at the back of his skull.

The Saxon toppled like a felled oak.

Gilbert cursed; lest he dismount, he could not drive a sword through the Saxon's head. And if he dismounted, Maria would surely try to escape him.

Still, with the amount of blood leaking from the Saxon's leg, and his own faith in the power of his blow, Gilbert doubted Rothgar would survive. He lay still as death, no muscle moving, not even his breath misting the air.

"Cease your squirming, woman," Gilbert said,

driving an elbow against Maria's skull just hard enough to daze her for a bit as he spurred his mount into a dead run, trailing the other horses. He made no effort to stem the tide of pure pleasure that bubbled forth in laughter. He'd accomplished at least part of what he'd set out to do. The Saxon lay dying as Gilbert stole Maria away into the night.

21

Maria fought. She fought Gilbert's strength; she railed against the cruel fate that miraculously restored Rothgar to her only to pluck her from his arms. She pummeled her heels against the innocent horse, she gouged backward with her elbows. Her nails raked harmlessly against his mailed arms, her teeth gnashed the air when he gripped her hair and tilted her head back, planting heated lips against her neck. She screamed, sobbing with impotent, outraged frustration, while Gilbert laughed, his muscular bulk easily containing her within his arms. Gilbert laughed, the smug, self-satisfied sound drifting back over the barren, moon-flooded fields.

He laughed, the grating, low-throated chuckles diminishing as he slowed the horse to a walk, as her heaving anger subsided into deep, shuddering gulps.

She could not bear leaning against him yet could not maintain her balance without doing so, so she bent forward and encircled the horse's nodding neck with her arms, ignoring the discomfort of the saddle horn prodding her belly, burying her face against the steed's sweating hide.

"Where are you taking me?"

"I am not certain. Stillingham, I suppose, until I can think of something."

"What will you do with me?"

"Only what we agreed, that day in the woodcutter's hut," he said. "I mean to take you to wife."

"Rothgar will come after me." *Make haste, my love,* she prayed.

"Afoot? On a near-severed leg?" Gilbert's malicious laugh rumbled again. "You'll be dandling my babe on one knee with another stretching your belly ere he stumbles upon us again—supposing he doesn't bleed to death first."

"*His* child might grow even now in my womb, and happy I would be to bear it."

"That matters not. Should you bear a babe ere nine months pass from this night, I'll drown it."

Gilbert meant to possess her, then, tonight. And as her futile struggles had shown, her strength was no match for his. Silent, aching tears trickled down her cheeks, melting into the horse's neck.

How wise of the church to call despair a deadly sin. Such was her despair now that she could think what blessed relief it would be to fling herself into the river, just as Gilbert threatened to do with her babe should she bear Rothgar's child. Together, she and her love child could slip into the cool, soothing wetness, and worry no more of crafty kings and hard-won lands and disloyal knights and . . . hopeless, doomed love.

"I promise I will not hurt you, Maria."

As if mere physical discomfort could override this torture of her heart! "I care not what you do to me,

Gilbert," she said, bitterness tingeing her words. "Fling me to the ground and take me now if you will."

"I would not!" His shocked dismay brought an ironic twist to her lips; what knightly code of honor deemed it permissible to hold her against her will but not to claim his spoils in the bare dirt?

"I love you, Maria. I have always loved you." Gilbert's voice sounded oddly strained. "You will come to love me, too."

"Never," she spat.

"Love will come in time."

"The only thing 'twill come in time is Rothgar. And Hugh." Maria raised her head, heartened at the thought. "Aye, Hugh will come, too. The abbess is sure to send warning to Langwald when she finds I never reached the abbey."

"Hugh is unfit," Gilbert said, though a note of uncertainty clouded his speech. "And his knightly force is decimated. None save Dunstan remains."

"Hugh commands every man within Langwald," Maria said with smug assurance. "Your own squire will feel duty-bound to slay you for this, as will the other young men-at-arms."

"Then," said Gilbert, reining the horse to a halt, "I needs must silence the abbess ere she goes to Hugh."

Oh, God, what had she done with her taunting? Surely Gilbert would not seriously contemplate killing a daughter of Christ, and yet his trained eyes raked the heavens, judging their position by the stars. Hauling the horse about, he dug his heels into the mount's sides, spurring it onward toward what she knew in her heart must be the abbey.

A shrill scream from her own beloved mare roused Gilbert's curse. His horse stumbled, its steel-shod hooves striking the mare's forelegs again, but both animals recovered their balance.

"We can make no speed while they're so close tied," Gilbert muttered. Fumbling at the gathered reins, he freed the trailing horses.

For a moment Maria knew a wild surge of hope, that one of the beasts might turn about and head back to where Rothgar would surely be relentlessly limping after them in the dark. But the horses, creatures of habit and herd instincts that they were, ignored their newfound freedom and contentedly followed along behind as though still bound by long, invisible cords to Gilbert's saddle. Even the injured mare hobbled along as best she could, her mournful whinnies carrying over the empty night as the distance lengthened between them.

Maria . . . Langwald . . . Helwyth . . . Edwin . . . Maria . . . Gilbert . . . Maria . . . Maria . . .

Sweetness, heartache, treachery, love . . . all a dream? Rothgar longed to groan against the ache in his head, but he knew that to make a sound, to release a plume of breath, would bring certain death. He must pretend to be like the others surrounding him, stiff and cold and dead, until deep dark, when he might chance his escape from his Norman wardens.

Maria. He could see her in his mind's eye, feel the silken texture of her skin, inhale her sweet essence. No, she was not a dream. He'd escaped the dung heap long ago to find heaven in her arms. So why did his mind plague him with the memory of corpses, why had his flesh and hair raised as if death stalked him? Reluctantly, he forced an eye open, and his senses crept back with the dim moonlight.

'Twas Walter's body he felt stiff and unnaturally chill beneath him.

Shaken and weakened, he rose unsteadily to his feet. Maria. No sign of his beloved. No sign of Gilbert, or the horses. Breathing hard, Rothgar freed his sword and retrieved Maria's dagger, partially embedded in Walter's neck. Gilbert had taken Maria . . . but where? Stillingham, most likely. He cast a practiced eye over the ground. Even frozen, the marks made by four horses showed a clear trail toward Stillingham. With Philip dead, there would be none to deny Gilbert entry and safe haven.

Given the state of his leg and the lightheadedness he knew came from Gilbert's blow coupled with his loss of blood, Rothgar knew he could never make it afoot to Stillingham.

He scanned the empty horizon. No Fen to spirit him mysteriously back to Langwald the short way through the black forest. Traveling crippled, he'd have a beard swinging to his knees ere he made it back along the road to Langwald for help. Nay, his best course would be to make for the abbey. Sister Mary Agnes would concoct a pain-killing draught to help him ignore his aching head and assorted wounds, and the stable was sure to hold a sound mount he could borrow for the journey to Stillingham.

He cut a strip from Walter's tunic and wound it around his thigh, hoping to stanch the bleeding. Limping along, using the sword as an inadequate crutch, Rothgar struck out for the abbey.

"Do not lose heart, my love," he whispered, willing his thoughts to carry to Maria. "I will find you."

* * *

Maria felt the horse slow as they rode into the abbey stable amid a flurry of activity. Black-garbed women clustered around two heaving, bone-tired donkeys, with Sister Mary Innocent the excited center of their attention.

She shrieked when she saw Maria sitting before Gilbert.

"Oh, thank God, my lady! We greatly feared for your safety."

"Where is your abbess?" Gilbert said.

"At prayer, giving thanks," Sister Mary Innocent answered while the other nuns murmured their disapproval of Gilbert's rudeness. "Who are you to speak so to me? You are not one of those who rode escort to my lady earlier this night. Thank God for that, too. We know the younger man to be a traitor to the lady Maria."

So Philip Martell had carried the news of Hugh's condition to the nuns. Maria winced as Gilbert ignored the nun's observation and dismounted, pulling her none-too-gently down behind him. He clamped his hand about her wrist, its viselike pressure biting into her skin. The warning she meant to shout to the nuns dissolved into a whimper of pain.

"Show me the way to the abbess," he ordered.

"I will not." Sister Mary Innocent squared her shoulders. "No man is permitted within the cloister, not even Father Bruno."

"Out of my way, then. I'll find her myself." Towing Maria behind, Gilbert shouldered his way through the ineffectually grasping group of women.

"Do you seek me, Lord Norman?" The abbess's commanding voice halted Gilbert in midstride. He whirled, his hand at his sword hilt. The abbess, her hands clasped around a rosary so that only the cross dangled free, tilted a brow and frowned. "You will not draw your weapon on this consecrated ground."

"He means to kill you, Mother," Maria screamed. With a curse, Gilbert jerked her against him, clamping a fist across her mouth.

The abbess seemed singularly unimpressed. She gestured about her at the hovering nuns. "Before all these witnesses? Reconsider, if you will, Lord Norman. I am sure we can resolve whatever troubles you."

"Cease your blathering, hag," Gilbert spat. "I mean to keep this woman. I'll not stand by while you send to Langwald for reinforcements."

"What do I care whether you keep her or not? And do our poor tired beasts look capable of returning to Langwald tonight?" The abbess cast a scornful glance at Maria, who wilted in despair. Her fleeting hopes dissolved as the abbess continued. "It seems a poor plan to murder me and then haul her thither and yon while the Holy Church seeks its retribution upon you for murdering one of Christ's daughters. Why not just wed her? None will question the how or why of what you do with her then."

"I mean to," Gilbert said, equal measures of stubbornness and uncertainty marking his speech.

"Then God has led you to the right place," the abbess said with a serene smile. "Do you forget that tomorrow is Easter, Lord Norman? Even now Father Bruno will be on his way to celebrate mass at the sunrise on this most holy day. Surely your strong arm can forestall a group of women for such a short time."

"The good priest himself promised to wed us on Monday," Gilbert said, nodding. "Very well. We will bide here awhile."

Gilbert's grip slackened and Maria struggled free of his silencing fist. "Mother, no," she begged. "Do not stand by while he does this."

"Women must make the best of what God sends them," the abbess snapped. "Cease your prattling. God blesses you with an opportunity any sensible woman would grasp this night." She tempered her tone as she addressed Gilbert. "And now, my lord, do you care for some refreshment?"

"Uh . . ." The abbess's quick acceptance of his dominance seemed to have unnerved Gilbert.

"Of course you would," she answered for him. "Sister Mary William, go to the kitchens and warm some of that excellent beef broth. And Sister Mary Agnes—Lord Norman has ridden hard this night. I can see his neck wound pains him. Perhaps you could run to the still room and fetch some of that special ointment the lady Eadyth asked you to prepare the other day."

Rothgar had learned, during his captivity, the valuable trick of disengaging his mind from pain, both of the body and of the mind. His body, leaning hard on the sword, soon found a choppy rhythm: step, thump, drag; step, thump, drag. He let his mind rove where it would: imagining Gilbert Crispin skewered at the tip of this sword, God willing his use of it now didn't blunt its piercing ability; imagining Maria in arms that still tingled from their embrace; cursing himself for falling so neatly into the Norman's trap; Maria, Maria, Maria.

When he saw the mare, it seemed but a partial manifestation of the memory currently occupying his mind, of Maria sitting astride this very mare, Maria's hair blowing wild and free as she stood watch over the work he did for Langwald castle. The mare moved, a short, stumbling step so like his own that he blinked his eyes to clear them. Reins trailed along the ground, and dark, glistening streaks trickled down the mare's forelegs. She snorted and tossed her head when she saw Rothgar, then pawed the ground and neighed accusingly, as if she held him accountable for some misdeed.

"Steady, girl," Rothgar called softly. He pressed the sword against a rein, trapping it against the ground, but the mare made no effort to run from him. She whinnied and pawed the earth, growing restive as he came closer. "What happened?" he crooned, crouching to examine her forelegs. Twin crescents of torn flesh marked each leg just below the knee. "Looks like you've been kicked right well."

Under ordinary circumstances, Rothgar of Langwald would never have mounted an injured horse. He did so now, sighing with relief when his weight left his aching leg. The relief, coupled with his change in position, served to renew his lightheadedness. He shook it off, every ounce of his being determined to find Maria. "We've a hard night's riding ahead of us," he said, slapping the reins and clucking the mare into motion. Toward Stillingham.

But the mare took no more than two halting, stumbling steps when he realized he'd not catch Gilbert Crispin mounted upon this horse. Like himself, Stillingham was beyond the mare's ability given its injuries. Still, its long-legged stride was bound to eat ground faster than his own, and from his vantage point atop its back he could see the pall of smoke escaping through the thatch over the abbey of Marston.

"Give it your best, girl." He sighed and headed toward the abbey, mulling the injustice of the fates that seemed bound to alter his course this night.

22

The abbess accepted a laden tray from one of the nuns and then turned to Maria. "Come, daughter, and help me with this."

"She stays with me," Gilbert said.

"The door can be locked. She cannot escape you."

Maria thought a spider might have difficulty escaping this bare, cheerless cell. No windows broke the dreary gray daubed walls, and the mean fire smoking in the corner did little to warm or brighten the oppressive chill. Even so, if she could but get free of his wrist, there might be a chance, however small.

"Lock it," he said.

The abbess signaled to the nun who had lingered, and the door swung shut behind her to the sound of a metallic bolt being pushed home.

"Daughter?"

"Will you release me so I might assist the Mother?" Maria asked.

With a snort of disgust, Gilbert freed her and went to warm himself before the fire. Rubbing her wrist, Maria went to the abbess, her heart threatening to hammer its way through her throat. Two tankards of beef broth steamed on the tray, the delicious scent wafting through the chill air and setting up a rumbling in her stomach. Next to the tankards sat a bowl of salt and the pot of ointment the abbess had bid Sister Mary Agnes to fetch, a duplicate of the one she'd used so effectively to diminish Gilbert's strength. *Thank you, Reverend Mother,* Maria longed to say, *but 'tis a wasted effort—the ointment takes too long to work through his wound to his blood.*

"I thought you might be interested in learning the art of preparing this ointment," the abbess said, her conversational tone belying the flinty resolve in her eyes. "Interesting, is it not, that the very beef tallow that forms the base of the ointment flavors this soothing broth, that one could not distinguish by taste between one and the other?"

"Most interesting," Maria managed to say, remembering the rigid, dead dog. Small wonder the animal had lapped up the ointment.

The abbess indicated a spoon resting alongside the pot, gestured toward the salt and ointment in turn. "Two measures of your choice, well stirred, will mingle with the hot broth and provide . . . adequate seasoning."

The dog had died after swallowing the ointment. Might Gilbert succumb as well?

Maria's hand hovered over the salt. Then she plunged the spoon into the ointment. One spoon, two. The waxy ointment dissolved in the hot broth, vanishing entirely as she stirred. An even more tantalizing scent of beef drifted from the tankard.

"Now, serve the man, daughter," the abbess instructed. "He deserves this sort of attention."

Gilbert laughed appreciatively, his eyes roaming possessively over her as Maria crossed the room with her deadly offering.

"I look forward to enjoying many similarly winsome scenes once we're wed," he gloated, accepting the tankard from her trembling hands. He tilted his head, taking a hearty swallow, and then grimaced. "Most flavorsome, but too hot," he gasped, flapping his free hand before him to cool his tongue.

It seemed an eternity ere he ventured another sip, a timeless space that allowed Maria to consider the nature of the eternity awaiting her once this deed was done. He swallowed, smacking his lips with pleasure, all unaware that he ingested death. Did she have the right to deprive him of life simply because he was ambitious when it looked like Langwald was ripe for the picking, because he desired her while her heart was set on another? Were the occasional bruises she'd be bound to endure sufficient cause to kill him? *Yes, yes.* Other women suffered worse. *No matter.*

He blew into the tankard and then lifted it again, a hearty swallow. He lowered the tankard; the firelight flickered against the broth's surface—half gone.

The image of the dead dog floated into her mind. Gilbert lifted the tankard. Did she allow this to continue, she was no better than he—

"No!" she shouted, slapping the tankard from his hand.

"What—"

"Oh, daughter." The abbess sighed, sorrow and a hint of respect shining from her eyes.

Maria stifled the urge to burst into tears, recalling what she'd thought as she entered this room, that not even an insignificant crawling thing could escape it.

Nor, it seemed, could she if poisoning Gilbert was her only way out.

"I'll fetch you the other portion," Maria said to Gilbert. "There was a . . . spider trying to crawl free of that one."

"This way!"
"Hurry!"
"Shhh!"

Whispering and shushing one another, their long gowns rustling against the floor, the nuns urged Rothgar toward the end of the hall, where a stout bolted door marked the end of the passage.

"You are certain it is the lady Maria in there?" he asked, his voice hoarse and trembling with excitement. To think that the very fates he'd railed against for his injuries, for the useless horse, had steered him unerringly in this direction! He sent them a prayer of thanks and hurried to placate God for having done so beneath this sacred roof by vowing to confess as soon as he had the chance.

"Aye, the lady Maria. The Norman, and Reverend Mother, too," Sister Mary Innocent whispered back.

"Let me through."

"Why?"

Rothgar stared at the nun, perplexed. "So I can save her."

"But they're locked in, Lord Rothgar, and the door is barred from this side. Besides, you're bleeding like a stuck pig. If anyone needs be saved, it seems to be yourself."

"Shhh."

One of the younger nuns glanced at Rothgar, blushed, and giggled.

"Shhh."

Sister Mary Innocent crouched closer. "Our donkeys were exhausted, so we put Sister Mary Magdalene on the Norman's horse and sent her to Langwald to fetch help. All we needs must do is wait."

"You cannot fight with that bad leg," said the nun who'd blushed at him. "I can tend it for you."

"Shhh."

"But he . . ." Rothgar's voice trailed off. One did not speak of the threat of rape before nuns. "He is much stronger than she is," he finished.

"He'd not violate the lady Maria before the reverend mother's very eyes," Sister Mary Innocent scoffed, provoking wide-eyed, interested looks from the other nuns.

The little nun looked at him again and buried her face behind her hands, stifling yet another giggle.

"I—" God's teeth, what was he doing, cowering in a hall with a gaggle of giggling, gaping nuns? Naught but a door barred him from Maria. "Stand aside," he said.

"But—" protested the blusher.

"Oh, he has that mulish man-look upon his face," said Sister Mary Innocent, shaking her head in resignation. "Let me slide the bolt free. I've had practice in doing it soundlessly."

"When did you practice?"

"Just slide the bolt," Rothgar muttered.

"I surely hope you didn't practice on me, whilst I thought myself safe from prying eyes," a nun accused Sister Mary Innocent, who only smirked in response as she proved her skill.

"Stand aside!" Rothgar roared, pushing past them. With a mighty heave he flung the door open with a loud, crashing boom that echoed through the abbey.

* * *

"Rothgar!" Maria whispered. "I knew you would come."

Gilbert flung his tankard against the wall. "What manner of trickery is this?" He took a pace toward Rothgar, stumbling over something Maria couldn't see. Rothgar stepped forward as well, lurching when his injured leg bore his weight.

Oh, why had she forestalled Gilbert's drinking the poisoned broth? Rothgar, lamed as he was, stood no chance against the skilled Norman knight. Sobbing in frustration and self-castigation, Maria scrambled about for a weapon while Rothgar and Gilbert took the measure of each other. She found one discarded tankard and then the other, flinging them both at Gilbert's head to no avail. They missed and bounced harmlessly from the walls.

"Reverend Mother, take Maria and lock the door," Rothgar ordered. He faced Gilbert, cold determination settling over his features. "Only one of us leaves this room alive this night."

"Nay!" Maria shouted, shaking off the abbess's hand. She would not leave Rothgar, ever again, even if she died to stay by his side.

Heavy swords flashed in the firelight, meeting above Saxon and Norman heads with a great clanging repercussion. The force of the blow drove the men apart, and they stood glaring at one another, gasping for breath, mustering strength for the next blow.

Maria hurled the ointment pot; Gilbert dodged it easily.

"Come, daughter, you are in danger." The abbess tried to draw her to the door.

"I will not leave him." Maria tried throwing the tray, but got a poor grip on its heavy, awkward bulk. It crashed to the ground scant inches from her feet.

Gilbert laughed.

"Maria, go!"

Rothgar raised his sword again and again, driving Gilbert back but doing no harm as the Norman parried each blow. Gilbert laughed again, but less confidently, and sweat suddenly sprang to his brow. Clumsiness tangled his feet. Maria watched with wide-eyed trepidation. Gilbert's sudden weakening could be a ruse. If only she had a weapon, but there was nothing left to throw, not even a chair to smash over his head, only the fire flickering in the corner.

Rothgar wielded his sword once more, driving hard enough to breach Gilbert's defenses, striking a telling blow against Gilbert's mailed abdomen. Gilbert grunted, and then with a roar of outrage charged toward Rothgar. Numb astonishment swept through Maria when Gilbert feinted sharply at the last moment to grab her, thrusting her before him as a living shield.

"Drop your sword, Saxon." Gilbert wheezed, out of breath from his exertions. Maria writhed in his grip but he simply clamped his fingers more tightly over her arms, subduing her efforts to escape.

"Bastard," Rothgar spat, but he did as Gilbert asked. Maria's mind echoed with the clanking sound Rothgar's sword made as it fell. This was all her fault, all of it. Rothgar had told her to leave the room. And now he would die—they would both die—at Gilbert's hand. She met his gaze with mute apology, but found no censure for her there, only watchful confidence, as though Rothgar felt certain he could save her from the dilemma she'd caused.

His confidence imbued her with new heart, enabling her to relax ever so slightly to relieve the pressure caused by Gilbert's painful grip.

The knight staggered, as though he'd been counting on her rigid stance for support.

"Bend to the ground, Maria, *now!*" Rothgar bellowed.

Obeying instantly, Maria collapsed from her waist, catching only a flashing glimpse of jewel-encrusted gold as Rothgar pulled her dagger from somewhere within his tunic, throwing it with fearsome accuracy. With a moist thud, the weapon buried itself to the hilt amid the chain links armoring Gilbert's shoulder. He howled in pain and sent Maria tumbling to the floor when he shrieked and pulled ineffectually at the dagger. And then his eyes widened in stunned disbelief. Clutching his middle, screaming as if he'd been disemboweled, Gilbert dropped to the ground.

Rothgar knelt beside her and gathered Maria against his chest. Her softness soothed him, her scent lulled his senses, gradually banishing the blood lust that urged him to gut Gilbert open and skewer his depraved heart.

"Are you hurt?" he asked her, when he had control of his tongue.

"Nay—oh, Rothgar, you are covered with blood."

But Rothgar ignored her frantic words, her searching hands, staring quizzically at the moaning knight. "I didn't strike him in the gut, Maria. Look, the dagger still lies in his shoulder."

"'Tis the ointment in the drink you gave him," said the abbess from behind them. "It twists in his belly."

"You gave him a potion?" Rothgar asked. "Here?"

"Aye. But I knocked it from his hand," whispered Maria.

"Before he drank the full lethal dose. He sipped enough to cause this." The abbess moved beside them, gesturing to the pain-wracked man writhing upon the floor. "He is at your mercy, Rothgar, completely. He'll not recover fully from this."

"Always in pain?" Rothgar asked, something within him pleased with the notion of a lifetime's suffering for the knave, and yet recoiling at the thought of such an unremitting sentence.

"Always."

"So be it." 'Twas a harsh penalty, indeed, harsher than the death Rothgar would have wished upon him, crueler than the violent death his outraged senses still demanded, but he could not in good conscience brandish a sword against a man in Gilbert's condition. Rothgar rose, pulling Maria up with him, keeping her cradled within the circle of his arms. "Come, beloved. We will leave him to the nuns."

The abbess nodded acceptance of the duty, and Rothgar guided Maria toward the door.

Gilbert's harsh, agonized voice stopped him.

"Saxon! Remember your oath."

Rothgar glanced over his shoulder. Gilbert had risen to one elbow, his face grayish-white, a death-sweat beading his brow.

"You swore in the stable to kill me if I touched her." Gilbert gritted his teeth; Rothgar fancied he could see the pain spasm through him.

"She is safe now," Rothgar said, knowing he could not strike at the Norman now, though the memory of Gilbert abducting Maria, of holding her before him to ward off danger, made his hand itch for a stout Saxon ax to bury deep in Gilbert's head. "I think she need not fear any more suffering at your hands."

But Gilbert would not let him turn away. "Rothgar! I . . . I beg of you. Hold to your oath."

Speaking so low Rothgar could not hear, the abbess whispered to Maria, who gently disengaged herself from his embrace to follow the nun from the room.

This would be between the two of them, Saxon and Norman, man to man.

"You would do no less for a dog who swallowed a belly full of putrid meat," Gilbert gasped when they were alone, his voice noticeably weaker. "I heard what the nun said. There is no honor in enduring the life she has prescribed for me. But I could die proudly, if the final blow came from one such as you—Lord Rothgar, of Langwald."

"You need not humble yourself so," Rothgar said, surprised at the Norman's form of address.

"'Tis not showing humility to acknowledge one's victor," Gilbert said.

Rothgar hesitated. His notion of mercy made it imperative he aid the Norman, but a curious lassitude had overtaken him, as if the vengeful spirit that suffused him while Maria faced danger had deserted him now she was safe. His head ached from Gilbert's earlier blow. His leg trembled from the wound in his thigh. He would show little mercy to Gilbert if he found himself too weak to deliver a telling death blow.

"Please," Gilbert whispered, misreading Rothgar's hesitancy. "'Twould be a kindness I know I ill deserve."

Rothgar knew no words to acknowledge Gilbert's plea. He merely nodded, praying God return some portion of strength to his arm.

Taking no chance that his thrust might fail to pierce the chain mail, Rothgar hefted his sword high above his head, clenching the hilt with both hands, and drove it with all his might through Gilbert's heart. There was a rattling gasp, a very slight welling of blood, and the dimming of the light in Gilbert's eyes to tell Rothgar his aim had struck true.

He waited a moment before leaving the Norman's side, wondering what God might do with the soul of a man like Gilbert Crispin.

"I love you," his bewitching Maria whispered, wrapping her arms around his waist when he stepped through the door of Gilbert's death chamber.

He felt a surge of raw, primitive emotion. Heedless of the reverend mother standing near, of the nuns hovering just beyond the door, Rothgar lowered his head and captured his beloved's lips with his.

When at last he lifted his head, his blood raging through his veins and overriding his good sense, he said, "Come away with me. 'Twould not be proper to stay beneath this roof with the thoughts swirling through my head."

"Please, Rothgar, let us return to Langwald!"

Rothgar's heart sank. Langwald. There would always be Langwald between them. "For a time," Rothgar said, in apparent agreement, to cover the sadness sweeping over him.

"But not overlong," Maria said, touching his face. "I need time enough to explain things to Hugh, so that he understands when I go away with you to seek a home of our own. Then we can be on our way."

Rothgar's spirit soared, yet he felt bound to caution her one more time. "'We will face many obstacles. 'Twill be fearsome hard."

"Fearsome hard, indeed," she said with a bold glance at the front of his tunic. He burst into delighted laughter; she slanted her brown-gold eyes upward and smiled a secretive smile.

"Rothgar," called the abbess as they made their way from the room, "dare I hope she might be the last woman you'll spirit from behind abbey walls?"

"That is certain, Reverend Mother." He smiled down at Maria. "I've no interest in provoking her jealousy. She's far too skilled in administering potions."

"Among other things," Maria said, smiling serenely.

Epilogue

August 1067

A hawk soared high above, drifting in slow, lazy circles, uttering its shrill, piercing cry. Maria shadowed her eyes with her hand as she watched it, wishing it were possible to shift minds with the hawk, to borrow its awesome eyesight ere her own faded from this ceaseless searching of the horizon. First a sennight, then a fortnight, now two full months gone. God keep Rothgar and Hugh safe.

"Maria!" Eadyth screeched, her hand cradled protectively over her belly in the manner she'd affected since missing her monthly courses, her voice shrill with excitement. "Fen's returned!"

Maria whirled, seeking where Eadyth gestured wildly. 'Twas Fen to be sure, gliding and edging his way into the courtyard. And then, over the low rise of a hill, the flash of sun against mail, the sharp, eager whinny of a hungry horse scenting its stable. Two men, one brown-haired like herself, the other with hair glinting gold in the sun, whipping against his neck, tangling with a beard of tawny gold.

Then she might have been the hawk, so quickly did her feet fly through the castle and across the moat to Rothgar's side.

And she might have had ten arms, so eagerly did she swarm over Rothgar once he'd pulled her atop the horse before him. Pressing close, despising the mail that kept her hands from touching his flesh, blessing the mail that had kept him safe for her; twining her fingers into his hair, she'd been right, that night a lifetime ago, thinking it would suit him hanging low against his shoulders; stroking his beard and showering kisses upon him, relishing his breath mingling with hers, his joyous laughter bubbling against her lips; and most of all his arms, clamped like iron vises about her waist, his hands, crushing her against him, trusting to the horse to carry them home.

"Have a care, sister," Hugh warned, despite enjoying a similar welcome from Eadyth. "'Twould go amiss with William to learn yon Rothgar'd been suffocated by a woman ere the ink dried on his pardon."

"He granted it." Though it should have been her happiest of days, Maria found herself forcing enthusiasm into her voice. "Did he approve the marriage between us as well?"

"Aye, we had gold enough to persuade him," Rothgar said. "It goaded him sore, but his need for ready cash outweighed all else. William finds England a costly prize, indeed." Rothgar fumbled in a saddle pouch and withdrew a parchment, limp and droopy from traveling against a sweating horse beneath summer's relentless sun. Bold ink strokes graced its surface, mysterious curling embellishments that somehow granted Maria the right to wed a

Saxon, granted the both of them safe conduct across the English countryside.

Now, they could leave Langwald.

Now, they must bid farewell to Hugh and Eadyth and the babe that nestled in Eadyth's belly unbeknownst yet to Hugh. To the castle, so newly complete, so forbidding in appearance and yet so wondrously comfortable for living. To Langwald's people, who'd shed their surly natures when she'd cast aside her tense watchful protection over Hugh. Leave it all.

And oh, how gladly she would ride out at Rothgar's side, her head held high, filled with love for him. Yes, now they could leave Langwald, but forevermore a tiny portion of her heart would yearn for the home she might have had.

"I have a parchment as well," Hugh said.

This bit of information roused Maria from her gloom. "You had no need of a pardon, Hugh."

"This parchment is for you."

Stunned, Maria took the document.

"Your brother's bravery extends beyond the battlefield," said Rothgar. "Hugh dared confess to William what happened to him and told him how you held Langwald while he mended."

"Yon Saxon seems overmodest to me," Hugh interjected. "I also told William I doubted these castle walls would be looming over me now had Rothgar not brought the villagers round. Nor did I neglect to give William a recounting of the day when Rothgar saved my men from the ambush in the woodcutter's clearing, and how he organized our defenses after Walter and Gilbert betrayed me."

Langwald Castle cast its huge, dark shadow over them, shielding them from the blazing sun, bathing them in blessed cool comfort.

"What had William to say of this news?" Maria whispered. To think how long she'd dreaded the information reaching the king's ear, only to have Hugh himself bear the tale!

Hugh smiled, a fond, proud grin. "William remarked that had all his knights done so well as one small woman and one sworn enemy, the land might be free of turmoil by now."

"So all those months of anguish . . . I had no need to fear William at all?"

"You were right to fear him, Maria. As soon as I spilled the tale, William announced Langwald was forfeit."

Though Eadyth gasped in accord with Maria's plummeting heart, both Hugh and Rothgar seemed unaffected by the loss of Langwald, but then they'd had their traveling time to accustom themselves to the loss.

"You women need not look so stricken," Hugh said. "William didn't leave us homeless. He granted traitor Philip's Stillingham lands to me, along with a nice parcel of acreage leading to the sea." He squinted upward at Langwald's walls. "It seems I needs must set to work building another one of these on my new holdings."

So Hugh had gotten Stillingham and more as a sop, but all Maria's efforts, all those months of uncertainty, all Rothgar's work, had gone for naught. And what of the love she bore this place? Futile anger rocked her at the unfairness of it all. "What becomes of Langwald, then?" she managed to ask.

"William said the one responsible for upholding Langwald throughout those troublesome times should be the one to hold it forevermore," Rothgar said, mischief lighting his eyes. "This parchment,

Maria, 'tis William's royal decree deeding Langwald to *you*."

She could not have heard aright.

Hugh snorted, oblivious to her confusion. "A secondhand decree, Maria. William first pressed the deed into Rothgar's hands. He declined the gift."

Maria turned a disbelieving gaze upon Rothgar. "The deed to Langwald . . . for me? You declined? Why?"

"Because your strength and determination held Langwald, Maria. I but helped you a bit near the end."

The parchment felt well-nigh weightless in her hands; such an insignificant thing, it seemed impossible it brought her all she desired. A home. Rothgar.

Hugh had guided his horse soundlessly away. Her heart slammed hard against her chest, considering the document.

Rothgar spoke softly, even though Hugh had ridden out of earshot. "And I must confess to a moment of doubt, Maria. I wondered, if I take her to wife when Langwald is again mine, is it me, or is it the land she weds?"

"So you give Langwald to me, so that I might suffer the same doubts?" she whispered. Rothgar had spoken not at all of love in these few moments. Might his feelings have changed toward her? "As my lord husband, what belongs to me will belong to you. I might ask the same question."

"I give Langwald to you, Maria, so you may decide. You have your home now, whether you marry me or not."

Oh, staggering thought, to think that she alone might rule these lands she loved! The very idea left her feeling like an empty walnut husk, dry and lifeless.

Some imp seized control of her tongue, drawing out words she would swear she had never thought, but which seemed immediately right for the situation. "Let us forget all this, Rothgar. Let us return Langwald to Hugh and leave here, make our own way as we planned, so there need be no doubts between us."

With instant, fluid motion, without a backward glance, Rothgar spurred the horse away from Langwald Castle.

The sun heated her face, but its heat was as nothing compared to the warmth suffusing through her at Rothgar's easy repudiation of Langwald. The air stirred by the galloping horse washed over her skin, lifted her hair, pressed her back against Rothgar's broad chest, as if it meant to wash away all fears and doubts, meant to show her the one solid refuge she could always count upon. It rumbled beneath her, this solid refuge of his chest; he was laughing as they rode away from his birthright.

"Do you think this is silly of me?" Maria asked, slanting her eyes upward to meet his.

"I dreamed of you suggesting this very thing, scarcely daring to hope you would," Rothgar said.

She peeped over his shoulder, toward the castle receding behind them. "Does Langwald mean so little to you?"

"Oh, nay, beloved. It once meant more than life to me. But now I find I treasure one possession above all others." Rothgar's voice turned husky as he tightened his arms around her. "Maria, Langwald is naught but wood and dirt and stones lest you are there with me. I realized that anew when William handed that deed to me. Langwald means nothing to me, unless it comes with you as its lady."

The power this man had, to send her heart soaring with only a few words! "My very thought as I sat night after night, waiting for you to return. Oh, Rothgar, though Langwald surrounded me and people crowded the castle, I felt so alone, so lost, as though I'd traveled far from home and could not find it again without your hand holding mine."

He planted a quick kiss atop her head.

"Rothgar?" she began timidly. "Let us go back. Let us go home."

He drew the horse to a halt but made no move to return to the castle. "Wherever we find ourselves together shall be home to us," he whispered.

His hand plundered her tunic, probing through the light summer-weight linen. She wondered if he could sense the added fullness to her breasts, the slight rounding of her belly, to realize that even if they married today, the arrival of their babe would prompt much finger counting.

"'Tis you I want, Maria," he vowed. "Not Langwald."

"And I want you, Rothgar. Not Langwald."

He frowned down at her, a mock frown belied by the teasing lights in his wondrous blue eyes. "William will be displeased to hear you spurned his gift."

"Then I suppose 'tis my unpleasant duty as his loyal subject to accept it," she said with mock gravity. "But what shall we do with this place neither of us wants?"

Rothgar urged the horse into motion, back toward Langwald. A ferocious scowl crossed his face, as though he were mired deep in disagreeable thoughts. And then his expression brightened. "There is one sleeping chamber within the castle where I *might* think of something to do. Mayhap we can spend all our time there . . . together."

"To please William?" Maria teased.

"Nay, Maria," Rothgar murmured, his voice a low, husky promise. "To please me."

AVAILABLE NOW

ORCHIDS IN MOONLIGHT by Patricia Hagan
Bestselling author Patricia Hagan weaves a mesmerizing tale set in the untamed West. Determined to leave Kansas and join her father in San Francisco, vivacious Jamie Chandler stowed away on the wagon train led by handsome Cord Austin—a man who didn't want any company. Cord was furious when he discovered her, but by then it was too late to turn back. It was also too late to turn back the passion between them.

TEARS OF JADE by Leigh Riker
Twenty years after Jay Barron was classified as MIA in Vietnam, Quinn Tyler is still haunted by the feeling that he is still alive. When a twist of fate brings her face-to-face with businessman Welles Blackburn, a man who looks like Jay, Quinn is consumed by her need for answers that could put her life back together again, or tear it apart forever.

FIREBRAND by Kathy Lynn Emerson
Her power to see into the past could have cost Ellen Allyn her life if she had not fled London and its superstitious inhabitants in 1632. Only handsome Jamie Mainwaring accepted Ellen's strange ability and appreciated her for herself. But was his love true, or did he simply intend to use her powers to help him find fortune in the New World?

CHARADE by Christina Hamlett
Obsessed with her father's mysterious death, Maggie Price investigates her father's last employer, Derek Channing. From the first day she arrives at Derek's private island fortress in the Puget Sound, Maggie can't deny her powerful attraction to the handsome millionaire. But she is troubled by questions he won't answer, and fears that he has buried something more sinister than she can imagine.

THE TRYSTING MOON by Deborah Satinwood
She was an Irish patriot whose heart beat for justice during the reign of George III. Never did Lark Ballinter dream that it would beat even faster for an enemy to her cause—the golden-haired aristocratic Lord Christopher Cavanaugh. A powerfully moving tale of love and loyalty.

CONQUERED BY HIS KISS by Donna Valentino
Norman Lady Maria de Courson had to strike a bargain with Saxon warrior Rothgar of Langwald in order to save her brother's newly granted manor from the rebellious villagers. But when their agreement was sweetened by their firelit passion in the frozen forest, they faced a love that held danger for them both.

COMING NEXT MONTH

A SEASON OF ANGELS by Debbie Macomber
From bestselling author Debbie Macomber comes a heartwarming and joyful story of three angels named Mercy, Goodness, and Shirley who must grant three prayers before Christmas. "*A Season of Angels* is charming and touching in turns. It would take a real Scrooge not to enjoy this story of three ditsy angels and answered prayers."—Elizabeth Lowell, bestselling author of *Untamed*.

MY FIRST DUCHESS by Susan Sizemore
Jamie Scott was an impoverished nobleman by day and a masked highwayman by night. With four sisters, a grandmother, and one dowager mother to support, Jamie seized the chance to marry a headstrong duchess with a full purse. Their marriage was one of convenience, until Jamie realized that he had fallen hopelessly in love with his wife. A delightful romp from the author of the award-winning *Wings of the Storm*.

PROMISE ME TOMORROW by Catriona Flynt
Norah Kelly was determined to make a new life for herself as a seamstress in Arizona Territory. When persistent cowboys came courting, Norah's five feet of copper-haired spunk and charm needed some protection. Sheriff Morgan Treyhan offered to marry her, if only to give them both some peace . . . until love stole upon them.

A BAD GIRL'S MONEY by Paula Paul
Alexis Runnels, the black sheep of a wealthy Texas family, joins forces with her father's business rival and finds a passion she doesn't bargain for. A heartrending tale from award-winning author Paula Paul that continues the saga begun in *Sweet Ivy's Gold*.

THE HEART REMEMBERS by Lenore Carroll
The first time Jess and Kip meet is in the 1960s at an Indian reservation in New Mexico. The chemistry is right, but the timing is wrong. Not until twenty-five years later do they realize what their hearts have known all along. A moving story of friendships, memories, and love.

TO LOVE AND TO CHERISH by Anne Hodgson
Dr. John Fauxley, the Earl of Manseth, vowed to protect Brianda Breedon at all costs. She didn't want a protector, but a man who would love and cherish her forever. From the rolling hills of the English countryside, to the glamorous drawing rooms of London, to the tranquil Scottish lochs, a sweeping historical romance that will send hearts soaring.

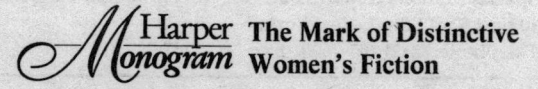

Harper Monogram **The Mark of Distinctive Women's Fiction**

ATTENTION: ORGANIZATIONS AND CORPORATIONS

Most HarperPaperbacks are available at special quantity discounts for bulk purchases for sales promotions, premiums, or fund-raising. For information, please call or write:
**Special Markets Department, HarperCollins Publishers,
10 East 53rd Street, New York, N.Y. 10022.
Telephone: (212) 207-7528. Fax: (212) 207-7222.**